R0202704896

12/2021

O9-BRZ-626

ALSO BY JOHN EDGAR WIDEMAN

LOOK FOR ME AND I'LL BE GONE

Stories

JOHN EDGAR WIDEMAN

SCRIBNER

New York   London   Toronto   Sydney   New Delhi

Scribner
An Imprint of Simon & Schuster, Inc.
1230 Avenue of the Americas
New York, NY 10020

First Scribner hardcover edition November 2021

SCRIBNER and design are registered trademarks of The Gale Group, Inc., used under license by Simon & Schuster, Inc., the publisher of this work.

For information about special discounts for bulk purchases, please contact Simon & Schuster Special Sales at 1-866-506-1949 or business@simonandschuster.com.

The Simon & Schuster Speakers Bureau can bring authors to your live event. For more information or to book an event, contact the Simon & Schuster Speakers Bureau at 1-866-248-3049 or visit our website at www.simonspeakers.com.

Interior design by Wendy Blum

Manufactured in the United States of America

1   3   5   7   9   10   8   6   4   2

Library of Congress Cataloging-in-Publication Data has been applied for.

ISBN 978-1-9821-4894-2
ISBN 978-1-9821-4896-6 (ebook)

To C—
with luv

CONTENTS

LOOK FOR ME AND I'LL BE GONE

ART OF STORY

TWO YOUNG PEOPLE, DIFFERENT COLORS, my color, pass me. Dark fist of her topknot, edges of his fro outlined by a soft glow above their heads when I first glance down the street and notice the couple busy with each other, strides synced, no hurry, not strolling either, about a block away coming towards me on Grand, a glow hovering, visible against early morning light of a clear spring day that frames the figures as they approach, pavement shadowy under their feet, the sky behind and above them stretching up and up into pale, cloudless, bluish distance, a sky finally no color, all colors, same and different, fading until my eyes drop, and when I look again to find gleam of halos, the couple is behind me.

Stories graves. Empty graves. Nothing there. All living and dying in them fake. Pretend. Even when someone reading or listening or telling a story, it's empty. Empty. No time in it. A person requires time to live and die in. Stories not time. Graves. No entering them or leaving them without time. Nothing to breathe inside a story. Nothing lost nor found there. No time. Only a story. Only words.

You pretend. As if pretending permits you to enter a story, to leave one place and begin in another. You let yourself believe you create time. Your time. As if your time not a story you make up. As if *time* not a word like others you make up to tell a story . . . *Once upon a time* . . . as if time ends or begins there, with words. As if time waits in stories or is something like them. As if a story contains the breath of life. As if words share time or time listens and reads. As if stories are not graves. Where we play with the dead. Play dead.

As if a something words make of nothing is more time. Time saved and not a story. A moment on Grand Street. Not fiction. Not a grave. Not a make-believe time, but time saved. More than time. Not nothing. Not merely words. Not mere story.

Maybe, I tell myself, this is one I can tell. And someone perhaps will listen. Will read. But a story does not become something until it ends, until I pretend it's over and that I am no longer experiencing a walk in New York City on Grand Street early in the morning. Me pretending these words I write, one after the other, are something like steps. Mine, yours, anybody's steps. Anyone who listens or reads and for some reason perhaps they may remember other steps, streets, and revisit how a morning materializes from nothing but steps. Step after step taken while darkness, brightness unfold or enfold.

You are nowhere, nothing until you are feeling, speaking, thinking one instant then another, one word after another, the next seeming to follow from the one before, no beginning or end, more steps, more street seeming maybe never to stop unraveling. A moment, a morning that materializes as fast and solid as certain crucial missing things suddenly recalled, things striking you as happy once or painful, familiar, odd, urgent once, though soon enough you also recall that nothing's there, that you are alone as always with your thoughts, always alone even with a busy headful of them, including anybody else's thoughts, aches, words, telling stories, pretending time at their fingertips, your fingertips, time ahead, time behind as you take step after step along Grand, and where oh where else could you be, where are you headed this morning if not to a physical therapy appointment at 450 Grand Street and two young people appear, the two of them together, content, focused enough upon each other to match strides, colored teenagers or very young adults coming towards you, intent on each other, soft crowns of hair that shimmer over each skull, visible against morning's brightness, floating light that is perhaps source or end or both of vast sky above them, surrounding them, but when I glance ahead and notice them coming towards me that morning, *mourning* also comes to mind. Mourning's sadness, and that *mourning* word mine, not theirs. The morning not mine, not yours, not ours. Not their morning either. Only a morning, one that only happens once, anyway, and belongs to no one, belongs, fits nowhere, is nothing except words, story, nothing, nowhere, only a story beginning that I might find myself in the midst of unexpectedly, but of course an empty story, over and dead, a true story since they all are true and are not, whether or not we tell them or listen or read.

Let me pretend, let me believe the glow, the auras seeping from or hovering above heads of two young people on a Lower East Side street, April 29, in the year 2018, New York, USA, signify hope eternal, and that light above them very same light I saw framing rows of heads, row after row in a crowd of people not stretching to the horizon, but backed up as far as where towers, stores, windows, and walls of a city abruptly resume, the public square ends, and Cape Town spreads gray across the horizon, pile of it rising until overtopped by light that reaches even the very last shimmering row of heads. Many, many heads maybe about to explode and demolish monumental stone buildings of the square enclosing them, many, many rows of heads aglow, perhaps ready to ignite the million or so fuzzy bodies indistinguishable one from another that have gathered to greet Nelson Mandela coming home after twenty-seven years of imprisonment, bodies igniting and incinerating old bodies that will be born again. A crowd whose size, whose yearning ungraspable by

3

me, despite the very present, very hungry witness of my foreign eyes peering from Cape Castle's balcony down into the packed square on February 11, 1990, Republic of South Africa. Inextinguishable hope one story I can imagine, try to tell, though a different story narrated by helicopter gunships stitching a dark net in air above the square, and barricades fortified by tanks and steel rhinos packed with shock troops in camouflage securing all streets, sealing every entrance and exit from the space of welcome.

Time unruffled by anyone's stops and starts. Returns. Entrances, exits. Stories. Two young people striding towards me. Grand Street unruffled as time. Going nowhere. My steps one after another vanish as I pass two young colored strangers, remember a square in Cape Town, the teeming, excited crowd in which perhaps I last saw the couple.

COLORED ANGEL LEVINE

For Bernard Malamud

A COLORED ANGEL NAMED LEVINE said to him, I have come to help you. But he had only half-listened to Levine. The name, the color wrong. Don't match. Unnatural. Beyond belief. He lost the angel until he desperately needed him and searched desperately for him and searched and searched and at last finds him and pleads for help that the colored angel had once long ago offered. A happy ending to my story, please, Levine.

When he steps on the water of the colored angel's voice, it does not give way. Feels solid as sidewalk, firm enough under him to place his other foot on the water, which could not be water, he was thinking even as he mounted it and stepped again, as if he could walk on water as easily as he crosses the kitchen floor. Accepts the ease of walking on water, accepts the oddness of pushing back in his chair from the table and standing up and no longer being a grown-up, old Jewish man. A boy again, surely, as he hears the boy's mother say his name or rather say her name for him he hadn't recalled for years, more years than she's been dead.

But walking on water impossible because water doesn't work that way, does it. You can't just walk on it, there is nothing to it, your feet get soaked, you splash, sink, you drown if water's deep enough and you are not careful and believe you are that boy again, there again in the morning with your mother in the kitchen, you pushing back from the table and rising up and turning to go to get more milk from the icebox to fill you up, fill your cereal bowl that sits behind you now on the table, sitting there still plain as day again after all these years of never thinking of it once, bowl there, you see it with eyes in back of your head, a gleaming white bowl circled by three deep blue bands, your favorite bowl even though a tiny, spidery crack looked to you sometimes like somebody had nibbled the blue rim and you wondered who, how, why when you had nothing better to think about those mornings before school, only a cereal box to read, a box read so often that nothing happens, words go nowhere, so you sit hunched at the table munching or crunching or just letting milk sog the flakes or sweet crumbles or pops or nuggets in the bowl until you can just about drink them down, going down easy, swallowing them easy as walking on water would be if a person could do it, he thinks, walking on water as solid as the kitchen's shiny linoleum floor that holds him up this solid moment he walks across it as if his life is not sinking, drowning. He hears his mother's long-lost voice, and he's sure she will be waiting, busy moving about the kitchen till he gets back and sits himself down again, finished doing whatever a boy thinks he needs to get up and do.

Simple as that, a colored angel promises.

LAST DAY

SOMETIMES GOING TO SEE MY brother in prison felt like when you hear a person call you *nigger,* a somebody you may not even know addressing you, a stranger who suddenly becomes intimately close by establishing a boundary, drawing a line and crossing it simultaneously with the n-word as if the two of you, separated by that line, have known each other a lifetime, and *nigger* declaimed by him or her restores with absolute authority a prolonged, familiar, shared history whether or not you have ever laid eyes on one another before, that person with *nigger* in their mouth announcing the presence of a line that divides, that claims a compelling relationship of intense distance, intense complicity, and neither you nor she nor he has any means, any right or reason to deny it, once that word *nigger* is up in your faces, both you and the other person are powerless to erase the line, erase the nigger word, powerless as colored boys or girls in Cleveland or Detroit or Los Angeles or Seattle who cannot erase or nullify the bullets police officers shoot into their bodies, guns fired for many of the same reasons in every case, though the news media say, and we the people say, too, don't we, each case is also, yes, yes, a separate case with differing, yes, extenuating circumstances, differences sometimes as obvious as difference between night and day, black and white, or different like different sounds of *nigger* depending on whose lips speak the word, different each time it's spoken, differences private, public, acceptable or not in terms of law or public opinion, differing acts, but all validated by the same rule, rule old at least as this country, a rule continuing to persist, and though we may disagree about its appropriateness or application in each circumstance, it persists predictably, along with its often unarguably fatal, direct consequences, that rule which originated when some of us in a position of power abused that advantage and enslaved people, used power's brute force to seize and imprison the bodies of others and treat them as inferiors, as if those enslaved others born members of a different group, a kind or variety or race not exactly deserving to be considered human beings, and once designated as such, treated as such, remain different forever, a rule that still rules today, dividing us into separate races, declaring that each person's designated race stays the same always, stays in force today, and though the rule may operate covertly or blatantly, it remains present every time in every case to reinforce and justify whatever other motives a person might conjure up for calling a person *nigger* or imprisoning niggers or segregating niggers or shooting many many bullets into a young nigger body, then it's too late, always too late, too long, bang, bang, victim dead, don't fuss, don't protest, the rule's the rule, a prerogative in place too long, suspects presumed guilty, no defense against being called *nigger,* nor do unarmed colored boys girls women men possess any magic to stop bullets that armed citizens of various colors designated as officers, deputies, cops, agents fire into them, no power except perhaps to remember always the time-honored, hoary prerogative, remember the rule of a line dividing separate races and embrace it, seize it, and turn it around as self-defense, as battle cry, use the rule to stigmatize and abuse others before they use it to hurt and destroy you, before they call you out your name.

It's never absent, and though I seldom hear anyone say *nigger* out loud in the prison visiting room, the word rings in my ears each time I visit. Need the word maybe, I admit, so say it to myself in order to deal with an otherwise intolerable situation. Need it to answer the question tearing me up inside when I look around and see a busy, crowded visiting room filled mainly with people my color, the many colors of my family. Why such an overload of us in this terrible place? *Why us,* a question with an answer I have been taught already, learned in childhood, in school, an ancient answer known before my very first visit to a prison and known for all the visits, all the years and years since. The answer is: This is the way things are, have always been, and shall be forever.

But that answer instilled when I was a boy beginning to ask questions about a world perplexing him, that answer too ordinary, not stunning enough, not satisfying enough in the prison visiting room and gives me no peace when I try to make sense, try to account for faces surrounding me, far, far too many faces colored like mine, and no answer truly explains our disproportionate presence, nor my outrage and sense of defeat, no answer sufficient to compel me to accept the evidence my eyes confront, no answer, only confirmation of a line drawn long, long ago, before I was born, a rule that divides faces I see into two groups, unalterably divides them into two separate groups, and then I am able to remind myself, say to myself, *nigger,* niggers of course, that's why, and no other explanation required. What else would I, should I, would anybody expect. *Nigger* the word we need to shout out loud or whisper inside ourselves and that word reveals why.

The line, the word always there. Hard, rigid, premeditated as the prison visiting room's bolted-to-the-floor, plastic seats arranged side by side, in aisles and sections, all seats in each section facing in the same direction so eye contact impossible with a person beside you unless you twist in your seat, lean over a metal rail that divides one seat from the next. You talk sideways, as close as you can get to a visitor's ear. Awkward conversations, minimal privacy in an overcrowded space that also isolates.

None of the humming discontent, the simmering helplessness and frustration a person experiences upon entering the prison visiting room is accidental. Room's layout conceived, like the rule to divide races conceived, in order to execute a plan. And plan works. The architecture's visible scheme—expressed by unmovable steel, by concrete of floor and ceiling, by locked doors, windowless walls—boxes you in. Visible lines repeat the ancient, invisible injunction to consider yourself either one kind of human or another kind. Choice drastically limited. No choice except to go along with a program long in place. Once entered, no exit. No way out except to scream loud enough to bring walls tumbling down. And who's prepared to spoil a visit. Prepared to risk imprisonment. To resist guards, sirens, clubs, guns. No. When you visit you follow house rules, rules posted on the walls, rules that define and reduce your choices, eliminate all other options. Nigger rules that humble and humiliate and impound.

At one end of the visiting area, far end from where my brother and I occupy adjacent seats, a play corner reserved for small children, an area supervised by an inmate and furnished with bright plastic toys. Good job, my brother says, nodding at the corner. Only trusties get it. Playing with kids. Out the goddamn cell four, five hours at a time. Wouldn't mind doing it myself, cept everybody knows the guys you see over there too tight with the guards. Only way you get the best jobs in here. Wouldn't let none my kids go to those guys. Don't mind me, man. Some them guys just guys like everybody else. But ain't nothing free in here.

Hungry.

Always. You know they starve us. Always hungry. Worse since they brung in that private company and started counting calories. As if grown men supposed to exist on what those company charts say enough. Everybody walk round here all day hungry. Hungry wake you up in the middle of the damn night. Shame how they do us, bro. Getting so bad some these guys kill another guy for a bag of chips.

Remembered to bring quarters this time. What's the rule now. You allowed to push buttons or not.

No, no. They see me much as touch a vending machine, visit's over. Ass outa here.

What you want, then. Knock yourself out. Plenty quarters today.

You know I like them wings. Package of chicken wings. A cheesesteak. If they outa cheesesteaks, a double burger. Bag of popcorn if any left. And some grape juice or some kinda juice, or pop if that's all they got. Don't matter really. Junk all they put in them machines, but you know something, it tastes kinda good, brother dear, after slop they be feeding us every day in here. And nice to feel kinda halfway filled up half a minute. Thank you.

I wait in line behind a short, very young, very pregnant woman who punches in choices like she's been here before, inserting quarters one by one from the see-through bagful she holds in her off-hand. Then wait my turn at a microwave oven on a table beside vending machines. Don't turn around to look at my brother, but I listen, and our conversation starts up in my head while I wait, while he waits, and I wonder how we always find so much to say, more to say, never finish saying it.

The tape runs in my mind . . . I hear it word by word. Visit again, smell the warmed-up bag of popcorn from the machine, taste apple juice, hear my brother beside me, here, there, wherever we are.

———

I wonder if he ever daydreams a last day, day a guard delivers clothes for outside, a paper shopping bag for transporting the property my brother accumulated inside, receipts he must sign for the bag and his possessions, wonder if my brother daydreams about that day and I want to ask him what he might feel if and when, ask him what he thinks he might be thinking when the steel door of his cell slides open, Spivak or Crawford or Jones or Valdez standing there in the passageway waiting, looking at him, less curious than I am about what's on his mind, looking through him, past him, past this task to the next, one task closer to the end of same ole same ole slog of guard duties imprisoning them with him night and day until punch-out time, one guard or two, three, maybe the whole dreary crew of them, living and dead, every single officer hired and fired by the state department of corrections since day one, every single sorry one of them in uniform again to escort him down long rows of cells, through more gates, then across the yard, vacant, quiet this early, to the final gate, rank after rank of silent guards crowded into the narrow corridor just beyond his cell's open door, guards stern-faced, grinning, scornful, accusing, no, no, no, just standing, just impatient, just wanting it over with, whatever, peering through him as if he's already gone, simply not there, or there like a shit smear in a toilet bowl their duty to maintain spotless, this day of leaving no different for them than any day they are paid to watch him, their eyes, the expressionless expressions soldered on their faces giving up nothing, as his eyes, his expression give nothing back, keeping each other at a distance way too vast to cross, distance any sane person has no reason to cross and decent folk know better than even to imagine crossing because everybody understands, don't they, what's over there across the line, nothing's there, an abyss, a bottomless pit over there in which people burn up, become nothing, vanishing fast as prisoners sentenced to life supposed to vanish from life, like him, like me, though I want to believe I might escape my cell by asking him how he thinks he would feel the last day, except idea of a last day nothing but twist, glimmer, less than nothing as it passes too quickly to follow and disappears into the abyss, the cauldron, and to protect himself from plunging even deeper into nothingness, would he allow himself even that idle thought of freedom, freedom an excruciating stab of pain until it's nothing again after a thought of free flies, slinks past, nothing again, he remains behind bars, in a cell, so why bother to think different, as if inside and outside not absolutely separated, as if there's a chance of release, of being elsewhere other than where he is, nowhere, nothing, consumed, disciplined by the business of survival while he perishes here, in this nowhere place where he is, there where it's impossible for him to take me or anyone else, except maybe in daydreams he dreams in his cell, so I teach myself to resist the temptation to ask certain kinds of questions, and instead of asking I pretend that we are both inside when I visit the prison, or pretend both of us are outside, pretend that words we speak, words I write bring us closer together, and for his sake and mine (my response a bit like the guards, I'm ashamed to admit) I try not to wonder too much about his daydreams, do not ask to hear them, nor ask if he ever thinks about what he might feel or do last day.

SEPARATION

I WAS A CHILD AND believed that if I stood alone, quiet enough, long enough beside my grandfather's coffin, he would speak to me. Tell me a story. But I lacked the courage to enter alone the room where they put the box into which they had put him. I was ten and literally frightened speechless for weeks by his death. Already half-orphaned by the loss of a father who had deserted us and now my grandfather, a second father gone, too. Afraid to enter alone a room's stink and dark and silence. Scared my grandfather would speak. Or not speak.

I grew up in rooms full of stories. Mostly women talking. Men seldom around during daytime when I was a boy with nothing better to do than listen to my grandmother, aunts, neighbor ladies, my mother. Listening though I never wanted to be caught listening. Best stories shushed if Mister Rabbit Ears around, stories I wasn't supposed to hear, not supposed to understand whether I heard or not. Stories as much about absent men as about women present in the rooms telling them. Stories that could embarrass or shame me because I was too little to possess any of my own I could tell myself or tell back at others when their stories made me feel in danger—naked, alone, angry, afraid. How could the women know so much about me I didn't know, couldn't speak. My story absent like the men, and is that one reason why I needed to listen so hard. Why women's stories that made me laugh could also make me want to cry. Or run me away, far, far away where the only voice I would hear my own. It's silence. Silence where men might be hiding. Talking. Laughing. Talking back.

Separated now by years, by death from all the people who once filled my life, people who filled my head with their stories and silences when I was a boy, I still miss them. Still stumble around today, looking back, needing them, needing words they said and didn't say. Looking for help to make sense of this accidental place in which, mostly by accident, it seems, I find myself.

Sarah, a woman interviewed in a magazine article about people who hear voices, names one of her voices *Tom,* and tells the author of the article that she and Tom have known each other a long time. Writer asks when did she meet Tom, and Sarah pauses, gives the writer a little smile before she replies, "He's saying, in the Sumerian period."

When all was darkness, the oldest story in Sumer recalls, there existed no thought of time. Each animal lived alone, and beyond alone nothing. No thought of other animals. No light. No sound. Total darkness and silence. No fear of death. No loneliness. All animals one. All free as a god. Until animals imagined time. Time an explosion of light that revealed sights and sounds of other animals inhabiting darkness, each animal separate, each a blur of clamor, motion, confusion, each stunned, overwhelmed by possibilities of seeing or being seen, by the shock of time's abrupt, mysterious presence that seems to open space where there is none and takes what seems to be space away, each animal needing words and time alone to think them, to separate themselves from time, each animal dissolving as fast as time dissolves, time sudden, implacable, invisible, time boundless yet caged in old, old darkness that promises nothing. Holds nothing.

Like Sarah's Tom story, mine could begin in Sumer. First problem, I do not speak nor write the Sumerian language. But language, it turns out, a convenience, not a necessity. Often more useless than useful, the second man I encountered in the city of R in Sumer assured me as his gaze swept over me, past me. Much more than language separates us, his eyes told me. Galaxies swirl in the space between your world and mine, he said, without uttering a single syllable. The man's silence louder than babble of buying, selling, braying, hallooing, bells, screams of a busy marketplace in the bright, hot middle of a day in which I am a stranger, so much a stranger I know better than to ask others in this crowd of strangers any questions about particulars of place or time or why they are here, why I am here, my eyes, ears, the entire piecemeal body that I am inside or it's inside me or floating just above me or me floating just above it, two more strangers milling, swelling the crowd and whatever question I ask, no one could answer because the language here is Sumerian and I don't speak a word and who does.

Sumer an empire I once read about, ancient as counting, ancient as words and writing, Sumer, and I find myself there, and Sumer holds my grandparents' row house, not really their house, they didn't own one, they rented, never owned more than a couple sticks, though my grandfather worked hard and drank hard enough year after year from the very first day he arrived in Pittsburgh, Pennsylvania, emigrant fresh from Culpeper, Virginia, to earn, to own the entire city where he grew old and died, still poor after decades of work and drinking gallons, tons of dago red, too poor to pay an undertaker to display his body in a funeral parlor after the undertaker did whatever undertakers do to preserve lifeless flesh as a kind of person-size doll, only enough in my grandfather's insurance policy to pay for the doll and have it delivered to my grandparents' row house, insurance paid in weekly installments to one of those usually bespectacled, usually Jewish men whose specialty insuring row-house dwellers like my grandparents, collecting nickel by nickel from them weekly for decades if the family could afford to keep up premiums, or if not keep up exactly, beg as my grandmother told me she did Mr. Cohen, a nice, really a nice, nice man, she whispered to me, begged him many a week, then sometimes the next two or three empty-handed weeks, to grant more time or more like take pity on her while profusely, sometimes not dry-eyed, she literally begged to the point of almost dropping down to her knees but he was nice and could see the abjection coming and a family man himself so desired no part of it and let her off with a weary nod as she stood there wavering in her housecoat, him always in my grandfather's easy chair just inside the front door where he'd settled and crossed one leg over the other and opened his coupon book first time she let him in the house, Mr. Cohen nice enough to shut sometimes the book propped on his knee, saying her name sometimes while he slowly wagged his head, a halfway frown, halfway smile, *Freeda, oh Freeda,* letting her off this once or twice or more until she saved the nickel or majority of a series of delinquent nickels, and seated now on a wooden kitchen chair, bare knees under her housecoat pressed together, on the piece of furniture furthest from the man, but too close anyway, she counted out coins, rose and delivered them to his palm from a kerchief in her lap she had opened as if opening Fort Knox, the way she might open her lips or legs to a stranger to feed her starving family then kill herself immediately afterwards or maybe not.

Not the way she opens that flowered kerchief with its twisted corners and withdraws blood money, a few crumpled bills smelling like talcum powder, and hands them to me first year I went away to college, but yes, open it she did to pay the insurance man so family and friends could come to pay their respects in a respectable way, in a respectable place, a living place scrubbed spotless clean so nobody tempted to say or think these trifling niggers never owned two sticks to rub together, that old man laid out in one of the tiny rooms of a dark, tiny row house, no windows for sun to peek through, dark, stuffy, and cramped as the box the old man winds up in after working hard, drinking hard every day of his life, and to show for it what—him and Freeda in this narrow-ass box of row house barely large enough to hold two old people and here come one his daughters and her three babies cramped up in there boarding with them, upset, crying daily, messes all the time everywhere and suddenly it's busy, noisy as a Sumer marketplace in the yellowish, shit-brown sand of a desert's vastness because the daughter and kids got no place else to go, my father deserted my mother and nowhere for us in this great big sprawled-out city my grandfather could have bought and sold a couple times over with the fruit of his labor if there had been fruit instead of just more labor till the day he died on the toilet in a bathroom too small for him to stretch out his long-shanked legs, they, his long legs I inherited, wind up laid out in a wooden box with a hinged lid so the lid's top third could stay open for viewing till they shut it down at night, peace at night from December's last fly in his face in that room I was scared to enter alone in that row house my grandparents didn't own but renting a lifetime, working a lifetime and after all that, still not a penny of insurance money for the undertaker's services except the job of draining fluids and pumping in embalming oil or whatever was in the body after the undertaker fetched it then brought it back home to lie in state in a dark, stuffy little room because all the rooms tiny and dark, except maybe the kitchen a little less so, one small window back there at the row house's rear end, sunlight back there in my grandmother Freeda's long, straight, gray hair, hair passed from her father, a German man I never met, an immigrant whose family perhaps neighbors of Mr. Cohen's family back in the old country, light frizzed up in strands loose from the bun my grandmother kept it tied in while busy cooking or cleaning, light floating atop her head if I looked up at her from the Bible days coloring book and crayons on the kitchen table one of my aunts had given me on my birthday or Easter I think I remember, but respectable people wouldn't lay out a body in the kitchen would they, even if kitchen the brightest room, even if no money to rent a room for three, four hours of one day and other services like programs with photos or sad music piped into a funeral parlor, but a certain old-fashioned dignity maybe after all about the old-time way some people down home and emigrants in the North, too, used to bury people, laying them out in the house they lived in until church, cemetery, a certain familiarity and roundness and appropriateness to being at home even if the dead person didn't own, just rented, just lived there, just occupied the cabin or row house, slept in it as I sleep in my body without owning it but get habituated to think of the flesh as belonging to me, as Sumer could belong to me and me to it while I'm remembering a day in Sumer, beginning to teach myself Sumerian as if it were a language a person in a story might learn to speak to write in another place and time.

Strangers pass by me on Homewood streets, Sumer streets, and I think each of them a carrier, each carried by time, each one as close to another time and place as I will ever get. Not very close I'm pretty sure. No matter how close, how like mine another's time seems. Or seemed in other places at different times. Cities, people's faces and lives impenetrable. Don't know their names, but pretty sure strangers in the streets have names, pretty sure they have breath, hearts, had a mother, a father, histories more or less like mine, begotten, born, mortal like me, passing by like me, evidence for each other of time's presence, time's everlastingness, but also each hidden by time's invisibility. Invisible as primal black darkness in the oldest Sumer story. Pretty sure I could be any one of these strangers passing by, or not be, and not know the difference if I was, if I was seeing me or not seeing me with eyes not mine, who would I be, where would my time be. Who could tell me the name of a city where I belong. Where we are. Who could show me time inside of them, time inside or outside of me.

To write my story I must teach myself the language of Sumer, the history of Sumer it inscribes when written. Learn new words for things I recognize with other words from another language, a process like forgetting and remembering my color, gender, age, or features of my own face, more or less, to recognize faces of strangers on the street. As Sumer forms, it shapes me. We grow thick as thieves. Lovers who need to be constantly reminding each other we are inseparable. As if the first word is also not the first step away and how we begin to disappear.

Many languages in Sumer. Many Sumers begging to be heard if you learn to listen. Listen to a scared ten-year-old, to a slave or a poet begging words to free them.

———

Though not exactly one of them, I served in a regiment of colored men born enslaved, then precariously free to fight in Sumer's Great Civil War, a prolonged conflict following many, many decades of vicious, bloody strife, ethnic cleansings, declarations of independence, tribal feuds, alliances, religious inquisitions, and massacres, the parsings into power blocs and political units and ideologies that precede a stable empire. Desert harshness characterized much of the land—few stones, few trees—yet reliable cycles of rainfall and drought deposited abundantly fertile alluvial soil along banks of broad, navigable rivers, and meant that Sumer had always supported and encouraged agriculture, commerce, a steadily growing population, rise of many towns and cities. The Great Civil War that did not end slavery as promised, but established Empire's unchallengeable military supremacy, transformed a patchwork quilt of quarrelsome, antagonistic neighbors into a vast tapestry spreading to the very edges of the known world. A colorful, ornate tapestry whose intricate design of gods, heroes, myths, its luxurious fabric, smothering weight narrated tales of Empire's fabulous wealth and power.

Orphaned at ten in this Empire, I had been apprenticed to an old couple. The man instructed me in skills of masonry. His specialty, until crippled by a fall, working on walls after they had reached a height too uncomfortable, too dangerous for ordinary masons. The old woman's contribution to the project of transforming an orphan boy into a useful citizen, aside from the usual dawn to dusk and then some more duties all women in families required to perform for husbands and offspring, duties I recalled my mother and grandmother performing daily, was to teach me not to expect reward or appreciation as I accomplished endless, exhausting tasks assigned to me, but on the contrary, to anticipate being treated as worthless, or worse burdensome, by those who assigned and benefited from my exertions.

If the old woman had once known a word meaning "tenderness"—and such a word must exist in the language of Sumerians—I would say she tried on rare occasions to express tenderness to me. Stuttering, frustrated attempts as when a person wants very much to express a feeling, and knows a word for it exists, and is sure she knows it, but the word stubbornly, teasingly eludes her, and she shakes her head, her eyes blink, wheel vacantly, then close, pondering a void until she remembers who she is and gives up trying to remember the word, angry that it has deserted her and will not serve her, does not fill an emptiness she, for a moment or so, almost desperately needs to fill, angry at herself then, her long lifetime of failing, again and again, she believes, to please anyone, to measure up to other people's expectations, and finally her anger directed at the one, at me, the person for whom, in whom, with whom the lost word could have initiated an exchange, a softer, clearer exchange, allowing her to be the sort of person she could be if ever given half a chance, but the stubborn, willful word floats a hairbreadth away, resisting her effort to recall it, the missing word that might express what is missing, if only she could force it to obey, as Empire teaches her to obey—word down on its knees, crawling through her lips.

Like most young males I was conscripted into Sumer's army when the Great Civil War began. Our heads were shaved. We were issued weapons and instructed in their use. I was eager to leave the old couple, happy to be relieved from drudgeries of a vocation, the threat of "tenderness."

Quickly, I distinguished myself as fearless, intelligent, willing follower or leader, first to volunteer for difficult or dangerous missions, deferential to superiors, unsqueamish, aggressive, no mercy or tears wasted on the foe. Rose through the ranks and was sent to officer school. Led a regiment of South Carolina freedmen by the Great Civil War's conclusion.

Sumer's endless wars in my blood, I guess you could say. Or say in the blood of all of us. My uncle, my mother's gentle brother, Otis, fought in America's Pacific War. "Pacific" an ironic name for any war, but especially for no-holds-barred, take-no-prisoners, victory-or-death struggles waged on hilly, jungled islands. Primitive combat, up close and personal warfare whose intimacies would be familiar to Sumerian warriors—mano a mano duels, horns blaring, drums thumping, screaming, charging with bayonets deployed like spears, kicking, punching, knives, slaughter in which Sumerians would have excelled and probably prevailed—yet war also waged with machines—kamikaze planes, aircraft carriers, flame-throwing tanks, artillery barrages, bombs raining from the sky—firepower that would have annihilated all of Sumer's proud, savage legions in five minutes. Thus a "Pacific" war not to suggest calm, but to distinguish one zone or theater of war from another, one featuring Americans killing *japs,* whose island empire lay in the Pacific Ocean, the other theater starring Americans killing *krauts,* whose empire, a large portion of it anyway, bounded by the Atlantic Ocean, a body of water much smaller than the Pacific, named for a lost continent, a lost empire, lost civilization that had disappeared into the sea.

I have fond memories of Uncle Otis. Uncle O T, we kids called him, my mother's younger brother. My earliest memory of him, his big hand wrapping mine, pale skin like my mother's, his voice soft, kind as some of the women's. Recall him reading to me, how he'd become someone not him while answering my questions. My curiosity turning on a light in him, a shine almost, making him, his words very distant but absolutely convincing. An uncle seldom spoken about in family gatherings once he started coming around less after he dropped out of art school and began tending bar, after prison time, after time in a federal facility in Lexington, Kentucky, to cure heroin addiction, then wound up for many years a short-order cook in a diner on Braddock Avenue so to say hi when I was in town I had to go round to the diner's back door. Reminiscing with my cousin about our quiet, favorite uncle O T, dead for years, younger brother of both our moms, and both moms gone too, and my cousin says he doesn't recall anybody in the family ever saying our uncle gay. *Gay* not even a word back then, my cousin says. Huh-uh. No. Like you when we were little, you know, we never thought of O T that way. Course once we got grown, we knew. But no reason then to talk about it.

My soldier uncle too gentle for his father, my wine-drinking, gambling, street-brawler, lady-killing grandfather, and part of my grandfather's love for me began there maybe—as rebuke to a son, O T, who displeased him. The grandfather I adored, who adored me, ignoring his shy, quiet, thus disappointing son, and skipping ahead a generation, father again for the next. My grandfather's love for me thus also remorse for failure of love. Him perhaps seeking a chance to redeem himself, his progeny, hoping to instill in me, a new boy child, all the manly qualities men like him worshipped in themselves, qualities stunted or absent altogether because of lack of opportunity to express them in lives men like my grandfather could not control, lives in which their talk and dreams treated by others as cheap, so never exactly worthy, never manly enough in their own eyes and certainly not in the eyes of those who controlled empire, those who had money to spend, who hired and fired, owned, bought and sold land, who despised, disrespected the sorts of lives they allowed or allotted to people like my grandfather who was quite aware and very punished by that awareness of being a lesser man in those others' eyes. Less worthy except a smart, tough man like my grandfather dreams an alternative version of himself and fabricates a separate story of who he is, and what he might become if things were different, sharing this Sumer story with others like him caught in a similar dilemma, sharing ideas, myths about who they are, sharing bullshit, approving in each other various shaky, shady ways of behaving to conceal and disguise the heartbreak of being perceived as not quite men.

They, we, improvise makeshift ways of escaping an inescapable trap, invent styles of hanging out, of lording over women, talking deep, deep, impenetrable shit, or silence or loudness or flight, commit acts of stunning selfishness, love, or pure violence or grace or courage. We hide or strut the streets like peacocks, lie, brawl, are renegades, invincible athletes, invisible men, whatever—men in spite of or because of perfecting such stunted expressions which are good for nothing much, finally, except perhaps to delay inevitable reckoning. Abruptly, in a single instant is how the reckoning frequently happens. A moment coming, sooner or later, that feels like truth because afterwards, a man never able to forget missing his chances not to be what he appears to be in the scornful eyes of others. Including the eyes of his own womenfolk and kids. That moment when he must ask himself, well, well, well . . . if I'm not the sorry-assed, colored creature other people scorn, then who am I—evil gangster on a throne that some boys, boys hell-bent on becoming just like him, believe he. Or perhaps the reckoning even worse for my grandfather when he realizes one day his boy, his male child, his son turns away because he wants to be nothing like him, that the boy owns a life at least as real as his, a life plain as day for everybody living in the row houses to see—a different life displayed in details of how the child cries, crawls, stands, walks, talks—a life that denies not only the Sumer my grandfather dreams for a son, but dreams of for himself.

Perhaps the story above true or partly true, but either way, anyway, I see my uncle as victim of it, see myself as a beneficiary, an accomplice perched on my grandfather's shoulders—his consolation, redemption, resurrection—as we tour Homewood, one name for our neighborhood of raggedy row houses. Me listening to my grandfather's stories, rhymes and songs, basking in the peace of his voice, singing "You Are My Sunshine," *My only sunshine*—while my gentle uncle O T fought on Okinawa.

Fought an inaccurate word for services my uncle O T, my grandfather's only son, rendered to empire. A ferocious, deadly, months-long battle raged around him on Okinawa, but since my uncle colored, he—like almost all colored troops on the island or in the larger war—was assigned to auxiliary, support duties, not combat. His job to bury *japs* not kill them, though it's not unlikely that as he guided his bulldozer's sharp blade through fields of corpses, he may have delivered a coup de grace, beheading or gouging open or crushing an occasional live *jap* playing possum until he could rise up and fight again or a *jap* who had not yet quite succumbed to the horrific wounding that had earned him a place among piles of maggoty, decomposing, fly-infested bodies harvested and stacked, bodies scooped up from where they had fallen in desperate, futile, sayonara last stands and trucked to where my uncle does his job, bodies whose stink clings to his khakis, cap, bandanna he ties over his nose and mouth, bodies of civilians as well as soldiers, most of the dead casualties of relentless allied assaults from air, land, sea though some executed as spies, some victims of self-inflicted mayhem once the general, reciprocal killing on Okinawa abates, violence wanes, and peace approaches for victors, the unthinkable approaches for the vanquished.

Many enemy soldiers, rather than face the shame and ignominy of defeat, threw themselves into the sea, into fifty-foot breakers like those that batter black rocks far below the cliff where my uncle O T pilots a steel-treaded machine. He's grateful for yielding soil that halfway inters or forms a breading of blood, gore, rags, dirt to coat flopping corpses, obliterated faces and severed limbs he shoves, careful, careful not to get too close to the runway's end and tumble over into the Pacific behind a blade-load of dead *japs*.

O T smoked Camels, he tells me. Endless Camels. Sumer camel depicted on each pack. Many smokes in succession. Rapidly. Like bingeing on greasy potato chips, one after another fast, grabbing a handful from a bowl, hoping no one notices him alone in a dark corner stuffing his mouth, chip after chip, munching, swallowing salty wads in somebody's basement party, music slow dragging, shadowy couples grinding, two hunched-over people, one lumpy shape, two wrapped so tightly together they must be pretending to be one, four feet stuck to the tarry floor, but their feet not stuck and sinking like his, their synced bodies sway, jiggle, glide in place to a thump thumping bump-and-grind tune spinning on a record player, rhythms intoxicating them, but for him inscrutable, intimate, hurtful as bumps, prods, piercing lacerations his blind machine delivers to dead flesh on Okinawa, an island in the Pacific where overhead a tropical sun blazes fiercely as Sumer's at noon, unremitting heat and sweat and white desert brilliance till suddenly sky morphs, cracks, torrential banzai sheets of gray downpour, everybody, everything drowning, swept away.

My uncle remembers munching chips like I remember munching potato chips in the dark of teenage parties, condemned to conquer girls or be conquered by them and both choices defeats, wars no one wins.

My uncle O T hears potato chips crunch inside his sore-gummed jaw, smiling though he hopes to god no one watches him eat. He keeps his lips pressed together just in case, ashamed of his mouth, mouth clamped shut even when he smiles or chews, so the gap, bottom right from a tooth knocked out, doesn't show, no dentist till he's nineteen years old, drafted into the army, quick, mandatory training camp inspection— keep the good ones, bad ones yanked—why you hollering like a big baby, trooper, don't you know this is war, what the fuck you expect boy your momma coo-cooing, holding your soft little hand, sissy boy, don't you speak the language, don't you hear me talking to you, trooper, next, next, why you pussyfooting, you in everybody's way, splib, over and out nigger get the fuck out the way bulldozers backed up to San Francisco and here you sit taking your own good time, blocking the runway sweaty niggers plowed up and pounded to get this war over quick and here you are sitting there like you got all the goddamn time in the world, like those fine bitches supposed to wait forever while you sneak around hiding in a dark corner chewing potato chips as if one them hos supposed to beg you to do the nasty. What's wrong wit you, sonnyboy.

Maybe Homewood public library where my uncle used to take me by the hand is where I first encountered Sumer. The word *maybe* means "maybe not" in this language I write now. No guarantee that in Sumerian it means the same. Or means anything. Maybe there's no *maybe* in Sumer. Maybe everything always there and not there inside every person. Black/white. Female/male. Right/wrong. Or not. Maybe nothing. There or not there. Nothing matters in a game or puzzle unless you invent rules. But invented rules don't have power, any more than language has power, to make something of nothing. Rules, like the rules for counting and thinking and writing, fall off the edge, tumble into an unfathomable sea of darkness that does not start or finish, that does not churn or spit skyscraper waves, that is nothing, and swallows you and your bulldozer machine.

Nights too hot to sleep on Okinawa, my uncle tells me, so he smoked instead. We called cigarettes *fags,* he says. Says fags a kind of sleep. Flimsy-ass sleep, really, but better than nothing when all you have is hours and hours of no sleep until morning and morning not another day just the same goddamned day again. Stink and heat and sweat and buzzing flies, invisible insects that bite like cobras you got welts all over your body you scratch bloody and draw more bloodsucking, mothersucking flies mosquitoes same ones feasting on the dead they can't get enough of, but smoke might help you try to tell yourself as you light up a night's first Camel, then another, then another, telling yourself la-di-da maybe it will help, knowing while you thinking that lie it ain't so. No way man, you ain't hardly gon smoke yourself to sleep you know better you know smoke drifts away, gone, gone, drifts apart, flimsy as a cobweb your hand brushes away, as darkness that you cannot see through but see everything in it, see the dead, see yourself burying them or not burying them, and know crystal clear you are one of them, the dead, the enemy you are shoving, scraping up, you see them, see yourself ride over them ride em cowboy ride your shiny little pony, patty-cake / patty-cake / baker man / put 'em in the oven / fast as you can. Drive these piles of stinking japs and krauts and niggers and fags into the sea today tomorrow same same.

You smoke more smokes, more fags as if they could light up the island, burn down the house, as if this Okinawa gone in the morning as if black sky not a lid on a skillet to keep grease popping, people frying. It was not easy is all I'm trying to say, after all, nephew, but no harder for your uncle than the rest of those poor boys hurting and killing each other over there.

———

Smoke floats, drifts, scene changes and doesn't. Grandfather gone. I grow older, larger, stronger, but no less afraid. Darkness abides. Like my uncle I pretend to build a wall, a thick solid wall of smoke. Old Sumer man, master mason, taught me how to build walls, didn't he, with clay bricks mortar cement row after row, story atop story it rises, and unafraid, you caper up there, teasing the edge, working, willing the wall higher, a man with nerves of steel who rides high above row after row of dead.

I am beside an ocean again, not the Pacific, but here beside the Atlantic with my memories of uncle, grandfather, father, old Sumerian mason. In France now where I spend summers and falls with the woman I love. A warning received—*Medusa coming.* Do not swim along Brittany's coasts. Poisonous jellyfish driven by currents, currents driven by powerful, unseasonable storms in the south. Hordes of a small, round, blue-black-purplish variety of medusa never seen before in these waters will soon infest them. Jellyfish that possess lethal bites. Nature upset by global warming and pollution just as nature goes haywire in the Last Days my mother used to say in the last years before she died, quoting the Bible's dire prophesies of Apocalyptic breakdown each time she'd see in the newspaper or hear on TV topsy-turvy evidence of things falling apart, of human beings and nature profoundly, wickedly, unforgivingly gone awry—three-headed turtles, a baby cooked in a microwave oven, floods and earthquakes, plagues, genocide, poisoned Halloween candy passed out to Homewood kids trick-or-treating in rich white people's neighborhoods, a man whose head grows beneath his shoulders.

As luminously calm, clairvoyant, compassionate as my mom could be in the last years before she passed, still I wondered sometimes if maybe she was seeking confirmation of a secret wish, a dark Sumerian wish which she believed should remain unspoken by her forever, her hope that since god obviously had chosen to end her life soon, perhaps he also intended to take us—the ones she loved and who loved her—along with her, take us and all the rest of the world and leave nothing behind when her turn to go, an unthinkably selfish wish, a hidden desire she was harboring in the back of her mind when she pursed her lips, shook her head, and cited with absolute, worried conviction some uncanny, freakish happening that proved the Last Days surely upon us, days warning us to get right, get ready not only to save our souls, not only because judgment day nigh, but because for her the thought of separation, of being alone—no family, no church—too awful, too unbearable and in her dark secret prayer she was beseeching her Heavenly Father, Yes, please, Lord, go ahead and do the deed all these terrible signs and wonders portend, and since you got to do it soon anyway, do it when you take this old woman, her weary body, famished soul, Lord—when you take me home to your bosom, sweep this wicked old world away, too. Take me, Lord, and everybody I love and loves me, please, in the cleansing whirlwind you promised would clean up all this mess.

She's gone. Darkness claimed my mother, disappointed her, betrayed or ignored her, paid no mind to her prayers, nor her guesses, nor her wishful thinking. Her pleas gone, her gone, forsaken by her god, but no better for me, for us left behind, than for her, though unlike her, I harbor no wish, expect no favor, believe in none, ask for none, I'm just here, missing her terribly, the world I inhabit chugging along hopelessly, cruelly broken, unfixable as she understood in her last days. The darkness, emptiness unfathomable now for me, mysterious as those Last Days her god prophesied. Darkness, emptiness swallowing us so maybe shared by us, though they separate us, too, render us further apart than millennia, those years counted in chunks of thousands to measure vast distance from this moment here, now, to Sumer. Coming and going from here to there and back and there again, the years, the moments I would if I could, use to build a city and a wall securing that city which holds us, my family, people loved and loving each other, safe, prospering within walls I construct to protect us, gird us, except the materials I have on hand, in my hands to build a wall are nothing, or less, just thoughts, words, just stories, just smoke, just counting, longing secretly for an end to toil and trouble like my mother saying her name, saying mine in the dark, saying the lost, forgotten name of a father who left one morning, never returned.

I check my watch. *Tick. Tock. Tick. Tock.* Are you checking yours. Wondering how long this story might be. Wondering if it ever ends. How separate parts connect. Does it resemble yours less or more. One story or many. Whose. Are stories truly there, or just noisy thrashing of another creature in darkness surrounding you.

I bought my watch several years ago, *tick-tock,* in Chinatown on Canal Street in New York City. Same merchandise displayed outdoors on Canal Street in one shop after another, endlessly it seems, stores not quite identical but selling the same if not quite identical stuff. How do they compete I often wonder, passing by, looking at more or less the same selection in each sidewalk bin, in each shop window, each shop's narrow, steel-ribbed glass door beckoning like the last and next, and how does anybody earn a living all selling the same goddamn shit only inches away from each other I wonder, but they must, is the obvious answer, or they try anyway and manage, it seems. Chinatown been here forever, right, I think when

I purchase a watch, luxury brand name, less than seventy-five bucks and the door tingles shut behind me, a little almost musical treat for those who purchase an item or those who just enter or just leave a shop empty-handed, its jingling breath an announcement that the shop lives and stuff stocked, displayed here gets bought and the peal of tiny bells or gongs also warns the clerk or proprietor, one and the same often for economy's sake, that a customer or thief has arrived or departed.

The tinkle-tinkle cheery mystery of Chinatown, of watches seductively cheaper than anywhere else in the city, but beware, you may not be getting what you think you're buying so better keep your receipt, if you receive one and it's not bogus or counterfeit as the item you believe you are buying, but you won't be able to find the shop or be sure you have the right one even if you bother to return to demand money back or at least exchange another watch for the watch that ceased telling time three days after you fastened it on your wrist and maybe you should consider yourself lucky, after all, because that false silver band or false shiny shiny gold band worn for very long would have turned your skin an unhealthy color, and maybe that solves the allure of Chinatown. Explains perhaps the Russian roulette attraction of Chinatown. Of Sumer's noisy marketplaces. Mystery of Chinatown watches. Mystery of what people bet on betting on love.

Here at an edge of the Atlantic, on a beach in Brittany we drive to almost every morning between 10:00 and 12:00, depending on the tide, I note our arrival time, *tick-tock,* on my Chinatown watch. My lover's time since she's the swimmer not me and she decides the hour we arrive. Ideal time from her point of view, time which seamlessly becomes ideal for me, too. Time usually when nobody or only a few people around, no victims nor sightings yet of medusa, a time before the tide at its lowest ebb would impel her to tiptoe gingerly across a hundred or more yards of slippery, treacherous rocks and stones to reach water.

Best like now when just the two of us and tides up and quiet enough from where I stand at the sea's edge to hear her stroke back and forth between two more or less parallel strings of yellow buoys, long, waveringly straight lines separated by about two hundred yards, each line stretching from shore towards the horizon, strings of buoys bobbing far out into the sea until they meet another string of yellow buoys barely visible from here, paralleling the shore and connecting the other two lines to enclose a zone for swimmers that boats are supposed to honor and mostly do.

She's a good ways out there in the sea, close, but not too close to the outer perimeter of yellow buoys floating there if she needs them, and though she's a very strong swimmer and does not depend upon them, both of us grateful for the buoys anyway. It's the sea, isn't it, and anything can happen. Beach deserted at this hour, no boats, no other swimmers, and me no help. If I dived into the water to try to rescue her, I'd only drown, too. Water where she is way over my head, me useless, drowning surely, even if by luck I managed to get out that deep. An imaginary lifeguard at best, we both understand and share the joke, the silly story of me on duty, keeping watch, pretending she's safer because I track her, walking back and forth, sneaker soles printing in wet sand while she swims laps I time with my lucky watch, lucky because here on my wrist still ticking seven, ten years after I bought it in Chinatown.

Us lucky, too, it seems in this story—a sunny day, time and tide right, lucky to have discovered this beach, to return here year after year. Water bright, clear, her arms splashing, lifted, dropping, cleaving a white path back and forth through the sea, lucky, but we try hard not to anticipate luck, not to presume, not to expect it, luck of her skill and luck of my wishful thinking that as long as I am a sentinel here on the shore nothing unlucky can befall her—after all, wouldn't I—of course

I would—leap in without a moment's hesitation and swim to her rescue, wouldn't I—yes, yes indeed—and couldn't good luck triumph over the bad luck I can't really swim, just love the sea, enjoy paddling around, brisk shock of Brittany's always chill water first plunge in, floating on my back, syncing my arms and legs like a frog the way she taught me to stay on top the water—both of us lucky enough, pampered enough by luck to make us as superstitious, awed, as afraid to jinx luck as my dear, lost mom who feared every scrap or streak of decent luck attaching itself to her—and like my mom we know better, don't we, and never speak aloud to each other nor even think aloud inside ourselves about luck that doesn't belong to us, luck that might just as easily bring sudden heartbreak, so we just hold on, do not name it, do not separate luck from Brittany, from roar of surf, good night's sleep, crisp air, her cutting through the water practicing, perfecting this stroke or that one while I keep time casually, for my own benefit, to entertain and distract myself strolling back and forth at the ocean's edge, counting until the moment she's coming up out of the water and then I holler, Twenty, thirty minutes, whatever, as if she didn't already know the number of laps and how much time each lap exhausts, time in the water a count she precisely, silently maintains as she glides back and forth, surrounded, immersed, vulnerable beyond knowing—her heartbeat, breath, strong arms, kicking legs futile as mine if luck we dare not celebrate, changes.

After the Great Sumerian Civil War (*civil* an adjective as inappropriate for war as *pacific*), that war which, instead of ending slavery, created an empire, I was decommissioned, rewarded, as a few lucky veterans were, with an opportunity to better myself by attending at empire's expense an institution of higher learning. By then I understood that I had been a fearful, powerless child before the War, and that knowledge, combined with a young man's surge of exuberance and optimism surviving war had released, combined with an old man's sense of fatality instilled prematurely by years of combat in which anybody's life or death, survival or extinction simply a matter of chance—a buddy shaking out a fag for me then blown to smithereens after he walked a few dozen yards away—that mix of fright, expectation, insight, and ignorance freed me, encouraged me not to go to school to learn a trade or pursue a profession, but to study Sumer's language and history.

In that story *study* means rules invented as I proceeded. No program of formal training, no apprenticeship, no residence in a community of masters and aspirants. Instead I granted myself license to wander Sumer's vastness. To listen, read, write, wait and see. Eventually, to support myself I needed to find work, and since in an empire, one cannot work and not work for empire, I began to serve empire as a messenger, a scribe of sorts. Employing the still clumsy tools for recording numbers and words extant during those ancient times, I crisscrossed empire's vast expanses, roamed deserts and hills, rode barges, ferries, rafts, boats with bladelike sails up and down the two great rivers, Tigris, Euphrates, trekked endless leagues on foot laden with clay tablets, my head full of weightless, invisible words, gathering and recording information in a language whose odd sounds and peculiar wedge-shaped script had been absolutely unfamiliar, literally foreign to me when I'd arrived in Sumer.

Back and brain overloaded, overtaxed, burdened down like any poor mule or camel, collecting and delivering facts and figures empire required to control its subjects (*enthrall* and *control,* synonyms in Sumerian), I became something like a soldier again, except the mayhem and violence of war's swords, guns, bombs—not usually visible in front of my eyes. No nauseating stench, no flames or smoking ruins, no groans, screams of dying humans and animals assailed my senses. But in the course of performing my duties as messenger, I encountered appalling results of a different sort of conflict. Empire ceaselessly imposing and enforcing brutal choices—win or lose, feast or starve, black or white, good or evil, female or male, rise or fall—upon its inhabitants, choices separating people from others and from themselves.

Atop one of those huge, black stones encrusted with razor-sharp, broken oyster shells, stones common along this coast of Brittany, stones bedded immemorially in sand, a menace when the tide rises and their dangerous surfaces are hidden underwater, elevated on such a stone so I'm a few feet taller than usual, I stare out to sea, towards scattered islands whose dim silhouettes form a kind of intermittent, shrouded horizon line beyond which the ocean stretches that feeds this gulf of Morbihan, and I can almost hear night descending upon sea and beach, night quieting wind and water. Feel myself drifting inside the darkness of Sumer's oldest story.

Just beyond the rock, beach full of unburied soldiers. Too simple and unexpected a sight, too present to pretend the dead soldiers might not be there. *There*, no matter how improbable and bizarre. No confusion. No frightened, dissenting voice inside me—please, please, this can't be happening, I must be dreaming, please—instead I see what I see—rows of shadowed corpses, unburied bodies night drapes, corpses left behind as the tide, the *marée*, as it's called here, runs out. Countless dead bodies here on a beach in Brittany, where just yesterday she was swimming while I kept a loving eye on her, my footprints in the sand tracing her path back and forth through the water, but I'm alone now, a pit stop to piss, then mounting a rock to stare at the sea, take a deep breath before hiking seven kilometers back to our cottage, and suddenly, below me on the sand, many rows and scattered piles of dead soldiers.

Maybe Japanese Imperial Marines, I think at first, thinking of my uncle O T, but no, no specific identities cling to the bodies, just anonymous debris of war, a mass of uniformed corpses no one's gotten around yet to clearing away. Perhaps no need to hurry a cleanup. Some of these victims of war probably very young and have lots of time, lots of patience. They could be alive in some other place, quiet, serene, content as they wait for whatever comes next, each of them in one piece, not stinking, not rotting, inhabiting an empire elsewhere, and whether young or old, why would they want to rush back here, here where I find myself gazing over rubble of them, where they have landed and litter the beach, layers of dead transforming a flat stretch of sand to dark, rippling, lumpy terrain beyond a black rock I had an urge to stand on to look out at the water. Less steady now, me not the rock, as I stare at a carpet of dead that spreads to the sea's edge, and more dead in the water, invisible beneath gently lapping waves of an ocean full of dead bodies and live bodies that consume them, uncountable bodies unseen, waiting.

Some of these uniformed dead could be U.S. Marines. Marines whose anthem I memorized when I was a kid. We fight our country's battles on land and air and sea. After my cousin and I watched Marines featured as young glory guys in some movie or another at the Belmar show in Homewood, we always pretended we were Marines when we played war. Our uncle Otis never told us his war stories back then, and we didn't quite believe our gentle uncle a real soldier, anyway, and we sure weren't practicing to be quiet Uncle O T in our endless, shoot-em-up war games, squabbling always about who should carry the biggest gun, who would die first, gloriously, and be the hero. My cousin almost getting his wish, enlisting in the Marines fresh out of high school, grievously wounded in an ambush that nearly annihilated his entire squad in Vietnam.

Marines from one country or another sprawled, heaped among these ambiguous, anonymous corpses here on the beach after their war ended, after it rages on to other places, but war still here, too, nibble, nibbling away at them while memories of them far away as Japan, Sumer, Homewood fade and become stories, separate stories, warring stories empire stitches together to make one story true. Row after row of butchered, maybe sleeping bodies, maybe hallucinations I think I see because my thoughts sneak up, whispering before I see them coming— "Look, look," beach littered by the dead who are not there. No. Bodies there. I study them and they do not disappear. I look and look, can't look away. Casualties not of one war, many wars, many murdered in Empire's Great War that never ceases. More substantial, more doomed to die again and again the longer I look and begin to notice details of age, torn uniforms, nakedness, a boot, limbs stiff in postures of agony or peace, an open mouth, open eyes, a gentle hand I could touch if I had the courage, or no eyes, no mouth, only black holes to count.

Sumer desert terrain. No ocean. No Marines. Except I recall an elite cohort standing tall, golden tips of spears gleaming a foot above plumed golden helmets, gold gauntlets above fists that grip spears, gold shields planted on the deck of the Emperor's cobra-headed launch, warriors at attention behind a red railing, unmoving as statues, warriors I never saw blink, though as a boy I couldn't quite believe they were live men and kept my eyes riveted upon them to see one blink when twice yearly on pilgrimages back and forth to the City of Temples, the Emperor's hundred-oared craft led a numberless procession of boats past our village, first going south on the Tigris, Emperor and court descending the waters to establish themselves in the Lower Kingdom at the commencement of planting season, bearing prayers, caged slaves and animals to sacrifice, tithes of gold and silver, then another imperial fleet returning north in the season of harvest to the capital city, Urez, back and forth as they have been going and returning since time began, and must always descend and ascend the living waters back and forth as the Law Songs command, back to Urez, after reaping what had been sown, boats laden with grain, spices, dyes, precious metals, new slaves, war stories, love stories, chants of gratitude and praise to Sumer's deities for granting prosperity and power

I happened upon this final story—or better to say this last Sumer story this story will tell—like I happened upon Sarah's story, only this one not in a magazine. I pieced together this final story over the years, and it begins around the time of America's Civil War, or just yesterday, so to speak, a love story I learned from voices present like voices Sarah claims she hears, voices bringing her gifts and loneliness in conversations with people no one else sees or hears.

In this story I meet a poet. We are both survivors. She had survived slavery, and I had survived bloody combat in a civil war fought to end slavery. One morning I received a letter from a faraway town, from a woman unknown to me, born in Africa. The letter's words all I have to confirm her existence, but immediately I feel her undeniably alive inside me, alive as my swimmer, my beautiful lady whose strokes daily carry her far away, too far until she turns, swims closer again, love of my life, but she's a different story, separate from this other story of love manqué, a ghostly bride-of-wishful-thinking, regret, a lost mother, stranger, poet, daughter, soul mate . . .

Stop, please stop, she says, says the woman I first meet in a poem

41

in a letter she sends to introduce herself. But since she doesn't sign the letter with her name nor include a return address, I guess it's truer to say her letter introduces me, not to her, but to her poem.

A poem framed by a formal salutation, *Dear Sir,* above it, and below it, instead of her name, she writes, *from a free woman of color born in Africa.* Poem of few lines, simple words, many dashes, lots of vacant space, its sparseness seeming almost to enact an apology for the presumption of its existence. Then following her "signature," comes a sprawl of sentences. Lots of words helter-skelter, continuing until they nearly fill the sheet's reverse side. Words barely legible, obviously rushed, contrasting with the poem's stoic reserve:

I entreat you to forgive—if by chance my words reach you—this unwarranted intrusion upon your precious time—I am very aware that my entreating you is itself another unforgivable intrusion—but please believe me, kind sir, I am not a bold person and understand the trespass of sending—unsolicited—my poor verses to you—a selfish, rash act not mitigated—perhaps made worse—given the extreme admiration and respect your writing has always aroused in me—I feel myself blessed—as grateful multitudes of readers and citizens have been—by your distinguished achievements— stop, stop, stop—I shall, must stop here—I lose courage here— no special pleading—your large accomplishments and stature do not offer the tiniest license to impose upon your time—I will stop here—I'm getting lost here—words piling up—smothering my innermost feelings—I have no proper excuse and can torture out no arguments for attempting to bring to your attention a fragmentary—quite flawed, my heart assures me—expression of gratitude for the gifts you have so generously bestowed upon me and so many others—your service in the unfortunate Great

War—your writing that condemns war's hollow, evil victories—the heartening memoir of how you recruited, armed, and officered the enslaved, living among them, as one of them in the struggle to overthrow their oppressors—please, sir—please do not be offended if I designate you a treasure, a monument upon which I cannot resist laying a bouquet, small and insignificant though it be—

Her attempt to communicate with him posted to the national magazine in which from time to time he published an essay or poem and whose masthead listed him as assistant editor. How many years ago. How many letters since. She raises her eyes to the same window in the same parlor, same house, same street where she had folded the letter, inserted it in an envelope, sealed the envelope then concealed it in a pocket of the gingham housecoat, a favorite once, its voluminous skirt filled the overstuffed armchair it was her habit to occupy while on duty, and gave her small body inside it a claim to settle itself and be comfortable in a chair dwarfing her, a housecoat within whose well-deep pockets she once had imagined caching a nephew or niece of the household playing hide-and-seek in the rooms around her, all her charges, all those years, children growing up then gone.

The family's little ones asleep, as were the adults when she wrote the letter by candlelight at the parlor desk then ferried it up the back stairs where it sat a week, a month until she remembered it, secreted between discarded sheets of piano music atop old books in a carton in the same dark corner where that old-fashioned housecoat had hung on its nail, old lady gingham housedress she had hated, then learned to love, letter and poem asleep till she forgot fear, walked them to the post office five blocks away, a pleasant, tree-lined, peaceful walk through a town he once had visited, dead as Sumer he had called it in an essay. A town *quiet, placid,* he wrote, but not unusually so for this region of farms and colleges she might have argued, certainly not quiet that day on her way to the postmaster, envelope humming, on fire in her black wool knitting bag.

Perhaps this morning she should have donned that ancient gingham housecoat—young again in it—age she was when she arrived first time at the house, barely older than the family's oldest children she was purchased to care for. Had the garment been torn up into cleaning rags or was it still here, musty, moth-bitten now, stuffed somewhere in the upstairs storage closet that for how many years had been the room in which she slept every night. If she entered the breakfast room wearing the housecoat, would anyone notice her this morning, notice how she was dressed. The hired help, maybe. No one in the household privy to her presence, nor to the fact an out of town person arriving today to visit her, a rare, more than rare occurrence, but who would care or remember, who in the family would be surprised that she expected a man to ride up on a snorting, black stallion, hooves kicking up a swirling cloud of golden dust miraculously generated from Number 7's brick walkway, a turbaned Arab snatching her up behind him on his panting mount, or a snarling, hairy beastman pounding on the front door, kicking through it to burst into the parlor and eat her alive.

Weren't they used to her odd imaginings, her peculiarities as she was tolerant, used to theirs, this family that had bought, then freed her (her eternal gratitude thinner each year, vanishing once she understood that human beings could only pretend to buy, sell, or free other human beings). A family at first extremely critical of her peculiar speech, peculiar ways, but convinced, more or less, as decades passed, that she was irreplaceable, that despite her annoying, incorrigible differences, she served them faultlessly as the family waxed, waned, as son or daughter departed to begin a separate household, as an infant grandchild or silent, almost transparent remnant of an elder generation died, as young people increased in size and disappeared into their rooms, each pretending to be a stranger to siblings, mums and dads, grandparents, uncles, spinster aunts, but not strangers to her. Too intimately acquainted with the body of each of her charges, every intimate detail of each one's history. They were fellow sufferers, witnesses, victims, beneficiaries of peculiarities that united and divided the family, set each family member apart, though none an island separate as she was in this miniature sea of family bounded by the walls of Number 7 Richmond Avenue, Amherst, Massachusetts. A family whose prosperity rose and declined with empire's fortunes, a praying family, charitable, pillar of the community, but one that mostly minded its own business of unruffled surfaces and facade, and her role, her place, her duty simple in a fashion—always to be there, available when needed, disappearing when not needed, following family rules, instructed by them how to act, what to say, do, and see or not see, especially when the sea of family business stormy or worse, turbulent beyond navigating. Her job to accept, to follow commands, compromise her own desires despite the losses, the broken heart such service entailed. Or surely she would drown. Perish hopelessly alone and unhappy. She must abide by family strictures, crushing at times but necessary always. She must persist, struggle, strive to keep herself ensconced in family, part of a family in spite of her peculiarities, the peculiar cruelties of family. No choice but to honor that bargain, and quietly, too, no fuss. She must either make peace with that choice or be alone, doomed.

Old baggy-sleeved, baggy-skirted gingham housedress, the tiny, naked, free animalcule scuttling concealed within it she became when she wore it. Not today. No tricks. No flights of fantasy today. No hiding.

Why had she waited decades for him, for his knuckles rapping the wooden door. Or would he be the sort of man who lifted the brass knocker of Number 7 and let it tap crisply, once, twice. Years of secret correspondence, letters sent and not sent, received, not received, and sometimes she could believe she knew everything about him, though now, in this peculiar moment of truth, she admitted she understood nothing, had perished waiting for him to enter the front door of this stone house and she still knew nothing, not his habits nor smile, not coolness, warmth, nor shape of fingers enfolding her hand if in fact he was the sort who observed the old-time, or was it modern, gentlemanly ritual of taking a lady's hand in his, turning her hand over, touching it to his lips. Dead, she needed no chair, no words, no kiss, no gingham dress, no hand, no family. Nothing required of her except waiting, waiting. Nothing except to exercise the talent she had consumed a lifetime teaching herself.

Is it ever truly over, ever finished, she asks, scanning the too familiar parlor, the trees framed in its only window, a door opening onto a brick walkway and town. That impossibly familiar scene. Clean, pleasant, neat, welcoming, even elegant in a modest fashion. She sees the house, the family, sees herself, safe in that harbor, that privilege, and didn't they all enjoy passing back and forth, swimming together in those family waters, the effortless to and fro, resigning themselves to whatever else might be troubling their minds, pleased that other family members are also resigned. Allowed not to speak of, or pretend not to notice regrets, disappointments. Waters stay the same. People come and go, passing by as close or distant as Africa or Sumer, but same, same water, same family.

Wouldn't she exchange in a split second, if she could, exchange the impossibility of being here, where she is for the possibility of being back there, with the family in those bright surroundings forever familiar. Wouldn't Phillis, as she'd almost signed her letter to him, weep to land there again. Eyes flooded by joy. Happy again to be waiting for his knock. Or better here now. Here where she needs nothing now. Dead now. In a letter he called twelve lines of poem she sent him a profound lamentation and had also scolded her for one dash too many. Teased her once: I will come join you, he wrote. Wrote that he imagined he might learn to like it in Sumer.

I watch my love rise then sink then rise then sink again as if waves buffeting her, buoying her, belong to her and not vice versa—imagine words of a poem she might address to a stranger. Imagine myself reading a page bearing bones of language, bones not fleshed by messy explanations and denials and promises and footnotes and postscripts. Imagine empire's dark power. Power to separate. Imagine the lightness of love as it swims, as it sinks. Imagine other stories. No stories. Many. Imagine no darkness, no war.

TILL

IN THE BACKYARD KIDS PLAYING TILL. She never really liked it, but played Till like everybody did growing up. Recites to herself name of each kid in the yard. Her one, middle sister's three, eldest sister's boy and girl twins. Kids. Cousins. Half dozen of them busy, busy, playing Till.

To start Till, first you kind of glide away, shadowy, pretending no interest in the others, and off you go to fake sleep or playing dead, then a snarl, a swoop, you're back, you holler *TILL,* and Till game starts, and the others shriek and scramble, and you grab and pull as if an arm, a leg the prize, and detachable, edible if you hold tight, twist, tug a limb, and never let go. Like not enough chairs in musical chairs, not enough arms and legs to go around and everybody knows that after each scuffle, each war of tangled-up limbs, greedy hands, screams, nibbles, bites, yelps, tears, somebody left armless, legless, with no place to sit. Somebody caught. Somebody lost. Somebody Till.

Never liked playing Till with her sisters, and now all the cousins playing, her little girl included, long-legged all of them, all with those high, tight, round little butts and that big forehead she liked to think hides a large portion of brains. Cousins all bearing telltale markings of family, though each body also a surprise—tall, short, dark, light, slim, pudgy. On this hot afternoon everybody in shorts and T-shirts going at their peculiar version of Till, the game changeable as each flesh-and-blood version of whatever dooms them to be family. Kids out the window, out there on the grass, under trees in her backyard playing the old, ugly Till game again that still chilled her. Waves of uneasiness irresistible as sweat in her armpits, between her thighs if she deserted the air-conditioned kitchen and joined the kids out there where they play, kids ignoring the heat and humidity of a July day.

Noted ichthyologist to lecture Sunday.

What kinda itchy-who-what you say.

Icky-thee-all-o-gist. Paper says he a big-time scientist studies fish. Sounds kinda intrestin to me.

Hmph. Ain't humpin nowhere to hear no colored scientist got nothing better to do than peepin in fishbowls.

Then guess you don't wanna see this picture of him and his pretty daughter coming to town wit him.

Lemme see that noospaper, Amos. Hand it here.

Fine lookin redbone gal, ain't she, Andy Brown.

Hmmm. Sho is. Sho nuff fine. Hmmm. Maybe we check out that fishman, after all, Brother Amos.

At the window she halfway hears the radio voices over her shoulder, enough to pick up the story, dumb as usual, just enough story to tease you into following what in the world Amos, Andy, Kingfish, Sapphire, etc., are up to in tonight's episode, what in the world they will find to talk about to keep your attention for half an hour and keep themselves entertained nonstop, show after show, same time, same station every weekday. Love listening to them get mixed up in one mess or another, and can't wait to tune in and hear them talking again, whether or not words they say make much sense, or any sense, and maybe no sense best of all, ha-ha-ha. Who wants sense. Ha-ha-ha better than sense. Best when you can just laugh and laugh. No rules, nobody in charge. Like kids out the window inventing Till again, drifting around each other silently, dreamily in a half acre of green yard until one snatches at another one and the Till game mauling commences, rough or nasty or fun or mean or scared. Playing almost as if there are rules, same Till rules she had followed when she played, though she had never quite figured them out (except one rule—*Till* rule—and every damned fool knows that one, don't they—not Till, no, no, never end up Till). Cousins playing almost as if there really is some deep sense, some deep purpose or deep understanding of the game within all those big foreheads, little hands, size of her hand her mother once upon a time used to smack, and now she and her sisters smack a kid's hand, too, if they catch one talking like Amos and Andy talk.

Cousins, how many cousins that day she tries to recall. Cousins riding to see their uncle. How many busting out the car that summer morning after the long drive crosstown, through tunnels over bridges lost awhile as usual in the final intersecting maze of many streets, highways, expressways, dead ends, construction, demolition over on the Northside to get to the prison. A jailbreak when car doors open, long-legged, half-naked cousins dash across parking lot to a cage outside the wall where visitors must line up and wait to enter.

Stop . . . stop. No running. Stop. Slow down, youall. Be careful. But the oldest cousins know the game and younger ones race after them across the asphalt to steel fence, barbed wire, immense, filthy, ancient stones. Break your bones. Step on a crack break your mama's back. Careful, youall, slow down she hollers at the posse disappearing in a cloud of dust. Waste of breath she knows. Who cares, who listens. Amos and Andy play behind her back.

ARIZONA

Dear Mr. Jackson,

Thank you for your music, and thank you for reading this far in a letter, if it reaches you, from a stranger. Though we have never met face to face, I could say that I've known you since I was a teenager growing up in Pittsburgh, PA, in the fifties, born fourteen years or so before you were born, Mr. Jackson, and I wanted to be you, or rather wanted with all my soul, a soul real to me as the faces of people in my family, to sing like you would sing the music we both inherited and you would keep alive in the eighties, nineties with your talent and gifts. Listening to your voice, I hear the old music again—the Dells, Diablos, Drifters, Flamingos, Spaniels, Five Satins, Midnighters, Soul Stirrers—and it takes me back to those voices on the corner, in church, on records, radio, teaching me the fires in my belly, dance steps in my feet, the hungers, fun, sadness, loves lost and found all around me I only half-understood and still don't, old man that I am today, but yearn so badly, teenager and now, to stay part of, that swirling, full-to-the-brim, overflowing life that sometimes fills me up, sways and staggers me, sweeps me off my feet, that elusive, loud, shaking, shouting world that could sometimes go silent and disappear, here then abruptly gone, passing me by as if I were nothing, nobody, less than a speck of dust or a tear no one sees falling, all of that, and more bitter and more sweet because, like you, Freddie Jackson, I was a colored boy and my world, my people, hemmed in by others not colored, others inexplicably mean, crude, intimidating, evil as death.

Anyway, I don't need to tell you about coming up colored. When I hear you sing I remember you were there beside me and here I am now beside you, listening once more to all the stories, facts, times, people, voices that the music passes on, gives back, recalls, steals, wishes for, touches, releases.

I should admit straightaway I can't claim to be a devoted fan or student of all your music. I'm writing to let you know one song in particular that you recorded, "You Are My Lady," seems part of a story I'm trying to compose. Composing now as we speak. Or rather as I imagine myself speaking and imagine we are speaking together. Pretending to speak with you my way of telling the story I wish to tell. Our silences, really, not our voices, engaged in conversation. Though I hear you singing. Softly. Clearly. Your song "URML," in my story, inseparable from it before there is a story.

Point of this letter is not exactly to ask permission to put you in a story I'm writing, Freddie Jackson. Rather, I'm letting you know (informing/fessing up/sharing) I have no choice. You are in it already without being asked, without any exit offered, like the color we share, color which this country assigns to us before we are born.

Story I'm attempting to put together concerns my son, youngest of my three grown children, a prisoner now, in Arizona serving a life sentence for committing murder in 1986, when he and his victim both fifteen years old. I have tried to write his story many, many times—as a short piece of fiction that stands alone, as an episode in longer narratives, fiction and nonfiction, published and unpublished. Each attempt failed. Failed probably for a variety of complicated reasons in each case, but the simple fact is none of my efforts to write my son's story freed him. And that one negative outcome they all share certifies their collective futility: my son remains incarcerated. Getting him out is the sole justification, if any legit justification exists, for me writing about him. Even a grieving, conflicted father possesses no right to ignore his injured son's request not to discuss in public his son's wounds, especially when at best the father able only to speculate, guess the nature of the wounds and their effects. No excuse for a story's probes, prods, provocations unless they promise to produce, at a very minimum, the possibility of a cure. Why else disturb a son's privacy (an inevitable result no matter how scrupulously I endeavor to avoid it). Why intrude after finally, expressly, he's forbidden me to write about him. Why discuss in public a horrific series of events unless the retelling, the painful, incriminating exhumation liberates my son, sets him free. None of my previous efforts to tell his story have disentangled him from the consequences of a crime beyond my power to change. My helplessness feels unalterable. I find myself unable to foresee a different scenario. So I'm asking myself, asking you, Mr. Jackson, if I should try a story about my son once more. And if I try to write it, for whose benefit, whose sake, on whose behalf, for what purpose would I be performing.

I ask you because you are an artist, Mr. Jackson, and because sometimes your singing achieves what the best art accomplishes. A song you sing creates a space with different rules, different possibilities. A space opens that doesn't exist until a listener tunes in and hears your voice, a sudden space that may disappear the very next instant but changes that instant, too, no doubt, and it doesn't matter that the previous moment and the ones before remain whatever they were and lock a person down with unforgiving, unalterable facts. None of that matters when I experience the undeniable presence, the unique truth a particular song can deliver—your song "URML" my best example. Your voice in that song reminds me there's more in any moment, more to the life I think I'm caught up in, more than I can ever know, ever understand, ever come to terms with, make peace with, survive, so much more and more and different and other than there had seemed to be an instant before the music. If I listen, if I let it be, let it alone, just listen to the music while it delivers inklings and intimations of things very different than I thought they were, are, sometimes I'm able to go there, into a different space, thank you, thank you, space the music uncovers, reveals, and I go there, can't help myself, because I need it, need help so much, I do, I do, I yearn, I hear the music and nothing is what it was an instant before or ever after, maybe, if I listen, keep believing, remembering that my life is less than nothing and also perhaps a tiny, tiny bit more than everything I believed I already knew, every damned body already knows, if I really listen, let myself hear when a song speaks.

How do you work the magic of your art, Mr. Jackson. What makes your music special when it's special. How do you offer a space with your voice that feels real enough for a listener to enter. What secrets have you learned to please

*an audience. How do you put all of yourself into a song,
but then disappear so there's only music and it belongs to
the listener. When your voice breaks silence, how does it
make silence speak. You did it at least once, certainly, for
my son and probably countless times for others, including
me. How does a song reach out and touch. Do you sing to
please yourself. When a song feels good to you while you are
singing, is that the best test. Is that the answer to all this
letter's clumsy questions. URML's secret. Or maybe only an
answer I want and need.*

*I had a friend once who killed his lady. Crime occurred
in Philly, about eight years before a song you addressed to
your lady reached No. 1 on Billboard's rhythm and blues
chart. Years before he committed a murder, I'd lost touch
with him, my former friend, occasional cut-buddy when I
was an undergrad at Penn in the early sixties. A guy who
hung out around campus, long-haired, scraggly-bearded,
a kind of sloppy, happy-go-lucky, sinister phony, a power-
fully persuasive and manipulative guy with a malodor-
ous charm about him, Charlie Manson before anybody
had heard of Charles Manson, other than my friend and
his coterie of fellow eccentrics and visionaries who cir-
culated among themselves counterculture news and views
through a kind of crude precursor of the Internet before
anybody else had heard of Internet or Manson. My friend,
a nice kid on the lam from middle-class, suburban Jewish parents, had transformed himself into a Philly street
character whose intimidating range of knowledge, arcane
reading, provocative ideas, and batty eloquence, despite
my reservations about his lack of personal hygiene, drew
me to him as he was drawn to me, despite or because
of our obvious differences, me growing up poor, therefore
street tough, street wise, he assumed, a jock who played*

college ball, physically attractive, smart enough, though intellectually underdeveloped, politically unsophisticated, naive, poorly read, innocently gregarious, but my new buddy soon perceived that I was ambitious, ruthless, and predatory in my dealings with other people as he was, my insightful, observant, preternaturally selfish, shamelessly inquisitive, greedy new acquaintance.

In the role of professor-guru he enjoyed explaining himself to me. Claimed he answered to no one. Responsible only to himself. Made it clear that nobody possessed rights he was bound to respect. Even in Powelton Village, Philly's wannabe version of the Village in New York—your city, Mr. Jackson, where you grew up in Harlem—we must have been an unusual sight: tall, fit Black guy, and squat, flabby white guy, the unlikely pair of us roaming neighborhood streets, parties, participating in rallies, arts festivals, demonstrations, defying cops and authority, hitting on women, getting stinking drunk in local bars, but welcomed almost always, anywhere we showed up, by the helter-skelter mix of all sorts of people that constituted Powelton's inhabitants. An odd couple, but didn't we embody, maybe, a new day, a new dispensation, a social and cultural revolution everybody back then wanted to believe they desired or at least were willing to accommodate since it promised better sex, better drugs, unbounded freedom and license, an option to be contemptuous of traditional styles, conventions, and rules, an inalienable right to hit the road, Jack, and head out for faraway, exotic destinations when the place where we find ourselves becomes unsatisfactory.

My former hangout partner, whom the cops arrested in 1976 for killing his lady friend, still maintains his innocence though convicted twice—once in 1979 in absentia because out on bail awaiting trial, he'd fled the

States, then found guilty a second time in another Philadelphia courtroom after being extradited to America
from a farm in France, a fugitive seventeen years on the
run, hiding under assumed names and fake identities.
My old intimate, my fellow bullshitter and I, both relentless pursuers of any pretty girl we hoped seducible,
including one he admitted he tried hard to catch and
didn't catch, but I did, a girl whose background mirrored
his, except her parents lived in Connecticut and much
richer than his, a girl I eventually married, mother of
my children, including my son in prison, the marriage
in name anyway lasting for thirty years neither party has
yet to forgive the other for inflicting, enduring, and even
so during those thirty-plus years, Mr. Jackson, on numerous occasions, I would have counted myself lucky to
have possessed a voice like yours and your song "URML"
to serenade her, which goes to show what . . . nothing of
course, as my bearded mentor would insist, except the
poor taste in choosing lovers certain pretty, seducible girls
exhibited back in the day and how fickle, how unfaithful
songs and singers can be.

My once-upon-a-time buddy complains that he is an innocent victim of a CIA frame-up organized to discredit and
get rid of him because the CIA knows he knows too much
about contacts it has established with an advanced, extra-
terrestrial civilization, contacts that notorious agency desperately wishes to keep secret from the American public. But I
bet if I visited him in prison and we got an opportunity to
converse in guaranteed privacy, he might not leak any nitty-
gritty about the CIA–Star Wars connection, but if the chance
arose, he would confide to me that he killed his lady for more
or less the identical reason that I attribute to you, Mr. Jackson, as a possible explanation of why you sing as you do. He'd

confess, just short of bragging, and perhaps with a wistful semi-grin, yes, he loved his lady but she split, and when she came back to their apartment to pick up her stuff, he believed that if he killed her, not only could he keep her, he'd please himself, and pleasing himself always good, so he did.

C'mon. Think about it, dude. Pleasing yourself always the best reason. Unless you wanna be a stooge for somebody else's bullshit. A stupido stooge. Doing what the man says cause the man says it's good for you. Go fuck yourself, what I say. Your wars. Your pissy little no brainer jobs, a whiny wife, litter of whiny, ungrateful brats. For them. Do it for them, man tells you. Family. God. Country. Any goddamn reason just so you do what you're told. Don't think. Just get in line, turkey. Bend over, turkey. BLAM. Gotcha. Well, not me. Not today. Not tomorrow. Huh-uh. I'll do what pleases me. Me. Me. Me, friend. What pleases me. Best reason and only reason. And I recommend strongly, old chap, mon semblable, my darker brother, that unless you want to be the man's bumboy chump, you best do as I do. Be insolent, abrasive. Extend to yourself bottomless generosity and benevolence.

CIA eavesdroppers or not, I bet he'd pass on the message I paraphrased above. Why should my old pal be shy about repeating his rule. Especially since no one, in the forty or fifty centuries preceding this one, despite what they practiced or preached, has come up with a more compelling, more self-evident rationale for how folks should behave in this best of all possible worlds. Mystery (a.k.a. chaos) *abides. Whether a person wants to shop for clothes or dinner, wage war, create art, fall in love, discipline kids or criminals etc., etc., no recipe exists that guarantees success. So why shouldn't my friend argue, Please yourself. Same rule for him, you, me, prison inmates or Presidents of the*

United States. Rule my pal would shout, scream, cackle, laugh, giggle, holler, preach. His rule today. Same one he used to expound, pontificate, rap in the middle of campus parties, street crowds, into a mic, into your ear, into a garbage can while he was barfing.

Let me quickly, unambiguously assure you, Mr. Jackson, that in no way, shape, nor form am I equating what might guide you to sing a song as you do and what guided my former friend to take his lady's life. An immense, immense difference between you discovering as you perform onstage that your audience is most pleased when you please yourself, and my old street partner discovering that terminating another's life and pleasing himself could go hand in hand. Rather, I'm illustrating and admitting my own confusions, worries, fears, my inability to decide my next move in this story. My next choice. Aren't the ramifications of any choice unfathomable. Whether a choice about how to sing a song or a choice to kill or not to kill. Consequences never exactly knowable before we choose. And often no less mysterious after we choose. Good intentions or not, we're involved always in guesswork, after all. Gut work. Trapped inside ourselves. Our minds. Our feelings. Selfish, arbitrary, dark perhaps as my once-upon-a-time friend's mind and feelings.

And that truth cuts much deeper than different strokes for different folks, I believe. Any point of view not the only possible one. Always many. Always changing. Smallest piece of something represents, replicates, renews, becomes larger, becomes whole. The whole always fragile, always shatters, incomplete as the smallest piece. Both the entire shebang and each infinitesimal byte forever exchanging places, and we can't have one without the other. World happening as fast as we remember it, forget it, and I often wish, Mr.

Jackson, Freddie Jackson, that I could sidestep, write away, sing away that endless simultaneity.

Distance from Phoenix to Flagstaff, Arizona, approximately 145 miles. A drive north of about two hours, eighteen minutes on I-17. If you are interested, time-lapse videos posted on the Internet can get you there faster, in anywhere from one minute and forty-two seconds to forty-seven minutes and ten seconds. The two lawyers who met my son's plane at Sky Harbor Airport in order to escort him to a jail in Flagstaff where he'd be locked up until tried for murder, may or may not have been in a hurry. Being in a hurry doesn't necessarily get you any quicker to where you wish to go. Nor does the wish to never arrive at a particular destination necessarily retard arrival. I wasn't in the car hauling my son to jail that day in Arizona, thus can't say who was in a hurry and who was not.

My son a fugitive for twelve days before he called his uncle and asked for help, before his uncle called us and we engaged lawyers. How do my son's twelve days of running compare to my old buddy's seventeen years of flight and hiding. I should know better than to ask such a silly question, Mr. Jackson. As if time consists of a given number of repeating, unchanging, definable units, like inches, miles, pounds. Aren't aging or loss or cancer or fear or mourning or despair also species of time. What units measure the length and weight of a boy's time fleeing on the road, a fifteen-year-old boy who maybe hasn't had sex yet, who hasn't attended a funeral or slept away from home a single night with no family, no adult, no companions keeping him company. A boy terrorized by killing, for no reason he comprehends, his roommate in an Arizona motel on a pleasure trip organized by an elite summer camp in Vermont the boy's grandfather owns. How could anyone not that boy grasp how time passed for him on the run or passes now in prison where *bars and cages do not stop the running, but torture and bend time further so time collapses, empties, or swells like a corpse decomposing, or towers like some suppurating beast many stories tall with bloody talons pawing the air. Stink, moans, a dreadful roaring that halts my son in his tracks, keeps him fleeing.*

Three days of running from the fact I did not know my son's whereabouts had broken me. A kid assigned randomly one August night to be my son's roommate, a kid from the pack of boys on a sightseeing excursion to the western U.S., boys who'd been summer campers together for years, that kid had been found stabbed to death in the room he shared with my son. My son gone. No one knew where. Perhaps a captive of the madman who stabbed my son's roommate, perhaps my son bound and being tortured somewhere by the kind of marauding monster who would storm armed into a motel room, kill one boy and kidnap the other at knifepoint or gunpoint to enjoy later. Maybe dismember, maybe eat him at his leisure, his pleasure— that's what I could not stop myself from imagining as I ran away from and ran after facts that might explain a vanished son. Three days, three periods of twenty-four hours each had registered on other people's clocks, but stretched for me longer than I could bear, and I slid down a pine tree I was hugging in a Vermont forest, crumpled to a weeping heap on the ground beside the tree's trunk, my lifetime abruptly passing, consumed. Enough. Nothing. More time than I could handle.

If I'd been an occupant of the car proceeding north on I-17 taking my son to stand trial in Flagstaff, I would not have been privy to what other occupants thinking, the lawyers' thoughts, my son's thoughts invisible to me then, and again now as I tap out letter by letter an invisible story to render it visible. Story to rescue my son. Over the many years following that car ride, Mr. Jackson, I got to know both lawyers pretty well, stayed in one's palatial Phoenix home once, commiserated often in my mind with the other as he suffered problems threatening to drag him down, out of his profession, until he got well and practiced law again and still may. On the afternoon I handed over my son to them, the lawyers absolute strangers to me, except for several phone calls exchanged and a high recommendation from a lawyer friend of my then wife, my son's mother. Two men I'd never laid eyes on before, but men into whose hands, literally and figuratively, I was placing my son's life while I waited for my wife's plane so she and I could drive to Flagstaff together. The lawyers' thoughts, my son's thoughts in the car they were riding to Flagstaff still unguessable for me today. Nor could the occupants of the car see each other's thoughts that day in 1986 on an Arizona highway, though each must have been wondering, more than wondering, probably actively searching for clues in each other's expressions, gestures, silences, maybe even asking out loud, Who are you, why are we here, where are we heading, what is happening to me, us, how will it end, whose story is this. The car's occupants like me trying to make sense of a senseless story, all of us rolling along towards Flagstaff, in a hurry or not, listening, imagining, speaking or not, trying to understand why. Would all our stories end or start once more when the car doors open and cops stand there waiting for us with handcuffs . . .

At some moment before that Flagstaff arrival is when your voice, Mr. Jackson, your song "URML" entered the car. I want to say filled the car, but I wasn't there, was I. Don't know who in the front seats, who in the back. Was the car radio on or music just in my son's portable tape deck and earphones. Car radio playing I'm almost sure, somehow. Pods wired to machines not so ubiquitous in young people's ears back in 1986. Element of surprise part of the story. "URML" enters suddenly. Unexpectedly. A moment altered. Who's playing the car radio. How loud. Who listens. No matter what else, where else your thoughts, how can a person help listening. Whether you wish to listen or not, could you ignore the radio, drift off through a window, study fractured, flat desert, gaze at spines of mountains rimming the distance. Remember another's voice you are missing or trying to forget. But how could you not hear it if a loud radio fills a car. Or a good tune fills it softly. "URML."

Did a lawyer or my son pick the station. Let the kid dj. Let him play with the dial, push buttons, let him make this terrible ride shorter or longer or make it disappear. Just so he doesn't drown us, sink us, minstrelsy us, mug us on some urban dark corner, some station very, very, overbearingly loud filling the car so impossible to think station. Remember, young man, not just you inside here, as big, as sorry as your big sorry story is, truly, truly, bad, large, and ugly—we heard about the other poor gored kid in Flagstaff, son—but there's three of us stuck together in here awhile, like it or lump it, and the dead boy, too, but do not despair quite yet, young man, maybe we will plea-bargain the judge down from firstdegree murder and death to life imprisonment (though Arizona looking for an under-sixteen to execute and thus lower the death penalty age threshold and here comes your son, a handy, colored killer to make the State's case easy, we warned your parents). Our job to save your life. Seems a nice enough scared kid, his skinny fear filling the car louder than anything he might punch in on the radio, but

*we are big boys, we can bear it, the noise, the heat, the
fear, besides he won't get that urban-station way-too-loud
stuff way out here middle of the desert, anyway let him
dj, seems a reasonable enough, smart enough kid, nice
parents, what in the world happened—and just about
somewhere in there, low, hills now to the left, one behind
another to a hazy horizon, to the right, dramatic contours
of frozen sand, countless cacti, layers of drab-colored cloud
climbing, clamoring an endless sky to heaven. Thickets of
thoughts coming and going, to and fro, battering air inside the car like wings of gigantic bats too large to see. Two
middle-aged, palish human men and one slightly colored
boy, three total to whom the thoughts belong, trapped on
the road to Flagstaff and suddenly there's Freddie Jackson
singing "URML," suddenly a song's in the car, and my
son, as if with sudden wings, wings not as big as the invisible bats' wings or so much larger, so, so much larger, is
lifted, rides the draft. Sucked out the car roof and gone.*

*And if such were literally the case—my son free, Mr.
Jackson—I wouldn't be writing this letter or story, would I,
Mr. Jackson. Yes and no, maybe. "URML" a beautiful song.
Worth a story at least. Many. One of my all-time favorites
so perhaps one day I would be tempted to try. Try despite an
incalculable sadness your song always invokes for me, whatever else. I keep going back to "URML" for the same reasons
I believe people want to hear again songs they love. Revisit-
ing unhappy songs as often as happy ones, and, strange as
it seems, people recall sad ones, my guess, more than happy
songs. Or perhaps no difference. Certain songs too deep to
be happy or sad. Both. (Smokey's "Tracks of My Tears.")
Neither. More. Less.*

Who am I to instruct you about songs, or singing. Or

audience responses, Mr. Jackson. But I admitted from the git-go, I'm writing this to myself as much as to you. Plenty people (all?) sing to themselves, don't they. I do. Even in the shower, or especially in the shower people sing—alone, wet, warm, soaping up, scrubbing up, usually not the worst of times. Rushing water's close-up noise in your ears if it's a good, strong shower, water to take the edge off false notes, water to swim in, drown in. Why not listen to myself. Though you are a pro and sing for a living, do you still sing to yourself. Do you listen, Freddie Jackson. In the shower. No offense intended, but could the shower be where you, too, do your best work. An audience of only one hears my best work. Hears the voice inside my head no other person will ever share. Better than anyone else's voice. Unspeakably good. Closer to what I wish to sound like than any sounds I'm able to produce. When I get it going in the shower, I give my voice more than the benefit of the doubt. All benefits. No doubts. Let imagination work between the lines, speaking a story for which there are no words, speaking for what's missing always. I imagine more than what's there. Fill in what's impossible, lost, searched for, those things a song desires to happen while it's sung and sometimes they do, things playing inside, when one listener only, only inner lips, ears, eyes, feet, hands working and the invisible elders busy remembering, reminding me how it goes, what it means and says, once and only once, audience of one, never exactly the same, never over while a person keeps it inside, alone when she or he sings, writes.

I couldn't help smiling, Freddie Jackson, thinking one afternoon about poor, long-suffering tough guy mafioso Tony Soprano on TV, romanced and undermined by his female psychoanalyst as vice versa he endeavors to undermine and romance her in her office. She sits, her big, nyloned legs crossed across the room and he leans forward in his chair straining to hear her saying what she hears him not saying and he can't say aloud even inside himself. Her office a shower of sorts, a spa where Tony goes to come clean, where every once in a while butt-naked Tony lets go, belts out his privacies, his innermost, imprisoned stories verse by verse, singing away, no holds barred, to seduce his shrink with beaucoup boo-hoos and hangovers from bad old days when he was coming up the hard way on mauling, murderous streets, and worse at home, Tony Soprano croons, chirps, coos to her and she hears, "URML."

I wonder sometimes when I watch the classic video of you, Freddie Jackson, totally fly in your pure white suit, serenading a young woman, "URML," with your eyes as much as your voice, if the face and body beside you in the video are the ones you are addressing or if, inside your head, in a song only you are able to see, there is another lover listening, not the pretty actress caught on tape smiling back at you. I wonder, of course, because I glide so seamlessly into the make-believe scene I'm watching, letting your voice be mine, wishful-thinking that voice into the ear of a woman you don't know, have never seen, but I adore her, want her to adore me. Room for us, my lady and me, though you and your lady don't disappear. Both of you professionals, more than convincing performers who reach out and touch, skilled, sticky as a tar baby, who once Brer Rabbit pokes in a paw, Gotcha, old Mr. Tar Baby say and he ain't never gon let go. It's once upon a time each time the "URML" video commences. Viewers see, listen, tumble live into a song's story. Shape-shifting. Black holes. Voodoo.

Rumors, speculations, full-blown conspiracy theories circulate on the Internet, in fan magazines, newspapers,

TV, and radio about the nature of your sex life, Mr. Jackson. According to the perspective of many commentators who get paid or blog to please themselves or maybe just can't stop themselves from pursuing and commenting on such matters, you have been coy, evasive, manipulative, fearful, not helpful to the cause, irresponsible, exploitative, naive, inconsistent, dishonest for the long duration of a very successful, very public career because you never flat-out declared your own gender identity, nor gender preferences when it comes to choosing lovers. I'm no expert on this aspect of your life, any more than I'm an aficionado of the entire corpus of your work. However, searching for examples of what your voice might sound like when you're not singing, I found an interview I particularly enjoyed in which you didn't—as I'm pretty sure I would have— tell the interviewer to go fuck himself, yet still in your dignified and uncompromising fashion let him know in no uncertain terms that your business none of his business. Your life, your privacy not material for interviewers to label, commodify for other people's consumption. You let him understand that simply because you possessed the gift, the art to sing your ass off did not license him to be coy, evasive, manipulative, not helpful to the cause, irresponsible, exploitative, naive, inconsistent, dishonest during an interview. Not forgetting to add your humble suggestion that perhaps in a contemporary world inches away from exploding or imploding there are more urgent, more germane issues for the media to attend to than the in-and-out gossip of your sex life.

Still, I'm guilty, more hungry than that interviewer to learn your secrets. But different secrets for different reasons, I hope. The most crucial reason being how much

I'm moved by your song's power to free my son. Not exactly envious, but more than desperate to figure out how you do what you do. Did once in a car on an Arizona highway and why not again. I want to learn to emulate your example. Rescue him. Please allow me to continue to wonder about the particular face or faces conjured up for you when you sing "URML." Maybe songs, stories, fiction or not, give solace, context, possibility, as much with their stable, recurring forms as with their infinitely various contents, and thereby produce examples of lives shaped, framed so they are recognizably distinguishable from emptiness, from darkness that seems always to surround and render lives unseeable. I'm reaching out, asking you. Do songs and stories create real shapes, colors, smells, sounds. Real even if futile vis-à-vis the absolute arbitrariness of what happens to be happening moment by moment, day by day.

I've had mummies on my brain lately. They keep cropping up unexpectedly. In unpredictable, unlikely, unavoidable places, Mr. Jackson. Mummification old as the oldest documented civilization and practiced globally. My old Philly buddy who killed his lady attempted to mummify her, sealing her corpse in a box with stuff he believed would preserve it, stowing the box in the ceiling rafters of his Powelton Village apartment, hoping to conceal his crime by causing his lady, poof, to disappear.

That mummy didn't work. Leaked, stank. Led to my friend's arrest. I have no doubt his extreme oddness, bookishness, dabbles in the occult, fantasies of invincibility, though they failed to provide him with a proper chemical formula for mummifying his lady's corpse, supplied him copiously with lore, ritual, history, chants, prayers for launching her into immortality. Whether my former friend believed he could arrange life after death for his lady, I can't say, but I know he thought a lot about his various projects. Often intelligently, with a meticulously organized, relentless, insane, patient thoroughness and self-assuredness. Mummification, that horrific launching my once-upon-a-time friend perpetrated, his attempt to spare himself from the consequences of his crime and spare his lady's body the indignities of decay and dissolution, his effort to save her and save himself, may have felt like an irresistible option. No matter what he was thinking, his actions profoundly unacceptable and worse, of course. Especially spooky and unsettling because mummification linked his crime to an ancient, sacred practice devised to prepare the dead for a journey that would be a continuation of life.

As I learned more about the traditions of mummy making—the secret formulas, mysterious protocols, the motivations that conceived them, their imagining of a voyage that connects life and death, their envisioning of immortality, their listing of necessities, that humans would require and desire during a perpetual trip—the innocence of those practices and beliefs touched me, Mr. Jackson, revealed to me how a similar willed innocence possibly underlies all arts humans practice.

Mummification an art. Art mummifies. With only problematic or no evidence at all that such reliance achieves desirable results, people depend upon mummy makers to ensure that the dead are ready and able to enjoy, to survive whatever pleasures and perils a journey which never ends might bring. With equally scant proof of positive outcomes, people rely on artists and works of art to act as guides. Art improvises and embodies instructions for negotiating imaginary worlds—defines rewards and punishments in such worlds—confirms the existence of imagined worlds where occasionally a person can hang out, vacation on demand, daydream, or chatter without sacrificing too much time or energy better spent on the business of ordinary living. As if art—mummy making, writing symphonies—changes time. As if certain artisans can lift the veil of mystery that divides life from death. As if lifted, there would be anything under the veil. As if art's hocus-pocus might trump time.

Mummies are intended to serve the dead. Just as a song you sing (story I compose) intended to serve the living. Make sense of treacherous terrain. Traveling companions on a mysterious, arduous journey. Helping people along the way. Opening time and space to inhabit. A choice to continue. Or not. And lo and behold . . . sometimes it works. "URML." Song in a car. My son heard it, Mr. Jackson. Thank you.

I hope my intrusions into your private business, my questions, worries, and insinuations about your art haven't chased you away. Who is this guy, what does he want from me, you may be asking yourself—if you've read this far. Let me assure you I expect no response to this letter that is not even a real letter. I'm asking you for nothing, Mr. Jackson, though I understand how you or other people might believe that I'm asking far too much. Asking for a piece of you. Like any parasite demands. You must have encountered plenty of parasites, especially when you were at the top of the charts. Notorious pests in the entertainment industry as elsewhere. Parasites. A word I looked up once and discovered its origins Greek. In that ancient language the word signifies folks who are always showing up at your table for a meal, hands empty, mouths full of gimme, *and* much obliged. *Parasites. A word associated frequently with artists. With art's arrogance when it proclaims art for art's sake. With the proverbial, well-earned reputation of artists for laziness, greed, selfishness, nastiness, irrelevance, fecklessness, and fickleness. Parasites one more compromising word in this letter, this story. A word getting in line with murderers, mummies, mafiosos to suggest art's unsavory and/or failed ambitions.*

Walking last fall in Brittany with a neighbor on a 10K charity trek to earn money for the local elementary school's arts program, I pointed to a stand of trees atop the crest of a low hill in the gently rolling terrain of mainly pastureland surrounding us. The trees I indicated were not quite bare of foliage but stripped enough for limbs and branches to reveal lots of roundish puffs or nests suspended in them, big blots, blobs within the larger, more or less oval-shaped crowns of five or six trees ahead in the distance. Gui, *he said after I stumbled through an explanation in English and halting French of what had caught my eye and wanted him to give me the French word for. Closer up, one could see they are networks of something like spider webbing or skinny threads of black bone on an X-ray plate of bright morning light.* Gui. *Mistletoe a loose translation. The word mistletoe carrying, mixing, and matching stories from numerous languages that the plant's name in each language suggests. Saying the word in English gets me thinking about Christmas. Saint Nick. Santa. Love. Lovers and strangers tempted, ordered to kiss under mistletoe. Nat Cole crooning about chestnuts and fire. Druids with their mastery of oak lore and oak magic in charge of forests. Deer. Wizards and Witches. Elves.*

Gui *are parasites, my neighbor said. Infest the host tree.* Gui *produced by poisonous berries, I learned later.*

Sticky berries that stick to a feeding bird's beak and when a bird scrapes them off on a branch, tiny, tiny patches of resiny stuff adhere to the tree's bark, gradually penetrating it, though some species of gui *in a hurry, I read, shoot missiles, clocked at fifty miles an hour, deep into a tree's heart where they begin to suck and grow and send back messages of food, water from the tree to nourish the microchip-size growth on the surface, and if the chip is lucky, it flourishes and becomes a shadow, a cloud, a thriving, bulky colony of new life like I'd been curious about in those trees on the hill, silhouetted against the horizon we walked towards.*

That morning in Brittany as my friend got me finally to repeat the sound of the French word he was pronouncing by spelling it aloud—g-u-i—and also explained in a slightly disparaging tone that gui *a parasite, I resisted my usual negative reaction to the word parasite.* Parasite. *What was not a parasite. Who is parasiting whom. From what privileged point of view do we decide parasite or host. Were* gui *parasites any more or less than those six or so trees, behind us now, scuffling for nourishment from sky, ground, neighboring trees, rain, stars, those trees feeding on birds, mice, cows, insects, microbes feeding on them, up and down the food chain, Great Chain of Being, the latter chain a concept originating in the fifteenth century, popular through the eighteenth, that I had come across when I studied the birth of the English novel, both chains signifying the same grand plan and interconnection and infinite coupling and interdependencies and eating and being eaten necessary to create and sustain each moment, everyone, everything large and small, past, present, and future, Mr. Jackson. All of us parasiting our way through.*

Chains linking, binding us, like slavery's chains link and bind us, though slavery seldom if ever mentioned by my Oxford professors in the early sixties, academics whose stories taught me the origins of fiction.

Chain, chain, chain . . . *like Aretha sings, Mr. Jackson. Like you sing.*

WHOSE TEETH/WHOSE STORY

Okey—how are u, where r u—did job offer come thru—did u take it—enjoyed seeing u again after so many years—a question, Okey—do u know exact Igbo words of proverb Chinua Achebe translates as "all stories are true"—is Chinua's rendering figurative, speculative, more or less literal re original—wondering how Igbo concept applies to Chinua's essay that pretty much dismisses truth of Joseph Conrad's famous Congo story—I'm starting a piece about a Virginia-born, African-American missionary who arrived (1890) at an outpost on Congo river same time as Conrad—even possible they encountered one another before they began their separate journeys upriver into heart of darkness—anyway, something like a story may be speaking to me and any help u can give with Igbo words greatly appreciated

English Words
Shepherd—sheep—black sheep—white sheep—black Sheppard—white Sheppard—black souls—black shepherd—

SHEPPARD

William Henry Sheppard, after twenty years of service as a Presbyterian missionary in Africa, was recalled in 1910 by the Church and returned home to America in disgrace. I don't want to start or end my story

77

there, where it ends for his contemporaries and most of us—unfair to this "Black Livingstone," this Fellow of the Royal Geographical Society, this investigator and witness who helped expose to the world terrible crimes perpetrated by Belgium's King Leopold in the Congo, this writer, lecturer Wm Henry Sheppard, born in Virginia, who taught himself Kuba language and art, who some Africans called *black whiteman,* and others named *Bope Mekabe,* because they believed him to be a reincarnation of a king's dead brother, this dreamer who attempted to establish a Congo mission, Ibaanc, run by American women and men of color, this preacher judged guilty by the Presbyterian Church of unacceptable behavior and summoned home, adultery charges against him kept quiet to spare the Church embarrassment and scandal, a church whose crusade to save African souls conducted while African bodies were enslaved and exterminated just outside its doors, a church thus compromised morally, ethically no less than its once-upon-a-time exemplary, celebrated, then all too human missionary—this WHS banned from preaching, close to broke until the Church relents and offers him a pulpit in Kentucky, where he serves till he dies, his fame fading, exploits nearly forgotten.

MY STORY

Though his wife, Lucy Gantt Sheppard, an American of color like him, joined WHS (1894) in the Congo and mothered their four children (two infant girls died of fever—Wilhelmina and William a.k.a. Max, survived), Sheppard confessed to Church officials that before and after marriage, he had taken numerous African mistresses and acknowledged himself father of Shepete, a son born to one of the women.

Rather than vilifying or vanishing S for his misdeeds, as I learn more about him, a man whose existence unknown to me until just yesterday, until now when I am old and approaching my own end, I imagine S as a bit like me, beyond fearing exposure, even if not beyond guilt and shame. I imagine him looking back, as I often look back these days, at the long, crowded passage of time within each moment, the details each moment recalls. S telling his story to himself, listening to other stories without beginnings or ends, listening to words he chooses, words choosing him, welcoming him, a long-lost brother, nearly forgotten, seeing himself again in words he thinks, makes up, speaks, words he believes he hears others say

Unlike the Church (or S himself, whose memoir *Presbyterian Pioneers* [1917] records almost nothing that occurs after 1892, year of the death of his companion and fellow missionary, Samuel Norvell Lapsley, scarcely a word about marriage, wife, children, the Ibaanc mission staffed by missionaries of color he recruits, popular lecture tours in America, meeting the Queen of England and two U.S. Presidents), I have no reason to engage in a cover-up. No need to distance myself, pass judgment, conceal Sheppard's private life in Africa or back home. I want to write a story that sails across the Atlantic, resides in Africa two decades, returns to America. But not a story content just to dog S's footsteps faithfully. I need a story that includes mine. Fly on the wall. My feet in S's shoes when they fit.

I grew up in the North, not the South like S, but his manner of coping with oppression feels quite familiar. He seems to have quietly accommodated himself to the strict segregation by color enforced in his region and in his Southern Presbyterian religion. Cultivated early the habit of minding his own business, of befriending, when possible, people not his color, ingratiating himself, thankful for their attention, praising their kindness and generosity, content to appear reconciled, undamaged by the fact that law and custom categorized him as an inferior kind of human. Content it would seem to keep within himself rather than impose upon others, whatever angers he might harbor. Habits of caution, survival techniques similar to ones I learned during childhood and practiced throughout a university career. Why wouldn't S retain those habits while a missionary in Africa. Strictly compartmentalize and discipline his feelings, his voice, his appearance. Allow others little access to his innermost thoughts. A shape-shifter, adept at disguise. Thus, no surprise S not always a vocal critic of Europe's plundering of Africa—that vicious regime of forced labor, kidnapping, expropriation of land, that abyss of murder and theft—surrounding him as he strove to convert Africans to believers in Christ. Yet when an international tribunal (1899) was convened to determine if King Leopold's administration of his Congo protectorate was just and humane, information—including photos—that Sheppard had risked his life to obtain documented a massacre committed by mercenaries employed by Leopold's regime. Nine years later in a Southern Presbyterian newsletter S publishes his eyewitness account of how a once proud and thriving Kuba kingdom was being destroyed by policies that European governments and companies deployed to loot the Congo's wealth. His testimony damning enough that one of the powerful international firms he accused, the Kasai Rubber Company, attempted to protect its reputation by suing Sheppard for libel.

CURIOSITY

In *Presbyterian Pioneers* S recalls a boyhood job working for a dentist he knew as Doctor Henkel: "In the back room of the . . . office was a box filled with teeth. It puzzled me to think how in the world people on resurrection day were to get their own teeth back."

Equally strange and puzzling for me to find S and Joseph Conrad passing simultaneously through Matadi, a station on the Congo River. Conrad had opened an early window on Africa for me, and over the years I had often used his Congo story as a model in my writing classes, but not until I retired from university teaching to devote myself full-time to my own fiction, and had begun to research S's career as a possible subject for a story, did I discover that S arrived in Matadi at more or less the same moment in 1890 as JC. A simple historical fact on one hand, but it struck me as an uncanny coincidence, arousing my curiosity, igniting a sense of wonder. The sort of hardheaded, unsatisfiable curiosity that I believe S shares with Marlow, the fictional character who narrates *Heart of Darkness*.

Curiosity unsettles M and S. Drives them both to take chances. Risk their lives in Africa. S's curiosity aroused by teeth. M's curiosity by rumors circulating about a Mr. Kurtz. S fascinated by the mystery of random teeth, mystery of lives lost, bones scattered and silenced forever unless one day they are reassembled and speak themselves again. M a storyteller intrigued by a notorious agent in charge of a Congo outpost, a man people feel compelled to tell tales about, K stories accumulating like teeth a dentist saves in a box. I can almost hear S and M conversing—whose teeth, whose stories once upon a time. To whom do they belong now. Asking each other why particular teeth or particular stories survive. Why and how do we encounter them. And wouldn't S and M share curiosity about other mysteries. About a second coming, for example. Or mystery of any person's living, breathing presence, here, now, man, woman, boy, or ageless it seems, or at least not dead yet or perhaps already dead once and resurrected, how could anyone know, know more than rumors, stories that circulate, assert claims. Curiosity piqued by shadows scuds across dark, empty spaces inside a person's skull. Mysteries within larger mysteries. Shadows leaving behind only words, voices, silence, mysteries. Teeth.

And here we all are. Curious. Tilting with shadows. Okey waiting to hear about a university job. Chinua Achebe outraged by Conrad's depiction of African people, by the fact the same old, same old Africa story gets told again and again. Sheppard a kid learning to ask questions and wondering how in the world any person answers them. Marlow the eternal outsider.

Conrad a disenchanted emigre, ole boll weevil looking for a home. Me searching for a S story. All of us tellers of tales, wanderers, emigrants, exiles, natives of more than one country, speakers of more than one language, *men,* as if that idea of calling ourselves men means anything without the idea of *women,* all of us equal heirs of confusion, of division. Pretending invented words might invent truth. As if any single word doesn't depend upon all words of all languages for meaning. As if truth of any word or story not a daydream. Implacable sameness always bearing down. Terrorizing darkness of absolute, indistinguishable sameness. No words. Nothing.

To my sister, once a good Christian before she converted and became a good Muslim, I confess I am enthralled sometimes by the idea that perhaps god waits in the bottom of a bottle of good French wine. That's why I empty my glass with slow, reverent swallows, Sis, taking my time, savoring god's good time, no doubt, while I drink sip by sip, in absolutely no hurry, each individual sweet but not too bitterly sweet sip tasting good, maybe better than one before, maybe even sweet as the final, culminating, very last sip of all those sips getting me to the bottle's bottom, Sis, though your brother's smart enough to know that he cannot taste the last drop until it comes, that last drop after which there is no more, but anyway, I tease my sister, and say it's nice to keep sipping slowly, nearer and nearer to her sweet god, and if he's not in this bottle maybe the next or next, and maybe bye um bye I will hear *well done* as the old folks claimed in their stories we would, or so say some people in their stories about old folks and what old folks claimed once upon a time.

LAPSLEY

Samuel Norvell Lapsley, Sheppard's fellow missionary, fellow Southerner, and Southern Presbyterian, companion on S's journey from

America to Africa, placed in charge of a projected Congo mission, his color a necessary condition, no mission on the dark continent in 1890 conceivable by the Southern Presbyterian Missionary Board unless headed by a man of L's color. No Presbyterian mission in Africa during numerous years S petitioned the Church to send him there, mission impossible until Church officials found a man of the appropriate color, a white leader for colored S to follow.

This Samuel Norvell Lapsley—born and raised in Selma, Alabama—father a staunch segregationist, judge, elder in the Presbyterian Church—stirs my curiosity nearly as much as S. Was the constant, necessary proximity of two men's bodies in Africa what encouraged L to forget taboos deeply instilled back home in America. L much smaller than S in a photo of the two men standing side by side, photo I must invent since the digitized archives accessible to me do not seem to contain the image I need to illustrate my story, an odd fact because archived photo albums hold plenty pictures of S posing with others—an eight-foot-long python, a water buffalo, fellow missionaries, African women, laborers, elaborately costumed warriors, crowd of dark, naked children, a camel, snapshots and formal portraits of S with his wife and kids, with African converts, visitors from neighboring tribes, from Europe—a lavish gallery of faces and bodies displayed in S's photo albums to illustrate his busy life and adventures, but no photo of S and L together—standing, sitting, posed, casual, whatever—and I can't help wondering why. The omission too obvious to be accidental, to go unnoticed by S or L. Despite obvious differences, they are great friends. In writing they left behind each speaks highly of the other. Daily companions. Worked, played, prayed together. "Thank god for S," L exclaimed in a letter to his parents. Side by side, S and L confronted dangerous wild animals, hostile waterways, hostile native tribes. Nursed each other through bouts of malaria. Cleaned up the other's vomit, piss, shit. Sweated together when the jungle temperature too high to register on a thermometer, "swimming wet as ducks in a puddle" as one or the other put it, under six blankets fellow missionaries piled on top of them to break a deadly fever.

Where are the photos that must have been taken to celebrate, commemorate this special bonding of S and L, their survival despite the odds. A camera available it seems from their first Congo days. But usually only the two of them (not counting Africans) manning the station, so if one operated the camera, perhaps I shouldn't expect both to be framed in a photo. Still, where is L. Plenty solo shots of S, none of L preserved in albums I combed. Why not. Is L camera shy, fussy about having his picture taken. Or maybe huge ego S, too busy posing, never thinks of asking his partner to pose. Why am I speculating about an absent photo, creating a mystery that may exist only because I invent it. A clear violation of my storytelling license. Like claiming in my narrative to see a photo I desire but do not find. Photo showing S much taller, broader than L. Both men captured in same blink of a camera eye.

Face of SNL appears in *Presbyterian Pioneers* and in a volume of L's correspondence and diary entries collected and published (1893) by his family after L's death. A very different face greets you, however, depending upon which book you open. Fine, almost delicate features, a young, attractive, sensitive individual, most viewers would probably agree, this L who I see in the full-page formal portrait S chooses for his memoir. L appears boyish—bare cheeks, bare upper lip, a face innocent and vulnerable, eyes that don't quite meet the reader's eyes directly. In the photo his relatives pick to introduce L's Life and Letters, he gazes right, almost in profile, bushy-lipped, cheeks adorned by elegant droop of a grown-up's mustache, a face more mature, mysterious than face of L that S offers his readers. Two views of the missing partner. No doubt L present in both. But mystery of his absence, if mystery it is, from photo albums that document S's African adventures not solved, perhaps even deepens. Clearly, by choosing to place an image of L at the front of his book, before the author's own picture and pictures of the author's parents and wife, S wishes to honor L as unique, crucial to the story he is going to tell. The volume of L's letters published by his family substantiates the two men's intense physical, mental, spiritual collaboration, tells the same story S foreshadows by presenting L's face at the beginning of his memoir. The recorded words of both missionaries confirm again and again how much they depended upon, and respected each other. Far from home, sharing a perilous endeavor that tested them body and soul, wouldn't both of them desire a photo, a concrete keepsake memorializing their rare intimacy and friendship. Or perhaps such a photo would reveal too much.

I don't need to be told everything. But do want my chance to listen to everything. Want my chance to tell.

CALLING

Sheppard and Lapsley, like Conrad's Mr. Kurtz, steam and paddle deeper and deeper into the primeval forest, searching for an outpost, for willing souls, for fertile ground where civilization might lay down its burden of history and start afresh. Re-enlighten and un-doom itself. K a believer, a missionary like S and L. A man stirred by the notion of a higher calling the possibility of constructing a better world. And though K, like Conrad, probably too intelligent, too jaded to think anyone, anywhere will ever truly achieve or inhabit it, K believes a better world, empty or not, should be humankind's goal. A future that will materialize, if and only if, a determined few seek it relentlessly and with absolutely no compromise. A dedicated few, missionaries conscious like K of their duty, of a higher calling, must articulate through their lives and work an impossible world, a world in which no one could ever live every day, day by day, but a place the elect (writers of stories?) must strive to envision.

A perfect world (perfect story?). Is perfection K's goal. Like perfect models that fiction writers and poets of older generations sought to construct and pass on. A perfect imitation, though centuries ago Plato, unconvinced, railed against such recklessness. Predicted fatal consequences for humankind's grasp of reality when art's imitations compete with nature's productions.

A friend asked me recently, "What does your writing say. What does it teach. What do you want to leave behind for young people coming up after u . . ."

I was speechless. Embarrassed. Outed for a fraud? No answers possible. Better to ignore or forget or both my friend's unfriendly questions. Weeks later, unable to fall asleep one night after rereading notes in my journal for an unfinishable story, I found myself jotting down a few "propositions"—not to respond directly to the friend's questions nor to prove anything in particular—just a few propositions (I call them *propositions* because I can't come up with a better word) to express what I hope readers and writers who pay careful attention to my work might find. On that restless night reciting, reiterating, a chorus addressing myself or maybe just a broken record repeating over and over my intentions, my wishful thinking about what and why I write, what I struggle to embody in fiction, I finally scratched into my journal—"words dance; silence speaks; language is music; silence dreams."

HEART OF DARKNESS

To narrate a story set in Africa, Joseph Conrad creates Marlow. M's role appears relatively simple. He relates an out of ordinary experience to a group of fellow seamen temporarily stalled with him on the Thames River in England's imperial capital, London. JC invites readers of HOD to eavesdrop on M's account of a perilous journey up the Congo River to find Mr. Kurtz, an ailing company agent, emissary of Empire, a saint or renegade or madman or supernaturally productive (his shipments of ivory prodigious) species of businessman, depending on whose tale M listened to last.

Different stories. In HOD Marlow narrates one story, and behind the scenes, puppet master Conrad tells another in which M is character, not narrator. Created not creator. A distinction without a difference in Achebe's reading of HOD, since for him both invented character and historical author assume the same privilege and commit the same unpardonable offense: treat Africa and Africans as if they have no rights Europeans are bound to respect. M and C too closely aligned in A's opinion. Both storytellers content to render Africa from the point of view of passers-through, passers-by. Exploiters. Discontent, wanderlust, restlessness, curiosity are embedded in a fictional M and draw him to Africa, while JC's interaction with Africa motivated by largely unspoken, writerly, aesthetic concerns of fabricating a good story. A thinks both M and C treat people not their color with about the same degree of compassion the Congo River demonstrates as it snakes through central Africa.

CRITICS AND LIES

Rage—enrage—outrage. Obviously, those three English words are related, but their relationship is complicated. Etymological studies indicate that *outrage* not compounded simply of *out* and *rage*, but derived from *outre,* a word that English overheard in its ancient conversations with French and Latin and then borrowed. A word originally suggesting outside or beyond the pale in Latin and French, but as the word incorporated into English, *outre*'s sound changes and the different sound becomes rendered in English spelling as *outrage*. Gradually the English word loses the specificity of its Latin-French origins. When French speakers designate something *outre*, it suggests that reason and intellect have been engaged, a judgment, at least partially cerebral and considered, has been passed, that standards have been consulted, weighed, before something is called out as extremely inappropriate, improper, or ridiculous. For English speakers *rage* and *enrage* are old, familiar words signifying a very different process, indeed. *Rage* an impulsive, visceral reaction. Violent. Angry. An emotional, unthinking, unpremeditated, frequently uncontrolled state of mind and body. Older words of a language often colonize younger words and new words contaminate older words. Definitions blur, expand, harden, die. This sort of history can infect or change the meaning of words. In English usage *rage, enrage, outrage* have become conflated. I want to make a clear distinction between Lucy Gantt S's *rage* re S's adultery and Achebe's *outrage* re Joseph Conrad's rendering of Africans. Literary critics too often treat A's carefully considered judgments of HOD as an emotional response. But I hear A calling out C's story on the grounds that it expresses, both implicitly and explicitly, invalid assumptions about Africa and Africans. Outmoded, racist assumptions of European superiority that A challenges as extremely inappropriate, improper, ridiculous even. A's outrage shouldn't be confused with visceral rage. When his voice, his essay are dismissed as simply outcries from an enraged African, the ancient, vexed relationship between Europe and Africa that A objects to becomes, one more time, a weapon deployed against him.

Though I support A's critique of C, I feel no necessity to alter my view of HOD as imminently worthy of reading and study. Near the end of HOD, M lies to K's intended bride, a woman who waited years—like S's LG—faithfully, patiently for a summons to join her man in Africa.

M tells a grieving, bereaved woman (unnamed in his story and in C's story also) that with his last breath K said her name. M does not tell the intended what C's story tells its readers—that the final words K actually gasped were "The horror! The horror!"

One triumph for me of HOD is how unprepared I am for this moment of M's untruth, denial, falsification, truth. The many ways JC loads it, orchestrates it so I am not limited by what M's storytelling voice says, but able to step aside, become responsible, an independent witness with my own point of view on a scene M's describing. Alone, but not exactly alone as I read because the author present too, disguised, embodied by HOD's intricate text, by light and darkness, metaphor, truth and fiction, disclosures and cover-ups JC has fabricated using M's words. But alone in that stunningly intense fashion I feel when responsibility for the weight of a particularly bitter loss or failure falls upon me.

In HOD, before he discloses his own lie to the "intended," M assures his listeners, "You know I hate, detest, and can't bear a lie, not because I am straighter than the rest of us, but simply because it appalls me. There is a taint of death, a flavor of mortality in lies, which is exactly what I hate and detest in the world . . ."

Yet, when lying convenient for him, M lies. Are his previous assertions about lies untrue. In his dealings with others, are there any principles M feels bound to respect. His lie to K's intended bride clearly a vote for preserving a false veneer of respectability, sentimentality, no matter the depth of evil, of horror the lie disguises. And despite professing almost metaphysical repugnance towards lies and lying, M also believes that lying is trivial and goes unpunished. "It seemed to me that the house would collapse before I could escape, that the heavens would fall upon my head. But nothing happened. The heavens do not fall for such a trifle."

M's unreliability as narrator (for A anyway) begins long before M lies to K's intended. What else has M lied about or changed, A asks. What's been contradicted or left out or inserted in HOD to make it a good story. What do I (I ask myself) leave out or insert or contradict in stories I tell.

Did S ever admit to his wife, Lucy Gantt, the trespasses that he confessed to Church officials. If/when S tells LG stories of his betrayals, does he share her suffering. Does he ever listen to her story. Understand her suffering. One story. Many. Would S suffer telling his tales of trespass to LG.

What Achebe particularly disapproves of, I think, what outrages him about HOD is the safety net JC provides for reasonable Englishmen, for himself, us. Like M, Conrad authors a soothing cover-up. Yes, it's true that M lies. And true, we all may profess that lying is wrong. But hold on, wait a minute, JC's story tells readers. Is M such a bad bloke, after all. Too gloomy sometimes, maybe. Maybe too ready to pop off to exotic, faraway places and get himself mixed up in business way above his pay grade, but he's not that awful, is he. Africa an awful, hopeless place. Isn't that the point. M's a hard worker, likes his pint, a decent chap, not a bad lad, not much worse than most of us, is he. Feels sorry for poor darkies here and there. And can't we forgive a fella a bit of a fib to sooth a damsel in distress. Besides, it makes her happy, right. And after all, M confesses the lie to his mates, don't he. And lie or not, isn't he entertaining. We would be sitting here bored stiff, stuck between tides on the Thames, without M's company. He tells a good tale. HOD a good read.

I hear A interrogating JC, Where does your story take place? Africa, you say? Whose Africa? Whose dark heart? Who is lying?

When A's eyes caught mine that day in Amherst, Massachusetts, I saw a look from him intently directed at me, not aggressive, not lasting very long, yet intense, expressive, a glance that plainly said I believe or rather hope, my new acquaintance, hope you know better than the remarks you just chattered to brighten the conversation. In CA's eyes meeting mine across the white, wrought-iron table where we sat with a mutual friend, Mike, a Jamaican writer who had brought us together, I read equal amounts of wary distance, weariness, distaste, pity. I don't remember what I said to provoke the look—maybe we were discussing Conrad's story in my backyard I called a *garden*—but I have never forgotten Chinua Achebe's look, my embarrassment and shame, a blot on my first encounter with him that haunts me, that blot and another—the bottle of decent scotch whiskey I chose to serve that late afternoon in Amherst before I had read A's fiction and knew him only by reputation as an "acclaimed African writer"—the scotch we drank that day because for benighted me, any acclaim granted an "African" author of fiction suspect, did not necessarily signify superior writing, and thus this A didn't necessarily deserve the very best bottle I had to offer.

By the time I met CA in Amherst, Jimmy Baldwin also in residence there, lecturing in one of the country's pioneering Afro-American studies departments. Similar programs at other schools were being inaugurated, recruiting writers, scholars of color. Still, abysmal ignorance of African history, cultures, politics, ignorance of the African global diaspora, the suffering, transformation, and glories of African-descended people everywhere on the planet, continued to reign in academia. A reign of ignorance plus arrogance since, according to many academics, any African story, missing or not in traditional university curricula, couldn't really amount to very much.

Little changed until some of us began to understand that we were victims as much as we were beneficiaries of an educational system which had chosen long ago to omit crucial information about us. A brutal choice that marginalized, stigmatized, or rendered us invisible. With missionary zeal some of us embarked on crusades to transform our universities, ourselves. Enlighten the heathen. Uproot, expose, eliminate lies and misrepresentations that marginalized our humanity.

Like WHS when he set off for the Congo, many of us believed we were responding to a higher calling. Though few had ever heard of S, we imitated him without being aware that we followed his example. S sporting pith helmet, white puttees, linen suit in the Congo, my brethren and I in Brooks Brothers' suits, repp ties, Stacy Adams shoes, displaying ourselves conspicuously on campus in costumes associated with people not our color. Our elegant dress and speech beguiling, unexpected mysteries calculated to seize the natives' attention, keep them enthralled. Though some of us did prefer to mau-mau the savages, strutted around in robes, turbans, or mimicked hippie, half-naked disarray, cussing out our pupils with polyglot ghetto profanities, scaring, cowing them (and administrators) into submission. Convert or else. Just yesterday I learned from an essay, perhaps written by a Bakete speaker, that the title bestowed on S, Mudele Ndome, doesn't literally mean "black whiteman" but "man clothed as people not us clothe themselves."

Crucial information, crucial perspectives omitted from HOD, A believes, so he supplies them in his essay. Invents a photo of JC. And why would I deny my elder, better brother Chinua Achebe a license I grant myself. Of course, A doesn't need my permission nor anybody else's to tell readers his JC story. He creates a portrait of JC. Like it or lump it. Here's an unpleasant likeness of JC, A declares, and accepts full responsibility for presenting it. Exactly the sort of responsibility he asks JC to take for the kind of Africans and Africa C fabricates through an opaque partnership with M.

And if A refuses to grant JC a reprieve for not thoroughly, consistently clarifying an authorial point of view distinct from the POV of his creations—from M or K or the factors, enslavers, executioners of Congolese people—who is in a position to prove A wrong.

SUFFERING

As artists of the word, both JC and A commit themselves to preserving the best of what's been written and said. A's novel *Things Fall Apart* takes its title from "Second Coming," a poem by an Irishman, Wm Butler Yeats. I he novel records the turmoil and suffering of Okonkwo, an Igbo man, when the inherited traditions that form him are suddenly disrupted by an alien culture's intrusions. To dramatize Okonkwo's fall from grace, Achebe renders with great precision the intimate, everyday details and cultural specificity of Okonkwo's world, but he also evokes, as does the Yeats poem, literature's Great Time. Time that transcends place. Time with no beginning nor end. Time's remorseless squeezes and widening gyres that doom all individuals, all kingdoms to rise and fall. In A's African story, I hear the cry of Shakespeare's Lady Macbeth resonating: "Out, damn'd spot! out, I say." Her words in the play are a desperate attempt to erase the blot of guilt, the stain that abides after committing terrible crimes to steal a throne. But the blot, the memory of crimes persists, drives her mad, despite an exemption she imagines for herself and her husband, the king: "What need we fear who knows it, when none can call our power to account?" A's essay calls Conrad to account. Literature to account.

When do stories become cover-ups. Are writers responsible for aiding and abetting crimes when, knowingly, they tell tales that conceal crimes. Do writers become self-serving accomplices to crime even if a lie (fiction) they tell is motivated by good intentions. With a Marlow serving up a lie to protect her, would Lucy Gantt Sheppard suffer any more or less than K's intended.

Who listens to suffering's ever-present wails. Who is wailing. Who suffers. Who profits. Story I want Sheppard stories to help me construct could start there. Not by supplying answers. Art at best a feeble address to suffering. No story prevents fresh suffering, removes old bloodstains from our hands. Still, A's essay demands that stories, including JC's, address their debt, the suffering from which they arise.

COLOR STORY

It could begin with a missing photo I desire of S and L, ocular proof of the men's relative height and size. The photo also might show whose skin is lighter or darker than the other's. Not show color. Color banished from old photos unless restored by technology. Kodak pictures from the 1890s in their pebbly-grained fashion indicate a multitude of shades and gradations of light. We can't see colors in the photos, only imagine them, as once upon a time we pretended to see colors on screens of black and white TV sets. Physics defines color as visible light reflected by a specific wavelength. Thus, black and white, according to physics, are both absolutes. Black total absence of anything to see, white too much of everything to see. Eyes blinded by absolutes. Colors disappear. *Black* and *white*—when employed to designate a person's color—are stipulations, culturally assigned labels. The skin colors black or white that we claim to see, claim to recognize, that appear to us shimmering, real, reassuring, are there and not there. Black and white are colors imagined not seen. Colors not definable by wavelength. Except as absolute boundaries of the visible. Each time we claim to see a black Sheppard, a white Lapsley, are we pretending. Seeing people not there, ghosts produced by wishful thinking, dreams, nightmares, hallucinations, mirrors, stories . . .

L's correspondence and diary record his fascination, his changing notions of skin color. On their way to Africa, touring London with S, L seems surprised that the color of S's skin doesn't automatically restrict an English person's perceptions of S's social mobility. L notices that a man of S's color at a concert, tea party, or museum doesn't appear to ruffle people's expectations. "The English," SNL remarks, "don't notice at all what seems very odd to us." Once settled in the Congo, L grows "used to black faces or rather black bodies," of Africans surrounding him. "Just like our own darkies," he says. Color "made me feel quite at home." L is even able to crack a color joke and make fun of the absurdity of labeling a person either black or white: "white man as they call S."

L notices more. More than black or white. Notices more and more of the unseen. Notices that putting himself on notice in Africa produces weight. Weight of noticing more world. A world color conceals. The weight of vanity in a man who wishes to annul himself, abdicate himself absolutely in service of his god. Notices vanity of the notion of his own importance, of inserting his color, his words, his eyes, ears, every sense alert at the center of whatever circumstance in which he finds himself. As if his notice, his attention, his recording of what transpires around him matters inordinately.

He notices vanity of basking in the praise of his peers and family back home in Alabama when they had remarked upon his poet's sensibility, painter's eye in descriptions of nature. A weight of vanity he notices he is able to temper only slightly in letters home by reminding himself he's working diligently to remember this Africa not to aggrandize himself, but for the benefit of others.

He draws maps. Records words of native languages in his journals. Shyly he notices the African way of squatting, men and women nearly naked, bottoms almost in contact with the ground, bare thighs splayed, legs steepled, knees wide apart, a position Africans assume and can maintain indefinitely it seems. Notices women squatting in the mission yard all day as they work and chatter. Notices they don't give a thought to the outrageous immodesty of a habitual posture he considers surely obscene, remarkably lewd at first as their lewd public dancing until he notices that like them he can take the display for granted, and notice, appraise agile bodies, graceful limbs, the workmanship of aprons of woven cloth or occasional flap of dyed animal skin, aprons fore and aft, secured by a string women tied round the waist. Two flaps and a string, he notices, the sole garment of grown-up women busy about the yard in the next to nothing covering them well enough in their own opinions, he notices, as they squat, freely displaying scraggles of hair, various holes puncturing a woman's soft nether parts poised just inches above stomped down dirt or grass. Notices he couldn't quite keep himself from thinking about these always hungry women's bottoms as they squatted, lips foraging, feeding on grubs in the mud or bits of vegetation or lips parting to relieve swollen bellies or bowels evacuating or spewing out babies and yet he also notices how in a surprisingly short time he became accustomed to absolutely naked little girls or their aproned mothers squatting before him, conversing with him, him busy filling notebooks with examples of their Kete words and phrases, his fanciful pictures of what hidden lips might be performing set aside to concentrate instead on animated features of dark faces, their white eyes, white teeth, agile lips pronouncing Bakete for him to learn. Notices he still forgets his modesty sometimes as he watches a woman sway with that characteristic alternation of wobble and metronomic swing of sturdy hump above bare legs, legs often thin, long he notices, skinny legs anchoring what's swaying fleshy above them and he'd wonder about the action concealed by flaps of apron when a woman stands, dances, walks, or squats, pursed lips, nibbling mouths absolutely none of his business of course, and noticing his indecency he would have to caution himself, more often than he found comfortable, repeat his mantra "mind your own business, SNL," yes, yes, but he also studied those perfect clocks wound just tight enough to keep perfect time till the end of time and beyond.

L notices the incredible varieties here in this Congo jungle of flora and fauna, of colors and landscapes and waterways and weather and skies and tribes. Notices more of Sheppard. And L notices if he is patient and studies a fly just landed on the back of his hand, the fly freezes, and if he outpatiences it, the insect will eventually stir, wriggle a leg before beginning to crawl, a preparatory minuscule dance before it explores or bites him, and precisely then, while the fly intent on its business, L could swat it, kill them with great proficiency he had noticed back when he was a boy in Alabama, and notices with great wonder and some pride how the same kind of patience, same old boyhood trick he taught himself and mastered, works here, too.

Throughout his *Presbyterian Pioneers* memoir S adroitly employs a variety of narrative devices that allow him to approach in his writing as close to L's color, as close to L as he dares. A formal letter of mourning addressed to L's mother after he learns of his partner's death permits S to frame, to conventionalize an intimate outpouring of grief and love. Throughout his memoir, S's curiosity about the difference and attraction of L's skin color is not presented as personal reaction, but recorded as the response, the fascination of naive African eyes, ". . . anxious to see his feet. They begged and pleaded with him—men, women, children— to pull off his socks they called bags, that they might get one peep at least. To satisfy the crowd Mr Lapsley exhibited his small, clean, white feet. The eyes of the people opened wide. They laughed, talked, and pulled at each other, so pleased. Then they got down on their knees and began to handle them. Mr Lapsley was ticklish under the bottoms of his feet and this caused him to join in with the admirers in a hearty laugh. The exhibition was to be repeated for newcomers a number of times daily."

Invariably, out of habit, respect, conditioning by the Southern tradition in which he was raised, or perhaps a desire not to offend the majority of readers and sponsors that he could anticipate would, no doubt, share L's color not his, S always addresses (the excerpt above no exception) L as "Mr Lapsley" in his Congo book. That unchanging formality starts to become funny, silly, like those irremovable black anklets on naked men's feet in old porno flicks.

Mr L performing a crowd-pleasing display of his color is the first "unseen sight" in a section of his memoir S titles "Six Unseen Sights." But S certainly sees it. He is a member of L's audience and unapologetically participates. Similar performances are repeated often, it seems, and S witnesses those as well. Though L's unveiling of his color may resemble striptease to me, S suggests none of the risks or unsavoriness of that word. No provocation, eroticism, voyeurism, objectification, commodification, homoeroticism threaten. The performance of L and his curious African audience gets a free pass. S included. L sharing his color, his "small, clean, white feet" turns out to be one of *Presbyterian Pioneers*'s best moments. S clearly enjoys it. The mood is uncritical, high-spirited, one of the happiest, most carefree interactions in the entire memoir. L's color a blessing. Yet another gift, another bounty and mystery missionaries bring to the Congo. L exposing himself to innocent African eyes doesn't conflict with but complements numerous other depictions by S of proper good clean fun he and L explore together. "We would swim . . . to a large sand bank and on the warm sand would enjoy hand over hand and leap frog and run races."

In 1917 at the age of fifty-two, S publishes the memoir of his African adventures. His story concludes in 1893, when he is twenty-eight years old, seventeen years before he will leave Africa for good in 1910. What occurred during those African years that he chooses not to include in his book. Too many disappointments, too much sadness, loss, a precipitous downhill slide. Whatever happened, S chooses silence, and he omits from *Presbyterian Pioneers* seventeen years of his stay in Africa. Though under a cloud in 1910, when he returned to America, his lectures unveiling the Dark Continent's perils, mysteries, and art to his fellow countrymen continued to be very popular. Good publicity for the Presbyterian missionary project. S could anticipate Church support for publication of a memoir whose benefits the Church could share. With the Presbyterian Church as sponsor and Church members as potential book buyers, S surely understood that what he wrote in his African memoir and how he wrote it would be closely monitored. Vetted. Censored. Why waste time struggling to re-create oppression, slaughter, rape, enslavement, corruption, failure, betrayal, lost causes, lost loves, stories, when even if he could get them down on paper, the Church would red pencil as unfit for print. Why would his book never not address L (who died March 1892) as *Mister* Lapsley, an entitlement of color enshrined in Southern vernacular that translated means—Sir, you are my superior, sir. I accept that fact of life and never will ignore it, sir.

SKY STORIES

God you talk to, Sheppard, who talks to you and Ntomangela and loves you both you say and you both love him you say and say he loves us, Sheppard, how is he our god and does not know our words, our names . . .

S sees a sky filled with floating souls. Souls formed as figures of tiny people. If he didn't have better things to do with his time, he would spend whole days watching souls drift, twist, spin slowly, fall . . .

Older I get, more certain I become the best moments are moments spent alone. The writer's calling maybe predisposes writers to that sentiment. Appreciation of time alone to imagine what happened, is happening, should happen, or will happen next. Ironic that during time alone I often wish for someone loved with whom to share the moment.

But if someone with me, whatever their color, I would not be alone, would I.

S sees a sky filled with souls formed as figures of tiny people. Understands there is nothing better to do with his time, spends whole days watching souls drift, twist, spin slowly, fall . . .

LUCY GANTT SHEPPARD STORY

A story gone missing. Absent like the photo I searched for, photo of S and L standing side by side. Lucy Gantt, college grad, after waiting ten years for an invitation, abandons a loving mother, a teaching job in Florida to marry S and labor diligently beside him at Luebo mission on the Congo River. After two infant daughters die of African fevers, she's desperate to save the life of a third, and returns with her newborn baby to America, stays until she believes her child healthy and safe, then, rather than risk her daughter's life by exposing her again to the killing rigors of a tropical climate, with great regret LG leaves her little girl behind to be raised by an aging grandmother and, at the risk of her own life, rejoins her husband at Luebo, only to discover from one of the African women or girls, probably a student befriended in the mission school where LGS teaches English and pupils instruct her in Bakete and a creole they call Kru-boy, in one of those exchanges that are an unpredictable, improvised mix of three languages and other local tribal dialects and a speaker's idiosyncratic personal tics, in other words in the typical mode of people conversing in any polyglot crossroads of commerce and foreign nations and native cultures, in such an exchange Lucy discovers that while she was away, her beloved husband S not faithful, not too busy with god's work to neglect the devil entirely, slipping off at night to this or that very welcoming wench, and his seed, Shepete, birthed by one of the women, people say and me I don no maybe yes maybe no he very very busy round here bery but I not no, not my busyness missy lady m'sahib but better beware all I be saying you cause you good lady nice lady all time nice tankee u please missy, and Lucy Gantt Sheppard nods back speechless, stunned clean out of words and too much a Christian to scream in the girl's lying black nigger face not true it is not not no how true how can you dare say it but I won't scream, not cuss out a child of god, god's daughter just like my lost babies his children, you, you, how girl could u speak such things the all-seeing eyes of god watching, hearing every word u say no no almighty god I will not curse her just allow myself please a deep half sob sigh suck up all the rest inside me and take to my bed lay myself down next to my poor faraway baby's empty cradle, lay in that marriage bed S fouled while I traveled cross an ocean to save a daughter he called his darling precious girl my tiny girl I didn't dare bring back here not for his sake not in his name to love and cherish in god's name for god's sake. Mama said you don't have to go back neither, Lucy, neither one of you, both youall stay here, let it go, let Sheppard do as he must do according to his lights and conscience but don't sacrifice one more sweet god's child to do it with him girl stay here with your daughter where you belong Lucy let Sheppard and god tend heathen souls your place here don't go back but I nodded yes said I love him trust god love him please I am only breath and bone and when the young wench finishes her speech no bone left and all the breath of me seeps out in a sigh unhappy as this wide, sighing, mournful, churning river we sleep beside, dying here beside this long, long river carrying so much pain and blood you can't help listening some nights to how it quietly lashes and scars and gouges at the banks flowing past and thank goodness no dirty water, no dark scraping weight, nothing to lift when I rise from this gerry-rigged like everything else around here, this supposed to be teacher's desk and nothing to it, to me as I float away rise and shimmer away let me reach out and touch my child and then I will breathe in air again for her sake, breathe in once and then let it all go again let go this girlwoman's African face thankful I did not rip it with my talons her black skin, black grinning evil words how do I know it wasn't her own self she was telling on and laughing inside the whole time up in my face her face so serious and sad god help me take me home to my babies . . . etc. etc. . . . . oh lord what a fool risking everything giving him everything and now Jesus save me . . . etc. . . . . story goes . . .

S still away in a long canoe downriver to recruit more bearers so he can travel far away again, story continues the day after LG makes her discovery. Three days alone or perhaps many more if rapids or cannibals chop him, swallow his dog-sorry ass, days for her to rage and rectify, to recompose herself, to destroy what reminds her of his presence, of love, days to smash and trash enough so that if S comes back he will stand stupefied in the doorway as he sees the damage she has wrought during his absence, see with his own two lying eyes things he prizes, possessions that prop up his vanity, his courage and strength and sense of superiority, singularity, divine calling strewn about the household in grisly chunks, clumps, a nappy shambles littering bamboo mats like Samson's proud hair after Delilah's scissors, and she prays, forgive me Jesus, and yes, begs her sweet savior if he pleases may the sight blind S just exactly at the moment he sees it, sees damage her long absence from his heart has wrought upon the orderly interior of a good wife, helpmate loving mother and Christian, see, behold, lookee here, look inside the walls of this shabby dwelling, walls of my flesh, you dirty, defiling, evil man . . . her story (his) continues about a terrible, ungrateful sneaky conniving S and what a shame he is before god and man fucking everything he can get his nasty fingers on, girl, woman, goat, chicken, any living breathing thing around here a snake or these wheezing, sweating, mincing, simpering, nasty pastors and priests and parsons, wouldn't they jump at the chance, black, white, old, young, Christian, cannibal, a hippopotamus, because if an African female why not males, anything, everything after she left here gone begging good god to spare her baby and S goes wild with lust chasing anything moving, her it them, that pretty dead boy she bets when she snatches up the photo books, surveys pictures of bare-breasted, long-breasted African women, of pale him, a pale boy lover, too, why not, thinking why in hell not as she rips out and destroys every image she finds of that smiling, smirking pretty little mama's boy in the woods saving nigger souls, screwing niggers, by god it just might, could be true, sweetboy sweet on her sweet S and S her once-upon-a-time sweet S, her twisted S, sweet on him every day god sends, however it is they twist up to make love to each other, ripping out, tearing up, spitting on, burning every crumbled picture of him of them together in books or stuck on a wall of what's spozed to be her home and never ever will be again when she finishes this story, nobody home ever again.

WILLIAM HENRY SHEPPARD STORY

Glory days surround him, swirl past him, and anyone looking at him— if they spoke his language and acquainted with the word—would think *beatific* if they observed the flicker of smile lighting up S's face an instant before he blinks. S blinks. He is sitting up. Rocker or bed, he's not sure. Tries to open eyes and still not sure his eyes open or closed while he searches for legs, dull weight of legs, remembering them, murmuring to himself, taking inventory—hand, arms, neck, back, head, eyes— two legs stretched out flat, leaden, sweaty under bedding or his knees bent, butt and back folded into the rocker's hard wooden seat, slippered feet on the floor, no, no, yes, inventory of numb, dumb body parts forgetting him absolutely as sometimes he's able to ignore them, these stranger's body parts he summons now, recalling parts of himself, parts of this room he occupies, scans before he's sure his eyes open or not. Fear. Rush to be somewhere. Not gone. Not nowhere. Suddenly. Dully. No one. Patience he thinks. No rush. Lucy's voice sooner or later will open a safe rabbit hole in this silence. He is sitting up in bed. Tea in a cup, cup on a saucer (here, kitty . . . kitty) saucer on table at head of bed. Cold. Dozed off. Hot. Blow on hot tea with his breath . . . careful, it's very hot, S, you be careful now . . . let tea cool some, u hear me, S, Lucy had said. Still very warm on his lips first sip after blowing, blowing softly, lips puckered as if he's fixing to kiss tea.

Lucy brought tea on a tray. Set tea down, teacup on saucer on the busy night table she tidies a bit before she goes. Hot sip. Cold now. Tea set down ten, fifteen minutes ago. Hours maybe days ago. How long to happen. To change. How do you know. Patience. No rush. Count . . . 1 . . . 2 . . . 3 . . . after you lock on the hippo, patience . . . it's your time, take your time, draw a bead, S, aim, hold steady, wait. If the beast slips underwater, it will rise again. Wait till you see fat, furrowed hippo brow again in your rifle's sights, keep the line straight, centered, a string taut like when line connects to a fish and you jerk, no, do not jerk, you squeeze *ka:pow* slowly, slowly let your lips unpucker, no taste of hippo yet, too raw, too hot, too fresh, too soon, too bloody, wait they say, the natives say hippo not a fish on your shimmering line. Wait for it to pop up again in the hole through the water into which it vanished. Do not jerk the trigger. Squeeze. Let it go gently as shot hippo gently sinks from sight and he Mr. Hippo he be back they say, back maybe hour, maybe more less the hippo you caught between the eyes or up one gaping, wider than a Sunday funny paper negro's nose hole straight up a nostril to tiny brain dead hippo meat cooking if you wait hippo pops up belly-first, wobbles downside up in the muddy current and we will swim to it, knives, spears hook it, drag it out, butcher it, meat for days they sing and dance and clap and pat your back, S, they yodel your name, Sheppard, Sheppard, Great Hunter, *Njela,* crack shot, deadly like a god's lightning bolt they love you love the sunken hippo wait S him will surely return and break river's silence S wait for it to float belly-up floating, fresh meat after they fish him out.

If you are patient S and wait two minutes two hours two years who knows. Who knows why/when African fever comes and goes. You burn. Chilled. Melt. Afloat. Shuddering, trembling, blow on hot to make it cold, blow on cold to make it hot, cold, hot, cold, hot swimming in your own terrible wetness and you never forget fever will return even as it breaks (the helpful Baptists at Matudi station warned Mr. Lapsley and warned you, Mr. L's colored staff, S, about the dreaded fevers as if you both didn't already know, already fear fever, dream fever months before you land in Africa) as if information, gossip, tips, science, words the practical Baptists dispensed—[three types: (1) *remittent* (2) *intermittent* (3) *bilious hematuric*]—were a prescription, a cure like 5 grains of calomel, 5 grains jalap tea, 50 grains of quinine, those powders, charms you had packed of course though they are no cure either, you learned, just buying time, fever perhaps will diminish, hide awhile before it resurfaces worse, worse, never-ending you learn, the hulking, skulking, raging fever beast crosses an ocean, never losing your scent, its ravenous hunger for your stinking sweat, chills, hot flashes, shivering meat, no, no, S, it won't go away it waits and you suffer waiting and suffer worse when it springs up, tops you, and you suffering drop down on your knees, crushed, legs totally giving out, melt under you, you suffer no legs and collapse in bed till in due time given god's mercy and grace you sit up again, fever wanes it seems until it leaps, finds you here now in this Kentucky thousands of miles, days, years away from a mosquito-breeding, pestilence-breeding

Congo River, no cure for fever, no cure for color or darkness or light or lies, for none of the names for sickness or pain or suffering the missionaries stick in you like pins, knives, spears, only a matter of time between one killing seizure and the next, how long, how long, do not ask, S, do not count, S, wait, S, squeeze, draw your deadly bead on the wrinkled brow, little piggy pop-eyes, long, whisker-stubbled snout negroid-tunneled like yours.

You wait for Lucy's voice—Sheppard, Sheppard . . . are you ok, Mr. Sheppard. Him will pop up, the cannibals promise, hippo my righteous bullets hunt to feed them. *Pow-Pow-Pow.* Floating in water's unbroken silence.

Dead floats they say. Life floats, too. S sees small splotches of light floating, miscellaneous patterns of splotches without a pattern in silent shadows where play of light and dark a sort of quiet, quiet, not quite audible music during walks when he used to walk and walk or walks now on rumors of legs, ghost feet walking a backcountry road with tall trees growing alongside and thick branches overhanging, deep shadows and quiet broken by sun's brightness that prints blackly, intricately many, many layers of backlit leaves in air, on gray tarred surface of a road.

But not exactly quiet, deeper silence than quietness, more complicated, nearly darkness except those scattered blots shivers echoes ghosts streaks spatters webs cries of light he walks through, steps on, listens to. On some long stretches of road no trees provide cover, only bushes, brambles, tangles of greenery not as tall as he is line a burning hot Kentucky road, no shade, no discs, spills, meshes, splashes of light tremble, floating here and there, yet S still hears if he's patient, even in withering heat and brightness, hears if he lets his legs remember remembering, silent music, as it were, of cool leaf shadows once upon a time while he, while we walk, walking, walking, eyes open now S is sure. No hurry. Fever comes, goes. Forever.

MISSIONARIES' STORY

Sheppard remembers a square of bare mud, stomped down flat, smooth in the mission yard, a yellowish red blackboard of ground and L presides over it with a long stick of bamboo drawing a large letter in the dirt, pronouncing the letter's sound, four, five, six times, then directing, prompting gently with words, stick, gestures, grimaces, and smiles the crowd of African children to repeat the sound after him. At first the response a motley array of sounds, a mixture of many versions of L's *ah* sound for the letter A, but the chorus of voices following L's voice also harmonized, rhythmic, a multitude of differing *ah*s interwoven, blending spontaneously, subtly as Bach counterpoint because the children all speakers of the same language, shared an old culture that predisposed, guided them to sync their different voices into song, the first few combinations of *ah*s music, even if clearly not what L wished from them, but gradually, quickly really, given the number of different sounds from different mouths and how far apart each separate sound—*ahh—a— ah—aaah—a-a—haaa*—from L's *ah*, after a few ensemble recitations patiently, gently elicited by L's stick tapping the letter and saying the *ah* sound again, the voices evolve into a unanimous *Ah*, an *ah* perfectly matching in L's mind sound of the letter in the dirt, unanimity pleasing to him and the children, an *ah, ah, ah*, a single sound repeated over and over, one voice, lots of dark, skinny, naked, hungry, dying children happy learning, and L happy and—*ah-ah-ah*—S watches him, L almost prancing at the end of stick that had traced the letter A in a dried square of mud.

On an April night in 1891, in a campsite on the north bank of the Lulula River, tributary of the Congo, William Henry Sheppard and Samuel Norvell Lapsley, two young American men in their twenties, newcomers to Africa searching for a location where a Presbyterian mission might flourish, find themselves overwhelmed by vast, all-encompassing darkness, sheer isolation, strangeness of being unimaginably far from home, far from people who speak their language, only howls of jackals, hooting of owls breaking jungle stillness, and in a tent their African workmen have set up, the two missionaries sob audibly, cling to each other, S writes.

I can't help myself from flashing backwards two centuries before that moment in Africa S describes, flash back to a plantation in a country yet to declare its independence from England. I imagine two young men newly arrived here after many weeks sick, hungry, chained, crossing an ocean surrounded by others their color in chains, confined in close darkness of a stinking ship's fetid hold, others sick, hungry, dying, pissing, shitting, moaning, women, men, children, a Babel of languages, except all speak the tongue of suffering, and hearing that unending suffering voice again at night in a slave hovel in a new world overwhelms two young men who sob audibly, reach out to touch one another, men captured by slavers raiding their villages, marched in coffles to the sea, sea crossed to a land shrouded in all-encompassing darkness, night or day, sheer isolation, strangeness of an unimaginable distance from home, from people who speak their tongue, only snarls and cracking whips of masters in this terrifying Virginny, masters as absolutely unworthy of service as S and L believe the master they serve infinitely worthy.

MY STORY AGAIN

You must have figured out by now—if you are still listening to me discovering and sampling stories about S, by S and other imagined voices—me adding bit after bit, story after story to this S story—that the point is I don't really want it to stop yet—I want to paddle downstream, upstream and back and down at least once more—searching, seeking a place of refuge, of welcome—to start, to begin again—constructing, like S in his memoir, like anybody—a womb of stories that protects, confines—

stories I discover or conceal or repeat or cannot forget—stories I hear others tell, transformed by each telling—imaginary doors through imagined flesh. Nothing beyond my flesh. Nothing inside if stories stop.

It is about 7:30 p.m. here. Sun still high in the sky. Sun will stay up there another couple hours at least before it finally descends. Early July and sky remains bright late on clear days here in Brittany during this season, but I get up from my writing table on the deck to take down clothes hanging in my backyard because even if sky bright, dew begins to fall or rise or thicken or do whatever dew does in Brittany, predictably about 7:30 p.m. these days, and clothes dried on a line will get soaked again if you don't take them indoors, so I do, as once I took down her clothes and mine, before lies, before betrayals, her clothes always gathered first from the line because they made her feel present, here, no matter where else in the house she might be, treating her clothes differently than mine, I had gently squeezed open clothespins and carefully took down and folded her things piece by piece, stacked them in their own neat pile on a chair beside a large wicker hamper set on the grass under the clothesline, then my stuff grabbed, half-assed piled or tossed into the hamper, and the neat pile of her clothes from the chair placed on top of my things.

Finished today with my clothes, I go back to the round writing table and chair on the deck, to the story I had looked up from earlier to see a washer-load of my laundry drying, kicking around in a smattering of 7:30 p.m. breeze. A big, cloudless sky above, still up there, and on a plate next to my wineglass I notice a green scrap left over from a tomato I'd eaten, tomatoes, a little bowl of grape tomatoes, slices of saucisson my aperitif, and I pick up the detached green whatever from the plate to examine it closer and it is exquisite, a small, wilting five-pointed star silhouetted when I raise it, dangle it by tip of one point against blue sky, and believe me, the word for it *exquisite,* though I have no words to tell how unexpected and unique this particular dying piece of vegetable matter, delicate, unerringly complete, no words to tell its story, but I see it, hear it, this stem, leaf approximately an inch across when centered in my palm, a green root or handle or cap or flower that once fastened its tomato to a vine and no words for how perfectly shaped, elegant, exquisite it is . . . so I shut up. My clean clothes stuffed in the hamper, mostly dry, ready to be put away later, her clothes absent, where oh where, and I go back to wine, aperitif, no words to tell the story, and even if I found some, they would not bring my *Lucy* back any sooner.

IGBO STORY

Igbo words: *Onwero akuko gb'aka*—Okey, an Igbo young man, a fiction writer who respects and revers his elder, CA, and had worked beside him in both Nigeria and America, emails me that *onwero akuko gb'aka* are Igbo words of proverb Achebe translated into English as "all stories are true"—Okey also shares with me his understanding of literal meaning of those Igbo words: "No story is ever empty-handed or No story is ever bereft."

NTOMANJELA'S STORY

"A Girl Who Ate Her Mother" may be S's favorite African story. Recorded in *Presbyterian Pioneers,* told and retold countless times on the lecture circuit, published by him once as a children's book. Why his favorite, if in fact it is. The answer to that *why* as inaccessible to me as names of owners of those teeth in a dentist's boxful that fascinated S when he was a kid. But anyway, what follows here is a retelling of S's favorite story:

Ntomanjela . . . Ntomanjela . . . the afternoon I returned from a trip south to recruit bearers, L told me that 3 days previously he had heard someone calling him, one of his Bakete friends using L's Bakete name, *Ntomanjela*, meaning pathfinder because they believe he found a way into their country, their homes, language, and hearts. The friend had come round to tell L a story heard from a cannibal leading captives to market. A woman slave's feet too swollen to take another step and she dropped down beside the trail and they camped there and ate her and caused the woman's young daughter to eat of her also. Of course, S, I was horrified by the tale, L said, and told me that when he learned the coffle would be passing nearby, he felt he must go and ask why they had perpetrated such hideous acts. L intended to ask them gently, he said, despite his outrage, his rage and I believe he probably did ask gently, since gentle always how L dealt with people, and also, being no fool, he feared cannibals. The chief of the party, though somewhat annoyed, halted his caravan, consented to speak with L, told L he had followed the usual procedure and that it also made perfect sense. If too weak to march, a slave becomes welcome fodder for the others. Daughter hungry, alive and valuable merchandise. Why should she not be fed.

L said he then implored the chief to leave the unfortunate orphan behind at the mission. The cannibal said he would exchange her for a goat. L offered instead a bolt of foreign cloth, and a bargain was struck. A mission woman took the naked child to the river, washed and clothed her. N'Tumba will be a student in our school, L said to me, and god willing, she will thrive.

N'Tumba became L's favorite. He kept her especially close about him for the final ten, eleven months left him on this earth. And from her very first days here in the mission, quite difficult days for her, she favored L with her trust, her smile. His hands, embraces, smiles the only ones she did not ignore, resist, fight, hiss at, or run away from screaming. She loved L immediately as we all did.

N'Tumba shy, but on occasion boldly affectionate, L confided to me once. If he wasn't wary, she would sneak into his bed, he said, and curl up next to him until he awakened in the morning. N'Tumba became Ntomanjela's quiet shadow. Serving him, nursing him, imitating him. At ease at last, and a favorite, too, in the flock of mission women, suffering women that L and I both worried about because they were neither exactly fish nor foul, not property, not protected by chiefs or family males, our crew of fearful, dependent women, a congregation of disconnected souls, misfits, always hungry, begging for more, semipermanent residents or nomads passing through, our female wards with some of whom I admit I expressed myself most freely, in a manner that gentle, shy L never would or could, and he admonished me, saying he feared that my attentions to the women endangered my soul, souls of the women, those clamorous women, dark Eves, innocent, shy, curious, wild in this wild, dark garden, women forever beseeching, squabbling amongst themselves, women who obediently sang hymns, obediently chanted prayers we taught, our pack of pagans who would worship a python or lie down with one if they believed they'd be rewarded with a meal or shelter. In L's eyes N'Tumba a quiet jewel amongst them. A blessed daughter, little mother, helpmate.

N'Tumba brokenhearted, I'm certain, when Ntomanjela did not return on the government steamer from Stanley Pool, and N'Tumba mourns him today, no doubt, if she is still alive. No telling what they might have become to one another. But that's another story . . .

SHEPPARD

SHE BRINGS THE GLASS TEAPOT into a room too full of furniture to breathe. A woman not small, not large, not exactly shrunken, though clearly not the woman she once was. Old but substantial as each piece of polished furniture, oversized for the room's modest dimensions, furniture whose every flat surface and each shelf visible through spotless glass, loaded with knickknacks, photos in ornate frames, painted crockery, vases, an old woman crowded, competing for air with all the stuff she's accumulated to surround herself, antiques, relics, an imposingly massive oak sideboard, figurines of porcelain, ivory, carved wood, a roomful of last things belonging to her that she no doubt cares for meticulously, years of gathering, dusting, shining, arranging, rearranging, attending these inanimate occupants dying with her in this old house, this overburdened space paid for dearly and dearly owned, this museum of purchases and prosperity perfectly preserved as her undulled eyes that remain curious and restless, a smile young despite papery, freckled skin, wrinkles, white wisps escaping edges of a kerchief tied to conceal bare spots and purple veins I picture atop a pale skull, a perfect housekeeper perfectly prepared to let the manner she cares for this room into which she invites me for a cup of tea, introduce her, display her, tell her story if I, or any other visitor, desires to hear it, and whether anyone asks for a story or not, whether she survives the room or not, whether it survives her, the room narrates who she is, was, these objects, her ancient possessions, each with its own history, destiny, speak for her while I sit and watch her pour hot water over tea bags into two cups.

Why me, a question she addresses as much to herself as to me. Or addresses to no one in particular, just a way of ending an awkward silence opening, then expanding between us, a pause after cups filled and she hesitates, handle of glass teapot gripped in one fist, pot holder in her other hand to steady the pot, as if she's lost track of what she must do next to complete a simple action she intends. As if adrift, unable to remember or forget until she asks, *Why me,* to end a silence suddenly become too long, too complicated for either of us, total strangers before this meeting, to ignore or negotiate. A brimful, wary silence inconsistent with polite exchanges. Silence a vast emptiness calling attention to itself, consuming more than its proper share of the room's sparse air.

On the round mahogany table a rooster-shaped metal trivet atop a circular mat accepts the teapot. Before she vanishes again, my host, this Lucy Gantt Sheppard I found after years of searching, seats herself on a chair matching mine, matching five others matching the table. Her posture perfect—back straight, shoulders squared, no droop to her chin. She's substantial again, not dead, as I'd begun to assume after failing to discover any trace of her in public records after her husband's death in 1927. Lucy Gantt Sheppard not small, though cut in half by a tabletop's black, shining immensity separating us in this room of a house on East Breckinridge Street, Louisville, Kentucky, a room, house, street, neighborhood all of which have seen better days, and worse, too, I heard in her voice, *Why me,* before she sat down, before she shakes her head slowly and sighs, All that time . . . all that long, long time.

I am in another room now. Sitting, listening again. Hear her words again. Write them. Revise. Word by word as if one word might be correct and another not. As if I'd know the difference. As if I have a choice. Going forward and backward as if a woman, Lucy Gantt Sheppard whom I'm imagining, and a roomful of things belonging to her are waiting patiently for me to make up my mind. But my mind drawn out a window on this coldest morning of winter so far, January 21, Martin Luther King Day. A nearly horizontal whitish plume of steam gliding from some furnace's rooftop chimney vent steals my attention. Plume twists, spreads thinner and thinner, and I notice other clouds of whitish steam pumped into frigid air. Some clouds rapidly, others gradually, turning gray. Some scooting off fast as high winds snatch and shred and lift them.

Or was it a flight of birds that distracted me. Explosion of birds pinwheeling, dozens of birds in sync a moment as they swoop towards me, then rising, dispersed, a swirling mass of birds in a patch of empty sky, just beyond the edge of a recently constructed skyscraper three blocks or so from my apartment building, from my ninth-floor bedroom window the skyscraper dominates each morning when I raise the blind. All seventy stories of it out there yesterday and this morning. But where was it a moment ago while I was drinking tea with Lucy Gantt Sheppard. When I look away, is the tower gone. And what had I seen first, birds or steam this morning.

Were birds in fact what drew my eyes out the window, away from words on a page. Flash of birds first. Steam later. Birds my first translation of movement perceived in a corner of my eye. Black pebbles of bird hurled at me by a gigantic hand, puncture wounds in empty air before the clump of them veers sharply right as if to avoid a barrier. Birds like many, many specks of light blinking on an instant before they change direction, scatter, blink off, a fluttering swirl of dots black then suddenly white again swooping past brick walls, shadows, row upon row of apartment buildings whose tops are silhouetted against the bottom of a sky that stretches up, up, forever, beyond the new tallest, tall tower of steel and glass. Same endless sky looming each morning.

Birds hurtling towards me, careening suddenly to avoid a wall invisible to me, flock of birds ascending above jumbled streets and sidewalks, then out of sight, disappearing, and now I'm unable to decide if the birds guilty, or was it banners of steam changing shape, rippling flags of steam stealing my attention before birds appeared. Whitish steam quickly graying, gray smoke swiftly torn and tattered by gusting arctic wind inflicted on New York City today of all days. Wind driving flocks of birds, wind revising, ripping apart steam, words, a tea party, a King holiday. Lucy Gantt Sheppard nothing, nowhere. Not reachable, not translatable, not recoverable. Nothing here except me pretending that maybe it's not just me in a room making stuff up, me pretending that maybe by-and-by, those things, those words I'm looking for are reassembled elsewhere in clearer, better order, in their own good time and place. Patiently waiting for me. To teach me what to say, how to say it.

Witness to my own witness. Best I can say for myself. Unsure of myself. So how can I convince anybody else my testimony accurate, true. A survivor. Alone. I surely get that much of your story, Lucy Gantt Sheppard. And some of the *Why me* part, too. Space between us, space within myself I can't enter. Maybe a single word stands for both spaces, yours and mine, inside and outside, or maybe any word a person thinks or says or writes always breaks up a single space and turns it into many. *Love* one word for many spaces—space shared by two people and space within each one of us.

While you waited for William Sheppard's love letter summoning you to join him in Africa, how often did you find yourself reading it, Lucy—may I call you, Lucy—how often perhaps with tears in your eyes did you reread his unwritten letter and while reading could not help yourself and find yourself writing a response, formulating unwritten sentences you vaguely see, hear while you see and hear his words, his imagined sentences. You responding to a letter, a summons you have yet to receive, but you read it anyway, again and again. His unwritten letter and yours ghost dancing, his words and yours glide across the page together, converse, embrace, finding a rhythm, space on a floor of air that supports feet, words, though you had yet to receive the letter from him for which you have been waiting ten years, letter you dream very often in your hands, words in his handwriting right there in front of your eyes, a letter accessible as your most familiar, intimate memories that leave no room for doubt. Letter substantial enough you risk not giving it your full attention and add your unwritten words to his, your words and sentences on the page looping in and out of his while you half-remember, half-read, halfway forget how long it's been, how many years you have waited for his letter to arrive.

Not the kind of day I would have chosen for an MLK birthday party. But happy to celebrate King, happy to join marchers around City Hall. I participate to honor him, the man he might have continued to struggle to be if his life, his time on earth had not been stolen. Way past the point now, of course, for marches, protests. King lost, and another and another shot dead in the streets, and protesting, marching, speeches won't bring them back nor stop the next one from being killed. Way beyond the point of needing responses futile as I was sure the King Day march would be. Futile as trying to stay warm outdoors on an icy, snow-flogged day at the end of January. Futile as pretending anything less than total erasure and starting again from scratch would change this town, its citizens, my people, my country. But I can't give up on symbols yet. A writer, after all. *Futility* and *hope* are both only words, both only symbols. Who can say, let alone know, what's coming next.

Thirty-seven trillion the approximate number of cells in a human body. To count them one by one would take thousands of years. *Apoptosis* a word for cell death. One million of my body cells die every second. *Necrosis* a word for cell suicide. A healthy cell, if separated from its neighbors, may commit suicide to avoid growing in wrong place.

Wrong place. Was I in the wrong place. No invitation to the postmarch reception hosted by mayor or city council or King's ghost. Once maybe I would have been an honored guest, back in the day when my honored presence was courted to honor civic occasions, back before my presence deemed stale news, before my distinguished career, distinguished books, fiery, uncompromising rhetoric treated merely as disposable adornments, instantly replaceable. City doesn't need me as it slouches towards a bright, benign future promised by mayors and city councils, promised to citizens who are taught to assume that their elected representatives desire only the best for them, citizens taught that politicians (and a couple distinguished artists perhaps) embody the shining best qualities of humanity, though all of us, everybody, anybody trying or not trying to live decently in these streets, beneath these steel towers, beside trees, a river, among cops, bankers, universities, the halt-and-lame, lawyers, homeless, merchants, students, orphans, criminals, demons, preachers, ignorance, superstition, liars and lies, bus drivers, schemers, statistics, rot, hunger, drugs, we all understand quite well the dream of a decent life not going to come true.

No invitation to the reception. Hope I don't sound bitter. I am not.

Quite the contrary. Grateful, rather, on Martin Luther King Day, invitation or no invitation, to get quickly out of bitter cold, into a heated room furnished with hot beverages, an assortment of sweet rolls and donuts, and however I managed to wind up there—rumor of a reception circulating through participants in the march, heads-up from an old acquaintance, or following a prosperous looking group that appeared to know where they were headed and in a hurry and confident they'd arrive I felt I belonged Appreciated warm cup of tea a young woman behind a long table draped by white cloth poured for me. A pleasure to blend in unobtrusively. No fanfare, no profuse exchanges of greetings, hugs, smiles, *ooh-la-la* kisses on both cheeks of ladies, my trademark, confirming my sophistication, my distinguished reputation not only at home, but abroad. Thankful, in this familiar setting where once I'd wasted far too much time, far too many words, thankful that no bullshit required today. Just me warming up, my tea cooling.

When I noticed Sheppard, he was standing near the mayor who was beside someone in a wheelchair. Shock of white hair what drew my eyes to fasten on Sheppard. Anonymous white of hair, then Sheppard. Unmistakably him. William Henry Sheppard. Too much space intervened between us to calculate precisely how much his face had aged. But white hair signifies ancient to me. Death just around the corner. Keep my few hairs cropped short, nipped in the bud to avoid telltale blooming of age in my sideburns or white sprinkling the corona circling half my skull just above and behind my ears if I let hair grow longer than half a quarter inch. White hair I often admire on other people's heads but dread on mine, caught my eye across the ballroom, a head covered by hair white as graying snow shoveled, banked along city streets to clear a path for the march.

I held my casual glance an extra moment, hoping no one noticed, wanting to assure myself, indeed, it was our tall Mr. Mayor next to a brown man in a wheelchair, and yes, near the mayor, Sheppard's face wearing an ancient person's hair. Sheppard not forgotten despite my not seeing him for many years, then wondering how long ago it could have been since I had last encountered Sheppard. Not recently, but not a hundred years ago either. Huh-uh, no, impossible it's been that long, I was thinking, trying to remember until I realized I was staring again and abruptly stopped studying him, looked away. Impossible, I couldn't help myself from thinking, because if Sheppard had changed so much, turned so white in the interval since our last meeting, then certainly I, too, must have altered as drastically as him. Perhaps dead like him.

Whether or not S a mirror, whether or not I'd discover in his face more undeniable bad news, I had no desire to approach him and confront whatever his white hair, his eyes greeting mine might reflect. Fact S my elder by many, many dozens of years did not allay my panic. *Panic* the precise word. Turned on my heels in a panic, fled through a crowd much thicker now after word of free drinks, free food had leaked out, careful not to step on a blue ribbon lying on the floor, ribbon once strung between two waist-high brass stanchions to barricade space between the ballroom's open double doors where I'd entered. Staff long gone now who had been tending the ribbon and checking names earlier as I'd nonchalantly sauntered in, veteran me knowing better than to stop, attaching myself instead to whatever notable or notables I understood would not hesitate, not offer their names and no attendant would dare ask.

I inhabit a transparent glass globe of immeasurable dimensions, sealed, no exits or entrances fathomable to me. An all-encompassing singularity of consciousness, of terror I cannot escape.

———

I'm assured by those in charge my color does not require me nor not *not* require me to be poor or in jail or afraid or male or female or rich or homeless . . . etc., etc. No rules mandate me to be, nor mandate me not to be . . . anything. Up to me, I am told. Free to choose. To write whatever I wish. Reassured that my condition is my choice. That's what makes this country a democracy, right. Freedom of choice. Equal choice for everybody. Except color. One rule. No one's color an exception. No exceptions.

Hair not as white, of course, as it first appeared. Color less a matter of actual color than associations color triggers. And *shock* not a very accurate word to describe what covered S's head. *Sprinkles. Sprinkles* not the perfect word either, not as exact as *necrosis* or *apoptosis,* but better. Like you might say *white* is how a street, a roof, a lawn looks after snow sprinkles it. *Sprinkle, sprinkle, little hairs.* Sheppard's snowy hair a detail I easily might have missed or ignored when I scanned city hall's so-called Ballroom from my chosen corner. Difference of his hair barely stopping my eyes, its pale color or lack of color a minor note within dull theme and variations of predominately brown, gray, occasionally black or blond, mostly blue-haired guests the mayor had invited. But more to white hair than its color. Sometimes while I'm shaving, if I happen to spot a white hair in a nostril, I have to stop immediately, pick or snatch or scissor it out. A hair whiter, more urgent than it actually is, and that's how I reacted to a whitish head I noticed in the reception crowd. Probably a tall mayor leaning down and talking to a brown man in a wheelchair equally responsible for arresting my gaze, revealing ancient Sheppard.

———

I'm ashamed of the question I wanted to ask him when just the two of us alone together in my sister's kitchen, waiting for other fundraiser guests to arrive, face to face finally with the brown man I had noticed in a wheelchair beside the mayor on King Day. I had learned his name, his intention to run for city council, and we'd corresponded by email. Our first private moment with nobody else around, no members of his crew, not even the young woman who constantly hovered behind his chair at public events, tending to his needs, anticipating them it seems maybe even before he does, wheeling him around, offering a hankie, pulling iPad, phone, book, or some mysterious gadget from a saddlebag slung over one wheelchair arm. She was quiet as a shadow, words between them, it seems, not necessary to get things done, crucial or casual tasks seamlessly accomplished, tasks probably daunting or impossible without her assistance, and she tended him unobtrusively, you could forget her presence, the sort of companionship I envy, anybody would, and maybe feel a bit jealous, too. Quite a pretty young woman. Her attractive, caring presence there beside him even after she had followed my sister into the dining room to help with setting-up chores. Unfortunately, another far less desirable presence also remained palpable to me as I conversed with the young man. I was tempted to ask him a question, one at least as thoughtless, incriminating, and regrettable as the question I had asked the first African I met.

When I had asked an African guy, *Have you ever seen a live lion,* I was a college student and knew better or should have known better, but the dumb question irresistible, possibly inevitable, so I had asked it anyway. The evening in my sister's kitchen first time alone with the brown man in the wheelchair, though I had managed to keep my question to myself and didn't exactly inflict my embarrassing curiosity upon him,

I heard my silenced question loud and clear: *How do you cope if dead, truly, completely dead down there below your waist, below the tartan plaid wool blanket draping your chair.*

Even as it formed itself in my mind, that absolutely none of my business nor anybody else's business, unanswerable question, I felt a wave of shameful regret pass through me. I knew the question not really directed at the particular young man with whom I was talking, but compounded of worries, memories dogging me about myself. So much pain, so many years, so many words and still pretending that writing permits me to be a ghost. A tourist. No dues to pay. Privileged to gawk, gape, handle, grab. Fly back home and forget. No consequences. As if unforgivable questions not windows revealing who I am. As if being a tourist protects and privileges me. Allows me to avoid self-examination. Here today, gone tomorrow, right. Why confront my own unfitness, my vulnerability, my history, my stories, the terror of an aging body's inevitable obsolescence and failure.

I had avoided William Henry Sheppard on MLK Day. Seeing him from a distance sufficed, I believed. Believed it would be wise just to let him go. If I didn't acknowledge Sheppard's presence, maybe he wasn't really there. He would disappear. A phantom like the cruel question I hoped I would be able to forget since I had not imposed it aloud upon the aspiring, wheelchair-bound candidate.

More than ironic that Sheppard had popped up, with his white shock or white sprinkles, on the January day of a march and reception for King, a day circled in red on our nation's calendar of forget-me-not commemorations. The sort of special day WHS deserved. I had written previously to an old friend, editor of an influential journal, describing WHS as more or less forgotten by the American public, a man I had recently discovered purely by accident whose story fascinated me enough that I immediately began to research his career. A letter to convince my editor buddy to initiate in his prestigious journal a campaign for a WHS day to honor the unique achievements of an extraordinary human being who absolutely deserved more national recognition.

Instead of assaulting the candidate with an ugly question, perhaps I could have shared Sheppard's story. Before Tarzan, before heart of darkness and natives surrounded by endless herds of ferocious, exotic beasts, natives black as chimpanzees, natives hopelessly, permanently mired in savagery with no culture, no history, with funny ugga-bugga languages, laughable ugga-bugga names. Before shaky governments unable to survive without Western interventions, without foreign corporations extracting and exploiting their natural resources. Before murderous dictators, genocide, apartheid. Before gilded safaris. Before drought and famine advertised by skeletal child victims. Before decades of *National Geographic* magazine photos pandering plump naked brown titties and bottoms. Before willed amnesia that obscures centuries of human trafficking, of buying and selling slaves whose skin color reason enough to ignore their humanity and spread slavery anywhere, everywhere across the globe. Before all the above, before those facts, fictions, neither and both, had established America's vision of Africans and shaped our enduringly unacceptable relationship with the African continent, William Henry Sheppard, born in Virginia, barely two generations removed from his African ancestors, provides in 1899 a different perspective, an example of a kind of relationship between America and Africa that might still be possible, if we could envision the past (present) differently. Imagine a courageous Sheppard crossing the Atlantic west to east, a middle passage in the opposite direction of ships that had transported millions of Africans on a middle passage to enslavement in the New World. S sailing away from the U.S. not to increase nor to alleviate, not to carry, nor to deny the White man's burden. S leaving his Southern home to be a missionary. To free himself body and mind, and dedicate his life to liberating souls. His soul. African souls he believed no different and every bit as precious to God as his own.

Took a while for the journal editor to respond, a whole lot longer than I expected, given our long acquaintanceship and what I had assumed was mutual respect. Didn't S's unique story speak for itself. A missing link. S connecting America and Africa in a rather startling fashion seldom acknowledged, seldom explored by traditional historians, thus unsuspected, virtually unknown territory for ordinary citizens.

Got my old running buddy on the phone finally and he pleaded, C'mon, man. You of all people must know this S dude poison. Me and a couple staff folks pretty hip to him, but soon's I mentioned your idea, the ones even a little bit aware of WHS rolled their eyes, start to wag their heads, huh-uh. Not one my people even sorta agrees with you. Yeah, yeah, S something else, an unusual brother, specially back in those times, those evil days, a sure nuff cooking brother, anybody got to be impressed. The dude way out there back then, but the baggage, his baggage, you know what I'm talking about, man. Presbyterians chased his ass out the Congo. Boy lucky they didn't lynch him when they got him back home. Lucky they only rusticated his randy behind and didn't flatout defrock him. Course we both know he ain't first colored preacher fucking colored church ladies, but shit, Sheppard steady humping African honeys and making babies over there. What's worse, brother let his wife and them cracker missionaries catch him red-handed. Least one little son named after Sheppard crawling round the compound. No no no. Almost ain't had no MLK Day behind shit like that, bro. So can't help you with this project, my friend. No way, Jose. Still . . . tell the truth, I dig the cat. Just like you do. But best forget about it, man. Leave it alone. Sheppard fucked up. Women round here would burn me at the stake and my little raggedy magazine, too, we start agitating for some kinda WHS day.

I would carefully explain to my new acquaintance who I hope will become more than just an acquaintance, that I had no intention of promoting a Sheppard whose story omits LGS, or disparages women. Admit to him that yes, initially, Mrs. S played a very minor role in my thinking about S, but now the Sheppard story I would like to write, like to share, I'd say to him, starts with LGS. Starts with my respect, my curiosity and fascination about her, my desire to immerse myself in her world. Starts at her dining room table in Kentucky drinking tea. Starts with sadness, too, at the prospect of almost certain failure.

Where is Lucy Sheppard's world (or WHS's world or mine or yours, young man)—where do I find it. Like . . . it's located . . . where . . .

No. I won't play tourist again. As if I don't know where or who I am. I am here. Where I always reside. Always here. In this place no matter what I name it. Perhaps I've never not known where. Same answer always. Same imaginary place, *inside me*. Here. Where else could it be. Who is with me now in this place. Where would this place be if I were in another world. If

I am not here and I try to remember this place, where would this place be. Who would its inhabitants be. Where would I be as I try to recall them. If I inhabited a different world, and asked the same questions there I am asking here, now, who would be here to answer. Whose story is anybody able to tell. Where is it. *Why me,* Lucy Gantt Sheppard asks. In this story I'm making up, attempting to enter her space.

Not easy for me, she says, sitting up board-straight, eyes fixed on mine across dark expanse of table, and if you are familiar, sir, she continues, even a tiny bit familiar with my history, and you must be some, because you found me, didn't you, and here we sit in my home and you're going to ask whatever you need to ask, but anyway, I will start by saying, even though I'm guessing you may already know more than enough about Lucy Gantt Sheppard, that no matter what else you found written about me or folks have whispered in your ear, I need to add this—it's not easy for me even now, after all the long, long years, to go back to Congo. Even going back only in my own mind. Congo hurt me once. And still hurts. More than words can say. Other people's words or my words, if I can make myself say them.

Person like you—a man as you are—and being a man a blessing for you, you ought to be grateful, I believe—you cannot even start to imagine how hard back in those days for a person like me in Africa. A woman, a mother, a wife, a lover. Hard enough anytime, anyplace to be those things, do those things. To do what others expect of me. What I expect and demand from myself. All that, and color, too, which I have not even mentioned. Africa. Congo. Beautiful sometimes. I loved how Africans spoke. Their voices reminded me of home. Taught myself an African language. Talk it still. Africa a special place, Africans special people S wrote in his letters. Beautiful and sometimes terrible here, he wrote. Hard lives for Congo people, for him and the other missionaries. Strangely, when I read his letters, they aroused no fear of what might befall me when I joined him. The killing fevers preying on missionaries, relentless heat, poisonous snakes and insects, wild animals, bloody wars natives waged upon each other financed by Belgium companies, floods, starvation, diseases cutting people down every day. All the horrors and perils of Congo Sheppard described seemed bearable, did not scare me nor warn me away. Haunted me only because a life for me here or there unbearable if S did not survive.

When the letter I like to remember as a telegram arrived finally, telling me, Lucy please come, and not exactly in those words, but that's all the message I recall, because nothing else in it mattered, nothing more I needed to start me packing and hurry-up, hurry-up, fast as I could to join him, marry him, go off with him to another world.

And that Africa world just as beautiful, as mean, as soul and body crushing as what I'd heard and read. As S warned. But S did not warn me about his fielde heart, icy heart, forgetful heart, about changes he would put me through if I joined him in the Congo, and now, going back again now, thinking about him today, well . . . excuse me . . . it ain't easy. S ain't easy, and I pray your soul may rest in peace, William Henry Sheppard, though you done me blacker, worse than Africa ever did. African fever took two my babies, but S took my heart. Ate it. Spit the blood in my face.

Don't misunderstand me, sir, please. I don't ask *why me* because I feel my share of suffering greater than other folks' share. Just talking to myself most the time. Then a person like you at my door. Wanting me to bear witness. Asking me about Sheppard. Asking about me, too, it seems. After all the years, all this long, long time, how come you think only me left to bear witness to the things you seem to want to know.

Yes. Just me living in this house years and years now. But old house not empty. When people have to go they just go on and leave here.

One by one they go away. Doesn't mean they are not around. Or do not return. Busy coming and going. Witnesses like me. Who else I'm supposed to talk to. Rattle round in these rooms long as I been rattling, you get used to bumping into people. People big as life, bright as day everywhere in this house.

Love my house. All these precious Africa pieces we brought back to grace it. They talk, too. My dream home. When I was just a tiny thing, promised my mother I'd buy her a beautiful house and we'd live in it together for ever and ever like happy people in those fairy tales she used to sing me. Last few years of her life my mama, bless her soul, lived in this lovely home with me. Good years. Happy years. My promise to her come true. My children lived here, too—smart, sweet, perky Wilhelmina till she left to start a home of her own and Max, worrier like his father, but frightened of people like his father never was frightened, Max here till he left and start to roaming all four corners of the globe. Sheppard here when he passed in his sleep. He suffered good days and bad days here. People put on earth to suffer. How else would a body know they alive. This house a woman-dream. Woman-dream a place where she can live with her people. Man-dream a throne. Nice, shiny place just for him alone to sit and pretend he a little king. Place he can puff himself up about, brag about so other men think he a big king on a big throne. No doubt about it, but I'm a witness also to the truth that there's some men dream home, some women dream a throne. Two different kinds of dream and, me, LGS, I just call one a woman-dream and the other kind a man-dream. What I suffered, believed, learned all those years with S. And without him.

Cops who stopped my car fired five bullets into my back, the brown young man in a wheelchair said to me. First it was operation after operation, me in agony in a hospital bed, gradually regaining enough consciousness to figure out what had happened to me, and that I was probably paralyzed for life. If I could have, I would have happily killed the cops shot me. Be lying to you now if I said I have forgiven them, but I hope to god I will forgive someday. Hope god will grant me strength to never hate any person the way the cops guarding me in that miserable hospital room hated me. Taunted, teased me. Them standing there beside my bed in their uniforms and gun belts watching me cry in pain, beg for medicine, laughing at me instead of calling a nurse because, like one said, Nigger thinks he's a special nigger.

I listened carefully to each word of his story. As carefully as I listen to LGS. His hurt, shock, the hospital room, the cops palpable enough to make me cringe as he spoke. Had the good sense not to intrude upon his privacy by asking too many questions, but the fact stands that when the two of us alone in my sister's kitchen, I did pose under my breath one unacceptably brutal, disrespectful question and it obligates me, sooner or later, to fess up, to request his forgiveness. I used his injuries, his suffering, his private business that is absolutely nobody else's business, to save myself from confronting my own. False complicity. Speculating about his pain instead of asking him, asking myself intimate, difficult questions that might expose my own suffering and fear.

I could give myself benefit of the doubt, and say my silent question was elicited by simple, natural curiosity or I could admit absolutely appalling, chilling selfishness drove me to pose it. Same utter selfishness I believe rooted in all people and keeps me, you, everybody unsatisfied, keeps us carrying on, working for what we want, keeps us alive, keeps us killing others and killing ourselves. I admit I was perfectly prepared, for a moment anyway, to use him, acknowledge his difference, not in order to understand more about him, but to serve myself. Let myself feel I was better than him. In a separate, better space.

Like you I have secrets no one needs to hear, though nothing others have inflicted upon me approaches the seriousness of crippling wounds you bear. But listen a moment, please, if you will, to this part confession, part apology, part tit-for-tat payback I believe I owe you, young man. Will offer to you because my cruel curiosity, though not expressed in words you could hear, remains a fact that you are unaware of, and thus my unspoken words tilt a playing field I want to be level as we attempt to get to know each other better.

I need to confess. Confess despite knowing that most likely you, nor anybody else, will learn very much from my coming clean. Confess my need to tell Lucy's story. Tell yours. Tell you mine. Confess my relentless curiosity. Not to seek absolution exactly. Not precisely guilt I feel. Complicity, yes. Responsibility, yes. And worse, maybe, I feel something like perpetual disappointment. Pretty sure that if similar temptations arise in my life again, I might not react differently. Of course, I will try to do better. Try to imagine how to do better. Silly ambitions perhaps, funny as a lab rat wishing to change its behavior under the glass roof of a maze while it performs endlessly a trick scientists conditioned the poor creature to perform. If you choose to listen one day to what I feel compelled to tell you—me in my maze or wearing my purple and pink skintight bodysuit, a ten-yard-long balancing wand gripped in my fists, attempting to tiptoe across a tightrope of guilt and responsibility—you may decide it's silliness you don't need to witness, a waste of your time. But maybe that's the point. Me taking risks so we can become more comfortable, familiar, even maybe silly around each other. My revelations about myself, grand or petty, getting you to frown or smile or shake your head. Maybe laugh. Maybe angry. Maybe hurt. Unforgiving, maybe. Maybe help us both get a wee bit more used to bearing our different bodies, our different stories, more used to each other's voices, hearing them falter, break, or bleed in front of the other.

I am an old man now. Old with grandchildren. Beautiful, precious grands. One in college, two little ones . . . my, my, my. But granddaughters are not what I want to talk to you about now, though my wish to assist your run for office is grounded in my sense that you are determined, committed to serve all young people coming up behind you. The better part of me understands that your commitment and determination, your value for this weeping city doesn't depend upon how much erotic energy you may or may not possess. So why did that question you didn't hear sneak into my mind. Maybe you did hear it without me posing it aloud, since it's the sort of question many people can't help asking. With good cause you may wonder always, when a person sees you in a wheelchair, what they are wondering.

What did I see first time I noticed you in your wheelchair, part of a crowd around Sheppard and the mayor. Did I see another human being in a wheelchair or see something else, something different, broken, negative, less. The way our fellow citizens view Africa and Africans. View the color of our skin. The way men often view women. But my concern here not other people's wondering. I'm taking responsibility—even if you didn't hear me ask it—for an ugly question I directed at you.

Aging inevitable as death, but I would like to imagine that hope inevitable, too. Desire still alive in me. Can't respond to my woman's body in the biff-bam way I like to think I once could, but desire still there. *Sexual* desire some might call it, and they would not be completely wrong. Urges stir in me almost as often, almost as powerful as they always have, pumping up body and spirit. I work at being smart enough not to confuse these urges with my capacity to care for others or care for myself. I work at sharing love that is not equated with nor measured by the performance (or lack thereof) of a tube between my legs.

When I asked my first African, a Nigerian man who happened to be from Lagos, I believe I recall, "Have you ever seen a live lion?" he smiled at me, a smile to keep from crying, I'm pretty sure now, and then he responded politely, British accent all up in my face, Why, yes. Yes, I have seen them. Live lions in a zoological garden, of course. As have probably you, my brother.

I could call my naive query addressed to that African and the silent question in my sister's kitchen I aimed at you—*conundrums*—to borrow one of Jimmy Baldwin's favorite words. Unresolvable puzzles. Ma Rainey singing, *How come you do me / Like you do, do, do* . . . Perplexing enigmas. Fraught with embarrassing baggage, myth, an unsortoutable mix of lies, truth, dread, cliche, ignorance, arrogance, wisdom, self-defeat, self-exposure, oppression. *You made me love you,* another song cries out. But *conundrum* doesn't absolve me. I realized too late with the African guy, as I stood there facing him once upon a time, monkeyshines of my words grinning out my mouth, that I could not unask my question. Same as with you just yesterday, when my unspoken words revealed not simply monkeyshines and foolishness, but trespass, deep, deep confusion. I regret, more profoundly than I'm able to express to you, regret the wrong words I found for whatever I was asking and thinking. And *thinking* probably way too dignified a word to describe my mind's unspoken aggression.

What I truly wished to know, I was afraid to ask myself. So I asked you. Asked silently like a thief in the night silently robs. *Is there an end to all this.* That's what I wanted to ask. To know. My fears and hiding places. Do they ever end. And how. This yearning, dread, excitement. Is there a final edge to this living and dying. And when I reach it, will I go over the edge. Gone before I know I'm past it. Gone. Peace at last. Or will I feel myself falling when I fall, or just fall. Or maybe I can choose to stay. Here. Choose to be here. Where we are. Be here again and again.

When and if I get the opportunity, I will say to you that I believe what you are attempting admirable. You remind me a bit of a man named William Henry Sheppard—you may have heard of him—a colored American like us, a young man more or less your age when he decided at the end of the nineteenth century to go to Africa as a missionary. A journey he understood would plunge him into uncertainties and deadly peril. Quite a trip. Quite an unusual individual. A trailblazer. Your decision to run for public office—despite what the cops did to you, despite what we do to you, do to ourselves when we pretend no knowledge and thus no responsibility, no complicity with past lies and crimes. The past that continues to shape us. That past which profoundly damages us. Your decision to be a candidate, despite those conundrums, those confounding burdens, reminds me of S. And reminds me as much, perhaps even more, of Lucy Gantt, a woman who chose to marry Sheppard, return with him to the Congo and raise a family.

I'm pretty sure that a better world not necessarily the goal of either Sheppard's precarious choice. An inner determination—deeply selfish and selfless—drove them. Desires irreducible to words the Sheppards nor anyone else can speak. I believe a primal, mysterious instinct drove them, and drives other people like them. Loneliness of characters who are surrounded by stories they understand they inhabit but cannot write the next page. That kind of loneliness convinced WHS and LGS to set out for new worlds. Varieties of newness only each of them, each Sheppard alone, could imagine, experience, and risk.

You have my absolute support, for whatever it's worth, as you set out. Please let me know if there's any way I can help your campaign.

PENN STATION

INFORMATION BOARD SAYS THE TRAIN is on time. No arrival gate posted yet. I'm running early. Not my usual habit. Perhaps I should admit to myself I'm a bit scared. Perhaps admitting will help. More than a little fear I'm feeling. Feeling dread. Deep down dread. Forty-four years since I have stood next to my brother anywhere outside prison walls, and if the train truly on time and he is on it and gets off and comes up the underground stairwell and through the steel entrance/exit portal guarding Gate 7/8 West, he will be here, beside me in Penn Station.

My brother had said to me once: *Worst fear, bro. My very worst fear is dying in prison. I know dead is dead. When time's up, it's up. But you can't even die right when they got you locked up. A man don't just die in prison. He disappears. He's ain't nothing. Nowhere. Gone like he never been alive.*

I'm remembering my brother's words and wondering if he's relieved now from his worst fear. He's out. Released. Back. I stare at Gate 7/8 West. Believing, not believing my brother on his way, that he will be among the passengers mounting stairs or riding up an escalator and then scattering, clambering for whatever reasons into Penn Station.

Longer I stare, the less I'm sure, and dread deepens. If I look away from the gate, will it vanish. Will I vanish if I continue to stare. How will

I distinguish my brother from the dead. Dead passengers. Dead people because I don't know them and they don't know me, and couldn't care less unless we get in each other's way. And if we possessed the power to drift even an instant inside another person, would we really want to, even if such a trick manageable. Why risk it, even if we could. Each one of us stitched tight into his or her dead uniform like the uniformed woman behind glass manning Amtrak's information booth who had told me train 42, Pennsylvanian, from Pittsburgh would probably use Gate 7/8 West, but check big board closer to arrival time to make sure, she said, her eyes riding a slow escalator to meet mine once, finally. Shape of eyes, shape and color of her face concealed by umbrella of a bushy fro until a single uptilt of her head, then a few words suggested that she might be paying attention to a person and not a screen in front of her, not totally absorbed or dreaming or asleep as she gazes down at the console that monitors streaming crowds in subterranean tunnels, the dead scheduled daily to arise and file through Gate 7/8 West's metal arch. Those many, many dead eyes reminding me there are good reasons for dread, for fear and trembling inside my excitement, my unbounded joy and expectation that soon, soon, despite impossible years of waiting, my brother will be here and free.

Anxiety growing as I wait. Later, when I tell people the story, I try to make it funny, but nothing funny about two brothers separated from each other forty-four years by prison, and then stranded in Penn Station for approximately an hour and forty-four minutes, each looking for the other and not finding him. Neither able to pick out the other from the crowd, though at first they stand only maybe forty-four yards apart. Frozen in place, neither one daring to budge and risk missing the other. Then wandering, searching the station. Where oh where could the missing brother be. Their situation funny, after all, when a public service announcement I request finally brings my bro to the Amtrak info window, and believe it or not, we almost miss each other again in a very small service area outside the service booth. But then our eyes meet, we hug and decide to laugh, not cry about a lost, anxious hour and forty-four minutes.

Same way we sometimes decided in prison visiting rooms or during phone calls limited to ten minutes, to laugh off all the lost years, all approximately ten-twenty-thirty-forty-some fucking lost years and counting. Ain't never nothing but a party, like Aunt May used to say when we danced her in her wheelchair. Her sweet boys, sweet mama's sweet babies, nothing but a party, Aunt May said.

Except somewhere in middle of the party comes a moment it's not enough party, not enough fun and dancing and laughing and in that sudden, unquiet quiet you are alone. And though not quite ready to jump, not quite ready yet for party to end, no doubt a plunge into dark, cold water strikes you as an appealing, even merciful idea maybe. Icy ocean water would wash away despair, you think. Ocean a color you can't name. Brownish green swirling to darker brown to black with moon-bright patches scudding, churning. Ocean water so gotdamn cold that probably cold, cold shock the last and only thing you'd know, final thing endured just a few seconds before you are beyond hurt.

Coldness of water that churns its cold way thousands of miles to reach New York City where ocean laps quietly at stones anchoring a newly constructed scenic walkway along the edge of Domino Park. I often wind up there, peering down at salt water forty-four feet or so below the walkway railing, and some days, leaning on the metal rail, I wonder just how cold the water could be, how long could anyone survive the cold's first shock. Wondering if I would go with dignity like Africans I saw in a movie on TV who leaped first chance from a slave ship. Heads bobbing a second or two in the sea, then both arms shoot up straight to the sky and they sink, no regrets, rather than let strangers steal them from home.

I kick, sprawl, bat water, float, go under, swallow, choke. Water couldn't stay impossibly cold very long I think. Maybe if you leap, water more like a fist in the face and knocks you out. If anybody watching, it could be kind of funny, I think. I imagine a somebody almost me at the railing in Domino Park who watches my silly, short struggle in the water getting me no place but gone.

Ten years older than my youngest brother when they locked him up. How much older or younger now. Not simply a matter of counting years. Me seventy-eight years old and how much older or younger now am I than my dead uncle Ernie, seventy-six, when he passed a couple years ago.

Prison strips away time. Leaves your body bare, bones shivering. No end or beginning to prison time, my brother schooled me. Time shrivels to routine, repetition. Time inverted. Longer a sentence, less time matters. Prisoners own no time. No time belongs to them. Their time overladen with rules, regulations, limitations. Artificial time like an artificial limb. Like encumbered, painful time allotted to visitors when they enter a prison. The State claims all time, declares an incarcerated person's portion null and void. Proves its point day by day as each prisoner's makeshift body shudders and disappears, a witness silenced, a life shrinking, becoming more and more invisible. More time not time while time elsewhere passes and relationships with family and friends dissolve.

They got it down to a science, man. Real good at making our lives miserable, bro. Time don't stop inside the joint, my brother said, but it's changed, squeezed down till ain't no quality of life in it. Nothing, bro. Even when guys released, time stays fucked up. Ain't real time. Halfway time in a halfway house like you still in jail. Time don't just start up again. You can't never catch up. Never get your time back.

Prisons constructed, the story goes, to combat the evil of crime. Prisons allegedly benefit people who are not criminals by separating them from people who are criminals. But prisons never free anybody. Not from crime. Nor from crime's terrifying consequences. Prisons divide and conquer. Conquer and divide. Like legal slavery once did, prisons split us into two camps eternally at war. Prisons are compelling evidence of war. Stone and steel confirmation of the State's absolute power that must be exercised to discipline, punish, and confine groups like *slaves* and *criminals,* flawed groups essentially different, essentially inferior kinds of humans who, if allowed to roam free, would prey upon us and eventually destroy us.

We are taught to fear that the balance of power between those others and us is precarious. Though membership in one group or the other permanent, the fate of no group exactly guaranteed. Subject to sudden change. Thank your lucky stars if born into the free group or curse the stars for abandoning you within a captive one. But don't dare rock the boat if you are lucky. Or unlucky. Water's full of people drowning, dying to climb aboard. Nobody survives if all those dark, desperate, grasping hands explode from black water and capsize the boat. No room in the inn. The way things work is how they should work and nobody's business. Except State business. And long live state of things as it is. It could be different. Then what. Best be grateful if you are not a prisoner. Grateful that prisoners remain where they belong. It could be different. Will be, if we don't defend ourselves.

That story around a long, long time. We believe it. Don't need to listen anymore. We are invested in it. By it. If asked who we are, we tell the story. We have forgotten the facts that don't fit. Or we choose not to remember. We become comfortable or not. Divided. Conquered.

So I fret. No peace for the entire hour and forty-four minutes I wait then search for my brother in Penn Station. Worrying about what could have occurred—accident, illness, an argument, fight, mean cops, or him just plain lost, or maybe he's changed his mind about a visit. Only three weeks since he's been released on parole after forty-four years in prison, released into a new, gadget-addicted world. Gadgets and world scarcely comprehensible to me. What would they look like to him. Though he was granted special dispensation by Pennsylvania's Department of Corrections for a two-day trip to NYC, why would I expect no glitches, no anxiety. Why wouldn't I anticipate something unimaginably terrible. Not fretting. True dread. Actual and unavoidable fear in a vast public space packed with strangers, each believing they are vulnerable, each certain that for safety's sake, no matter what it requires of them, they'd best keep alive in the deepest recesses of themselves, at whatever cost, a reliable core of reassuring superiority, hostility, of distance, difference. Loyalty to their own kind. Story they depend upon to separate and guard them from hostile others absolutely unlike them.

In Penn Station's traffic of living and dead I search for faces of family. Mother. Father. Grandfathers. Grandmothers. Kids. See my great-grandfather posed in his preacher's robe in a faded sepia photo from Promised Land, South Carolina. See two of my three brothers, both dead now, faces hovering in shrouded middle distance, then flashing crisper, brighter than life, snapshots on a phone shoved too near my face, as if I don't remember, as if it's necessary to remind me. As if I don't know already my brothers gone. Gone. Gone. See my sister still very much alive, despite being born in the middle, squeezed between her two older, two younger brothers. I see her grin. Hear her special way of calling her football star brother *devilish*. Brother with his soft, green-eyed gaze, Superman biceps. Brother two years younger than her, eight years younger than me when he held on to my elbow, shuffling his Parkinsonian shuffle down a long corridor inside a nursing home. I see the face of the brother four years younger than me, two years older than Sis, still quiet, dignified, handsome, shy as he had always been, when I saw him last in a casket in Atlanta. Is my youngest brother, a survivor like Sis and me, wandering ghostly somewhere unseen in Penn Station. Stray hidden in the crowd. Invisible to me unless crowd disperses. Unless it outs him. Me probably as ghostly to him as he is to me. Both of us a bit afraid to see the other or afraid of looking past or seeing through the other's flesh and bones. Same kind of silly fear that keeps me from saying my siblings' names aloud or to myself in Penn Station. Or writing their names down here on this page, as if names are simply words.

Among the passersby, my father all skin and bones. Lifetime of menial jobs consumed his body, embittered his sharp mind, and he's nodding off, head slumped against elevated backrest of a hospital bed. Sliding deeper into waterproof sheets beneath a grayish, papery blanket. Has his sharp mind finally forgotten that he had never been granted an opportunity to flourish, never held a job commensurate with his considerable talents and ambitions. Or maybe his mind still aware, still yearning, determined, but he's just so, so tired, needs to rest, to shut his eyes till an awful world succumbs, a better world glides in to take its place. Isn't that the man I heard in his voice even during those last times towards the end when he could barely stand up without help. Man undefeated still, whispering at me once from the bed to take him with me. Please, he said. A *please* too close to begging, and his words, that last *please,* too close, would have broken my heart, but I was my father's son and I could let it go. Leave him behind. Not answering him. Not wanting to hear any more. My back turned, father's son walking away, not looking back. Not letting my father, not letting my brothers drag me down. I will my heartbreak into deadweight and bury it within myself. Promise myself to carry it no matter what, for however long, wherever I need to go next. Shape-shifting my way out through guarded doors of the ward that locks down my father.

Waiting in Penn Station, hopefully and with almost no hope at all, to meet my youngest brother, I watch him enter the prison visiting room, fresh from bending over for a rectal inspection. Four or five other inmates accompany him, their assholes just frisked like my brother's, and they all line up at the guard kiosk to sign in. Lil Bro suddenly too old, too frail inside an orange jumpsuit, standing next to his fellow prisoners, all of them colored guys, on average forty-four years his junior, guys who pad their bulky, shapeless uniforms with pumped-up jailhouse muscle and arrogance, decorate them with gang marks or styles they invent—one sleeve rolled up, a zipper unzipped a precise length—differences it could cost another inmate his life not to recognize, and I see my youngest brother's son, my nephew, tall, gangly kid shot dead in front of a pregnant girlfriend, her one-year-old, my little brother's first grandson, my grandnephew, cradled in the screaming girl's arms. See a niece weeping, cursing out a daughter who's in the street trading pussy for crack, a cousin's kid selling drugs, an in-law who returned from war an addict and deals big-time now to support his family, his habit, and one of his sons in Cleveland following in daddy's footsteps, dead or in the slam for murdering some other mother's son.

Faces, facts of my life materialize, no mere headlines or mug shots or musings on human nature or theories of culture, no talk-show interpretations, no recitations of numbing statistics, no citing of other holocausts to diminish significance of what is happening here and now. Simply pain I see daily in the street, in this train station, in many faces, colored faces, family faces damaged and punished, generation after generation of echoing pain that incarcerates and kills my people. Pain operating patiently, like the microscopic wound in my mother's breast that grew large enough to swallow all of her. Gone. Gone. Who's next. It chokes me, makes me short of breath.

When I let myself listen, I hear trains running at night. Trains packed with my doomed people, people stuffed into nasty, wobbly stacks of chicken-wire chicken crates, *clackedy-clack-yackedy-yack,* rolling along night and day. During daylight hours the noises I make to keep myself company usually drown out the sound, but now, within these cavernous spaces of Penn Station, despite din of public address announcements, loud chatter of passersby, their muttering, hollers, giggles, collective sighs, and solitary screams of dismay, I hear clatter of trains in and out. Same trains clackedy-clacking if I arrive alone somewhere, too late or too early, or when I'm overtired and need to rest, to empty myself of distractions, need to slide down naked finally into that immense tub of black oblivion, so much more of it than there is of me, down, down where it waits quietly, where I hope to dissolve my small portion into its measurelessness, me sinking until I am among those missing persons I do not miss when I sleep.

In Pittsburgh, PA, lying awake at night, listening for trains to pass on tracks atop a hillside just across from Finance, our colored street, trains close enough to rattle windowpanes in my grandmother's raggedy little house where our family boarded *cause your mama and daddy not gettin long,* I'd hear Cleveland. Hear China. *China* and *Cleveland* meaning somewhere else, anywhere far away and different, where the next train might be headed. On my long-awaited first trip outside Pittsburgh, outside my state to another state, to Ohio with the Shadyside Boys Club twelve and under basketball team, I wanted to kick the ass of the first kid I saw out my coach's car window because the boy no different standing there in his stupid Cleveland backyard than the stupid Pittsburgh kids I'd been seeing my whole stupid life.

Imagine yourself very, very hungry. You're starving and exhaust your last bit of strength to reach the only restaurant in Cleveland, and a sign in the window says closed.

LeBron James, world famous hoopster, busted out of Cleveland.

Celebrated his liberation like it was Christmas, like he been in jail those seven years playing for the Cavs. Cleveland guys in here used to love bad-mouthing LeBron, my brother said. Said he told those guys, Gwan. Get the fuck out my face. None you chumps shoot a basket to save your life. Leave the boy alone, I'd tell em. You in LeBron's big shoes you woulda done just what LeBron did. Ain't about Cleveland. It's about the gotdamn man got niggers locked up every gotdamned where. Man saying, My gotdamn way or the highway, and LeBron said—I'm gone.

I hold no grudge against Cleveland, despite the fact everybody in my family Steelers fans and always hated the Browns. Nor the fact that dope my youngest brother copped in Cleveland was bad and robbed him and his crew of every penny they'd stolen and saved up to buy it, ruining their scheme to get rich quick dealing Cleveland's copiously available cheap dope in Pittsburgh. Bad dope launching them into a free fall of blunders and crimes that wound up with a man dead, my baby brother serving forty-four years in prison. No need to pick on Cleveland. Cleveland rule not exception. LeBron returned home to Cleveland and won an NBA championship, didn't he. Prison far older than Cleveland. Older than America, older than China. Old as classifying people according to color. Old as stealing human beings and selling them. Older than decisions by America's founding fathers or NBA owners to treat some people like livestock—to breed and trade and purchase and distribute them to markets.

Crime scenes swirl. Prisons fill up. Swell. Rot. How can I invent a point of view from which to grasp the scale of damage or assess the extent of responsibility. Many people who might have helped me assess and measure damage, the blows, crushing losses have been removed. Passengers on trains I still hear running so loud some nights I think I'm a boy in bed again in Pittsburgh, or tied to a rail on that hillside across from Finance Street waiting for a locomotive's wheels to rush out of darkness and free me.

Couple years ago on a visit home to Pittsburgh, I ran into a guy, a long-time-no-see, large, heavy man (soon to die of a heart attack) I used to hoop with back in the day. He'd been a warrior on the court. Several inches taller than my six foot one and three-quarters inches, and about my age, my color, except several shades darker. In a Kmart parking lot we shared our anger and frustration about the story going round of two cops who, for no reasons anybody could justify, had recently shot and crippled a colored young man from our neighborhood. I shook my head, asked my old hoop buddy why these awful things keep happening. Wondered aloud what we could do to stop it. His response was to nod, shrug his broad shoulders, raise both big hands chest high, extending them to either side of his body, fingers spread wide as if to display clean, empty palms. A gesture of helplessness or vast acceptance or maybe surrender or defeat. Shit happens, he said. Not just to us, my man. Shit just happens. Yes, I replied. Shit happens.

In the fall of 2015 I had received an email. Printed a copy, saved it along with manuscripts, correspondence, family photos, and documents of various sorts, etc., stored in our apartment building's basement until shipped off to a university that pays me to deposit my personal stuff in its archives. That email happened to surface while I rummaged through boxes to liberate old family pictures and records my brother and I could check out together during his possible visit to NYC. I'd been in France the day he was released so our first reunion in forty-four years outside prison walls might occur here in NYC rather than Pittsburgh. Even before PA's Department of Corrections granted permission for my brother to travel, I had hauled up a couple cartons from the basement to test their contents. As if I could foresee my brother's reactions. Probably as much to satisfy my own curiosity. Items I'd choose might be a real treat

for him. Then again, maybe not. Simply old news. Or reminders of
news missed. Raw news. Hurtful. Bad news better left resting in peace,
maybe. Anyway, an email from 2015 had surfaced:

> *In 1972 your brother held up my pizza shop in the Shady-
> side section of Pgh one evening. I testified at trial where I
> met you briefly. I saw your brother a couple of times after
> that. Once at the Univ of Pittsburgh gymnasium. This may
> seem strange but I have thought about him many times
> over the years. There was something gentle in his eyes at
> times and I had hoped he would turn his life around. Is he
> doing alright. If you're still in touch with him please let him
> know that I forgave him a long time ago and I hope he is
> well. I live in the Pocono Mountains now after 18 years
> in NYC, 94th and Riverside. I am 66 years old. I was 23
> at the time of the robbery. Its funny how some things stay
> with you. Regards . . .*

Brother in that email not the one I will search for in Penn Station,
but my middle brother, the football player, two years older than his little
brother, the younger one's hero, a street legend, big, fearless, who carried
a bullet meant to waste him lodged in his chest, too near his heart to
be removed. Brother who was protector of his tagalong, skinny lil bro
until they got to be equal partners in street hustles, chasing ladies, drugs,
performing in doo-wop singing groups.

I didn't reply to the email. Seldom write letters of any sort. Though
on sleepless nights when the rattle of trains too loud to ignore, I find
myself composing countless emails and letters, pretending to post them,
imagining them being read. Words obsessively yet meticulously written
in air, each draft melting, drifting as I drift. Perhaps the way my father

drifted into deeper and deeper levels of almost sleep. Words bending, stretching, disintegrating. On one restless night like that my wife awakened herself with a volley of coughs, and I asked her if she was okay. Told her she'd been coughing as she slept and snoring loudly. My feisty French wife doesn't like to be reminded of her occasionally noisy sleep, and quickly accused me of snoring ten times louder.

An intensely private person, she resents the fact that marriage allows a spouse to spy on her sleep. Extremely intelligent, wood-nymph shy, swimmer strong as a mermaid, she steps out of the ocean and strolls towards me on the beach at Toulindac, on the gulf of Morbihan in Brittany. Wide shoulders, waist deeply cut. Water-darkened hood of Medusa snaky curls frame her face, drip on her bare chest. Lapis-lazuli sheen colors her skin, same color it is on nights I can't sleep and she glides quietly from our bed to go pee, her naked body illuminated, *lapis-lazuli*, only an instant before bathroom door closes. Too late, black middle of the night, I can't fall asleep, and did I catch a glimpse of her or not. Did she leave my side. Did she come back. Have I lost her. Was she ever truly here beside me as I write sentence after sentence invisible as her going or coming. No early morning glow from curtained window when she passes through the room, no true sighting. She's there and not there. A rumor, a story. Venus atop a scallop shell risen from the sea.

Lapis-lazuli aura of her skin not a color any dictionary can define, a color like certain sounds I hear in the speech of my colored elders. Sounds shimmering inside me, invisible yet substantial. Unforgettable. The opposite of my imaginary replies to letters, emails hovering, dissolving in darkness, my words unable to carry weight, unable to paint pictures, unable to sing, breathe.

Often, I sit wide awake, alone in the dark, waiting, wondering if the woman I love, woman my hand afraid for the moment to reach out and seek, has returned safely. Wondering about the fate of words

I publish or deposit in an archive. Wondering if anybody touches the pages. Reads. Are words dead things. Alive. Do they change, grow spontaneously, self-destruct. Will I ever recover from some archive the lost tickets (invoices) that once moved my colored family north from South Carolina, Virginia, Georgia, and remove us now on trains to wherever we are disappearing again.

My wife teases me about my papers stashed in Harvard University's archives. Do they pay for laundry lists, grocery store receipts, toilet tissue. I'm a bit more sentimental. There in boxes, along with my journals, diaries, handwritten drafts of unpublished novels, sparse correspondence, manuscripts of my earliest tries at story writing, are poems I scribbled on miscellaneous scraps of paper before attempting my first stories. Small poems with exotic words like *lapis lazuli* which I hoped would disguise my colored voice. Words that I had never heard anyone say and whose meaning I barely understood. Words for things I'd never seen with my own two eyes but believed because poets I'd been taught to revere in school were witnesses. Great poets used those words, and didn't I want to be great like them? Those great writers who could put any word in a poem because all words belonged to them. Hungry, envious, I tried out their seductive words, as if by learning them and writing them, I could make them mine. Used words to hide my face, decorate my people's faces, the way ancient Egyptians, wealthy ones, anyway, buried their beloved dead with scarabs of lapis lazuli framed in silver to protect them in the underworld.

No peace, no more magic or less magic in foreign-sounding words than in familiar ones. My last surviving, youngest brother returns or not. My wife returns to our bed or not. Lost forever or not. Her skin not lapis lazuli, but the color it is. The dead don't hear words. Remember nothing. Go nowhere. Words don't belong to me or anybody else. Only borrowed, preserved in places resembling unvisited museums. Or cemeteries.

I own no words in this underworld where my people are being systematically imprisoned and destroyed. My words do not stop the killing. Nor open prison doors. I am permitted to name people, places, things only because the powers that be have decided people like me less dangerous, less of a threat, perhaps, if we believe words and languages belong to us.

Adrift in unsaid words, silenced languages, words of lost witnesses who heard and saw and acted. Voices ignored. I need their words to understand my own, my wishes, guesses, intuitions, fears. Intimations received of a plan that produces losses, atrocities beyond words. Crimes that cut down my people. Where are those words. Who says them. Saves them. Are there any words for this. This writing, this silence, this waiting for a train, maybe with my brother on it, to arrive in Penn Station. This knowing and not knowing what's coming.

Email you sent to university caught up with me—don't recall meeting you at my brother's trial—but I appreciate your effort to reach out and communicate your memories and thoughts re ugly events occurring so many years ago—my brother became a victim of Parkinson's and spent his last two years confined to a nursing home—fortunately, as you guessed he might, he managed to turn his life around, so to speak, before disease struck him down—after prison, he graduated college, married twice, fathered 3 kids I know of, designed and administered an award-winning program in Boston for teens attempting to turn their lives around after juvenile incarceration—you declare that you forgive my brother—forgave him long ago—thank you—I am impressed—envy your generosity

and wish I could be as generous—of course I wish you
and yours continuing health and prosperity, but I don't
forgive—unable to express precisely what or whom I don't
forgive, and your note is not a request for forgiveness,
is it—so I'll just say that I'm much more confused than
you seem to be about who should be forgiving whom
for what . . .

Should I write more? Tell him that years before his email, I had received from a woman a very different sort of message, one as unexpected, unsolicited as his. Oddly enough, she could have been a victim of the same crime, or witnessed a second holdup in the same Shadyside pizza joint on another day, another year, because once my middle brother decided to become a predator, no rhyme or reason motivated his stickups. He could just as easily have been attracted as deterred by the circumstance that our family lived just around the corner, down the block from a strip of stores ending with a pizza take-out place he robbed. Worried or pleased that his face, his sister's and brothers' faces probably quite familiar to anyone who worked in or near the pizza shop. Especially familiar since our faces colored differently than those of most people browsing upscale Walnut Street.

For years my brother a danger to himself and others because he understood deeply that society applied its rules and dispensed its rewards perversely to people of color. He reciprocated the favor. Acted upon impulse, or perversely by intention. No fear of consequences. Doing whatever the fuck he felt like doing. Answered to no one but himself. A self he improvised moment by moment to express whim, anger, shame, deception, self-deception, resignation, illness, boredom, curiosity, whatever. An unstable self he hung out with the way you can find yourself hanging around with a crazy partner who infatuates precisely because she or he unpredictable, erratic, dangerous, a surrogate self who fronts for you and frees you from responsibility for who you are. Or not. Was his tagalong little brother present at the crime scene. Collaborator posing as innocent bystander inside the pizza shop or standing lookout outside.

The woman who wrote to me, like the email's author, described my middle brother's eyes. Except she wrote to inform me that she still suffered nightmares in which green eyes stared at her, cold, merciless as she remembered them during a stickup a decade before. She did not forgive my brother and clearly did not forgive me, either. In her view the fact I taught at a university and wrote books increased my complicity, my share of guilt and blame for the ordeal at gunpoint my brother forced her to endure. She meant to punish me for the terrifying abyss she encountered in those green eyes. Evil eyes she was certain I never could have seen truly nor truly acknowledged because he was my brother. Should I admit to the email writer whose store my brother robbed, that in spite of all the venom and bitterness the woman directed at my brother and at me, I preferred receiving her message to receiving his.

> You are/were about the same age as my middle brother—
> what did you guys think of each other when my large,
> handsome, slightly brown-skinned brother with green eyes
> entered your pizza joint and you both stared across the
> gap separating you—a vastness guaranteeing that one of
> you was much, much more likely to have a decent job and
> success—the other much, much more likely to be unem-
> ployed, poor, die young—I don't forgive that divide, those

unforgiving depths into which my people are slipping and disappearing—if in a dream I catch my brother in one of his good moments—sleepwalking the abyss, that powerful mind of his still generating flashes of withering lucidity— should I ask him if he remembers you—what he thought of you—should I ask if he forgives?

PS: You mentioned owning a pizza shop when you were 23—how shall I deal with that fact—ignore it—treat it as incidental—what about the apartment on NYC's expensive Upper West Side where you resided 18 years or the home in the Poconos—what about the feeling of belonging in those privileged places and feeling they belonged to you and the feeling of mul- titudes of others that they do not belong anywhere, never belonged, just hanging on, hanging out, accept- ing what comes or snatching a fistful of what doesn't belong to them and running, hiding, a fistful of nothing, going nowhere . . .

In the cab on the way to my apartment on Grand Street, after the dumb mix-up and tense delay in Penn Station, my brother asked, first thing, if I had been to Arizona lately to visit his nephew . . .

Your nephew and my son, I answered. No. Been way too long since I've seen my son.

I worry sometimes me being in jail mighta messed with him.

He's my son and your nephew. And thank goodness for that, is what I say. He loves us both, and has learned like you—probably partly from you—to be strong. He won't let prison destroy him. I'm off to Arizona in two weeks . . .

———

In Penn Station, after I had noticed my youngest brother's obviously painful, gimpy gait was not improving, after forgoing the subway ride I'd looked forward to as a treat for my bro and me, an instant, exhilarating immersion for us in the big city's unpredictability, the pair of us united again, inseparable forever, shoulder to shoulder, ready for anything NYC could cook up in its subterranean bowels, two fearless adventurers explor ing a jungle, the moon, whatever . . . after I had begun to regret even the relatively short detour I'd led my brother on—up stairs, through dense crowds, more steps and more colliding with bodies hurrying to reach the subway—after becoming more than angry at myself for missing or worse ignoring how each stride, precarious and halting, taxed my brother, only after all that did I even begin to understand that my brother was back.

Inside Penn Station, arms around my brother's body, how easily I'd forgotten forty-four years, forgotten how those years had changed him, me, and how unforgivable it was not to remember and not make appropriate adjustments for his sake and mine. I repeated to myself the necessity of reconnecting slowly, with extreme care. Repeating the fact that I must listen to a brother who had already forgotten more than I would ever learn about being forgotten. How much he knew. How for forty-four years he had no choice but to suffer precisely what was pos sible and not possible for him, what was impossible for anyone else to understand.

His role for forty-four years to endure, accommodate, survive. To be grateful when the spirit in another person (brother, sister, keeper, stranger) seemed willing to pay attention, to assist him, and no matter how wrongheaded it caused the other to act, my brother must respond. Needed them as I need him now, as he requires me, and many other souls, people better and stronger than me, to aid him, help him unbreak himself, put himself together with severely damaged parts, fabricate new models of himself for a new, nearly incomprehensible world.

Going along to get along he'd told me once, the phrase guys in jail used to exchange when they were wondering, thinking aloud about how, if and how, they could get through one more excruciating instant. Then another. My brother probably would have limped step by step beside me, or behind me for miles in Penn Station till he dropped, if I hadn't figured out the obvious and let go my fanciful subway excursion—Cab, fool . . . a goddamn C-A-B, you damn fool—

And after the cab, after a bumper-to-bumper creep through Midtown then Lower East Side streets, after a big hug for him from my wife, the two of them embracing, not wanting to let go, all smiles and tears looking like smiles, standing, swaying in the middle of the living room as she hugged him and he hugged back, after he had settled down on the couch and kicked back and tried maybe with one deep, deep breath to make up for forty-four years of never enough air in his lungs, and then leaned forward, elbows on knees a couple minutes I think I recall, until he settled back again, still not speaking for a couple more minutes, resting awhile in one corner, not middle of the couch, shadowed a bit in that shadowed corner of couch, of room, and after the room had become as quiet as he was quiet, my wife and I each seated in a chair facing him across the round dining table that divides our apartment's kitchen from living room, after nobody saying a word it seemed for a very long time, my brother said, Bro, you know this the first time since I been out I feel really free. Really, really free. Here sitting on your couch and no place I got to be tomorrow morning.

DEATH ROW

THINK OF LAYERS WITHIN LAYERS. Within layers. Think of getting dressed in winter for a long walk in the cold. Think of undressing to make love. Think of covering yourself after having your clothes ripped off and being raped. Think of layers of chain of command in an army. Think of layers of give-and-take layering who wins and loses in an economic system. Think of putting on makeup. Think of layers of fiberglass insulation to seal warmth in a home or think of the bulge of absorbent cotton and waterproofing material layering a baby's crotch inside a cute jumpsuit or bulge of adult pamper layering an old person's bare skin before underwear and other layers of clothing picked out as presentable for a given occasion on a given day in a given life in a particular place and time layered within countless other possibilities of time and place layered one within another that we pretend to negotiate with each choice we think we make, as if our choices are not layered within countless other choices we make or choices others make for us, choices far beyond our reckoning, but we choose anyway, and must, no doubt, continue choosing until we die, continue to pretend and attempt to keep track of where we are by assuming to understand where we have been and where we are going next, as if such an understanding possible through layer after layer surrounding us, confounding us.

> *Dustin Higgs was lying flat on his back. He was strapped to a gurney by bands across his wrists, ankles, chest, and waist, and his body, beneath a sheet from the neck down, formed the shape of a cross. A heart monitor was attached to his left index finger. One IV line had been inserted in the back of his right hand, and one in a superficial vein in the crook of his left arm. The lines ran into a slot in the green-tiled back wall, behind which was the chemical room, the unseen chamber in which sat the executioner.*

That paragraph, italicized to distinguish it as not my writing, but someone else's layered in mine, is strong writing, I believe. Lifted it from an essay in which the writer deftly exposes layer by layer the horrors of capital punishment. Good writing is rare, and that's one reason it's here. Good because the writer's witness conjures me as witness. Creates me in the execution chamber. I'm there, standing next to a gurney, staring down at the doomed victim, closer to him than even his family members, press corps, prison officials, and guards gathered inside the chamber or observing through three windows in the death chamber's side walls. Closer because the writing offers point-blank details for me to observe and absorb. Offers again and again a fresh look, another opportunity to attend the execution and form impressions before what I am experiencing becomes memory and begins to fade. Me watching, me present word by word as I read. Inhabiting the death chamber long after the event has transpired and actual flesh and blood spectators of the ritual gone about their business, living or dead, wherever they may be.

Layers of rules and regulations determine how and when and where a prisoner of the Federal government may be killed. The somewhat bewildering, occasionally conflicting mix of Federal and state laws that choreograph each execution is meant to ensure the illusion—just as rules requiring Americans to be either colored or white—ensure the illusion that each condemned citizen is treated separately and equally.

While a condemned prisoner waits in the wings, lawyers, who are also offstage, often litigate, up to the very last excruciating, fatal instant, exactly which script will guide a particular performance. Prerogatives—for instance limiting who and how many may witness an execution, or what cocktail of poisons will be administered—are fiercely, jealously guarded and debated. Governments (and politicians who run them) compete to protect and defend their own interests. Endeavor to appear innocent despite bloody hands. Nothing occurs in these ceremonies, those in charge assure us, except what law allows, what law demands. With layers of impenetrable, often contradictory statutes, elected officials distance themselves from the unpleasantness of murdering their constituents. Take credit for maintaining Law and Order while also taking pains to minimize, by any means possible, legal or not, public awareness of all the dirty work necessary behind the scenes to mount a successful, convincing production. But no, no, no, declares a crusading writer. With my pen, my words, in my solitary cell connected no doubt to the vast, vast prison you govern, but beyond its panopticon gaze, freed for a few moments, perhaps, from your surveillance and supervision, I will expose the hideous rituals you perpetrate while concealing yourselves behind layers of law and custom. No. No hiding place. No, no, no, the writer asserts.

I applaud the good writing and good intentions of the essay quoted above whose author chose to entitle "The Lightning Farm." No doubt the writing's power part of what's inspiring me to contemplate accepting the rather grim assignment of attending an execution at the same federal facility in Terre Haute, Indiana, the author had visited. Only part, since I must admit I have a brother and a son who are both serving terms of life imprisonment, and that fact together with the fact that a life sentence is just about as grim and unforgiving as the death penalty, are punishment enough to compel me, without any extra incentive from reading an article in a magazine, sooner or later, to go and observe an execution. Go as journalist and report. Despite my dread, my deep repugnance, distaste, disapproval of treating capital punishment as a spectacle for public consumption. Go and report. Go though I'm certain whatever eye-witness account I might publish would not end executions, but serve only as a potential source of profit for the newspaper that employs me. Serve readers whose appetite for mayhem, murder, pornographic voyeurism and violence seems insatiable.

And there's at least one more layer driving me both to attend and not attend an execution. Daily, during random moments before sleep obliterates me once again, I'm overwhelmed by an undeniable sense that as a matter of choice, as a convenience, I am betraying my son and brother. Palpably fearful at least once every day that son and brother (and you and I) are being destroyed by our complicity, by our willingness as a good citizens of these United States to authorize and benefit from the worst kinds of damage a government can inflict upon a human being. A government itself, guilty of systematically, self-righteously, habitually suppressing truth with countless layers of lies.

Does a particular perspective rendering a person or thing visible convince or enlighten most effectively when that rendering also blinds the viewer to other perspectives from which the person or thing might be rendered.

———

Do you believe this . . . believe this place . . .

Mr. President, sir. Mr. President, I . . . [they warned me at the the guard desk, *Sir, you best address him as Mr. President or he ain't even gon speak to you.*]

Mr. President . . . perhaps . . .

Pretty damned incredible. Gotta give it to 'em. Crew did a helluva job. Looks just exactly like a prison visiting room, though of course, I've never been in one, except in movies maybe. But look around. They got it absolutely right for once. All the big stuff, and little details, too. Wait till you see the tacky, urinal-green tiles inside the death chamber. Loved them, first sight. If I didn't know better, I'd believe we're in a sure-enough pokey. In a real death row visiting room in some godforsaken prison in some godforsaken place in the middle of gotdamn nowhere. This gotdamn, cramped-up little cubicle belongs on death row if I ever saw one. Helluva job. Set they built outside for the camera to pan on the way here, damned convincing, too.

My, my. Got our own little Abu Ghraib here, don't we. And that would make you an interrogator, right. Too tall for an interrogator. Specially an Arab interrogator. I wouldn't have cast you as interrogator. Way too tall. Stretches the frame. Distracts from me. Not a good idea. But we'll be seated, won't we, for most of the interrogation. The interview. Wink. Wink. Anyway, lots of tall folks mostly leg so when they sit, they shrink. Do you shrink. You seem a bit high-waisted. But anyway, here we are. They picked you. Who knows what's on writers' minds. Why I have to do most their thinking for them.

Kind of a writer myself, have to admit. Quite good at it, too. When I have the time. My ideas behind most *Truth No Consequences* scripts. You recall the show, no doubt. Biggest blockbuster reality TV show ever. Borrowed the title from a radio show I used to listen to when I was a kid. *Truth or Consequences.* Very popular. Crossed over to TV, folks loved it so much. I tweaked the title just a little bit. Who needs copyright problems. Could say I invented reality TV with my show. Would still be number one and me still the star, but politics more fun.

Till not much fun anymore, so back to TV. New show will be a sort of sequel, you might say, to *T No C.* Why you're here, right. To spread the good news—He's back!

Sometimes I look at myself in the mirror and say *Geez, that guy reminds me of some famous person,* and he looks back at me and smiles and I smile at him, and *wow,* hotdamn, he really is a really famous person.

Knuckle-brain writers wanted to name the new show *Deathrow.* Do you believe it. Sounds like—Jethro—that hillbilly clown. Jethrow Pew. Or Jethro Pugh. Betcha he smelled like pew. *Deathrow.* Who the fuck they think's gonna pay good money to see their president locked up on death row. Death row's a place for trash. Worse than the looney bin. Most the scum on death row can't read or write. Morons. Outcasts. Misfits. Baby killers, serial killers, mental defectives, degenerates, homicidal maniacs slavering for another body. We all know how they got there. And who wouldn't be happy to flush them all away, Swooosshh. Gurgle, gurgle. Gone. Good riddance.

Everybody loves sci-fi and fantasy shows and cartoons. Folks need to kick back and let TV daydream for them. But who in their right mind believes an American president could wind up on death row. Forget about it, I said to the writing crew. Not associating myself with that lame title in any way, shape or form. Huh-uh. No. Told 'em we'll call the new show, *Reel to Real.* Or *Real to Reel.* Haven't quite made up my mind yet.

Would you believe the writers trying to talk me into calling this initial episode *Deathrow.* No way in hell, I informed them. You journalists, you jokers and degenerates and gentlemen of the press and whatever else you are, you writers never give up, do you.

But Mr. President . . . sir . . . my research, my notes say you were indicted and convicted of thirteen murders. Not by your own hand, granted, but deaths resulting directly from premeditated conspiracy, a blunt weapon you and your attorney general fashioned in cold blood for the express purpose of extinguishing thirteen lives in a hurry before your presidency ended. Thirteen lives—one of them, special shame on you many say, a woman's life—terminated during a seven-month period, a killing spree from July through January 2020. The evidence from trials, impeachment proceedings, appellate courts, special congressional hearings, independent investigative commissions, etc., is incontrovertible. All legal appeals are exhausted. Your execution scheduled for dawn tomorrow. No pardon coming from your successor in the White House. Ugly story of your crimes, your efforts to deny or avoid punishment have been featured nonstop for months and months across the globe on TV and in the press. Your efforts to exonerate yourself and pleas for mercy or forgiveness have failed utterly. That's why I am here today, Mr. President, sir. Here on death row to record and preserve what you might finally wish to confess about your actions, your intentions, your victims, this terrible, unprecedented tragedy that has gripped our nation . . .

Can't wait, can you. Writing copy already. Practice makes perfect. Sounds close to a final draft. Why bother interviewing me if your pissy story already finished.

Don't bother hemming and hawing. Forget the prefab tale you carted here in your carpetbag, and listen up, sir, cause it's the President speaking. Honorable President of these United States and his story not over yet. Just beginning as a matter of fact. Those perk sniffers and dandelion-hearted sycophants in DC won't dare touch me. I know too much. Could blow all of them out of the rose garden— petalled water they swim round in cooing and fondling one other. Believe me, they're all quite aware I can wipe them out. Could and would destroy them in a second if they were really coming after me, coming down on me, and not simply providing free-of-charge, tons and tons of free publicity for the first episode of *Reel to Real* or *Real to Reel*, whatever the hell I decide to call it. Those pansies won't dare lay a pink finger or pink glove on this chief executive. Guilty or not of thirteen executions.

By the way since you claim to be a journalist, and journalists claim to know what people are thinking, tell me why, please, sir, why folks upset because a woman one of the thirteen executed, when if it had been thirteen gold medals the President awarding and none went to a female, same bellyachers be on my case for being sexist. And while you're at it Mr. Syndicated Truth-teller, how come all the bleeding hearts crying over thirteen dead convicted killers don't shed a tear for thousands, tens of thousands of innocent babies executed in their mama's wombs every year.

Do you consider thirteen an unlucky number or lucky number, my tall friend. What do your notes say about that.

Problem is nobody really likes strong rulers. Who wants somebody telling them what to do. Brits figured it out long ago. Royal family not rulers. Damn sitcom. Royals give the Brits something to gossip about. Queen and her court in the palace are ghosts not rulers. People want their own knucklehead ways to rule. Hate a boss ordering them around. Over there across the sea in England, Parliament just a sideshow, too. Blah-blah-blah. Bunch of fancy guys fancy blah-blahhing at each other and nobody listening. Brits pay 'em to gussy-up in robes and sit there blabbering and doing nothing, then they got Parliament to blame for no jobs, for everything wrong with their grubby little lives. People over there just like people here. Want everything their own way. Fuck rules and rulers, people say. But that's bullshit. If people want a country, they got to let somebody run it. Brits got it figured out.

Can't get over how real this place looks. Crew did a helluva job, didn't they.

Many years ago when I was a young whippersnapper not much older than the extra who escorted you in here, a guy passed me on the other side of the street and hollered, You remind me of somebody famous. Hey, I hollered back. Somedays I remind me of somebody famous. But, truth be told, I often wondered back then if I was ever gonna be more than the smartass, spoiled brat son of a millionaire daddy, a very, very rich daddy cause back in those days millions, not billions made a man very rich.

Mister President, my first question is. . .

——

You stay in character don't you. Even when the wrong character. A bit boring, but a useful habit, if you plan to stay in this business. And no biz like show biz, is there. So go right ahead. Do it your way. Interview it is. And I'll play dead president. Till I'm bored. Then back to the script I edited and okayed. The real one. The cliff-hanger. You the evil interrogator sent by my enemies to plague and harass. Me the patriot unjustly accused and persecuted, perilously close to death, until at the very last instant, a bugle tootle-toot-tootles and the cavalry thunders in to rescue me.

Mr. Pres . . .

Huh.

Mr. President, I . . .

I . . . I suddenly feel very tired. Where were we . . . are we . . . oh yeah. We were getting into character, weren't we. Or you were already in character. Never too soon. Play's the thing, to quote the Bard again. Best actors never out of character. Where do we start. Or pick up from. Where did we leave off. I think I was sleeping when the knock . . . then . . . or no . . . to be honest, I . . .

Naps my advice. And staying in character. I strongly recommend both if you want to succeed in this business.

———

Sir. Mr. President, as you must have been informed, I'm from the *Times*, and the *Times* so grateful, and I'm so grateful, sir, that you consented to give up a few moments of your time. Especially now. Precious time in the midst of, at the end of . . . Thank you, Mr. President, for agreeing to speak exclusively to me, to readers of the *Times* . . .

Did I. Did I say that. It's crazy around here. Absolutely bonkers, banana crazy. Rush. Rush. Rush. No wonder I was napping.

Let me clarify the record. I have nothing against tall guys. Even tall fellows miscast as interrogators or tall reporters. I like tall guys in a way. I'm tall. My wife's tall. We expect and pray to the good lord our son will be tall.

Invited the NBA champs to the White House once. Knew they'd be tall. Lots of very tall guys and just about all black. Tall, black guys no surprise. Huh-uh. I don't like the game much. Never played. Too fast. Too helter-skelter, happening everywhere at once for my taste. Too many NBA games and too long. Can't recall last time I watched one, if I ever did, from start to finish, but knew like everybody knows, game about tall, black guys, a few quite world famous, lots of tall, black guys shooting big balls through small hoops, and when you get a teamful of them all together at once in a room, even an extra large White House reception room designed for graciously greeting foreign delegations, a bunch of tall, black players seem even taller, blacker, seem to grow, spread, hog every bit of available space and the longer they dawdle around, the more they grow, more of them and taller, blacker, more and more of them it seems and if you're the sort of person has a hard time breathing, like me since I had awful asthma as a kid, you'd probably almost suffocate in a room full of them, the air you have to breathe full of them in their suits and ties, cologne, zany haircuts, gold chains, jewelry, and more seem to keep coming, more and more of them even after the door closed behind the few league execs and coaches who trail whitely after them, white escorts smiling like the tall, black players for cameras rolling as they strolled through the West Wing, Hi, fellas. Congrats fellas, Well done, champs. You gentlemen ought to be proud, I said loud and clear for the nation to hear. Nothing against tall, black guys, though to tell the truth, couldn't f-ing wait to get them or me out of the reception room. Congratulations, you guys, but never again. More than enough of them, too damned many, tall and black hovering around, shrinking and heating up the air, except a few of them voted not to turn up, not turn out, you know, choosing not to attend in order to diss me, not showing up, *showing out* as those tall, black guys say, so fuck you I say, never again, fuck em all, I say, even when same team champs again the following season no White House invite. Hell no. Never again. No breath-stealing, smartass mob of tree-top tall blacks smothering me in my house.

But not here to talk sports, are we, sport.

No, Mr. President. I'm here on behalf of the *Times* to record whatever you wish to say at this extraordinary moment. To preserve in this exclusive interview your words for posterity. Feel myself quite privileged, quite honored to be a witness, to be in your presence, Mr. President, this last precious day as the clock winds down. An unprecedented moment in our nation's history. Though to be fair, and to reciprocate the frankness so far of your words to me, I must admit that I am here also because I read an article by Caroline Hester in *Harper's* magazine mourning Dustin John Higgs, one of the people she claims you murdered. Article's author obviously a staunch opponent of the death penalty, and thus, very likely a biased witness. Yet her words are convincing as she renders in painstaking, meticulous detail how you, Mr. President, in performing what you may have believed were your appointed duties, went unreasonably, unforgivably far beyond the responsibilities your high office demands or permits. How you, along with your more than willing attorney general, sacrificed lives, violated the public trust, committed a heinous crime in the service of personal agendas of the most narrow, self-serving, amoral kind. Invented a scheme to perhaps gain a small advantage over political rivals or perhaps simply out of pure spite and vanity. Pumping yourself up, cleaning up after yourself, with the blood of condemned prisoners incarcerated in the Federal prison at Terre Haute, Indiana.

Must admit, Mr. President, I remain more than terribly perturbed by Ms. Hester's account of your machinations. Her words, her accusations one reason I'm here with you on death row, standing here—yes, I'm standing now, preparing to leave now, unless you, Mr. President, say something to change my mind.

You're behaving as if Diggs your first execution. It was his first, too. Makes you brothers. Is that what you think. Except Diggs way too short and dark to be your bro, I bet. Maybe bros under the skin. Soul brothers. Is that what you think. Well it was his first *and* last execution. Haha. Same for all thirteen. First and last execution. Just like yours when it comes.

Everybody born on death row. Next sixty-seven to seventy-eight years time spent trying to beat the rap. Or ignore it, la-de-da, la-de-da. Have a little fun. But everybody born on death row. Everybody condemned.

Even if all allegations 100 percent accurate, and I'm 100 percent guilty, what did I do wrong? Thirteen, right. Lucky or unlucky number. Go head. You spin the wheel and tell me. Okay.

Anyway, always a matter of style. Of she said, he said. He said, she said. Audience chooses. Truth no consequences.

If we are all born sharing a common humanity, when do we begin to form layers of fear, of ambivalence and indifference that disconnect other lives from ours.

Evil as they are, those exalters of one particular group, or color, or race, or nation or religion as superior to all others, or those deniers of the worth of any group or color or race or nation or religion other than their own, those evil souls are less dangerous enemies of the project to establish secure common ground that supports all humanity equally, far, far less dangerous enemies of all of us, than people who ignore or forget or erase the value of a single person.

You *are* a good actor, aren't you. And determined to stay in character, even when you're cast wrong. But surely in your heart of hearts, or brain of brains, your headquarters or heartquarters, as it were, the control room of your chain of command, you don't truly believe this is real. This stage set, these actors, technicians, coolies, directors, gapers, producers, sponsors, etc, etc. And for heavens sake—I'm almost afraid to ask—you don't believe you or I actually exist. This reporter. This president.

Hasn't it occurred to you, sir, none of this possible. A globe-trotting, bunny-hopping, prize-winning correspondent, and you're taken in by this sham. Shame on you.

Who on earth would dare perpetrate this farce, if I wasn't willing to play along. Who in the blessed universe could snatch me from the pinnacle of power and install me on death row. I am in charge until I decide not to be. In absolute charge. If I appear to step back or step down a peg or two, it's because I can change my mind in a split second if I choose, and step up again or down, higher or lower at the snap of a finger. In charge again *shazaam* because I'm never not in charge. Snap. *Shazam.* One man one vote, right. And the vote is mine, right. Me in charge of all you see. And don't see. My tall, made-up friend.

How many armies, navies, air forces, cops, casualties, bombs, missiles, cyber attacks do you imagine would be required to displace me, dislodge me as commander in chief of the biggest, baddest country in the world. To change my rules. Change the game. It's my game always. I'm the gotdamn warden. I own the casino.

Hey you. You slouching beside the door. You get paid to work here, don't you. Then why you just standing there whistling Dixie. Bring me the goddamn potty. Hurry up.

C'mon, my tall friend. Think seriously. Who can vanish a president. Banish one to death row. Especially when the president a very tough guy like me.

But you've caught me on a good day. Lets continue our live, exclusive interview. Let's do it. Curious a bit about how you'll, *wink, wink,* end it. So soon as I finish here, let's begin. Nothing better to do today. My calendar empty for a change. Good riddance.

RWANDA

More a game than a question, he thinks. Then thinks maybe not much difference between games and questions. He decides to call it a *thought experiment* when he tries it out on a friend. If he can find a friend willing to play. Friend he wants to play with. He's old. Few friends left. A stranger might do. Start the experiment by asking: if you were one of those in charge of running the world and you learned in secret from unimpeachable sources that life on earth is going to terminate abruptly, very soon, within weeks, months, six months at most, if such incontrovertible information existed and you had the power to reveal it or keep it hidden, would you inform the public.

Thought experiment goes on from there as one question leads to another. If, for instance, politicians in power were now certain that the deadly plague we are experiencing these days means that all life will soon, very soon cease, no exceptions, no reprieves, no second acts, no escape, would they announce or withhold the news. Why. Who would benefit or suffer. Would those leaders you imagine, or would you, yourself, be governed by a moral, ethical imperative that outweighs all other considerations: to tell the truth. Do you trust anyone in authority. How would people react if such awful news were made public. Would chaos erupt. Total anarchy, panic. A violent, uncontrollable, global orgy of immediate self-gratification. Everybody determined to snatch whatever they can before it's too late. Constrained only by the fear of other people's strength and violence. Law of the jungle prevailing—eat or be eaten. Or would some of us stay on the job, attempt to maintain a semblance, at least, of order.

He would argue that everybody, whether conscious of it or not, engages in a version of the thought experiment daily. Because, of course, deep down, we all are aware life is temporary, and that anybody liable to die the next instant. Which means each morning as we awaken and open our eyes and begin sleepwalking into our usual routines, we choose either to confront or to suppress the dirty secret of mortality. For obvious reasons, most of us choose not to start the day by reminding ourselves of our utter vulnerability.

But issues raised by his thought experiment—death, time, truth, responsibility—impossible to ignore or resolve, he's sure. Sure that his responses to those issues are unsatisfactory and incriminating. And just as sure that his evil habit of taking advantage of others won't be cured by nattering away in so-called thought experiments. As the ultimate authority in the only world he can even pretend to run, he must admit, he reminds himself, that he exploits rather than shares his knowledge of the end. In this fragile place with everybody passing through faster than the speed of light, with the end never more than a heartbeat (or lack of one) away, what rules apply. None. Isn't that what he has convinced himself of. No rule except pleasing himself. His actions speaking louder than any thought experiment's words. Acting as if the certainty of everybody's imminent disappearance exempts him from responsibility.

Time. Less of it the older he gets. Very little, next to nothing left now, so why does he worry so much more now about time. Why does time frighten him. More time or less time equally unsettling. Though it feels as if it unfolds endlessly, time always relative, unquantifiable.

Always limited. Not guaranteed no matter how precisely people attempt to measure, ignore, worship, save, anticipate, or prolong it. Time not something he can count or count on. Time mysterious and brief as any next instant that he imagines will follow the briefly present instant already lost. He doesn't possess time. Time possesses him. Locks him up like his brother serving a life sentence in prison.

Ahh . . . all these deaths. *Ahhhhh* . . . all these deadly days. He can't help it. What's inside him sneaks out loud as a pitiful groan. Are these dire days (didn't his mother warn him they were near at hand) the biblical Last Days. He's positive lately, his feeling sharp and unambiguous as a nail through the bottom of a bare foot, that the last days have been entered upon, but, to spite the vanity of the virulent, all-conquering virus ravaging the city, he keeps his feeling secret.

Careful, Uncle. Careful you don't get hit by a car, walking around up there in the big city having one those deep conservations like you do with your own self, she hollers at him. His smart pretty niece, a gift by way of a smart pretty niece, her mother. He missed them. Mother and daughter. Missed all his people. Only phone calls. Couple a month or so. His people far away. Too many gone for good now. Dead and gone. Seldom sees the ones left. Too bad. He likes his pretty niece. She likes him back, no doubt. She'd be a perfect partner for the thought experiment. Next time he sees her he'll try to get her attention. She's the sort of person who might understand what enormous power anybody holds in their hands when they consider seriously the issues his thought experiment examines.

But an irony lurks within the thought experiment, always threatening to emerge and spoil the fun. With the end just around the corner, why bother to share thoughts with anyone. Why pretend anybody's responses are worth discussing. Or mean much. Or matter at all. Knowing the end on its way, and not knowing how to change it, what's the point of making up more stories, writing them or reading them.

He instructs himself to ignore the irony and try to draw out his favorite niece anyway. Woo her to talk about what she might do if she knew the world about to end. Should he remind her of Rwanda. Warn her about the terrible old man. Colored man he followed home and watched undress.

Why Rwanda. Because the horrors, sweet girl, unleashed in Rwanda, expose the stakes, the power and chaos, that the thought experiment confronts. Rwanda a country whose authorities announced the end of the world coming immediately. In days or weeks at most, life on earth would be finished unless certain Rwandans, designated by Rwandan officials as the cause, as agents responsible for the dreadful obliteration of all existence, are removed immediately. Hurry, hurry, the government said. Not a moment to spare.

An old, colored American man was summoned by Rwandan officials to do work in Rwanda, he would tell her. A man who is our ancient enemy but poses as a friend. For centuries, that man has been convinced of colored people's worthlessness. It shames him and he is ashamed of us. A traitor. Fattens himself consuming the flesh of others. He can never be trusted. His treachery unforgivable.

When the man returned home from his mission in Rwanda, I crouched one night outside his window. Watched the old fucker undress. Dim light. No naked glare of a single, lynched bulb like burns in the cell of my brother, your uncle. Near darkness okay with me. Kept me invisible to him, and I sure didn't want to see too much of a deteriorating old man. His movements encumbered by age. Yet he also resembled an obedient child as he went about his business as kids do, attentively, earnestly, endeavoring to imitate their elders. To earn their praise, obtain their permission, the bounties they grant. Doomed forever to spy on others, spy on himself. To report progress or lack thereof to his superiors in their language he'd been taught to mimic.

In Rwanda the old man had been first passenger off the plane. Got weeks of work in before the other commissioners disembarked and passed streamlined through customs. He was expected. No. He had been on the ground waiting. Been there before. Always. Never departed. His presence necessary. To authorize, facilitate slaughter. Argue justness. Righteousness. God's will. Proclaim the urgent necessity to eliminate fellow citizens. Not a visitor. Home. Home boy. Home again. Honorary *Interahamwe. Impuzamugambi*. Machete ready in hand. Government sponsored radio voices in the run-up to the executions had borrowed his gravity. His long-dead, once youthful spirit pranced onstage at rallies. Cheerleading killings. His expensive shoes splashed through blood, splintered bones.

Weary and decrepit, back home long enough to forget he had ever left, the man hangs up a grayish suit, embalmed stiff by dry cleaning fluids. Submits each gesture for scrutiny, approval. Brown man, colored like him. Sufferer. Suffered. He listens to him breathe, to sounds of him farting. Spares himself the smell. A coon-aged coon honored by being appointed to a delegation invited to investigate, twenty-five years after the fact, Rwanda's genocide. Crimes of, by, for its people. Rewarded for his decades of labor in America's gulags—hard work, impeccably high standards, a guard many years, then assistant warden, a warden twice, chair of board of pardons and parole, expert witness, judge, jury, executioner—you name it—old man had been there, done that. Loyal. Steady. Unflinching. Why wouldn't Rwandans be happy to host him, toast him, solicit his advice and benefit from his lifetime of service, experience, knowledge, etc. . . . of incarceration, the incarcerated . . . etc. Him singled out, rewarded for achievement, for persevering in his chosen trade just as your uncle has been rewarded in the writing trade he practices, even granted permission to publish an occasional book. Lucky and colored . . . etc. Despite or because of color . . . etc. What's the difference.

Should he tell his niece how sorely he was tempted to throttle the man that afternoon when he conjured up just the two of them alone in a Rwandan courthouse men's room. Disappointed himself, when he didn't finish him off then and there. When the hateful old man's time up, wouldn't his moans for morphine or death be music to my ears, he thinks. *Mehr Licht* the last words attributed to a dying Goethe. German words, Niece, meaning "more light," and still sounding a bit like *Mehr Licht* when translated into English. "More dark," that old darkie will gasp. Darkness to hide him, to cover up his fears, his rage, his betrayals, his shame.

But no point, he had decided that day in a faraway courthouse, no point in killing a nasty old man. Tutsi corpses don't return to life no matter how high the piles of Hutu corpses. Or vice versa.

At home in his bedroom, old-man eyes stare into emptiness between remembered/forgotten steps of untying his tie, loosening laces, removing shoes, rolling down crusty-toed, silk socks. Why commit a crime, he had asked himself. Risk freedom killing the bastard when surely disease will rot his old body and perform a more impeccable, patient, subtle, sustained, excruciating assassination than he could ever hope to achieve.

Story of any country's citizens massacring fellow citizens is many stories coming true, he will say to his niece. Also many stories becoming untrue. Yours. Ours. Thought experiments. Many stories redone. Stories crucified. Halal. Kosher. Bled white. Sanctified. Eaten. Goodness born inside each person along with evil, my dear, but goodness doesn't prosper like evil prospers. The woes an old, naked man—warden, keeper of the flame, keeper of coloreds, fellow colored, colored fellow—has inflicted upon others defy words. Best revenge not to take his life, but to wish more years on him. Life everlasting interrupted daily, every hour on the hour, by death of one thousand self-inflicted cuts.

Maybe more mercy than he deserves, his niece or someone else might suggest. Too much mercy for a person who remains until their dying day, willing to abuse others. How many times to please himself, had he, like the old man, violated another person's trust. Acted as if he knew the world going to end in a quick minute and no consequences that matter would follow his actions. As if whatever comes next could never matter more than the sweet pleasure of pretending no tomorrow for him or his victim to fret about. No questions asked. No hesitation. Just a game, after all.

Of course, more than contempt had motivated him to spy through a window on an evil old colored man fumbling around in a dark room. Whose story was he attempting to tell anyway. To whom. He already understood more than enough about the man. Knows him much too well. Bitter, bitter knowledge. Studies him because he fears him. And you should fear him, too, girl, he will say. Always, he will say. Beware. Beware. Sorry as I am to admit it, dear heart, yours truly is very much like him. Both of us men who should know better. No excuse. Way, way, way too greedy. Too busy. Way too selfish. Too accomplished at getting what we want. Everything. Nothing. No matter who or how many we destroy.

II

A few days ago on his early morning walk—no risk of getting hit by a car, sweet niece—dawn and streets more quiet and deserted than usual, even at dawn, even during the unnatural calm of lockdown and sequestering the city has imposed upon its residents to slow the spread of an epidemic sickening and killing thousands. He'd encountered almost no people, no traffic. Nearly absolute silence on streets leading to the walkway along the East River.

Close to the water's edge, he turned left, headed uptown, in the direction of Harlem, not on the paved, guardrailed, concrete walkway, but on a path through growing things—grass, bushes, shrubs, moss, flowers, weeds, trees—life someone had the good sense to preserve or plant and create parklike stretches paralleling the river. On his side of tall, black cyclone fences that protected tennis courts, running tracks, and ball fields, he saw the same discarded paperback book he had been noticing for a couple days, a pale, bulky lump still lying there atop late May grass, near the mud-colored path scuffed into brown earth by many, many footsteps, the skittering trail he was negotiating, only a bit wider than a shoe's length, a mile of path, improvised about a yard away from fifteen-foot-high black wire fences. Curiosity he had managed to resist on previous sightings won this time. He stopped, used a foot to turn it over, and discovered the book's title, *Snow,* on its torn cover, a novel by coincidence he happened to have read, its author a famous Turkish writer, and he was trying hard to remember the writer's name, remember more about the book, unable to take another step until he forced himself to remember more, embarrassed, ashamed when he couldn't. Silence of the morning, stillness of the streets on his way to the East River all he could recall.

Then snow. Instantly the green grass, the brown earth, the book are buried under whiteness. Huge snowflakes filling the air around him. If it had been a scene he read in the novel's pages, he might have dismissed it as "magic realism." But no, it was not words. No. Snow present. Snow a deluge of giant flakes slowly descending, snow dropping into the East River, turning edges of water into icy sheets, snow beginning to obscure tall towers—most completed, some under construction, crowned by skeletal arms of cranes—looming a half mile away on the river's opposite bank, snow falling until it buries that distant cityscape and all the building disappear.

Will he ever be able to express to her (or maybe she already understands—smart pretty niece by way of smart pretty niece—and maybe she will help him understand better) the painful complicity—inhabiting a world that holds his imprisoned brother, and holds another brother who *is* a prison.

III

Not exactly reparations, I say to my brother during the second phone call to me he's been permitted after a hearing that denied parole, an old colored man (is he a soul brother of bête noire my dreams spy on) presiding. My brother turned down for the fifth straight year since he had become eligible, after twenty-five years, to apply once a year for parole. Not exactly reparations, I smile and wag my head, though my brother can't see me do it nor do I quite hear his little laugh nor see that smart-aleck smirk that wrinkles up my brother's face since he was twelve. Silence on the other end of the phone line connecting us, him trapped inside, me trapped outside stone walls, but I keep talking, carefully of course, since our conversation's monitored and my words can be used against him. Say the story I saw on the *NBC Nightly News* not exactly reparations after four hundred years of damage, but maybe a step in the right direction. Whadda you think, man. Story the feel-good bit in these godawful times Lester always tacks on at the end of each broadcast. A project in a laundromat to teach preschool ghetto kids to read. Good idea, huh, though maybe a better idea, the best idea, just to stop pretending altogether they give a fuck. Excuse me. Give a damn. Probably my own bad mood as much as anything else, bro, but that piece made me so mad, so ashamed, I wanted to scream. Cry. Enslavement a terrible crime—just about everybody concedes that fact today—but all the victims and perpetrators dead, we're told, if we ask. Not spoken about if no one asks. America's gaping, cosmic black hole and here they come with another Band-Aid to patch it. Cringed when I saw those video clips of kids listening to grown-ups read, kids spozed to be learning to read inside some ugly fuck . . . damn laundromat in a raggedy-ass neighborhood. Let it bleed, I thought. Better to let it bleed. All of us falling one day, sucked into a black hole, but some of us encumbered with all the shit they've stolen will fall through faster, and the rest of us left behind, separated a blessed minute from those ruthless, greedy, toxic thieves at last, and maybe then at the end we might get a little smidgen of peace then.

Laundromat. Yeah. Yeah. Huge, barn-ass, noisy room and preschoolers stuck there anyway on wash day with mamas or grandmamas or aunts or big sis or whoever washes everybody's clothes so why not. It's available, cheap, plenty clients on hand regularly. Just bring in a couple volunteers and organize the locals, encourage them to read to the little burrheads instead of just sit around half the day smoking dope or doing nothing while all those machines rumbling, tumbling. Why not get the women involved who spawn too many colored kids. Teach them to sit their babies down and read to them instead of letting them run wild inside a filthy laundromat. And if Mama missed that alphabet class in school, teach Mama the alphabet, too. Makes perfect sense in a way. You know. Like, yes, please give our children a little extra head-start push. So niggers don't fail because they start out—first day in kindergarten—far behind other kids. Except everybody knows ain't no rule says niggers got to catch up. Four hundred years and we ain't caught up yet.

Makes sense and no sense. Teaching ghetto kids to read a couple hours a week in some loud, crowded, funky laundromat, bro. As if it's the best school the richest country on earth can afford for them. What kind of fucking catch-up is that. Four hundred years and counting of starting out unequal. That amounts to some serious left behind. Four hundred years' worth. And we spozed to catch up while our clothes getting clean. Why not slam up every single colored one of us into laundromats and lock the doors. Only let out a few, now and then. Ones who read well.

IV

She sticks the check from her uncle back in its envelope, envelope in her bag to deposit next day in the bank after work. Money her uncle sent for her other uncle, the one she's seen only a few times in life, and never outside prison, where he's been since before she was born, money her uncle had asked her to begin taking charge of this year, money in a lump sum he sends for her to dispense to his brother, her uncle said, both to connect her more closely with her imprisoned uncle and to encourage more visits to the prison, his hope. Requesting that she dole out to his brother in small, regular amounts the money he sends her, either when she visits and can put cash directly into a prison account or JPay it through Internet, the second option equally available to her college-educated uncle wherever he is, she's tempted to remind him, though he always claims Internet "befuddles him." Smallish portions, he schools her. Best not forward too much money at one time because my younger sibling has a fondness for gambling and we don't want to tempt him, do we, dear heart, my uncle said. Little bro's fondness for risk and his boundless optimism ensure he'll keep chasing after other folks' bad money until he loses all the little taste of good money in his hand, my uncle says, talking over the phone in that odd, elaborate way of his she thinks he must be as fond of as he claims his younger brother fond of gambling.

Her uncle had asked her once, Do you truly believe you're colored. Hey. Don't be looking at me all cross-eyed, young lady. A serious question. Do you, we, all of us still believe we are colored just because they keep telling us we are. Colored. Different. A damned shame.

Her odd uncle, book writer, wanderer, seldom in town. Her dead mom's uncle, really, Grandma's older brother. Her dead mom her grandma's eldest daughter, the man's actual niece, and that makes her what—great-niece, niece-in-law, second niece—whatever to this man she's standing next to on her grandmother's porch and always called Uncle since she was a baby, the wannabe front porch not much larger than a final step up to Grandma's house. Her house, too. For many years, she and her mom, after her beautiful mom got divorced, got sick, living there with Granddaddy and Grandma, her grandma who still misses a lost daughter seven years gone, mourns her lost daughter as fiercely, unconsolably, it seems and does not seem possible, as she does, daughter of that lost daughter who misses and mourns her mom, yes she does, still does very much, especially now, on this narrow, crooked front porch where she stands in the dark after family had gathered to talk and eat and drink themselves holiday-silly and each one finally at this late hour has had more than enough and begins peeling away into smaller family groups. Or a few, like her, alone, though her uncle beside her now, middle of the night, isn't it, and dangerous out there in the streets, and Uncle makes it his habit, whenever he's around, to escort each solitary family female outdoors, a sentinel on the porch until she's locked in her car, motor running, lights on and car rolls off, up or down the dark, steep hillside upon which his sister's house perches. Uncle there, bodies lightly touching when his arm goes round her shoulders and he leans down, kisses her cheek, and if her cheek just a wee bit higher or he leaned lower, his lips might have brushed hers, but didn't, no lip brushing because she's tough like her mom, though also unafraid like her, and believes, like her mom did, neither in sin, nor in everlasting romance of any mouth, uncle or anybody else on her mouth, knows better, raised better by her dead mom who nods gently, whispers best not, of course not, girl, best go on and get your behind down those treacherous slabs of broken concrete serve as steps up and down from the sidewalk to your grandma's red front door. Glad now she chose sneakers and jeans not heels and dress for the family party. Don't break your butt, girl, careful, careful now, get yourself down step by step till your feet on solid street and your car door locked, and you got yourself sitting behind the wheel, girl.

Her uncle tall. Not as tall as tall, gorgeous Riley. Thirty smiling foot of Riley in skimpy running shorts, T-shirt, fanciest of training shoes postered for months up on a wall next to Kmart entrance to the mall. Liked Riley lots. Maybe still with him. Maybe if he shared fewer of those dumb notions about women guys his age, especially fine ones like finest Riley, share about women. *Gimme some. Get me some. Cop me a piece of pussy.* What in the world did they think we carry around down there between our legs, her mom asked once, think we can break off and wrap it up and send it home with them or they can grab and show off to their friends.

Her uncle had asked her, If you found out, a secret, no doubt about it, world going to end very, very soon, would you tell other people. With that knowledge buzzing around in your brain, my dear, what would you do. Then her uncle had stopped talking. Stopped explaining experiments or games, stopped asking questions. Looked at her. Waited. Waited. As if he expected an answer. Since she had no idea what to reply, she asked him, What would you do, Uncle. He smiled at her, then closed his eyes and whispered, If I knew sure enough the world about to end, think I'd probably kidnap you, girl, and run far away with you, and my, my, wouldn't that be a trip, and wouldn't people talk.

And she had smiled back, smile deep as his smile because she believed her old uncle just talking, just teasing. Long, long way for both of them to go.

IPSO FACTO

I WISH TO TELL IPSO FACTO'S STORY. Write a biography of the famous photographer Ipso Facto who disappeared into the wilderness of New York City. He disappeared just at the moment when what had been understood as a "pandemic" began to be recognized as the end. As excruciating evidence of the end's beginning, the photos of Ipso Facto remain unsurpassed. All witnesses agree. The witnesses who survive and many who became blanknesses in the oblivion that swallowed the photographer and pictures he invented. In these days we endure, days when the end, like the pandemic, has come and gone, when nothing remains except the ruins each of us sees for ourselves, ruins each individual must accept and account for alone, the loss of Ipso Facto another kind of death worse than death.

Problem for a biographer is: No one believes anybody's story anymore. Or all stories are believed. Leaving us, creatures who wish to write biographies, as well as creatures dependent on stories to weave lives for ourselves, leaves all of us bereft. Words we speak or write or dream drain into a vast reservoir containing nothing. The reservoir itself, less than nothing. Itself a story, a figment. Containing truth and no truth. As a famous African writer warned us, all stories true. No accident, I insist, that *Vast Reservoir* is today one of Ipso Facto's photographs most discussed, whose disappearance most lamented, most mourned. Embraced by those who have encountered it as a revelation of truth discovered in nothing. Though just as many witnesses affirm the same revelation in reverse: nothing discovered in truth.

Some commentators argue that, paradoxically, by confirming what it eliminates, *Vast Reservoir* consumes the mighty, outrageous Internet clamor of all stories recited simultaneously. But does any life, any photo, any work of art ever end that deafening roar of nothingness people swarm about in, darting, feeding, dying, breeding here and there, treating ourselves as if innocent, as if we've been dropped into a bowl whose glass walls secure us, as if nourishment from above will forever trickle down, as if the water's benign temperature will be eternally maintained. As if the cozy, vicious bowlful of us, all competing sizes, shapes, colors, genders, ages, friends and enemies and dead will never be dumped into the sea of utter darkness that we choose, not only not to believe that we would ever be abandoned in, but from whence we deny we emerged.

When the pandemic pumped up the deafening silent roar of ordinary lives extinguishing themselves, and the beginning of the end silenced noises that each person generates inside to make sense of themselves, the universal quiet became unbearable as our memories of media clamor and howl. Enveloped now in silence of an IP photo, silence of all photos ever taken, we are lonely beyond words, estranged beyond, beyond, beyond words, of course, since words that don't exist can offer no consolation. Words nothing, too. Not *too*. Not in addition. Simply nothing. Nothing plus more nothing equals nothing. An empty silence in which absence of words once upon a time might have been a welcome state, as distinct, as needful to ears as occasional shocks of noise, but the constant silence of words both missing and unrecoverable deprives us, reduces us like Ipso Facto's lost photos. His remains impossible to retrieve from the ruins of wilderness, from the emptiness beyond ruin.

But if I truly believe all that shit I have labored into words, why am I attempting a biography, wasting your time and mine chasing Ipso Facto with more words. *More Words* the title, by the way, of another Ipso Facto photo only slightly less known, esteemed, regretted than *Vast Reservoir.* So what. Why write more words that vanish. More words, more silence.

Perhaps you may find room in your heart to sympathize with my predicament—those words you have just read, if you did, are not the title of another lost Ipso Facto photo, but like an IP photo (IP my abbreviation going forward of Ipso Facto's name since IF, his actual initials, might be misleading) those initial thirteen words of this sentence could be read not as an admission of defeat, but understood as an entreaty begging for your forgiveness and complicity, if you imagine for a moment that those words which appeared before the dash, thirteen of them exactly, an unlucky or lucky number depending upon whom you ask, imagine that for arguments sake, they do entitle a photo, and imagine them capitalized, italicized, centered on the page,

Perhaps You May Find Room in Your Heart to Sympathize with My Predicament.

and maybe the words will still sound a bit like me copping a plea, but also me fessing up to you that I am well aware, as you probably are, that all words and writing fail, and thus it makes perfectly good sense to expect failure and disappointment each time I begin a sentence, understanding in advance that there will always be much a sentence can't express, too much it cannot say, too much missing, many things belonging in it, but not quite, or things absent I cannot say even to myself, and thus a dash interrupts this string of thoughts or fragment of wishful thinking or whatever's forming in my mind, and after the dash, I offer again the words preceeding the dash, *Perhaps you may find room in your heart to sympathize with my predicament,* this time as a sort of prelude and invitation. I'm guessing that very likely you, too, may have experienced previously, a terrible loss or have encountered an indelible image captured in a particular photograph that breaks your heart if you do or do not not let it enter, and that traffic jams and regrets and chaos impossible to negotiate, might be recalled for you, perhaps, by an imagined IP photo and its italicized title, *Perhaps You May Find Room in Your Heart to Sympathize with My Predicament,* or recalled perhaps by some other work of art, a song, painting, or sculpture you can recollect that puts you in IP's lost shoes or my shoes, and therefore, gains maybe an iota more of your attention and time and patience for my attempt here to communicate with a reader, since who among us, after all, is not regularly flummoxed and betrayed by words, words betraying us as vanished photos betray us, betraying us even if found and in our hands once more, because photos remind us that we are frailer than nothing, that after we have looked and looked at them, trying to recall some fragment of whatever is missing, what we wish could or should be there, but ahhhhhh, *my-oh-my,* we remember so much more not there, and where did it go, and what wouldn't a person give to restore, to recover, to find it again.

And thus, here I am, I confess, still trying to get words to speak, but ahhhh, a dash intervened, and started a well-intentioned interruption that will last until another dash appears, the second dash signifying the intervention over, the sentence resuming, or perhaps no second dash will appear, a period instead, and the sentence will conclude, finished, at last, at last, and everything extra lost and found that I had wanted to include, to mention or suggest or meditate upon or tease out or holler, everything that for some reason still seems to be tumbling, rushing out of me into this sentence, everything disguised and/or naked appearing here before your eyes and mine, before the termination of this sentence, before a period mercifully ends it, and everything unmentionable or unimaginable or unsayable stops trying to crowd onto the page, as if world and time enough, and somewhere maybe, there is room perhaps, for all the many, many ghostly presences alive and shimmering within this extra space I am allotting to myself, hungrily, greedily, a space following a dash that splits open a sentence and precedes a second dash or another sort of punctuation mark that would close or rather enclose much, much, incalculably way too much fugitive stuff belonging mostly elsewhere, all of which stuff goes probably nowhere, except into invisible space between a pair of dashes, space that eerily resembles, and recapitulates space eternally between any two people, between us, for instance. And now after I have sought your complicity by inventing for you an IP photo that could be entitled *Perhaps You May Find Room in Your Heart to Sympathize with My Predicament,* I will add a dash—then proceed with my probably futile search for what is missing.

The story of IP's life doesn't begin here, with my distress and maundering, confessions or pleas. Everybody, even an extraordinary exception like IP, requires first a mother and a father and a birthplace to begin. Fortunately, or unfortunately, depending upon what you are looking for and why, no records have been unearthed of how exactly IP managed to acquire those basic necessities for starting a life. Or some would say he wisely avoided entanglement with them. One theory promoted by a handful of influential biographers and philosophers explains the lack of information about IP's origins as the product of his lifetime of intense picture taking, so many photos snapped for so many years, that the photographer's eyes consumed everything possible that could rise up and appear in front of them, consuming, internalizing, anticipating so voraciously each picture he seized until one day nothing of the world's plenitude left to present itself to him, no place for IP's eyes to go, and he plummets inside himself, his photos change direction, is how certain theorists explain the phenomenon. IP's subject becomes what exists behind his eyes, not in front of his eyes and camera lens. An inexhaustible subject, IP assumes, since always more it seems behind his eyes, in his past than what constitutes his present. He could plunge backwards forever, immersed, free-falling, gleaning without fear of exhausting what he perceives through his camera, what his camera perceives through him. Thusly, the critics argue, IP's art consumes his past before anyone else is able to hurry back there, catch up, and record the details. Unless the universe decides to halt. Unless the past ceases to accumulate and the ride terminates and all the cars of the train smash to a crushing, jack-knifing, shuddering, then absolute stop.

The overwhelming likelihood that his life story will proceed in that predictably ugly fashion, is what IP must have understood or feared in his photographer's heart. Fear of the plunge backwards could end an artist's life since it would reveal that everything coming before IP's camera undertakes a plunge and everything coming after could be equally exhausted, extinguished, frozen, immobile, piled up, nothing ahead on the tracks, nothing behind, only one more shrieking snapshot of wreckage he's unavailable to capture. Man wrecked, dissolving on a bridge in a Munch painting, an image echoing, lurking here and there in IP's vanished work, various experts assert, though none can cite exactly where. Scream appearing then disappearing into wilderness somewhere, as if wilderness always waiting outside the frame patiently, as some experts claim it is. Why wouldn't IP, if he ceased picture taking, find himself within the wilderness of Munch's famous scream.

On the train going to meet and interview IP's mother, I can't stop myself thinking about his father. I'm fairly certain I won't find his mother (IP's) in the city where I'd read or heard a rumor that she used to live and may perhaps presently reside. Father (IP's) so much on my mind because thinking about him better company on a long train ride than contemplating the futile prospect of seeing a mother I have no good reason to believe waiting for me at a destination I've chosen arbitrarily to believe she could be. I ignore the father long enough to ask the mother if she retains her initial memory of him (son not father) after all these years, a number of years I do not quote to her exactly since the precise date of IP's birth unknown. And some scholars, as I've already mentioned, don't think he required birth. (The ones who concede a birth insist unanimously upon the sixties.)

At some point (post–train ride) it strikes me that the sixties began sixty years ago. Anybody twenty or so when the sixties began must be eighty or so years old now if they are still alive. I was nineteen in 1960, so what's truly striking to me, I guess, is the fact I will be eighty on my next birthday, if I live that long. No wonder the pale image of a young man who looks to be nineteen, twenty, sneaking, skulking around, hunter or hunted, carrying in one of his hands an automatic rifle, maybe an AK47, the young man caught by an outdoor surveillance camera in one of America's cities (Chicago, NY, Atlanta, Seattle, etc.) shot up murderously over the recent Fourth of July weekend (in Chicago alone over one hundred shootings, fourteen known fatalities) is both achingly familiar and unfathomable as they say IP photos are. Young man revealed though not positively identifiable, lucky for him, in a blurry image. Blip on my screen, swept away as quickly as I would be wiped from his phone by streaming blips of news and ads if ever I showed up, skulking or not.

Why is the young guy doing whatever it is he thinks he is doing. What does he think he's doing, and what do I think of him and/or think of what he is doing and thinking. An enigma. Countless enigmas impacted. As I would be to him. Our mutually unimpenetrable time on the same small planet. My mind-set and his. Mingling and not. Wuzz-up, pops, hey old head, or him oblivious, ignoring me, a silent ghost in a barbershop chair or me shuffling by him on a street in the hood, or him yessir, nosir to a respectable, almost deceased elder, or he winks at a crusty, funky homeless old dude or grins at a fabled ancestor in ancient family stories everybody sposed to laugh at and wag their head in wonder. Does difference of age clarify our difference. Or bring us closer together before we both are stopped in our tracks by uncrossable distance between us. Where is he, where am I. The need we share to hug, or high-five, or bump or just nod or not nod, or not any of that stuff, both of us confined, incarcerated, forgoing all ceremony, no-contact visits in this contagious climate of rampant, deadly infection. No hello, no goodbye, just go on and get it on alone in an appalling, unspeakable present and future here and now.

Why kill kids, young man, babies even, why kill anybody any age standing around on a street corner, sitting on a stoop, in a playground, in an alley, the poolroom, at a party or funeral or picnic, or strolling your sis or mom's block or enemies, your competitors way over crosstown on the south side or north side who would need to be gunned down. Is shooting and killing a duty, thrill, pleasure, crime, fate, penance. Or is killing simply what you do and best not to think too much about it. Who taught you to kill. Who taught them. And who in your hood or city or country is sure you need to be killed. What's love got do to with it. Or age.

Does it matter truly to which kind the skulking young guy on TV belongs. Which generation, race, gender, nation, class, etc., etc. . . . kinds invented, assigned, maintained by words. Kinds claimed by words to divide humans into primal, stacked, lowest up to highest groups. Unchanging kinds that truly matter. But isn't time what truly matters. Time. Not kinds. Not age counted in years. Time that separates people into only two groups: alive or dead. Time's irresolvable mysteries that separate people absolutely, each one of us from every other, every one of us from ourselves. Only two kinds. True kinds that words, biographies can't create or alter. You are alive or dead. Here, breathing, playing games of the pretend sorts that we play. Or gone. Nothing. But since we live and die daily, simultaneously, the two kinds often seem similar to us in confounding ways. As if they could almost be the same. Familiar to people as emptiness of an IP photograph is familiar. But difference separating life from death absolute. Final. Difference unknowable, untouchable as time.

I don't know the mother's name, but she doesn't know mine either, and neither does anybody else, so it's an even playing field when I ask her on the train why, given such a world-famous son, no one knows her name. "Obscure origins" . . . is how one oft-quoted account of IP's life begins and also basically concludes its story of IP's earliest years. First time reading those words *obscure origins,* I recall attributing them to the celebrated author's laziness. At best her eagerness to get on with her tale. After my own diligent decades of research, I realize that no dependable facts available to piece together IP's beginnings. Ipso Facto? Does his name tell all. All anyone will ever know, unless they undertake the task of telling, writing, making up his story or choose to believe stories about him. Not a mystery. Just nothing there. Or like some people say, and I concur, the only truth regarding IP photographs: what you see is what you get.

Funny when I look back, see me hunched alone on a train, engaged earnestly, even furiously in keeping track of competing conversations with a mother and father not there. I wonder what they looked like. The two of them. Me. Did we ever raise our voices. Did I sleep for part of the interminable trip. Dream. Why have I forgotten lots. Or not. Did my companions directly address one another. Ignore me. Did they argue. Sleep. Have fun. Eat in the dining car. A dark, elegant Pullman waiter serving them. Smooch. Hate me for intruding. Resent me for imagining them alive again if dead then. Dead now. Alive. Where are words that we exchanged stashed today.

Choo-choo/Choo-choo-choo. Does a life count for no more than that. Noises. *Choo-choo-choo* noises until we all fall down. Go boom. Like a flashbulb when IP employs a flash as experts argue he must have, given what some experts hypothesize must have been the impossible conditions from which he wrenched those fabulous images of war and peace, night and day, tempest and calm, etc. . . . one shot including all and nothing, nothing less than the likes of which nobody has ever seen or never seen, some insist. Some agree.

I must admit I've come very close to shutting down my pursuit of IP and his photos. My project once saved, nay, *reinvigorated* a truer word, by a book, *Short Life in a Strange World,* I happened upon. Book about "Peter Brewgill" as the author (Toby Ferris) playfully rewrites the name of Peter Breughel. That painter (Peter Breughel the Elder 1525/30–1569) the author's subject only in a peripheral fashion. Breughel an excuse, a sort of off-center center the book staggers around, seeking its footing wherever/whenever each shoe lands, a wide variety of shoes, like the unpredictable shoes and hats of Breughel's famous dancing peasants, shoes stirred up by the writing's thumping beat, a bit of a breathless, dizzying performance for writer and reader, especially since the book clearly prefers to stagger and grow additional feet as it embarks upon almost miscellaneous and/or circuitous journeys from city to city, museum to museum, where Breughel's canvases hang, his wooden panels and roundels displayed. A book constructed from pop historical anecdotes of the painter's life and times, the author's quirky, provocative analyses of various renowned canvases, his prose buttressed by learned elucidations of scholars and critics. Ferris's words, his intentions occasionally fading and dissolving into blah-blah streams of self-consciousness and trying too hard, but then jump to up-close, intimate, engrossing remembrances of his family, nuclear and extended (drunk father struggling up steps and managing to set down without spilling a drop his tumbler of booze on the very top step an instant before he dies). Book a mini-cry from the heart expressing the love writers lavish on their writing projects and presumed subjects of those projects. Love anybody not a fool knows is feckless and will be unrequited. The book doubtless a meticulous, falling-down, resounding, stumbling-around labor in the spirit perhaps of IP examining his past, a book that lured me back to my IP project, to IP's photos in which pursuit of nothing better than nothing at all, as numerous viewers perhaps have beheld within them.

According to the dictionary, *ipso facto* means (a)—By the fact itself; by that very fact: *An alien, ipso facto, has no right to a US passport;* (b)—By that very fact or act; *ipso facto his guilt was apparent;* (c)—By the fact itself; by the very nature of the deed: *to be condemned ipso facto.*

Of course, on the train I asked both mother and father about the son's odd name. Didn't learn much. Neither parent went by Facto. Neither recalled that surname adorning any members of their extended families nor ever mentioned in family stories. Neither understood Latin. The father laughed outright. What you say, man. *Ipso,* you say. *If-so . . . Ip-so.* Don't even sound like a name. Mother admitted she had not been overly elated after her period gone missing and the doctor informed her why. Could hardly call it a blessed event, she said, not given when and how it got here, but I sure wasn't the kind of bitter person then or now to hold a baby responsible for my mistakes and stick the poor thing with a name people would make fun of for the rest of the little bugger's life. Never ever heard, she added, anybody say either word, *ipso* or *facto.* Certainly never heard it's anybody's name till you asked.

Uncertainty, unsupported attestations and allegations, philosophical speculation, ingenious hypotheses, guesswork, abysmal ignorance, mere meretriciousness and prejudice, sundry pure and unpure fantasies constitute the totality of information available to any good soul researching IP's private, personal life. That plus the sort of wistfulness and wishful thinking would-be biographers of IP's life share with those who yearn for just a single glimpse of one of his fabled snapshots (not *of* him, *by* him—*of* would be selfish and far too much to hope for).

I can offer no exit, no solution to the dead end confronting those who wish to learn more about IP's life. A dead end, a puzzle as described in the paragraphs above. His life a conundrum as elusive as the meaning of the adjective *Black* applied to a human. Except to say there is more to learn always though probably more you won't see coming till it's there, ipso facto. Or not. For instance, in a collection of Kafka's fiction, some stories previously published, some not, some long, others a few paragraphs, some only fragments K never completed, I discovered one called "A Little Woman" (seven pages—original pub date 1923—and by the way, "Tiny Lady" in my opinion would be a better English title).

K's story imagines a young, very Jewish, very lonely, extremely sensitive, and witheringly intelligent person in a virulently anti-Semitic Prague between the Great Wars. The meticulously crafted words of "A Little Woman" render a male narrator/lover's doubled life when love feels unrequited, when his urgent questions and his anguished persistence go unanswered. Gradually, as I read and reread K's tiny tale, I realized I was learning, maybe even gaining insights about any person's inner life who lives among strangers, who fears and conceals the presence of an incriminating inner life. With and between the lines of an invisible narrator's voice in "A Little Woman," K drops clues to create another, separate version of a man's undocumented private and personal life. Clues that enhanced my vision of the photographer IP tiptoeing silently as K across a catastrophic void. As if thin ice not widening daily, wider and wider under his feet.

Given fictitious differences that words invent, assign, maintain between certain alleged kinds of people and other alleged kinds, is an actual private life possible for anybody. Or only doubled lives. Ipso facto lives. In stories, photos. There and not there. Not you. Not me. Nor anybody else either. A photo. Poem. Love story. Or story of no love. Or what you see, what you get. Or not.

Two confessions now. Both of them equally intimidating and embarrassing. First (did u guess already), I am, ipso facto, IP. Second, I am not a photographer, not writing a biography, but a fiction writer and these words are my characters, my story. And here is how it ends—

One day in the park along the river on NYC's Lower East Side, a squirrel spoke to me. Then another. And suddenly, much, much faster than the speed of light, a multitude of squirrel voices chattering. Then pigeons, and rats, and birds, and ants, and butterflies, and trees joining in. No not trees yet. But all the creatures hidden in the trees howling, tweetering, baying, hiss and hoot and pecking and scratching, a tumult, tsunami suddenly of shouting of nonhumans and humans speaking too, faster, loud, louder, no warning, only a park's welcoming, nearly utter silence, then a single squirrel then infinite voices all at once suddenly rising and falling, shaking, rattling the foliage of the trees so leaves seemed to have voices also, as if a vast, beyond vast wilderness not there a millisecond ago had burst up and surrounded the riverside park, surrounded me instantly and now all the animals plants stones within it talking simultaneously, a din you'd think frightening, overwhelming, winds and oceans speaking, too, and me on a park bench scared, screaming, the cry of Munch's poor soul swept away by or within storms of thunder and lightning voices, but no. No hands over my ears. What happened, what I did was/is slowly rise, rotate slowly, steadily within the calm whirlwind center of all those speaking suddenly at once voices suddenly everywhere around me and inside me and, *Click . . . click . . .* take their picture.

BTM

IN THE MIDDLE OF A HOT, humid afternoon, a cluster of people here, in New York City, mustering along the East River, just beyond a service station often crowded with taxis filling up with cut-rate gas as I pass by on my frequent hikes. Cluster almost all female, many clearly overweight, most sporting fancy outfits they must have chosen to display on a pleasure cruise, women of all ages lining up at a pier where a dozen or so charter boats are moored, colored women of various colors, sizes, shapes, absolutely resplendent, gleaming, decked out in competing costumes of dazzling variety. Designer jeans fashionably holey and tattered, leggings and tights featuring an astounding array of zigzags, stripes, checks, polka dots, rainbow swirls, and splashes. Skintight miniskirts, shorts, short shorts, halters showing plenty of flesh, or dresses and wraps draping, clinging so you don't see much flesh but notice it anyway, since the outfits, whether exposing or covering flesh, entice your eyes. Sisters, daughters, moms, cousins, aunts, nieces assembled at the water's edge, more than a few of them showing off a round, fully packed, proud butt, all the ladies shimmering in afternoon sunlight, lovely and innocent and fragile as those antique, glitter-sprinkled bulbs my mother saved and set out in their raggedy cardboard cartons on Xmas eve for us to hang on the tree she hoped my father would find on last-minute sale and drag home if he was inspired enough after work to drag himself home, instead of to his favorite bar, everybody called Bucket of Blood.

Cluster of women disperses and fades, but not gone exactly. I see them everywhere, singly or in pairs or small groups, women of color decked out in casual finery, in work uniforms, everyday clothes, business suits, many, far too many, overweight, here, there, everywhere in the city streets. Women who are victims of a plot organized to exterminate them. How do I know? Weight the yellow star that marks them for early genocide. Though not a believer in conspiracy theories, I can't deny the evidence of my eyes. Less a matter of knowing than seeing. I watch lots and lots of big colored women pass by every day—young, old, light, dark, tall, short—being fattened for the kill. Lots of them, no doubt, immured in impoverished lives. Poverty of resources and options.

Far, far too many fat beyond dispute. With the slightest effort you can look around for yourself and see. Count the heavy, doomed bodies. Don't take my word. Use your own eyes. Big. Big. Big bodies. Some hard. Some soft. Big booties. A few bloated, obese. As if plenty of fat is ordinary and natural. As if way too much fat no cause for alarm. As if unnecessary Weight nobody's business except those who lug it, hump it around. Don't ask. Don't tell. Weight is fate. Like being designated Black is fate. Cradle to grave.

So many women Black and heavy. It can't be an accident. Is the same somebody who's responsible for the label, *Black,* responsible for the fattening up. Who. Why. And why do the rest of us participate quietly in a plot to tag and remove women of color. Why pretend not to see fat. Why not warn women and men about the damage and imminent,

mortal perils of fat. Any color fat. Why blind ourselves as we blind ourselves to calamitous excesses of wealth that are consuming the nation.

Not totally blind. More a matter of: Now you see them, now you don't.
Sidewalk full of overly large women one moment, and next moment none.
How, where do they disappear. Why do we ignore them and the burden
they bear. A sort of magic trick keeps us from speaking up when we should.
A cheap carney sideshow trick. Devilishly simple and ancient. Sleight of
hand. Willing suspension of disbelief. Trickster snaps a finger and *Presto*,
plays the race card. The fat women are Black women. We are distracted by
whatever cute fripperies and fatal deceptions of race the trickster dangles in
front of our eyes. Black. For a moment the weight, and the ongoing plot to
exterminate women of color become invisible. The long, deadly history of
enslavement and history dogging Black women evaporates.

Black victims of overweight, of race are not victims of a murderous conspiracy, the trickster's card assures us. Race card reminds us the fat ones
are victims of themselves. No one to blame but themselves. Those too
large Black women we see everywhere are not like us, card whispers. Different kinds of creatures going along to get along. Going along to get
along as they usually do. As they must and should, says the trickster. No
other way for them. Going along Black until gone. And gone soon, let's
hope, trickster winks. They are, after all, what they are, aren't they. Black.
Not us. Never us. No matter how desperately they want to be us. Pretend
to be like us. They always remain Black. Thus different. Going along
Black, fat, dirty, loud, hostile, greedy, in heat, dropping baby after baby as
they usually do, and sometimes Black even cute, even having Black fun.

Plenty of paying customers convinced by the evil trickster's magic
show-and-tell. Customers amused sometimes, and also often outraged
by the Black women's antics. The nuisance, obstacles, problems, threats

Black women pose. But not to worry, the trickster comforts his audience. A plan's in place. All those heavy Black bodies crowding the sidewalk not exactly real, not exactly there, and soon they will vanish. Going, going, gone. *Presto,* says the card. Streets, city, country, *presto,* will belong again solely to you, my friends.

If not exactly willing accomplices, most of us are silent accomplices, and our silence lets the show proceed seamlessly. Just as the trickster intends. *Presto.* Fat Black women there or suddenly not there. Trickster's choice. Silence a reassuring habit as we cede to the trickster again and again the right to decide what is in front of our eyes. Surrender our power to deliver reality. Shed the weight of deciding who matters and who doesn't. Who exists or doesn't exist. We see what race tells us to see. Women. Men. White. Black. Fat. Black fat. Yes. No. No. Yes. Going, going-going, gone.

Trickster plays the race card. *Presto.* Street full of fat Black women. Plays it again. *Presto.* Women removed. *Presto.* Plot never sleeps.

Not long ago here in NYC some fucked-up somebody or crew of fuckups decorated a wall with twenty-foot-tall letters: BTM. Sloppy work on the weathered white exterior of a mostly abandoned, six-story building whose ground floor houses a shop selling recycled electrical appliances, and always a jumble of stoves, refrigerators, freezers, their doors removed or propped open, crowds the sidewalk just across from the Williamsburg Bridge after it crosses the water and dips into busy Williamsburg's clutter. Bare, blank, high expanse of wall obviously an eye-catching spot if you wanted to advertise, but I had no clue what the huge white letters BTM, outlined in black, quite hastily it appeared, might stand for. Then about a week after they showed up, one letter was changed and BLM hollers at me from the wall each time I pass.

Given the wall's height, prominent position, its accessibility (you could say inevitability) for eyes gazing from constant streams of traffic back and forth over the bridge, easy to understand why somebody would choose it as a billboard. Easy to figure why the twenty-foot-tall, twenty-foot-wide letters were not neat, since the job of applying them probably would have been hurried, surreptitious, probably perpetrated at night. Easy to speculate that whoever sponsored the job must have been very unhappy until one letter changed, replaced, and all three letters filled in with black paint, so you see BLM now. The bold black letters BLM don't pose a riddle, do they, but I remain puzzled. Stumped by numerous questions about BTM, questions whose answers continue to elude me.

Did some careless or crazy or illiterate or all of the above person(s) carting heavy buckets of paint and willing to climb or scale or dangle at night, roped to the top of a sheer wall on a shaky scaffold, a courageous or well-intentioned or bizarre or wannabe Banksy simply botch his or her assignment and leave behind the letters BTM instead of BLM. Maybe. But before the letters were transformed, before their transformation made up my mind for me and the minds of anybody else encountering them what the letters were supposed to proclaim, the day I saw BTM for the first time on the first leg of a hike and then saw BTM again recrossing the bridge in the opposite direction home, I was mystified. What in hell did BTM signify. What movement or corporation or poor soul needed to impose its identity on a gigantic shithouse wall in Williamsburg.

here I sit lonely hearted/paid a nickel and only farted.

Read that poem long ago, a boy inside a pay toilet in Kennywood, a Pittsburgh, Pennsylvania, amusement park featuring thrill rides and picnic groves where our family celebrated a once a year outing, and I never forgot how silly, how sad, dumb, how small and helpless the words caused me to feel.

Of course Black Lives Matter crossed my mind on the day I discovered giant letters painted on a wall near Williamsburg Bridge, but B T M demanded a life of its own. Independent. Separate from BLM. Many possibilities intriguing me as I dreamed up words which might explain and decode the particular combination of letters somebody saw fit to print on a page of wall. Black Thighs Matter one tempting option, though I was a bit ashamed of myself for thinking it up, trying it on for size, smiling, repeating it a couple times because I liked the sound. Maybe because it brought back how boys talked about girls back in the day we were growing up. And still Jive-talked to each other about girls or to girls, sweet-talking them or street-talked with other guys about girls. Those sweet black thighs matter.

Or maybe BTM appealed because it was my nasty revenge upon the annoyingly ubiquitous, precariously confusing BLM mantra. Confusing because if all lives matter, if all lives precious, why is it necessary to declare BLM. Are people shouting BLM to convince themselves or persuade others. Confusing because I already know good and well that my life matters. So why would I need to solicit somebody else's agreement. Or be grateful if they agree. And anyway, who decides what a color indicates or whether a life matters or not. Who assigns a color to my life? Why? Why Black? Does Black celebrate or condemn my color. Confusing because if those who are attempting to convert people who doubt or outright deny the worth of my life, why would those friends who wish me well, choose the word *Black* to describe my life, the very same word that for centuries in America has embodied inequality and inferiority. A word employed to impose and enforce *race*.

Are Black lives different. Yes and no, the ambiguous reply of BLM. If I chant BLM, am I asserting, whether I intend to or not, that Black absolutely separates and divides. Isn't separation already the problem. One of the ugliest facts of life in America.

Imagine a sign that proclaims in huge red letters, SLAVE LIVES MATTER, a sign painted high up on a white wall in Williamsburg. Once upon a time throngs of Americans in the streets chanting SLM might have pricked the conscience of the master class, and maybe helped to alleviate a few of slavery's most cruel conditions. But the problem is that both slave owners and abolitionists could have shouted SLM enthusiastically. The words don't demand slavery's immediate extinction. SLM doesn't declare that categorizing a person as a slave is a crime, an absolute evil, unacceptable in any way, shape, or form. The words indicated by SLM don't condemn unconditionally a nation that profits from stealing a human being's freedom.

BLM like SLM stops short. Business unfinished, unclarified, unspoken because a critical word—*Black* in one case, *Slave* in the other—is conceded instead of examined and contested.

Just yesterday BLM an inspired rallying cry, then a crucial energizer of efforts to organize, fundraise, and continue a struggle that had temporarily galvanized and unified millions of people who claimed they desired a society free of destructive discrimination and oppression. But maybe BLM has worn out its welcome. Today, in the hands, the mouth of the evil trickster, *Presto*, the words Black Lives Matter become a weapon to divide and conquer. Trickster nods and announces, See. Told you so, didn't I. Race matters and even Blacks agree. Listen to them cheering for their race as they try to jack our lives.

Amen for all the good a BLM movement and logo accomplish, but what if the battle cry BLM also keeps the myth of race alive. Black equals race. And race equals Black. And Black indisputably bad, the myth warns. Thus a campaign to eliminate Black women and Black fat a therapeutic cleansing, not genocide.

The equation of Black and race in American minds continues to matter more than any words anybody can say or unsay. Day I crossed Williamsburg Bridge and was confronted by the letters BTM, though I wasn't exactly dissing BLM, I temporarily retired BLM, and allowed BTM to keep me company all the way home. A kind of singsongy, outrageous refrain I couldn't help repeating, even as each repetition also embarrassed and incriminated me. Mmm-mmm. Black thighs matter. Lives. Thighs. They surely do, bro.

You don't have to live truth to write about truth. You can write and think about the truth as you believe you see it, and not know what truth is. Is that a blessing. Perhaps it is. Yes, it might very well be. Yet finally no consolation. No reprieve. No way out of yourself. You are never forgiven the lies of your life.

Lie of many, too, too many, very large Black creatures not exactly women. Truth of too many women of color bound in chains of fat, marked for slaughter.

Twenty years ago, same year the Twin Towers burned, I published a story entitled "Weight" in a prestigious literary magazine. "Weight" won a national prize and has been reprinted often since. I relate these facts not to brag nor to impress you with my credentials as an expert on the subject of weight, but offer them as a confession of sorts to warn you that despite my earlier disparaging remarks concerning tricksters I, too, am one. And on occasion a successful trickster, paid to keep an audience enthralled. Keeping them distracted while murderous chaos rages round about us. Trickster myself, but not beyond being tricked.

Main character of my prize-winning story a version of my actual, factual mama, and it so happens that Mom was a slim, trim woman, though she thickened some through the middle of her body as most of us do as we age. "Weight" was thus not about the kind of weight measurable in pounds. Its subject metaphysical weight. Weight of the entire world my mother carried around on her shoulders. Her unrelenting determination to bear the burdens and troubles of her colored family and not let the terrible weight crush her or us. In a sense then, I guess you could say the story's subject was weight after all, but only if you translate the word to mean both a particular number of avoirdupois ounces and pounds, but also a numberless amount of them, pounds beyond counting. Impossibly vast beyond words heaviness my mother somehow managed to lift, keep off our backs, and, now and then, while she balanced that incalculable weight on her small, incredibly strong shoulders, she could even perform the miracle of a dance step or whisper a lullaby in my ear.

The hopelessness of railing against race and Black and fat and tricksters finally gets to me one day and wipes clean the slate of morphing, dueling BLM and BTM slogans. Demolishes instantly all my ancient, professed concerns and future plans—including the crusade against fat I presumed I could wage on behalf of too large women of color, my campaign that I supposed could bad-mouth Black fat without bad-mouthing heavy colored people, as if I could dump out dirty bathwater from a tub and not dump the baby sitting in it.

Here's the sight that shuts me up and delivers a final verdict on any pretensions I've ever entertained about what our country could be or what it is, about who I am or could be or wanted to be. Four bodies sprawled facedown in the street, two with hands cuffed behind their backs, a colored mother's kids ages six, twelve, and her two nieces, fourteen, seventeen years old, four bodies flat on the ground so you couldn't tell if they are overweight or not, but could hear them on a police body cam video crying, screaming, pleading, cursing, praying, sobbing after being rousted from their minivan at gunpoint by a bunch of cops responding to the suspicious license plate number of a vehicle in the parking lot of a shopping center just beyond the city limits of Aurora, Colorado, in the middle of a bright afternoon, August 2 in this year of our lord 2020.

Me absolutely helpless, afterall, to terminate atrocities played out in front of my eyes. Helpless, powerless as those helpless, traumatized folk at the mercy of police officers whose professional judgment and humanity go hopelessly missing once they see the colors of young women and girls sitting in a car. Cops believing the colors are Black and thus the females dangerous criminals who must to be treated as such. Cops unforgivably guilty of willingness, readiness to act as judge, jury, executioner when dealing with Black bodies.

I wish for an overwhelming bunch of people, lots of them of all colors, people with large fat sticks to arrive suddenly, materializing within the video framed on my TV screen. I yearn for irresistible waves of good citizens intervening who humiliate, shame, hurt the cops, bruise and bloody them in public on millions and millions of screens like mine, until the cops perhaps awaken. I can imagine no other remedy, no other way to teach that the evil cops perpetrate on others, sure as shit, punishes them likewise. Not exactly a remedy or a cure. Nor a chance to get even by inflicting pain. Not the false, futile, Old Testament, eye for an eye, tooth for tooth revenge that sanctions more destruction but never restores what's been lost. Instead, I'm demanding stunning ocular proof that alerts everybody on this occasion and forevermore, to a line in the sand. Sure, swift consequences if it's crossed. Like the lines power draws and dares anyone to ignore or violate. The lines power maintains violently to maintain power.

But here I sit. Tricked again. Poor, confused, sorry me watching powerless as those pitiful kids on the ground moan, thrash, whimper, beg. Powerless as the mother (is she wearing a BLM T-shirt) flailing, screaming at the cops. What horror's coming next—gunshot, knee on the neck, nightstick, taser, tear gas, or the unspeakable rupture of being captured, stripped naked, transported, exiled to an alien planet.

Why does it always happen one more time, despite years, books, schools, jails, songs, corporations, courtrooms, slogans, governments, banks, churches, protests in America's city streets. Stupid me imagining fat or lack of fat matters. Imagining something should matter. Me daydreaming of exposing a trickster who eradicates lives. Me asking my dumb, hopeless self whether Black lives or black thighs matter more. Or if they're the same. Imagining eyes, weight, words, votes, truth could end the killing.

GEORGE FLOYD STORY

The breath goes now, and some say, No . . .

So let us melt, and make no noise,

No tear-floods, nor sigh-tempests move;

'Twere profanation of our joys

To tell the laity our love

"A Valediction: Forbidding Mourning"
(John Donne)

GEORGE FLOYD IS DEAD WHILE I write this story. If I had written these words approximately a year ago, GF alive. In a year he will not be alive, whether I write or don't write this story about him. Except perhaps alive in the way stories *live,* or alive as people say people are *alive* in stories. People saying that as if they do not understand dead once, dead forever. As if they don't know that once is all the time a person ever gets to be alive. As if they don't know GF doesn't hear, doesn't desire mourning, clamor, and cries. As if they do not comprehend that their millions of bodies piled up or kneeling in prayer or prostrate in the street next to

GF weigh less than this sheet of paper on which I scribble, and that the commotion, agitation, exercise of their millions upon millions of hearts and minds will not summon a single breath of air when GF needs it.

I will not pretend to bring GF to life. Nor pretend to bring life to him. GF gone for good. Won't return. No place for GF except the past. And past not even past, a wise man once declared. Same abyss behind and in front of us is what the wisecracker writer signifying, I believe, and if I truly believe what he believed, where would I situate GF if presented an opportunity to put him somewhere alive. Not here. Not here in this story where I know better.

Better to forget GF. Better to let go or simply leave GF alone, thank you, than attempt to invent the point of view of a person not here, not where I am, a person who somehow possesses the power to see GF breathing, moving around, hear GF's thoughts. A person also able to observe me here, myself performing this grief, this terror and anger, this attempt to console myself and define and control and locate myself, establish myself as one who is offering a story about GF, a true story confirming my suffering, my connection to GF, a story about who he is, who I am, a story about myself, as if I am not here, where I am and he is not where he is. As if the two of us are not permanently separate as life from death. As dreams from objects dreamed.

Better to acknowledge impenetrable darkness surrounding GF and me, black darkness blinding me when I pretend I can speak with the authority of a kind of winged observer I imagine whose perspective absolutely reliable. Why write as if I can access the power such an angelic being might possess. As if I am able to employ that power to see, to enter GF. Power to convince myself or anybody who might be paying attention or reading or simply curious, that my feelings for GF, my performance, outrage, my rituals of claiming and disclaiming an unbreakable relationship to him are valid. Serve some useful purpose. My eyes, words reliable, convincing as words, eyes of that imaginary observer I proposed a few sentences ago. Why call upon some sort of supernatural observer to bear witness. Attempt to own that point of view. Imitating it to move closer to GF. Move outside myself.

I find each move unsatisfactory. A kind of presumption. Wishful thinking at best. Guilt and avoidance at worst. Pretending not to be here where I am, here with many millions of others upset over GF, people who watch online, in lines, who march, throng avenues and streets, behind mics, on TV, in front of TVs, assuming they may be rightfully, righteously blamed perhaps, but also hoping to be spared, forgiven. Given another chance. Here in this place where I am, too. Whether or not I pretend I can inhabit some impossibly different space. A place elsewhere in which I am neither exactly dead or alive, where I am suspended, invisible, yet able to observe myself and observe GF as neither living nor dead. He and I special beings like the one I imagined above, endowed with the power, despite absolute darkness, to observe GF here, to observe me here, despite or because we are not present here, but elsewhere, nowhere in fact, or wherever anybody chooses to imagine or not imagine she or he might be. Wherever I'm pretending I am.

For example, pretending not to breathe. A cop knee *(I know him—know the motherfucker's name)* pressing down on neck. Choking, suffocating me. How long. How long. Hands cuffed behind back. Cop body sits on my body pressing it down in a city street. Many shoes, boots shuffling too close to eyes. Wonder if they will stomp my eyes. Wonder what street. What city. Wonder how long dead while wondering.

How long. How long. How to make it real. Not to bid a victim, loved or unloved, adieu. Not to say farewell. Not leave-taking, not goody, good, goodbye. But return to scene of crime. Recount each blow like a Senator on the Senate floor who produces cinema verite for his colleagues—pounding rostrum POW-POW-POW-POW-POW—56 times in 81 seconds—like cop fists, cop feet strike Rodney King's body 56 hard, loud times—for 81 seconds—ignite cities. Like the 400 blows—*les quatre cent coups,* as the French saying goes—*dirty tricks* delivered blow after blow in a black and white movie for viewers to silently regard—400 uncountable blows beating a boy to his knees. Different strokes for different folks in different countries. Same pain always. Whose. Whose blows. Aghhhhhhh. Whose language did the recorder hear who said Truffaut said: I demand that a film either express joy of making cinema or agony of making cinema. I am not interested in anything in between.

I learn as I read to learn more about goodbyes, farewells to the dead, about narrative art, about protests, protesters, protestations, learn that singer Esther Phillips, née Jones, born colored on December 23, 1935, in Galveston, Texas—two days later and you could call her an Xmas present—learn she recorded, *"Put No Headstone on My Grave,"* a Charlie Rich song in 1981, same year GF turned eight with numerous more live years ahead of him before he's on his back on hard concrete or asphalt of a Minneapolis street begging for more breath, more life than he's going to get. Wondering how he hears, of all things, a blues/church voiced woman singing words he can't quite make out, words gone quick as they come, quick as they go, but slow, too, and sad words no doubt, very gotdamn sad brushing past, he whiffs thick sad on them, sad in a voice sad as blues and church, sad, slow, quick as a very last breath nobody ever hears anyway neck squeezed in a vise or not . . . *Oh, don't, don't, don't/Don't put no headstone on my grave . . . all my life I been a slave . . . just put me down and let me be . . . free from all this misery . . . tell my mother not to cry . . . tell her I'm finally free . . . don't put no headstone . . .* words passing, dangling, no place to go like the man seen dangling from a rope ain't going no-place else but there where he sways in that old south story old people tell, and some soul long ago snapped photos still scare the shit out me, out GF, but ain't him, ain't me, is it exactly she sings to, sings for. Timing all wrong, and anyway another country, bro, and besides, (August 7, 1984) the bitch dead. And we outlive King, too, don't we—drowned in his own swimming pool (June 17, 2012).

ACCUSED . . .

WHEN IT STARTED THE SNOW looked like rain . . . when snow started it looked like rain . . . snow looked like rain when it started . . . looked like rain when snow started . . . it looked like rain when snow started . . . looks like rain when snow starts . . . snow when it started looks like rain . . . snow starts and looked like rain . . . when snow started looked like rain . . . it looks like rain when snow starts . . . snow when it starts looks like rain . . . and twenty minutes or so later motorcycle after motorcycle drifts down slowly through the air outside the same window where I had seen snow start . . . motorcycle after motorcycle falling, floating in the sky . . . and an hour or so after that I gaze up again and nothing out the window until I push away from the table where I write and stand staring at a maze of treetops visible each time I look from nine floors up, clusters of trees doing their quiet business of decorating spaces between identical, twenty-story, redbrick towers of the complex in which I reside, or canopy of trees decorating a park visible from my window, a couple blocks of park until city resumes, endless stacks of city spreading towards rivers, bridges, jutting skyscrapers, toward more and more seemingly endless stacks of itself beyond the few blocks below organized to contain slides, swings, volleyball, tennis and hoop courts, benches, fences, walkways, public toilet, etc. . . . trees looking each time the same way I saw them last, a second ago or seasons ago, trees both different and same each time always except now every bare, black branch crusted white and I swear I can almost hear the particularly silent lost and found presence of them as if I've never seen leafless trees the color of snow before or will again.

When I was a boy growing up, if I played the game of stopping in my tracks very close to the one of the buildings whose street-level floors held shops and businesses lining Homewood Avenue and craned my neck backward until all I saw was sky and edges of the highest rooftops and let my eyeballs go backward even further into my skull while I stared up, I could trick my eyes into believing the stores, bank, church, every building whose uppermost edge I saw above me was beginning slowly, slowly to move, starting maybe ever so slowly to lean away from me or topple over on me or maybe beginning to rise and drift, higher and higher, it seemed, maybe forever it seemed till the instant my eyes tricked me back for playing a trick on them and slightly dizzy, uncertain whether buildings were swimming in the sky or not, I had to look down at my feet to be sure they were planted firmly on sidewalk where they were supposed to be. Why remember that now. Or remember a wind-whipped white bedsheet, the star for a few seconds in a scene from a recent TV movie, some anonymous Turkish somebody's anonymous sheet on a line hung out to dry between high windows of some anonymous multistoried tenement in Istanbul, a single white sheet flapping in the breeze, stunning me to forget myself, then stunning me back to myself just as quickly to remember a boy daydreaming some unnameable power changing everything.

Why, you ask. Tell me why, you say. How could you, you ask. But I have nothing to say. Once accused of doing something awful, what is there ever left to say. The accusation, spoken aloud, sits there undeniable, unchangeable. A fact hard and cold as terrible acts committed or not committed. Undeniable, unchangeable like all acts, all facts that words attempt to piece together or undo.

Rain . . . snow . . . wind . . . or simply *weather,* simply let me say weather because weather always true, always simply there, isn't it, no matter how many different people report differently what weather was like. Or not like. Not like, I say, not like you think, I insist, even if you had been there and not here, not here sinking with me in this fucked up city where rats nest in treetops and pigeons, blind as bats, trapped underground where they swoop and flutter and can't find a way out, scampering across subway platforms or wobble-wobble along a rail, wobbly like drunk like pigeons wobble tilting sideways from one tiny foot to the other, pigeons streaking catacomb walls and and station floors with shit everybody knows is white and nasty, but can't see, and steps in it, brings shit home on shoe soles, but too dark down here to see the color white or any other color or lack of color or see gigantic predators, gull-winged, pelican-beaked, who also glide and feed in the daylight of city streets above but are as invisible up there as in subterranean darkness pursuing and consuming pigeons that coo and crash and burn cooing in tunnels where rats will migrate again once summer's done.

So weather. Weather, I will say. No. Not *whether or not.* Just weather. Weather. Or say once upon a time . . . begin there. Except we both know better, don't we. Both of us tired of this exercise, these word games . . . my tunnel vision . . . two wobbles forward, two wobbles back. No end in sight. Let alone no light at the end. Let alone blind, anyway. Or worse . . . please. Please forgive me . . . please . . .

ATLANTA MURDERS

TWO CHICKENS (UNCONCERNED ABOUT THE metaphysics of why) cross the road, and once safely on the other side, one chicken says to the other, "I'm confused. I try hard to make sense of how they treat us, but it just gets more confusing the harder I try. A message in green letters on a package of sliced, smoked chicken breast wrapped in see-through plastic and distributed by a company called Applegate, claims that all chickens Applegate kills, butchers, and sells are *humanely raised.* If you know in advance that you are preparing captive, living creatures to be slaughtered and eaten, how in the world can you raise them *humanely.* Does *humanely* mean keeping your victims ignorant of their fate? Pretending to yourself you don't know their fate? Minimizing their day-to-day suffering? Organizing their extermination so it's swift and painless as possible? Or does *humanely* simply mean nothing. Except whatever human beings want the word to mean. Whatever serves the purposes and desires of the kind of gods they imagine themselves to be."

The conversation between chickens recorded above (actually, more like a single chicken's monologue) expires in far less time than either chickens or humans can conceive. Why shouldn't it. Who needs it. Why should words be preserved once the conveyor belt carrying them (and carrying talking chickens, their conversation, my attempt to reproduce it, me, you, etc.) passes the point of no return, and instead of a couple of chickens chatting, there are two eviscerated fowls dangling from hooks along with countless others of their kind all in a row. Like those four & twenty blackbirds or *naughty boys* baked in a pie in an old nursery rime who ride the belt, too. Plenty room for naughty boys, for music, rimes, tales, betrayals, opinions, for empires to rise and collapse during a conversation between chickens. The truth being, afterall, nothing lasts longer than that, because everything fits or at least seems to fit into space occupied and generated by a single thought. Everything expiring as fast and gone as quickly as each moment anybody uses to get here or there or anywhere. For instance, me thinking about how James Baldwin felt about being asked in 1981 by an editor at *Playboy* magazine to write about murders of colored children in Atlanta.

Before the conveying belt moves an inch further, he, Mr. James Baldwin, after flying to Atlanta, will find himself back home in Harlem or Saint-Paul de Vence in the south of France puzzled by the fact a man suspected of killing two young guys was convicted of those crimes after a grueling trial, but also presumed to be guilty, without a trial or evidence, of slaying twenty some other colored children, two or so of them female. Who knew how many more than four & twenty murders of young colored people in Atlanta had been ignored. Who knew why it was okay for those killings to remain unsolved.

How many murders had James Baldwin been paid to go to Atlanta and investigate. Comment upon. Make sense of. The killing of each Atlanta child a conundrum, as he might say, at least as deeply mysterious as the ancient one concerning which comes first, the chicken or the egg. And Baldwin discovers, of course, that neither he nor anybody else able really to shed much light on moments passed by once, never seen again, because the belt moves on. Leaves behind only metaphysical, metaphorical, unanswerable questions and worries and missing children, and plucked, decapitated chickens dangling. But since faith, like superstition, requires no evidence, and hope is enough to substantiate belief, perhaps it's good enough, in lieu of ocular or any other species of proof, to begin examining Baldwin's puzzlement and frustration in Atlanta by quoting a conversation between two chickens on their way to having their throats slit or to a bath in electrified water that stuns them senseless or gas that chokes them quiet.

The words quoted above, spoken just as two chickens arrive on the opposite side of a road they cross, occupy the same space, occupy an instant inseparable, indistinguishable from this one or from the instant in which all chickens and the rest of us will meet our maker. A place as good as any to begin thinking about terror in Atlanta. To begin thinking about stories James Baldwin, among others, invents to convince readers he was there in Atlanta and appalled. *Evidence of Things Not Seen,* Mr. Baldwin wryly entitles his book. His witness of troubles he reports. Troubles both unseen, and ancient and everlasting as faith.

On assignment, poking around in the ruins of a city, a nation, Baldwin could barely contain his rage. His eyes, his sentences recoil from atrocities committed long before, during, and after his stay. There seemed no end, no beginning to evil work perpetrated in Atlanta. Killings of colored children, discarding their bodies, the terror and shame of finding them goes on and on because killing cannot accomplish what it is determined to achieve: absolute separation of Blacks from Whites. Whites from Blacks, etc. And thus the work continues, even though it reeks, and decent citizens disapprove. The work's presence and momentum irreversible, Baldwin observes, no matter how many see or don't see, or how many perceive the work finally, clearly as curse and abomination.

Sort of work, I'm ashamed to confess, I, too, a colored brother, embarked upon at least once, fatally poisoning myself with an idea of separation I dreamed up to serve myself, protect myself, and rule all I surveyed. I labored for most of my life to sustain the illusion I had no brother. Or none, at least, I was obligated to respect as an equal. I called again and again upon every means at my disposal, fair or foul, to separate myself from a brother, from a shadow I believed dogged and threatened me. Eternal vigilance necessary to sustain separation. Permanent separation to preserve absolutely the distance and superiority I desired.

Such a brother, the kind I was, grows up fearing the brother he denies and refuses to acknowledge. Brother whose existence he also desperately needs in order to reassure himself and to prove to others that he, the firstborn, is the better brother. The deserving one. Keeping track of his brother becomes an obsession. Surveillance of his brother as relentless and consuming as that of a lover whose deepest worry is being unloved, insignificant, less than nothing in the beloved's eyes. A lover's eyes, brother's eyes avoided, never interrogated because unbearable truth may shine in them.

Uncertainty about what his brother's eyes might reveal can drive a brother a bit crazy. He invents magical encounters in which he's totally in control of what his brother thinks and feels. Plays games of coaxing, teasing, tricking a brother to draw him closer, to make him join in the games. Then hurt him. Cause him to disappear. Until needed again and summoned once more. Again and again. I stand convicted of this murderous hocus-pocus, and I believe the killer of Atlanta children probably practiced it, too. Most likely he enjoyed the games. *Hey, guy. Where you headed. You like ice cream. Wanna ride in this nice car, lil buddy.*

When I think about colored children murdered in Atlanta, more than a score of dead children in less than two years, I hear trains loaded with crated chickens clucking on the way to market. I hear Malcolm, November 22, 1963, welcoming chickens coming home to roost. Hear hum of the conveyor belt on rails I'm riding with everybody to hell. But I also hear sometimes John Coltrane playing his horn while he rides, making music to keep pace, stay steady, or even occasionally leaping ahead, *Out of this world.* Same music of the first language I experienced as a child. My mother's voice not unlike warbling noises chickens cluck-cluck softly at each other. People saying, *Hi . . . or Bye, bye . . . Bye, bye.* Bye-bye waved to each other with silent hands. Eyes dancing bye. Bye and hello. *Bye 'n bye a place, a destination unnameable, but reachable* with words my people sang, words their bodies formed. A place where, when I was a child, I believed and hoped I would arrive one day to join the conversation. My people's words not exactly words nor a language, but exchanges, a back-and-forth instilling, constituting a sort of faith within me as I listened to them spoken or anticipated them or found I could echo them, feel them, then speak them aloud inside, into space where I believed there were others listening, others who heard words, sounds, heard music I heard.

Bye'n bye. Bye, bye, baby, goodbye. Rockabye, baby / in a treetop. Doo-wop. *A Love Supreme.* "My Favorite Things."

Last time in Atlanta I traveled there to attend my brother's funeral, brother the first of four siblings born after me, four years younger, the brother closest to my age. Least close to me in most ways other than age because when he arrived I desperately desired no sibling and managed quite adroitly the atrocity of ignoring a brother's existence, from the moment he was born until the last time I viewed his face in an open casket in Atlanta, Georgia.

James Baldwin, surrounded by evidence of dead colored kids in Atlanta, explains to you quite precisely why I pick the word *atrocity* to describe work of keeping my brother year after year after year invisible within my heart of hearts. Hard, atrocious work for sure. Denying him, denying he was my brother, denying myself an opportunity to change, to grow after four years in which I had reigned supreme, only child in our three-person household of mother around always, father sometimes. Then a new brother. Precious chance for me to start unlearning selfishness. To grow up and stop pretending, as my father reminded me more than once with a cold stare which pierced and menaced, *you best stop your going round here acting like ain't nobody else here but you.* But I couldn't stop coveting, guarding my turf, acting like someone had anointed me lord and master forever in our tiny empire of family. Dirty work, and despite my mother's tears, dangerous stares now and then from my father warning me to cease and desist, I continued my work undercover. Constant vigilance to detect, to anticipate, to destroy any threat to my sovereignty a brother posed.

An emptiness exists inside me that I share with others so I don't mind others seeing it. That implacable emptiness filling and surrounding all of us, eternally in place, it seems, to ignore and mock us, especially when we strive to better our lives. It is that universal emptiness I strive to make visible when I write or when I shrug off some national or international calamity or foolishness or open my arms wide in despair to lament collective loss, public failure. But then there is another emptiness, deeper, unshareable, belonging solely to me, that I conceal. Often from myself, always from others. I dread the unique, empty loneliness hidden inside me. If it is outed, I will be gone. Vast emptiness will prevail, and I will vanish. Consumed like those fifty billion chickens humans devour yearly. Sometimes I worry I may have disappeared already, swept here, there, and away. Gone in the same quick, quick breath of air the conveyor belt moves past too fast to remember I need.

Mothers of Atlanta's slain children learned James Baldwin in town. Squabbled about whether or not to contact him. Famous colored writer could publicize their plight. An ally. His celebrity voice empowering their campaign, encouraging silent fellow citizens to acknowledge the mothers' brutal loss, fright, misery, grief. But is he trustworthy. Shouldn't it be him seeking out the mothers. Begging their forgiveness. Pledging allegiance to their cause. Could a writer's words truly bring to Atlanta that divine justice the world allegedly contains.

How long will he stay. What does he really want. Could he help mothers expose and shame the city officials who avoid them, ignore their pleas. Officials who do little or nothing then claim in a press conference during a rare visit to a colored neighborhood long ago abandoned to its ghetto fate, that they, mayor, cops, city council are doing everything possible to catch a killer, stop the killing.

Who would use whom. And who is this writer, anyway, the mothers ask. This dark-skinned, small man. A stranger, or maybe more like some kinda pussyfoot talking alien from another planet folks say. Him flitting around, groping around, asking questions about Atlanta anybody with a brain already knows the answers to. Odd-looking fellow, rumored to be a preacher's son, writer whose pages, some readers swear, burn with Old Testament fire and eloquence. But how many missing children will his words find and restore to their families, how many dead children resurrect.

Atlanta, city of mourning mothers, also *city too busy to hate.* Enlightened capital of the new South. City renowned for compromise. Mothers might think themselves trapped, besieged by poverty, ignorance, and violence, but better days a-coming, aren't they, if mothers practice patience. Teach themselves and their offspring to wait and hope. The president of Tuskegee University, Booker Taliaferro Washington, delivered that famous opinion in 1895, in a speech known forever after as the Atlanta Compromise. But William Edward Burghardt Du Bois, busy at work in Atlanta University, disagreed heartily, vocally with BTW's blueprint for transforming separation and segregation—those immemorial Southern facts of life—into benefits for people of color.

Whoa, hollered WEBD. Get real, BTW. Just how are we supposed to stop being victims of separation if we lower our expectations of equality, if we surrender the vote, our civil rights, and accept second-class citizenship. Accept the very terms of separation and powerlessness our oppressors chose so they could reimpose slavery upon us after slavery no longer the law of the land. Why are you advising us to willingly agree to a bargain that institutionalizes separation, a compromise which destroys independence and dignity, forfeits the only tools we posses to combat a condition of perpetual, demeaning segregation. Are not you, Mr. Washington, putting cart before horse.

Set down your buckets where you are, replied BTW. Burn down the house, Jimmy B concludes.

My younger brother, first sibling born after me, left Pittsburgh, Pennsylvania, where our family raised us and most of our clan still resides. Went to Atlanta to work for American Airlines as a baggage handler and raise a family. Didn't return to Pittsburgh very often for visits. Money short maybe. But I believe he also enjoyed being far away.

I ask the quiet chicken (though both of them probably quiet by now) who I spied crossing the road with his talkative chicken friend, if he shares the confusion his companion expressed.

Me. Shit no, he replies. Never believed a word you *humanes* said. Always knew I was a chicken and I knew, whatever else came out youall's mouths or whatever else you stuffed in your mouths, you motherfuckers ate chickens.

Funny you put it that way, sir. Just yesterday I was sitting at my writing desk, doing my best to stay still and quiet so I could overhear what I was trying to think about, and the simple fact came to me that as far as color goes and the question of what I am, Black or White, shit, like you just said about being a chicken, I always knew the answer. Or rather it didn't matter which color, Black or White, because if the question arose in an uncomfortable situation and maybe got me confused a quick minute, no problem—somebody always there who knew the answer, no doubt about it. Some good soul more than ready to enlighten me, you know. So like you say you always understood you were a chicken, me, from my kid days on, I always knew I was Black. And knew even if I got to be king of the world, I better watch my black ass cause I would be a *Black* king.

You are correct, Mr. Chicken. Everybody agrees. Agrees, just as you assert, Mr. Chicken. Agrees about color. Agrees about chickens and brothers. The only thing I can do is beg your forgiveness. Forgive them. Forgive me. Just like the fact a person's got to eat, there's the fact a person got to be one color or the other. Even if one color mixed up with a bit of the other. So yes. No. Not confused about what I am. Being a color no problem for me. Just like being a chicken no problem for you.

Uh-huh, the chicken replies. Chicken what I am. Always knew I was. Even if I didn't like it, I liked knowing it. That's what they call me, anyway, chicken, in the chicken eaters' language. So don't matter much what we call ourselves. They rule. They decide we are subject to be eaten and most of us are eaten. Unless we're allowed to hang around awhile and lay eggs. Which some of us can't, and no telling if the ones who can lay eggs very happy about them extra days they earn. Days they see their babies scrambled up, boiled, fried. And anyhow, sooner or later, mamas wind up with the rest us riding the slaughterhouse belt.

Now I may only be a chicken, but try to pretend a minute we're more like friends, friends together in this shit. And listen closely, please. This is important. Any creature can learn any other creature's language when necessary. Learn to speak it quite well. We both know that, don't we. For instance, *them* not the proper word to place in front of *extra days* in my little speech above. I may not talk their damned language perfectly, according to the book, but what I'm saying is lots of times my mistakes are on purpose. Not to *keep it real,* as some crossovers believe they keep it real when they steal a ghetto phrase or try to imitate old Southern down-home rhythms and syntax to spice up whatever lie they trying to tell. Huh-uh.

I mess with the rules of their language because I don't trust language. Any goddamned body's language. Language not substantial evidence of anything. Ain't never been one of the faithful who believe it is. And I sure don't believe any talk, any writing closer to real than any other kind. Even a chicken can figure that out.

All daydreams equally daydreaming. Equally unreal. Not about real. So my fuckups, my departures from the official sanctioned script of some expert's idea of what's supposed to be correct, may be sins of chicken ignorance, but often also are intentional signs of me working to keep my distance, working to remember my distance from whatever language, from whichever set of assumptions and superstitions I happen to employ. Ain't nobody truly listening, anyway. Why should they. Nobody gives a flying fuck whether a chicken expresses suffering eloquently or not. Correctly or not. In Igbo or Mandarin. Or with numbers, statistics or algorithms. People eat chickens. Including people who devise and corrupt and police language. The way it is, was, and gonna be.

I'm a mere chicken. Not my place to suggest to other creatures some universal guilt trip or reformation of ancient ways. After all, I'm well known to eat whatever I can get my beak on, even wormy remains of an Atlanta child if a murdered one disposed of in garbage I forage that litters the barnyard where I'm incarcerated. Does confessing to having no scruples locate me a tiny bit higher or lower on the evolutionary scale than creatures who claim scruples.

But I do have something to say about Atlanta and confusion. Just after you noticed me crossing the road with a loquacious road buddy, I interviewed the creature who would be convicted in an Atlanta courtroom of slaying a pair of colored males, males too old to be called children, but definitely childlike creatures of the same *Black* kind, newspapers said, as the one who murdered them.

Interviewed maybe not exactly the correct word for the exchange between myself and the killer. Happened so fast don't know exactly how to describe it. But everything flies past that swiftly, don't it. Isn't that the point of your conveyor belt image. Insufficiency of human enjoyments, or words to that effect, I believe is what you wished to infer, didn't you.

Anyway, after I had been rubbed with salt, spiced, basted, roasted in the oven, there I lay steaming, cooling finally, my breast nicely tanned, thighs scorched dark, my feetless legs splayed, asshole stuffed with cornbread stuffing, displayed on a large platter with tiny painted chickens decorating its scalloped edges. Platter resting on a table in the dining room of the Atlanta murderer's family. A prayer was muttered by the three of them, father, mother, killer son. Then absolute silence lasting way too long. I could feel their eyes appraising me. With admiration, perhaps, or awkwardness, or begging forgiveness, or perhaps for a split second after praying, they had forgotten or recollected far too clearly what came before or comes next, or most likely, the lunkheads had become hopelessly distracted, befuddled, restless. I'm certain they were hungry and desired fervently an end to the prayer ritual, and deep, deep inside wanted to believe that their work, their exchange of words with me truly had been completed, once and forever. That finally they could consume me in peace. Anyway at that precise instant, into their silence I injected myself.

Summoning the courage of my convictions, courage that had overcome oven and a carving knife, I stood, feet restored, and shook all my colorful, missing tail feathers. Strutted up and down that table, clucking and cock-a-doodle-dooing loud enough to wake up every sleeping soul in Atlanta. And though it may have come a little too late to do much good, I sure did enjoy that *Amen*. That good riddance. *Amen,* I cockle-doodled. And it ain't quite over yet, youall.

SOMEONE TO WATCH OVER ME

I HAVE ALWAYS THOUGHT *FIGMENT* a funny word. Not ha ha funny. More like odd, strange. *Fig* plus *ment*. A fig a fruit and I can almost see one when I read the word *fig*. But *ment*. What's meant by *ment*. What happens to a *fig* when you add *ment* to it. Sticking *ment* on words doesn't always create odd, new words. Quite common for language to add ment to words. Off the top of my head I can think of plenty. *Establishment, entertainment* for example. Perhaps what's strange about the word *figment* and some other words ending with *ment*, is that when the piece (segment) or word that precedes *ment* is familiar, a noun or verb with its own obvious meaning when it stands alone, sometimes those words do and sometimes they don't undergo unpredictable changes of meaning when *ment* is hooked to them. Which is to say you can't depend upon what you know about a word once *ment* gets attached to it. Quite a confusing situation if you think about it.

More than confusing. Chaotic maybe. A pig or a fig are familiar to most people, but pig doesn't mean an animal when you read *pigment,* and *fig* not a fruit when it precedes *ment. Seg*, on the other hand, doesn't ring any bell in my vocabulary, and probably foreign to most people, because *seg*, unlike *pig* or *fig*, is not a noun, and thus has little or no meaning when it appears in a familiar word like *segment*.

But who knows. In due time *seg* may be incorporated into the language as *frag* has been adopted and become a new word. *Seg* standing alone one day like *frag* stands alone now. Like *seg*, *frag* had little or no previous history as a noun or verb. But nowadays *frag* is often used as a verb to express a peculiar nastiness humans inflict upon one another, and though *frag* still not quite a noun yet, not like *pig* and *fig* are common nouns, I bet *frag* sooner or later will come to signify a piece or part. Such a possibility likely because the word *fragment* has been around for ages, and thus in the future, a *frag* may come to be understood as a portion or piece or part or remnant of something that used to be a larger something else, until somebody blew it up. None of those various confusing, perhaps random, goings on that transform the meaning of words or nonwords when they precede *ment,* helps to clarify the meaning of *ment,* do they. Language a predicament. Creates as many impediments as inducements when one tries to understand what words mean. Or understand the entitlements language grants a word.

Consider, for instance, how many permutations, combinations or algorithmically determined mutations of meaning language can produce by combining in a single sentence words that start with *fig, pig, seg,* or *frag*. Consider how in our society a figment of pigment segregates and fragments a society.

Perhaps language never makes sense. We just get used to it and used to pretending that it does. Used to pretending we are content, whether contentment does or does not make sense. Because who, afterall, doesn't desire what I desire. Someone to watch over me.

JORDAN

MY NIECE NAMED HER SECOND son Jordan. A magical name, she must have been thinking. A name to connect her son with Michael Jordan's magic on the court, his fame and good fortune. A name with more in it than she or I or anybody could have guessed. Power to raise the dead in the name my niece chose. Power of the dead to raise the living.

For reasons that I am not proud of, I have lost track over the years of my niece's Jordan. Haven't keep up with MJ either. Except recently, a documentary, *The Last Dance,* whose subject is the vexed but ultimately victorious pursuit of a sixth and final NBA championship by Jordan and his Chicago Bulls teammates, revived my romance with MJ's fabulous exploits, my hero worship of him that verged always uncomfortably close to idolization, and thus inevitably tinged by envy, insecurity, vanity, unrequited love.

My niece's Jordan was about six years old in 1998 when the Bulls danced off into the sunshine of eternal glory and MJ retired. By then I had met Michael Jordan and his fellow Bulls, written articles about them for national magazines, and basically lost touch with my nephew. We lived in different cities, and usually Jordan was in a swarm of other family kids when I saw him—smallish, his skin a few shades darker than most of the others, a bit shy and quiet. Beyond the fact that he loved turtles, liked reading and school, and never forgot to remind me that I'd promised all the kids a Christmas holiday in Disney World, he remained a cute little stranger. From his older brothers he had picked up the habit of watching sports on TV, pro football mostly, since everybody in Pittsburgh loved the hometown Steelers, but I had not noticed nor had anyone ever mentioned any particular aptitude or ambition that Jordan possessed to follow in MJ's footsteps, to *be like Mike*, unless you counted the extra incentive that might drive a boy to achieve something special back then because his skin color was MJ-dark and marked him as a sort of outsider.

Jordan still resided in my niece's belly in October of 1992 when I arrived in Pittsburgh to pick up my father and travel with him to Promise-land, a small, virtually extinct town in South Carolina from which, in 1900, my father's father—my grandfather Hannibal—had migrated to find work in Pittsburgh, Pennsylvania. Going to Promiseland was long overdue. A return-to-our-roots trip I had promised my father and my-self. Just as once upon a time I promised Jordan and the other kids a trip to Disney World. Grandpa was dead at least a decade, so he wouldn't be accompanying my father and me on the journey I had originally envisioned for the three of us, and no time to spare, since my dad was clearly on his last legs, only question being: Which would fail him utterly first, body or mind? That powerful boxer's body and swift hands, or that even swifter, tougher mind he had exhausted fighting every day of his life for the dignity and space that were supposed to be a guaranteed birthright (in theory, anyway) for all Americans? For my father, because color was a rule always there lurking behind the scenes—hidden sometimes, though sometimes definitely not—his life was a battle commencing each morning to find self-respect, fighting for room to breathe from the moment he opened his eyes till he closed them at night. A tiresome, wearying, consuming struggle he waged daily to endure.

Never got round to a Disney excursion with Jordan, and almost lost the chance to have my father accompany me to Promiseland, but set off finally we did, limping, you could say, my father already almost a ghost of himself, but not quite. Him—body holding pretty steady, mind faltering often—still the daddy and me still the son, he let me know. Although my father was a son too: my father's father riding with us, Grandpa's presence materializing more and more the closer we got to where our trip would take us. To Jordan, it turns out. This was not the destination my father nor I had anticipated, but we would find Jordan—another Jordan besides the boy who would be born in Pittsburgh while we were in South Carolina, and not the hoop star Jordan either. A third Jordan who'd been around long before MJ was born, long before basketball was born.

A Jordan we would find present in Promiseland. Someone my father and I were unaware of when we departed Pittsburgh. A surprise like the news we would hear when we returned to Pittsburgh and learned that my niece had delivered a son and had named him four or five days before she heard our news that the most ancient ancestor we had unearthed in South Carolina, my great-grandfather's father, was *Jordan,* an enslaved man. His name, age (twelve years), and price noted on the original bill of sale dated 1841, deposited in an Abbeville archive.

And that could be the story. Jordan's story could end there. An odd, entertaining coincidence. A glimpse at how the eternal, celestial spheres play games more magical than even the legerdemain that MJ exhibited on the court.

Omar says, C'mon, little man. You the one wanted to go here so bad. C'mon. Keep up, knucklebrain. Jordan looks beyond ole mighty mouth Omar who got something to say bout everybody, everything. Looks past

Om and the string of family kids, siblings, cousins various sizes, but none shorter, none darker than he is, looks ahead to where their tall, tall uncle Jordan in the lead hustles them on to the next ride, next exhibit hall, next sweet treat Uncle has in mind, touring the whole huge Disney World park when all he wants, Uncle Jordan please, please, is lemme go back please and get at the end of the line again and go again on one those tall, fast-turning, scary wheels, Uncle, no need to hurry, to hurry up hurry up and see all the rest, happy if we go no further than that single great ride one more time, Uncle, it fly you, squeeze you, scary enough make you bout to pee, don't it. Jordan doesn't bother to shout out what he's thinking. Best not. Who would hear, care? All the Disney World noise and musics and bells and whistles and screams, how anybody sposed to hear what you were saying let alone hear what you were thinking all that long way away his voice would have to run to catch up with his uncle Jordan strolling quick, far up ahead, all the kids trailing him in Disney World. Probably it's me just dreaming anyway and who in the whole wide world hears you when you asleep? Don't make no sense, do it, anyway, he thinks. None of this. He ain't in no Disney World anyhow, him wanting to go there so bad and now a dark, real dark uncle, dark as his real father got all the kids in tow. Too much. Couldn't be true. Gwan, turn over and go back to sleep, boy.

The day my niece and I took two cars and carted Jordan along with a bunch of family kids, and a few who are not, for soft ice cream at the Dairy Queen off the Boulevard of the Allies in Pittsburgh, it breaks my heart when I realize he is scared to say what flavor he wants. Tongue-tied, Jordan just stares and stares at the costumed colored girl serving behind a counter almost tall as him. Stares and stares up at her as if dumbstruck or spellbound or maybe instantly in love, engaging in a silent exchange with the pretty server, back and forth a couple few times before he freezes and his gaze drops a final time, deeper than shy, deeper than she can follow, and I realize Jordan can't summon a word—*chocolate* or *raspberry* or *blueberry ripple* or *pistachio*—not because he hasn't memorized every flavor or because he can't read them perfectly well from posters on the wall, or even that he doesn't know exactly which flavor he desires, but because he doesn't want to risk people laughing if he calls out the wrong one.

Back to the dead. With my father I discover that they, the dead, are all the family we have left in the little ghost village of vanished shacks or whatever it is exactly that some locals still call Promiseland. Gone except for maybe a couple hundred folks spread out here and there on land once belonging to the old Marshall Plantation, land surrounding a school erected in the empty space where Promiseland used to be. That's what everybody told us. By luck we were able to visit a school on the very day set aside by the local people of color each year to gather and picnic and celebrate and commemorate the ancestors who had founded this place. A school, an abandoned gas station, a few collapsing shanties, a shed that formerly housed a grocery store, perched on a few acres of bare ground memorializing the site of Promiseland.

Two thousand seven hundred forty-two acres of Marshall Plantation purchased in 1869 by the South Carolina Land Commission may have been intended originally for the benefit of colored people who had been enslaved. However, the state legislature's mixed motives, corruption, the shameless and systematic collusion between politicians and old-regime landowners diverted state funds appropriated for settling the newly freed. The Commission's project gutted rapidly. Land to help the needy plundered by the greedy.

Land the Commission was authorized to buy and redistribute could have been conceived not as a gift but as righteous payback, as proper compensation or reparation, but instead the Commission offered freedmen small plots of land for sale. Though full of aspiring folks hungry for a chance to own land, to farm and start new, independent lives, the defeated Confederacy did not contain many colored consumers with ready cash or credit. A war-torn, bleeding South contained instead legions of destitute colored people. Homeless, penniless women, men, and children roaming the countryside or adrift in war-ravaged cities. People whose unpaid labor just yesterday had sustained the South's economy, people whose subservient condition in the previously dominant social structure had reinforced the idea that *Whites* belonged to a superior race. In such a context the notion of creating communities like Promiseland has always been chimerical. Especially since, in its heart of hearts, the wounded American South did not desire a prosperous, free colored population. Rather, the South was desperate to restore absolute control over its former property, recapture their labor, rebuild a slave economy, reduce colored people once more to a subhuman status that would reassure Whites that their *whiteness* signified superiority and thus entitled them to command, buy and sell, transport, whip, fuck coloreds as they pleased.

Except for a few colored families both extremely lucky and extraordinarily endowed with fortitude, courage, wisdom, and stubbornness that enabled them to buy a plot of land and retain it even until the present moment, Promiseland was a species of wishful thinking. A rumor like the gift of forty acres and a mule promised but never handed over for even a temporary, trifling while to those whose labor in the fields and forests had created a Cotton Kingdom. No, unh-uh, that promised land, those rumored mules never belonged even an instant to the newly, officially, *free at last, free at last,* free people the U.S. government had chosen to designate as slaves.

So in the once-thriving colored community of Promiseland, my father and I discovered only dead family to greet us. Host us. And magically they did just that. Did not disappoint. Their names and stories were spoken and welcomed us in the tiny gym of the building where a lucky few had attended school when they were allowed. Though of course my father and I also shared a sadness beyond words with all those dead who once upon a time had conceived us and sent us north, south, east, west to make lives for ourselves they would never see, lives as mysterious to them as their ghosts would be to us.

Do you remember the story of the Boy in the Bubble? I do. Quite well. Big news back in the early seventies when I was in my early thirties. People fascinated by a newborn who had to live every moment of his life confined in plexiglass. A boy who would die unless ingenious doctors and machines kept him separate from the air normal human beings breathe and walk around in. A kind of sci-fi story. Evoked wonder, awe. A sadness too. His extreme isolation pitiful. A horror story. Boy touchable only with rubber gloves fitted into his capsule.

The harder they tried to describe the world outside his plastic cage and tried to explain why he could not survive there, the more the boy wanted to go there, I bet. I'm only guessing, of course. Guessing about what he thought or felt. Can't ask him. Or see him. Wonder if the bubble he inhabited still exists in a museum somewhere. Emptied of him. As now he's free of it.

The boy's situation was an obvious, painfully appropriate metaphor for the bubble of color and race I was born into and had never escaped. His story reminded me to feel sorry for myself. My self-pity, my identification with him might have afflicted me much more drastically if I had not had the father and mother I did, if I hadn't already accumulated thirty-some years of life before I learned about the boy's plight. Grown-up enough to accept the fact that all stories (including my own) were species, more or less, of sci-fi. Fairy tales laced with devils, angels, monsters, magic. Each of us time-traveling blind as we negotiate a vast darkness.

Eventually, NASA engineers constructed a miniature space suit so the boy could venture outside the bubble. But since this opportunity frightened him and encumbered his freedom of movement without truly releasing him, he tried the clumsy gear only a few times. Death almost certainly the outcome if the boy attempted life with no bubble or suit, the experts predicted, but the experts could devise no other options. As year after year passed, the boy's unhappiness and restlessness increased, his dissatisfaction and misery deepened, and so despite being aware of the probably fatal consequences of their choice, the boy's parents finally acceded to his wishes and demands. Gave him a chance for a life shared with other people, an uncaged life beyond the artificial skin sealing others out, sealing him in. He lasted just hours outside his tent.

Jordan knew better, knew that despite his not-great size, he was too big a boy to cry. But cry he did for Om, his large, rough, strong, funny cousin he always had wanted to be. Omar not twenty and shot down. Ambushed in the stairwell, probably hollering, *here I come, here I come, youall*—on the way up to pay a visit to his lady and their baby too new to have a name (or had a name that Jordan had not heard yet, probably more likely). Name Jordan would not have forgotten if he had heard it once. Iron-head Jordan never forgets, his mom told everybody. Her iron-head baby Jordan, too sweet for this world, for his own sweet sake sometimes, he had peeped her whispering once to her sister, his auntie.

Auntie sweet herself, like his mom could be sweet when she chose to be, and Auntie nice, very nice with him, to him, so if anybody besides his mom knew he snuck off and cried out loud for his dead cousin Omar gunned down by a gangbanger cause Om, they say, kicked the guy's ass one night outside a club in a fair fight, if there was one person, only one person Jordan wouldn't mind, after all, catching him doing something he understood he was too big a boy to do, it would be Auntie.

I don't remember Jordan at the family party when I danced with my niece, his mom. He had to work I think, but maybe he was there, invisible in different rooms. More a matter of me simply missing him, because J was quiet, shy as he usually tended to be, except one-on-one, and then he just might wake you up with a thought you'd never thought of or hardly expected anyway till you caught on and remembered oh yeah it was J talking and if he didn't usually have all that much to say, still it was J, and you never know what's coming out that boy's mouth. Anyway, I danced with his mother that evening and aside from how slim, how graceful and how hip she glided and spun, how fine her moves caused me to feel, I also felt like we had been dancing a long time before, warming up, getting ready long before our glances met and I walked across the room toward her and she rose up smiling off the sofa, and offered her hand, preparations in advance seamlessly in place so we got smoothly into the middle of it long before we started to dance together, and how grateful to her I felt. And I also recall kinda checking out the room, and now I'm sure it was to spy if Jordan was in it, or coming or going or watching from a doorway, a corner, a shadow, watching the dance.

———

I come in here to say I'm sorry, baby, truly, truly sorry I smacked you, Jordan, his mother whispers, and then says, but I got to tell you, baby, Ima hit you again, baby, harder next time if u ever call your brothers and sister, half brothers and half sister again, boy. Where did u get that word, Jordan? Your sister and brothers not *half* nothing. No half brothers, half sister in this house. You are all my beloved children, brothers and sister, my beautiful children, brothers and sister living in this house together and I love each one of you very much and will long as my feet walking God's green earth and longer, baby. Any man come round here to visit me or stay with us must love all youall, too, father or not, love each one of your brothers and your sister and they better and they will, or won't be stepping through our door ever again.

In South Carolina my father lost it. Badly, embarrassingly, more than once. Talking out loud, quite loudly to himself in public, not the worst moments. I understood that conversations with himself were a necessity, especially in South Carolina where for four hundred years nobody, except maybe family or those we embraced or embraced us as a kind of extended family, had chosen to listen to a single word he said. I understood, no problem, that eerie sometimes whine and sometimes stern, peremptory TV announcer or preacher voice that issued suddenly from him, telling everybody what they needed to hear, what to do, where to go, what belonged to him that they had stolen from him, what he'd returned to South Carolina to claim as rightfully his. Fragments and elaborate set pieces my father's voice performed down there in the South as unself-consciously as birds sing or birds shit, Daddy, I heard you and do now, your words, as they should, surprising, teaching, piercing me like seeing you, a large, brown, grown-up man drop down to his knees and pray each night beside a small bed. One of two—one yours, one mine—small beds in the small motel room in Greenwood, South Carolina, we shared.

Worse by far than your outbursts or cooing or pronouncements or crooning to yourself, Daddy, or you fielding looks people dared at you or stole at you or received from you, wagging their heads behind your back after you passed by. Worse than the truths you bore within yourself and I had managed over the years to avoid or neglect or speak or mirror only rarely, only when I summoned up the courage not to forget what I choose not to remember. Worse than all those speeches and posturings in South Carolina, worse than any of that by miles, the very worst was your bewilderment, your empty hands I could neither fill nor reach out and squeeze in mine. For fear of awakening you. Of frightening you. Of losing you. Awakening you in a more terrible nightmare whose raging truths harder to bear, harder even to inhabit than the one shaking you to pieces right there before my eyes, the two of us inside miscellaneous municipal buildings, museums, coffee shops, libraries, bookstores, churches, dinners here and there in somebody's house to which we were invited and politely declined, walking the streets of little sleepy Southern towns beneath which our dead were buried but not dead.

Omar. What you think of Jordan?

That ain't no hard question. You already know the answer. You a butthole, lil Jordy. Like you been since you born, Midnight.

Fuck, man. You know I ain't be asking you that shit, man. You know who I'm talking bout. Michael Jordan. What you think of MJ. Really. Seriously, Om. C'mon.

Seriously. Serious as cancer. Boy can do it.

Is he the best ever?

No. You the best. Best little nothing of a little tagalong nothing butthole walking round here on two legs I ever seen.

Shoulda known better than to ask you, Chump-ass. Shoulda known better.

Fuck you, Omar. No, Omar. Sorry, Om. Didn't mean it, he almost shouts out loud. Not *fuck you, Om.* Just wanted to know. Asked you to help, that's all.

Jordan runs the names again in his head—sorry, Omar. Poor Om shot down dead. *Jordan.* Poor, long-time-ago-slave-boy Jordan. Sorry. Sorry. And sorry me. Sorry me, he thinks. *Sorry Jordan.* Jordan. Shame on crybaby me. Sorry me. Helpless. Tears sneak, drip, roll. Burn.

LOST AND FOUND

WHEN YOU WERE BORN, BASEMENT full of stuff. Junk most folks would call it. Basement full of junk, and I agreed. Hated to go down in there. Down in the *cellar,* your great-grandmother called it, where Uncle L G, her husband who was not your great-grandfather, not my granddaddy, but nice to me, nice as any grandfather could be, him only grandfather as far back as I could remember I ever had, Uncle L G filled up the basement with so much stuff on top of stuff I hated to have to go down in there. Only one light down there goes on when you open the kitchen door to the basement and hit the switch. Light on and still dark down there. Hardly see those rickety steps supposed to be under your feet when you standing at the top and hit the switch.

Going down the steps into that dark you had to be careful or you break your neck, your great-grandmother, Gramma always said. Not much more light than you'd get from a match once you got down in it to do whatever you needed to do. All that stuff, stuff, stuff down there. So much junk you couldn't see past it or over it or through it to see where you going.

Like a scaredy-cat little girl when I had to go down there. Usta worry always somebody might come up behind me blow out my pitiful match and there I'd be. Alone with all those rats and roaches and whatever else in the dark creeping and crawling and sneaking round under my feet. Lost in those piles of junk, holding my breath in the dark till I did it enough times didn't need no light to make my way. Wouldn't never go down in there unless Gramma for whatever reason I didn't want to hear, told me I had to go, and then I'd always have a plan in my head. A plan such as stop after you go down the steps from the kitchen door. Stop and get your feet solid under you again, then turn so the tallest piles of junk behind your back, and shuffle halfway sideways towards the back where there's a bulb hang down from the ceiling, bare bulb if you twist it a tiny turn sposed to light the far end where a dead washing machine and two lines Gramma used to hang clothes on, but no reason for me to go that far and mess with that bulb Gramma said don't you never touch it, girl, lectricity fry you crisp, girl, so plan says don't, and you don't, no, you just shuffle according to plan, seven, eight slow sideways steps, careful your knees, your chest don't brush boxes and stacks of stuff, going along till you hear a tiny wet noise behind you and you know a kinda bathroom back there where only Uncle sometimes does his business, room with a drip, drip, leaky sink and a toilet you flush with bucket beside it, and if you need more light for some job Gramma sent you on, the plan says stop here, halfway turn around there where it's even darker than at the bottom of the kitchen steps, reach up and feel for pull chain dangles just inside a doorway with no door. Pull and two lights on now down there and everything, plan says, be a bit better.

Asked Gramma once why Pops keep all that junk down there. Disgraceful down there. Barely room to move round, Gramma. You could say that she ignored my question. Except for one those cold Gramma looks go straight through a person like the person ain't there. Like when Mama and me lived here and Gramma catch me doing something she knew and I knew good and well I should not be doing and she stare off into space while she making up her mind to tear up my little behind or maybe let me slide this once, and either way I knew best to get out her way. Quicker the better. But more than that in Gramma's look the day I asked about Pops's mess of stuff in the cellar. More than the usual reminding me of something I already knew quite well. More even than when she repeats one her favorites she never gets tired repeating like God don't like ugly, or Plenty goes on in this house not your business, miss, and unless I ask your opinion or give you mine you best just leave it alone, miss.

Day I put Pop and that junky basement in my mouth, Gramma's eyes telling me more. Much more. Too much for me to hear. Did she really and truly say—*you ain't nothing*—*why you alive and my daughter dead*—*just cause same roof over both our heads don't mean I got to abide your foolishness forever*—all in a stare didn't last longer than two blinks before she cut her eyes, cut off my breath and left me standing there wondering why in hell I ask her anything. Guilty, no doubt, of every crime I could think of, even if I couldn't say exactly which particular crime she caught me in red-handed that day. Me standing there like a damned fool, standing in the kitchen feeling naked as the day I was born and Gramma long gone, very busy wiping a counter clean wasn't dirty. She didn't bother to turn round and look at me. Took her own good time before words come over her shoulder. Plenty room down there for another box with you in it, if your Uncle L G's boxes don't mind your mouthy company.

Your great-grandmother, bless her soul . . . *Bless her soul.* Listen at me. My, my, my. You heard me, didn't you, blessing her soul. Here I am starting to talk just like she talked.

I remember me fussing about the basement, remember how Gramma's stare, then Gramma's words made me feel, Son. Remembered it yesterday when poor Miss Etta sneak up on me tending to my handful of flowers in the little patch of ground next to the house I had the nerve to call my *garden*. Old frail Miss Etta always lonely and her mind ain't been right for years, maybe never, and poor lady get in one them fogs come over her she be wandering around the neighborhood in the dead of night or you liable to find her anytime night or day in your yard if you have one or kitchen or dining room or bedroom didn't make no difference to Miss Etta, all the same to her, your house, hers, anyplace she happened to wind up all the same to her.

Pretty sure Miss Etta fond of me, much as she show up uninvited or maybe less a question of whether she likes me or not, I guess, probably more about the fact I don't shoo her or throw things at her or holler or call the cops, that last thing, by the way, a thing nobody around here, I believe, mean enough to do. Maybe yell to chase her away, but not call cops on her, don't care how pesky Miss Etta got. Pretty damned pesky if truth be told. Creepy, I suppose, to some folks. Damned nuisance if she turns up at a bad time. But Miss Etta had nobody's keys. If she in your house you musta left a door open or unlocked. Never heard of her stealing. Might pick up something and set it down in a different place and probably you don't miss it till you see it and wonder how it moved and then maybe you remember a Miss Etta visit. But Miss Etta no thief. And you could curse her out till you blue in the face, she never say a nasty word back. Though sure enough she could talk. Think maybe she never stops talking. Little chatter engine running inside her keeps her going. I said she was lonely, but truth might be long as she hears that little talk motor purring inside her, that engine talking loud enough sometimes for another person to hear and join the conversation, or just her lips and eyes busy with words you can see not hear, Miss Etta never alone.

Not even the plague stop Miss Etta making her rounds. Strange thing, people in deep lockdown scared their own shadows, but nobody feared Miss Etta. People must have thought there's not enough of this little, frail woman to carry no germs. And just as strange, she could pass through those nighttime detector eyes like they not even there, those detectors everywhere catch and zap everybody else.

Anyway, what I'm trying to explain to you ain't exactly our strange neighbor with her ghost visits and ghost voices. Trying to explain to you how my grandmother, your great-grandmother could make me feel sometimes. Like time I complained about Uncle L. G's stuff in the cellar. And I got the same scared feeling just yesterday listening to Miss Etta. Me all the sudden not knowing where or who I was.

Started with Miss Etta asking me a question. Her talking before I noticed her. You inside sleeping away in your bed. Me outside. I might have been bent over, maybe down on one knee, touching or trying to smell my flowers. Room for so few of them in that scanty bit of dirt, I could have given every single flower a name and remembered all the names, and called them by name, if I was that kind of person. Stooping down sorta, comforting my babies, comforting myself when Miss Etta come up from the street. Not quiet as a mouse like usual, not quiet as those creatures scuttling in the dark basement, cause this time she don't just arrive and stand there the silent way she does lots of times, till *boom* you turn and notice her, or sometimes just remember her there even if she isn't there, when you turn around to check. No. Miss Etta not quiet yesterday afternoon. And for Miss Etta, in a kind of hurry, too. Heard that skinny whisper of voice, *Hey-you, Hey-you,* her name for me she always calls me by, *Hey-you* a couple times before her short little self in front of me talking, few feet away after I straighten up.

She standing there in front the house next door, house with yellow aluminum siding belonging to Mr. McCullough who didn't mind me leaning a trellis against his wall because he likes a rose too and my red and white ones climbing up from my little garden squeezed tween our driveway and his house, pretty he thinks. But when I give my attention to Miss Etta and try to figure out the frantic hand jive, frantic batting and lowering and lost expression of her eyes, no trellis standing tall, no yellow wall behind her. Just sky and jumble of fallen flowers and quiet emptiness on both sides of the street climbs the hill our house sits on. Steep hill where the yellow McCollough house used to sit, too, till it got shrooped away like the rest the houses as far down and up the hill as I can see.

Nobody home. Nobody home nowhere, Miss Etta mumbled at me or mumbled to voices I couldn't hear mumbling inside her. She still sees the houses. She thinks they are still there, I said to myself, explained to myself. Bet Miss Etta must have just paid a visit six or so houses down the next block, to her very best buddy Valery and Valery's family, where, even if a visit not exactly welcome at the moment, she was always welcome to come try again, but today nobody home, nobody waving from the porch, no greetings, none Val's kids and big ugly dogs playing in the fenced yard, no yard, no porch, no house all the hours Miss Etta waited, shaping a house like Val's again and again with her empty hands till her arms tired holding up the weight. Saying Valery's name out loud or to herself so many times and no answer till Miss Etta couldn't wait any longer and hurries away, hurried past house after house, houses maybe there, maybe not, maybe she's starting not to trust her own eyes, then she finds me, and watches me weeping and fumbling in my garden, and decides to try again. Try to find company. Ask me where Valery. As if I understood any better than Miss Etta what has happened. Why she and me and you and two, three dozen mostly broken-neck flowers all that's left pretending the neighborhood not gone.

Why just about everything, but not quite everything, gone, what she asking me. Shrooped away. *Shrooped* a cartoony-sounding but definitely not funny word people started to use on TV for what they had witnessed—till TV gone, too—when hot, swirling storms of dirt, pebbles, dust, wind took away houses and everything once inside houses. The furniture, people, knickknacks, food, clothing. And took streetlamps, power lines, trees, billboards, cars and trucks, snatched all that up too, whole city shrooped up maybe. Could be the whole damned world soon, carried off in giant fists of shroop hitting so fast, faster, faster than bolts of lightning so you almost can't see them coming or going, just hear them, *Boom*, drumbeat, heartbeats exploding louder than a atom bomb, only you can't tell when next beat coming, minutes between beats or hours or days between, or strings of strikes, *Boom-Boom-Boom* one greedy shroop after another, rattling the sky's bones. Whether a silent, eerie sky bright and blue or black black sky above layers of cloud and storm, *Shroop* finds sky's bones to rattle.

Why, Miss Emma wants to know. Where's everything, she wants to know. But why she asking me. Why she thinking I know why she and me and you and broken sticks and broken flowers in my so-called garden got left behind.

Sometimes I wonder why I tell you terrible things, little one. Must be because you gon hear them sooner or later and I want to be the one telling. Ways and reasons for a mother, if she lives to see her child, if a child lives to see its mother, ways and reasons a mother got to tell her child the very worst things she knows. Ways and reasons I believe no one else but that child's mother understands. She tells it different. Tells the truth even though her words can't change terrible things she knows coming for every mother's child born on this earth.

Gramma, who could behave just the opposite of mean sometimes, was quite a reader, by the way, and she told me once upon a time she was reading a book written by a dead colored woman, a book about pain and loss and floods and dying, all sorts of awful things just about bring tears to her eyes, and then she come upon some words Gramma called down-home, old-timey words. *You got to go there to know there.* Words on a page in a book Gramma said made her grunt and rock and start to wag her head, sitting there alone all those years and years ago, sad book in her lap, *Amen,* she said she had to say out loud, then smiled she said and smiled again telling me about finding those old-folk words talking in a book. *You got to go there to know there.* Message in those words true, Gramma said. No doubt about it, Gramma said. You got to go there alone with your own damned self.

The way it is, my son. And maybe I can't stop bad stuff surely gonna come for you, but I'm your mother and got my ways, my reasons for stories I tell you, baby. Stories you won't hear from nobody else. Hearing terrible things in those stories help you or not help you, but I just want for you to hear them first my way, for my reasons, from me. And just like when Gramma telling me those words in a book, just like her saying amen and smiling, not everything I have to tell you terrible. How could it be with you alive to hear and me alive to tell.

Miss Etta standing in the driveway got me to thinking about Uncle L G. Uncle L G a street merchant. Pops I call him, but you know that, don't you. Pops spent his whole life buying and selling and trading stuff at street fairs, swap marts, yard sales, outdoor markets, sheriff sales, auctions, going-out-of-business sales, pawnshops, junkyards, evictions, black markets, open-air bazaars, fire sales, back-alley, middle-of-night, back-of-the-bar dealings with junkies and thieves, church and temple rummage sales, not only here, but driving to other cities, him alone in whatever piece of car he owned, or caravanning to special events with his Moorish brothers in their red Arab caps on regular yearly trips and weekend hit-and-split routes they had figured out. Pops buying, selling, trading, storing in the basement what he couldn't move on one day to move maybe another day. That's how Uncle L G earned a living after his hoodlum hustling days and drug days, after jail years, after he joined the Moorish Brotherhood and married your great-grandmother and they settled here in this house on a hill, house where my grandmama helped raise me after her daughter, my mama arrived with a baby, me, in her arms, after my mama had runned off to live with the wrong man in Philly. Mama running back home to her mama, scared, tail between her legs. My mama wishing she'd listened to what her mama and Uncle L G said about the knucklehead she runned away with. Then here she come running from him, scared of him till Uncle L G speaks with him. Uncle L G with ivory clasp of his straight razor gripped in his fist I bet, arm hanging down alongside his body and never raised it, but razor probably very seeable as he opens the front door and stands barring the way while he talks, talks I bet as Uncle L G usually talked, his bargaining tone of voice you might say, suggesting some good in this, a bargain for both us if we use our heads and fine-tune this exchange, talking calmly to the man at the door, man who was maybe your granddaddy, my daddy maybe, the man Mama once thought she loved, but he never knocked again, never darkened the door of this house again. Not once during the years before I left here with my mama nor after I was grown and we came back here, started living here again when I needed help to take care my sick mama. Your grandmama, Son. My Mama who, sick as she was, stayed beautiful. Just as pretty everybody says as when she came back here with me in her arms from Philly all those years before. But Mama got sicker and sicker in this house anyway, no matter how hard she tried and we all tried to help her, Mama died here anyway, and you born here and here we are today, my mama gone and all Uncle L G's stuff still up under us in the basement.

———

I say *maybe* the man Uncle L G talked to at the door was my daddy, your granddaddy, because that might not be the only story. My mama shy, tended to keep her business to herself, but she talking to me one day and one word led to another and next thing I know, Mama saying . . . there was a boy . . . back in Philly . . . and I kinda liked him.

I believe the cancer had Mama down that particular day I'm recalling. Think she may have been in bed, in her blue nightgown, propped up on a special pillow come home with her from the hospital. She feeling beat up real bad, barely able to catch her breath, seemed to me. Then seemed like weather all the sudden changed. Sky clear. She didn't scoot up higher in the bed, nothing drastic as that, but Mama perk up a minute, maybe hearing her own voice or seeing what she saw in her own mind clearer, closer than the pain, closer than me and the stuffy room. The boy, Mama said . . . a student. He worked like her in the university cafeteria that fed the students, she said. Said . . . not like me really, not like me scuffling, serving food, washing pots, pans, dishes, mopping floors, scrubbing tabletops and chairs nine hours straight, not counting time on the bus each way, six days a week so I could eat and keep a roof, pitiful as it was, over my head. His job only took away a couple hours from his day, work he had to do to keep a scholarship paid his student bills, he explained to me when I got round to asking. Took me a while to ask. Shy, you know me. And him shy, too. A colored boy where hardly any colored around except ones like me working slave jobs for the university. So of course I noticed the boy. He was cute. But so what. Got my hands more than full with another man and didn't really pay much attention to a colored boy busing tables lunchtimes till they moved him to a different dining hall and didn't see him for a couple weeks, then here he come in line with other students across the serving counter from me and I'm thinking about the silly net pulled over my hair and frumpy smocks we had to wear at work over our own clothes, and why you be thinking any of that, girl, I had to ask myself, with everything else you dealing with, girl.

Turns out nothing ever came of it, Mama said. Boy just start to coming by. Regular enough, Mama said, some the other girls start to cut their eyes, grinning, teasing me and teasing him too. Till he got to be a daily customer, and them nebby noses paid us no mind. But like I say, nothing happened. Met up couple times on campus. Movie once. Holding hands. Couple talks, couple walks where we the only colored where all those white students strolling. Boy very nice to me. Kind. Very smart. Night and day different compared to the fool I was trying to make sense of. Fool never home. No job. Drinking and drugs. Dared to put his hands on me once. Warning me he break my neck if I try and leave. Treated me bad from the start, then worse and worse, as if I had no choice but to take it.

Miserable in Philly, Mama said. Why wouldn't I be, she said, when the man supposed to be loving me made me cry when he was around, made cry when he not around. Made up my mind to get out the rattrap apartment we lived in. Find my own place, start over.

Weird thing, the nice boy I met in the cafeteria, Mama said, just as miserable as me. Hated the university. All he wanted to talk about in a way. How school broke his heart. Working so hard to get there, then finding nothing there. No others like him. No real welcome for him. Lies and bullshit. No classes about places you and I come from, he said. No professors look like us. Bullshit and lies, he said. Not an education teaching you how to make a new life. Education teaching you same old life with no room in it for you to live your life. Wasn't really him when he talked bitter, bitter. But I knew he meant it, and wanted me to understand, and that's why I can still repeat some the very words he said to me. But university world not my world. Lot I couldn't understand then and never will, but I felt his unhappiness, sure enough. Almost as much sometimes as feeling my own.

And don't you know that damned campus blew up. Him and a handful of other colored students, call themselves Nat Turners Army, occupied president's office in Wilson Hall. Didn't shut down the university. I was in the cafeteria all week, dishing out mush like nothing special happening on campus. Snuck past Wilson couple times. And not much to see. Students carrying signs, couple pairs of campus cops hanging around, students strolling by, a few stop, curious a minute. Not much did happen, except on the seventh day, and then I was home by the time they dragged them out Wilson Hall screaming and kicking. But that night on TV I saw fires, bottles thrown, broken windows, sirens, students chased by cops or maybe students chasing cops or each other. Worried a little bit, but stuff like that starting to pop up regular everywhere round the country. Then they said on the morning TV news black boy shot down. Killed in the street. Heard his name. Said they caught him trying to torch a cop car and he didn't stop running when ordered to stop. My sweet boy lying bleeding to death in the gutter. On Spruce, same street I walked up every day from the 34 bus to get to my work. Street where White Castle, Smokey Joe's, Ho Chan's, and all the rest those little fast-food and take-out joints for students used to be lined up there. Still are, probably.

That day Mama got to talking, telling her story to me, she faded fast as she had perked up. No chance to ask her more about Philly or her cute boy. But anyway, like Mama said, she was shy. And Mama was. In some ways, sometimes, anyway. Of course, it crossed my mind to ask: Mama, did I have a daddy lying dead on that Spruce Street in Philadelphia. Couldn't help asking myself the question, and halfway answering it, too. Question in my mind still, if truth be told. Here I am asking it again, out loud, talking to you, my son. Asking as if the answer makes a difference.

———

I said once to your great-grandmother. Said, Gramma, I wonder why you never speak about my mama. I miss Mama so much, Gramma, and I know you must miss her, too. Miss her probably in a way even more than me, and every once in a while I think maybe it might help both us to talk. I mean you do say her name every now and then. Or if I ask you a question about her maybe you answer. But short answer. Yes. No. Or *hmmm*, sometimes. Like maybe you know more answer or maybe you don't. *Hmmm*. But you don't want to go there. You got something else to do. *Hmmm*. Then you're gone. Letting me see you got more important things to do than talk about Mama. Then she's gone again, too. I mean I don't mean to say it's your fault, but we don't never really talk about Mama, and I miss her so much, Gramma.

Just cause you grown enough to have a baby and grown enough to come here with your baby, come to my house and Uncle L G's house just like she did after she run away and then one day there she is back with a baby under her arm and her eyes full of tears. Sorry, Mama, and mouth full of gimme, gimme, please, Mama when I open the door and she opens her mouth. And just cause you think you grown cause you got a pretty little baby breaks my heart to touch, to see me, holding him, counting each tiny bump of breath and praying his next breath will come, and just because your mama dropped me, and a precious child dropped from her, and another precious child dropped from you, and here we are now bumbling around in this terrible mess people call a world, call God's Heaven and Earth or Allah's Heaven and Earth as if that's all there is to it, as if there ain't no rotten, lying Hell-Beast under whose nasty behind this world sits, and nobody, no babies, no nothing pass through here that don't get dirty and worse, and just because things got to be like that and got to happen again and again, and just cause Uncle and me took you in, it don't mean you are grown today, young lady, and don't mean I want to talk with you, about your mama, or talk about you, me, all the beasts and devils and saints, ghosts, everybody, everything falling and rising and running away and come back or never come back. Why in the world you think I would want to have a conversation today about all that with you or anybody else on this never again green earth. Let alone speak of my only child. Speak of her to her child. Hard enough to speak to my own damned self, girl, about things that don't change no matter how long, how much love, how much talking.

Don't get me wrong now, my girl. Come closer. Lemme pat your nappy head. Sometimes a person can't help theyself. Sometimes I be stirring round alone in these rooms. Uncle out, you out with the baby somewhere, and me cleaning or cooking or just sitting reading one the magazines Uncle brings for me or laying cross my bed and there she is. Your dead mama, my lost daughter sweet again as the sweet baby she brought here, there she is, my child standing here big as life, smiling at me or frowning or paying me no mind the way she used to do me quite often, if truth be told, her all wrapped up in or tore down by her own business, by whatever that girl be thinking about in that busy, busy, smart, pretty head of hers. But here she is and I need to speak to her. Ask her where she stay. When she coming home. What did she eat this morning for breakfast or eat last night for supper. Ask how's my little one when I know good and well she can't tell me even if she wanted to. Gone. Gone. Gone.

Except once when I thought it was Miss Etta creeping around in here. Turns out I was listening to my daughter. My babygirl all grown up. And me not just thinking I'm listening to her. I watched her moving in the shadows. In the room I was in or the shadows in the next room. Didn't matter. I could see my lost girl again and hear her again through the walls. Wasn't no Miss Etta. Huh-uh. My girl back. Not Miss Etta. My baby, sure nuff. And she stays for a long, long time. Long enough with me, holding my breath the whole time, till I had to let that breath go or die. And when I let go that holding-on breath, my daughter, your mama kept on doing a minute what she was doing. Hardly making any noise really. Quiet like Miss Etta can be. You know how Miss Etta be all up under you and so quiet you not aware she's there. And after I let go my breath, everything stay quiet awhile. Outside and inside me. Barely hear my own self when I spoke, and didn't truly understand why or who I was talking to. Just sat there or lay there or stood there waiting for my sweet girl to answer.

You dozing off, ain't you, sleepyhead boy. Sleep on, little guy. Talking mostly to hear myself talk now anyway. Sleep on.

Pops always had lots of jobs besides being a street merchant. By the end, mostly working at his Moorish temple, but always busy, double busy his entire life. Managed a little kinda grocery store around the corner from here, jitneyed, sold encyclopedias, a counselor to boys released from juvenile court, drove for a funeral parlor and did the fingernails and toenails of the dead waiting to be buried. Curious as I was as a kid and later, too, when I was grown, always asking him about his jobs but never could ask Pops the thing got my attention most, ask him what he thought about touching those cold hands and cold feet of the dead, their toenails and fingernails he got paid to trim and paint. Ask him why anybody cares, painted, trimmed or not. Specially since dead people have socks on when a body in a casket at the funeral home or in church, socks I'd heard grown-ups talk about taking to the undertaker along with a nice dress or nice suit and tie, clean underwear. And the hands probably hid under a fancy, silky white blanket they tuck in round the dead when they laid out to view. Didn't matter my questions dumb or not, Pops give me the benefit of the doubt and answer.

Whether anybody else cares or not, not the point, I can hear Pops answering that question I never asked him about trimming and painting dead people's nails. Ain't about if anybody else cares or not cares, dearheart. If it's a job I'm doing, he'd say, Ima do it right.

And I got to tell you this story right, little one. Tell it so it's maybe yes, maybe no. Tell you the man I think is my father, might or might not be him. Is or is not my father. Or maybe both. And is he your grandfather. More than a likely chance, I don't and won't ever know the answer my ownself, and that's what I want to tell you. Tell my way. My way so story not cut and dry. Not black nor white. Not over. Not over. Never over for a mother and child. In these awful times, does any story matter. Only answer I know is to tell my story. Tell it so it's not finished. So I can start again tomorrow, telling and listening again tomorrow not knowing what the end gon be. Not exactly my story. Nor one daddy or another daddy's story. More to get to. More to say and hear. Fingers and toes Uncle L G, fixes up, not cold, not dead, he'd say. Alive while he's doing his job.

Tomorrow morning, you still here, me still here, in this house, on this hill, we got something to do together, don't we, baby. Start up the story again.

Story didn't end the day them buses come by here and lined up at the curb, buses full of Uncle L G's red cap Moorish brethren and their families. Maybe if I had really been listening all the times Uncle L G had tried to tell me about the Prophet and Prophet's prophesies of Last Days, maybe if I had changed my ways, changed my name, put Bey in front of it the way your great-grandmother been calling herself Bey longer than I can remember, maybe you and me on one the buses going to Cleveland. *Cleveland,* Uncle L G kinda winking as he answered, *Cleveland,* when I asked him where he and my grandmother going that day they left. Bear hug from Gramma, then shy pat, squeeze of my arm before she turned and said over her shoulder as she walked off, Don't you fret none bout us while we away, girl. Everything you and the little sweet puss need down in the cellar if you can't find it nowhere else, she said, stepping up into the yellow bus.

Wasn't long after the buses drove away down the hill before plague started. Terrible fevers and dying everywhere at once cross the whole wide world it seemed. Lockdown ordered. Got tighter and tighter. Whether locked-down helped or not, who knew. Lockdown got tighter still and more mean. Seemed like locked-down gon last forever. Till graybeard Mr. Shroop blam his fist on the High Table. *Enough,* he said. You free, he said. And then not much left. Just about nothing, nobody. Only us, this house, a few stray souls hiding here and there. But I bet Great-Grandmother and Pops come back for us or come stay with us, when and if they can, baby.

Your uncle L G and his Moorish religion and Moorish brothers with red *fezzes* on their heads—Pops told me call the little red cap a *fez*—they a mystery to me to this day. Trailer truck pull up one morning couple years ago, parks, and whole bunch of Brethren scrambling round unloading a huge black box, bigger than two, three big, fat Frigidaires, a carton they muscle out the back of the truck and set down on the sidewalk where used to be a driveway between our house and the McColloughs' house, where further back a ways in the dirt alongside the driveway I'd planted my little garden.

Now wasn't door nor window in this house even close to large enough to get anything through big as that black box they unloaded, so don't know what they up to, but I whispered to Pops after he come from helping them to get the box down off the truck, Youall men be real careful of my flowers, please, Uncle L G.

Had somewhere I needed to go that morning and did and when I got back three, four hours later, no humungous black carton on the curb and Gramma and Pops sitting at the kitchen table, Pops drinking a glass that lemonade Gramma fixed fresh for him most every day. Pops look up said, Box in the basement and didn't touch a hair on the head any your pretty flowers, sweetheart. You know me better than that, dear.

And I sure knew better than to ask any questions about box or basement, especially with your great-grandmother sitting there. To this day don't know what was in the black carton or what they did with it. If they opened it and carried whatever in it piece by piece into the house and down the kitchen steps, lugged stuff and stuffed it down where wasn't room for a bird, let alone a huge-ass black box or huge-ass boxful of god knows what that truck brought that day. Bowed my head to keep my feelings to myself, but couldn't hold back a quick little grin watching Uncle L G sip his ice cold lemonade from a green glass mug, the green glass pitcher dripping sweat down the sides, resting tall on the table tween Uncle and Gramma, and wondered if maybe Uncle L G, like ole Froggy gone a-courting, just twanged his magic twanger and *Twang*, oop-poop-a-doo. Everything he wanted in the cellar dancing down them dark steps, *Twang*—oop-poop-a-doo.

Sometimes a person got to wonder how it ends. Wonder like during the worst days of lockdown when everybody's house worse than a prison because the government had got very, very good with guards, guns, and never-asleep screen eyes. Folks starving. People stone sick of each other. Hate each other. Not nuff water nor power. No way a person sneak outdoors when not allowed to go and not get zapped or shot down, no questions asked, dead in a minute. All them digital machines, electronics, scientists, engineers, mathematics, computers, and politicians who can't figure a way to stop the plague from raging and killing thousands, then millions of us everywhere cross the globe, that plague keeping people half living, half dying in prison so long, it start to feel like *fuck it,* dying quick be better than living this way, this miserable, unbearable, worse than hopeless way, not really sure you live or dead, during those bad days steady getting worse, a person had to wonder why those fools supposed to be in charge of saving, organizing people's lives, those so-called leaders who can't protect us from a teeny virus, a person had to wonder why we let those same leaders and experts build foolproof eyes, foolproof weapons to silence people, automatically execute people who dared question or break rules meant to keep us locked down, isolated and separated.

Zap. Crackle. Pop. Ziss. Noises in the night. Invisible murders. With nothing better to do, I count them some nights. Or am I dreaming. Or caught breaking curfew and listening to my ownself, zap, crackle, popping, zissing as this world breaks, and no other world begins. A dream. Sound of murder in the night another blast of shroop will mercifully silence.

Before shroops started, everybody believed the immensely rich ones buy their way out of lockdown. Believed a few spots left on the globe clean, green. Believed if the plague ever ended, the rich would reappear and run things smoothly again. And believed miracles can happen, faith can move mountains, and meanwhile . . . etc., etc. . . . But maybe we shoulda started believing one more day locked down far too long to wait. Too long to keep on suffering too many terrible things . . .

More story tomorrow morning. Not finished. That's how I want to tell it now. More to tell when we wake up tomorrow.

LOST LOVE LETTERS—A LOCKE

(1954)

Books. Art. White People. They can kiss my black ass.

(1922)

Dear Boy,

You chose to leave early, but let me assure you, my special friend, your presence stayed late. Lingered beside me as I lay an hour or so in my bed. An hour or two, if truth be told, then sad time alone until sleep rescued me from the terror of your absence, a terror bearable for me only because I pretended that you had chosen not to leave, pretended that you had simply stepped away a moment and in the next moment you would return. Beside me again, if I kept imagining your warmth, smell, breath. Tasting, stealing, savoring as if I was not alone. Imagining hands, lips I yearned for did not belong to a stranger in a faraway country, a land I had never visited except in dreams, a stranger I would never encounter except within the kind, peaceful sleep which finally, mercifully I slipped into last night. Your presence and mine meeting there, crossing over. No separation.

The two men had enjoyed the concert. Stroll afterwards for a night-cap at the smaller man's second-floor apartment tucked between brick row houses on a quiet street. Sickle moon gleaming in DC's black sky. An unpleasant usher dead on plush scarlet runner of concert hall carpet. Poleax the small man had wielded to fell the usher vanishing into a bespoke suit's vest pocket as swiftly, efficiently as the weapon had appeared at the box seats' entrance after the reluctant negro usher leading them had halted and peeked in to be certain the booth not occupied by white patrons who might be offended if joined by the two men whose tickets in the small one's brown hand had claimed the negroes paid. Late into the second string quartet, just before intermission, a white couple had brushed by relatively politely and quietly into a brace of two empty seats adjacent to the men's brace, settled in without raising objections about negro neighbors inside the box nor a negro usher's prostrate body lying outside the box, an obstacle that possibly could have impeded the tardy couple's progress to their seats at least as much as two pairs of shined negro shoes and negro knees, but management, no doubt, had removed the corpse by the time the nicely dressed couple had arrived.

Morning after the concert, after usher slaying, after nightcap and shared peek through barely cracked door at his mother under a white sheet, lying across the foot of her bed, awaiting a tea party and viewing next evening at eight when her uniquely arranged and embalmed body, gowned, gloved, reposing on the living room couch, would greet mourners, after a cordial invitation to the wake extended to his visitor by the smaller man, not only shorter by a head than his companion of the previous evening, but a tiny man, smaller than even most small men, closer to boy-size he would smile and admit from time to time only to his dear mama and to himself, but now, yes, only to himself, and after all that he's wondering on this lonely next morning if somehow during the busy night of the concert, he had provoked unintentionally an obviously bright, but also obviously immature young man's rather sudden, regrettably premature departure. *Spooked him* an unkind yet perhaps not totally inappropriate phrase as he listened to a spiteful voice inside him blurt out the ungenerous words, *you spooked him, fool.*

At the apartment door his visitor had politely declined attendance at the wake, citing an unavoidable, urgent engagement, smiling briefly at the hand held out to him, brushing it only with a single fingertip, before he turned his back and headed towards the hallway stairs. Since a second rendezvous had not been scheduled, and the exhausting business of closing down his mother's affairs endless, no opportunity would soon be presenting itself for him to pose directly to the young man the worrisome question bothering him since the evening of the concert. A note must be addressed to his new acquaintance, a note in which he would make a point of asking, Please . . . tell me why . . . after a lovely concert, why such an abrupt leave-taking, my young friend. Honesty between himself and each of them, each special friend, the best policy. What he always desired, demanded of them and of himself. Absolutely. Honesty in social relations between himself and others a requirement always, if possible. To enable a fruitful *next,* and surely there must be a next. Next even if his ferocious need the sole reason for believing a next might materialize. His ferocious need for connection, for continuation. Whether a next bore fruit or not. In the present case, he felt more than a crucial need for a next time. Extremely attracted to this new one who is still special, still—except for crude yet soft, baby-like edges—unknown. Mysterious still. A note, a next meeting necessary to clear the air. Open one heart to another. Next, then more, more next time, more, more nexts and more. No other way. Until one. The one who appears and becomes as he was to his mother, she to him, as her God had been for her. The only one. First and last and forever. Could this new boy be the one.

[1885]

Born dying on September 13, 1885, doomed, I suppose, like my father and his father, I never had a chance to be other than I have turned out to be. Body and breath and color bequeathed by a Gracious Creator, amen. Wonder of wonders. *Thank Jesus,* as some of my mother's old-lady church friends might have proclaimed, had they been there for the blessed event of my birth. But not many old ladies, nor young ones either who attend shouting churches among my mother's acquaintance, though plenty shouting churches in Philly where I grew up. My mother's circle preferred the kind of church where you could hear a pin drop during services. Where tranquillity reigned supreme. Where pastor and congregation engaged in brief, exquisitely enunciated responsive readings. Crisp, nearly abrupt, nearly martial hymns. Where squirming in my seat as sinful and unthinkable as jumping up and dancing in the aisles. A church old and distinguished as my mother's family, established in Philadelphia before the War of 1812 in which her grandfather, a colored combatant, had earned a medal.

My father a Locke, Ishmael Pliny Locke, who fancied himself a proper parent because he read Virgil and Homer to me. Epic poems extolling exploits of Greek and Roman heroes to nourish a sickly son during endless afternoons the boy confined to bed. A man vastly disappointed by life, by himself. Same father who, once I had regained a fragile semblance of health, enough at least to stand and hobble about on my own two feet, beat me down again, an unforgettable thrashing I will never forgive, occasioned by some sin I cannot recall. Small sins evidence always for my father of sin unspeakably large. Barbaric, repeated blows battered me, nearly killing me, not ceasing till my mother's screams, tears, frantic body wedged son and father apart. A smallish man bearing great expectations his old Philadelphia family of strivers had expressed in names bestowed upon him at birth. *Ishmael. Pliny.* My colored father certain from an early age he could perform demanding intellectual tasks equally as well as, probably much better than, any white man. Just as certain he would never receive a fair opportunity to demonstrate his superior gifts because he was negro. Trapped by stultifying blackness forever. With such a father who loved and hated himself prodigiously and saw the color that plagued him reproduced in his son's brown face, did I ever stand a chance to be more or less than I turned out to be.

My parents named me Arthur Leroy. Thus my initials spell *ALL*. I never asked my parents if the small joke on purpose, smiling, gazing down upon their precious, tiny—*All. Arthur* a renowned British king seated at the head of his Round Table surrounded by legendary knights. *Arthur* got lost early and at home I was called Roy. Both parents quite aware that *Leroy* derived from French *le roi*. I wonder how my parents, if asked, would say they spelled my nickname. Saying it, did they see *Roy* or *Roi*. At age sixteen, upon entering high school, I decided people should call me *Alain. Alain* French, too. A name I associated with nobility, with fair-skinned, handsome French lads. Many years later, a grown-up man, I surprised myself by becoming a fan of a comic strip,

The Little King. My odd little king with his Jimmy Rushing, *Mr. "Five by Five,"* roly-poly body wrapped in an ermine-collared crimson robe, minaret-shaped crown tilted atop his tiny head, long black tentacles of mustache curlicuing above lips that never spoke a word. Despite myself, I adored the round little man who always appeared to be quite pleased to be alive, idly wandering daily through his kingdom.

Consider my father's given names. *Ishmael. Pliny.* I often have. Considered his names, my mother's name—*Mary,* the holy mother, *Hawkins,* a notorious English pirate—and considered who else may have said, heard, written, considered the names. Biblical *Ishmael,* Abraham's son, of mixed blood, and as a consequence, banished, exiled with Hagar his African mother. Wanderer in the desert, yet Ishmael's loins seeded a new nation. *Pliny* a Roman scholar who helped invent the discipline of history, whose son Pliny would watch while *Pompeii,* a great city of an empire whose origins his father had chronicled, was burned crisp, buried by flaming ashes from Vesuvius.

PROFESSOR LOCKE'S MEMOIR IN PROGRESS . . .

At Oxford University I observed how the clannish, self-satisfied, self-congratulatory, palsy-walsy, slovenly, chatty lingo affected by my fellow American Scholars was generally ridiculed and despised by the English students. Brits viewed their American visitors as loutish and uncouth, as large, exotic creatures much too anxious to hurry off and run the world, not waste time conversing about it in university classes, tutorials, tea parties. A world those American backwoodsmen, athletes, provincials, faux aristocrats, entrepreneurs inexplicably assumed it was now their destiny, not England's, to rule.

Habits imbibed at home from my mother and father, habits my parents reinforced rigorously, severely if I didn't practice them assiduously enough, habits of dress, comportment, of speaking always carefully, properly, each sentence grammatically correct, each word clearly pronounced, displaying an extensive, precise vocabulary, those habits separated me in the eyes and ears of the English from my American peers. An acknowledgment of difference that for once, in this rare case, redounded to my favor. As a result of their preference for my styles of speech and behavior, my English colleagues eased, even welcomed my entry into the social and academic life of their ancient citadel of learning. I became, of course, even more fastidious about how I represented myself. More demanding of myself. I had no wish to revert to the practice of contenting myself with books of philosophy and the Bodleian's blue, multivolume *O.E.D.* as my most reliable companions on dreary, chilly Oxford afternoons and nights. My fellow Americans had little patience for what they deemed my stuffy manners, fussy way of talking. Since most of them firm believers anyway in segregation of the races and absolutely convinced of the innate superiority of their race and the innate inferiority of mine, their disapproval of the distinctive character I fashioned for myself did not alter how they behaved towards me. How they generally ignored, avoided, or openly insulted me.

Gradually, I discovered the partiality shown towards me by Brits, especially colonial Brits, a few whose skin colored like mine, more than compensated for absence of comradeship with the vast majority of my fellow American Scholars. My difference at birth and differences I cultivated, instead of treated as obstacles, aroused the curiosity of my foreign colleagues. Being treated as distinctly un-American a privilege and pastime, one might say, granted by my three years at Oxford. Privilege and pastime splendidly expanded, gloriously enhanced during semester breaks when I crossed the channel to explore the Continent. And those positive advantages, those exciting possibilities of being something other than an American, certainly not lost on me when I returned to the country I had grown up calling my home.

My dear mama, who, when I had announced I had won a prestigious scholarship to study abroad at one of the world's great universities, cried out, close to tears, *Alain, Alain. How marvelous. How proud of you I am, my son,* the most unrestrained display of her emotions I had ever witnessed, same dear mama, several weeks after my arrival home, on the day I finally mustered up courage to admit to her that after three years spent in pursuit of an Oxford degree, I had returned empty-handed, revealed in her expression, her eyes, absolutely no indication of her feelings. One blink, a nod, before she said, *I'm not surprised.*

If you have been paying attention, you may have noticed that in my description above of my time at Oxford, and in related remarks, I did not state the famous name of the alleged benefactor responsible for paying my university bills. An intentional omission, and not a case of benign neglect, I assure you. Though I am eternally indebted and grateful to those who oversee and administer the Trust, those dedicated Trustees whose labors insure that funds are available to aspiring, accomplished young people from all over the globe to educate themselves, better themselves, and lend their strong shoulders to the collective effort of improving life on this planet we all inhabit, I must address to the able Trustees a plea which will surely discomfort them. It seems to me imperative at this moment (as well logical and wise) for the Trust to sever all ties with a so-called founder who was an undeniably evil man. A man, of course, no more evil or good than I am, a man who was a creature of the era that spawned him, just as I am molded by my times, but a ruthless, driven man, blessed/cursed uniquely by the King Midas gift of turning whatever he touched to gold and killing it.

Why should my paltry personal defeats and successes in the world's great fight, the public contributions and derelictions of duty I and my fellow scholars achieve, be linked forever to an unscrupulous businessman who in the name of self-aggrandizement and Empire sought to transform the entire southern end of the African continent into a so-called sphere of influence granted unto himself by himself, a personal fiefdom in which he and white supremacy would reign.

Indulge me just a moment longer, I entreat you, honorable, esteemed Trustees. Imagine an unimaginably wealthy corporation. Imagine it the proprietor of an immensely popular, enormously profitable, internationally distributed brand of athletic products, and for example, let's say that the product line is called *Nike* because in ancient Greece that god's name stood for victory, power, speed. Now suppose archaeologists and other scholars of ancient, extinct languages, cultures, and history discovered they had been all wrong about Nike, that in fact Nike was not the deity signified by a statue of Winged Victory, but the tutelary leader of an outlaw cult of child molesters and murderers. I bet that corporation would be more than anxious, more than well advised to change the name of its brand as rapidly as possible.

. . . is that him passing by, over there, yes, yes, over there, but don't stare, it's him ain't it (the tiny, dapper dan prof notorious on Howard's campus for his mincing walk, suspicious invitations to tea or private tutorials extended to slim first-year boys, his classes welcoming as quicksand, his peculiar style of speaking that smart students mock and snicker at, dumb students envy as it puts them to sleep) him . . . Locke . . .

How can I, or anyone else, be a Rhodes Scholar. *Rhodes Scholar* more than a misnomer. A contradiction in terms, isn't it. Or oxymoron, certainly. How long must I and my fellow scholars submit to the indignity of serving as advertisements, as props in an ongoing propaganda campaign to enshrine the memory, enhance the reputation of a bandit, a brigand who appropriated vast swatches of Africa, removed, exploited, dispossessed, virtually enslaved millions of African people. Why should my name, humble and obscure though it may be, be exploited to further glorify his name. Why should the word *scholarship* be kidnapped, forced to pose naked next to his naked, brazen name. As if such a perverse juxtaposition does not shame the word *Scholarship*. Divest *scholarship* of its positive associations with education and learning, with the disinterested search for knowledge that enlightens self and society.

A scholar-athlete at Oxford? Well, not me, precisely, I should admit. Although, I did try. Suffered through a determined effort to display athletic prowess the general public assumes all American Scholars naturally possess. Second term I auditioned for the role of coxswain in the Hertford College boat. Performed tolerably well, a favorite with the crew, I later learned, until my utter lack of success in swimming lessons disqualified me from competing for the job. Pity, since my body type ideal for a coxswain, and I had discovered that rowing my kind of sport. Quite marvelous to skim along the Cherwell on a bright, spring afternoon, perched in the prow like a Little Prince or Cleopatra on her barge, counting aloud to encourage and invigorate the strokes of lean, well-muscled, young men at the oars.

PROFESSOR LOCKE LECTURES ON NAMES

Does it all begin with names. If we desire to be truly free, free to forge an identity based upon qualities we freely chose, free to invent art and institutions embodying our choices of what we perceive as

beautiful, useful, worthy, we cannot afford to be, as the vast majority of colored folk and most whites are, ignorant as barnyard animals
about the history of our names. If you, as I believe you are, my young
friends, are indeed serious about becoming educated human beings,
I must insist that you cultivate the habit of treating names, especially
the ancient ones bequeathed to us by antiquity, as sacred trusts containing instructions and possibilities. *Ishmael* and *Pliny* are names my
father inherited from two previous generations of his colored family,
but of course the names stretch backwards much further, to countless
generations lost and found, to stories reanimating, retelling, encap-
sulating achievements in countless societies and cultures. Universally
experienced losses, promises, warnings, premonitions, guidance, wisdom, despair.

Names may guide or immure or mock or condemn or warn us, but
unless we choose to be blind as whites who giggle or laugh outright at
niggers with highfalutin handles, or whites who tagged us as they tagged
pet dogs with tongue-in-cheek names like *Aristotle* or *Clytemnestra*, we
must teach ourselves to confront the past that names embody. Embrace
the privilege and responsibilities of names and naming, as I urge all
my students they must, in this lecture I believe my responsibility to
deliver early in each term to every one of my classes. We must disrupt
the process that transforms names to labels, to conveniences for others.
Names contain mysteries. Prophecies. Teach yourselves to peer into
them. Interrogate pasts and futures they bear.

But in a world constantly changing faster than the speed of light,
are names and words ever more than arbitrary signs. Blips, blinks. Futile, illusory handles with which we attempt to grip what's not, what's
never there. One person's *Devil*, another person's *Angel*. The names, the
words employed to identify things expose the unresolvable paradoxes
and presumptions of language. Any language speaks of and reveals only

itself. Repeats, elaborates, reconfirms its initial assumptions. A language teaches a language. One possible language among infinite languages, and no one of them any closer than another to uncovering, authorizing, conferring absolute identity and verification we seek with words and names. No absolute identity. No verification. No match between word and thing final. Necessarily temporary. Relative. Meaning gone with the wind that brought it to our attention. Bereft because a word, a name, though it may momentarily hover and illuminate, does not halt the unceasing flow.

Names appear and disappear. Change. The meaning, the significance of any name or word depends upon circular reasoning. Reasoning that may seem to operate quite dependably, seamlessly, consistently within a given language or culture, often turns out to be patently illogical. Faulty reasoning because it starts with arbitrary assumptions. Assumptions arrived at, not through logical deduction, but by simply constructing motley blends, at best, of fact, fiction, myth. For instance, consider how Europeans view African art or Africans view European art. The source of each group's assumptions about the other's art may be a commendable urge to make sense of another's world, but those assumptions remain, afterall, unproved premises. How else can we proceed? Mortal creatures as we are, we must search for ourselves here. In this place that must be *someplace,* we think. Even though it and our thoughts about it hemmed in by impenetrable darkness. But anyway, we say to ourselves, let's assume this darkness a place, a beginning, a start. Perhaps light will come. Words. Names. More light.

What's true of names, true also about all words in any language. Names are words, and words names, afterall. Arbitrary designations, afterall. Still, they possess the power to form and transform us.

Does answering to names or words others call us mean we have accepted them: *Negro. White. Black. Professor. Scholar. Nigger. Bitch. Father. Artist. Daughter. Brother. Sister. Dead.* Do our names, our words belong to us. Can we deny or refuse them. Buy or sell. Is it possible to compel our names to be answerable to us. Are we able ever to attain the power to name ourselves. Will language generate answers to such vexing dilemmas.

My training in the academic discipline of Philosophy, my years of teaching Philosophy leave no doubt in my mind that language a mixed blessing. Language confuses and silences as often as speaks and clarifies. The problem is, my friends, we are captives of language. And that problem exacerbated beyond measure for some of us by another problem. People of color were, are, and will remain an enslaved people, our bodies and minds captive, unless/until some future, unforeseeable cataclysm, equally as brutal as enslavement, liberates us. Sets us free to say who is beautiful. Who is desirable. What is sweet. What forbidden. Who matters. Who doesn't.

But until that tumultuous day, the names and words we inherit won't free us. They remain signs of damage inflicted. Of defeat. Depleted soil which will continue to yield only a paltry harvest. Until/unless that soil cultivated by New Negroes we must dream and become.

PROFESSOR LOCKE'S LECTURE ON AESTHETICS

We are born heirs and founders of our arts. Heirs and founders of ourselves. Yet doomed to operate at the margins always in our search for beauty. Beauty at the center, the source. No-man's-land of birth and death. Beauty the source, the center that Aesthetics interrogates and contemplates. Never owns. Never ours.

Consider Africa. *Africa* a word. A name. In the art of African-descended people—no matter how many decades or centuries or cultures or miles removed from Africa, no matter how many memories lost and found or erased by force or rekindled purely by dream or wishful thinking, superstition, or religious acts of will and faith—do traces of the African Garden, the Eden, a Motherland, Fatherland survive. My good friend, consummate artist, and collaborator Winhold Reiss, said his friend Professor Keesch, a renowned critic and student of traditional arts and crafts indigenous to the African continent, grew impatient with the otherwise insightful, gifted American sculptor Aaron Douglass who admitted to K his uneasiness, his resistance to African influences because of "doubts and fears that seemed to loom so large in the terrifying specters moving beneath the surface of every African masque and fetish."

What is Africa to me? That initial line of Countee Cullen's poem "Heritage," struck me the first time I read it, not quite as an epiphany, but close, very close to holy writ. Embracing, entangling, and lifting me. In a sense the words felt like mine. A thought I had often pondered. But my thoughts, no matter how compelling, exciting, or earthshaking, or crystal clear they strike me at the moment they occur, are also, always furtive, fleeting, confused. Accessible, comprehensible to me only in a fragmentary, fleeting fashion before they swirl away, absorbed back into the infinitely fertile, inexhaustible ether that produces them.

Countee Cullen's words not my thoughts returning, not thoughts belonging to me unveiled, but words touched, blessed, substantiated by the medium of poetry, poetry's form that allows me an opportunity to slowly, clearly contemplate and interrogate what I perceived only slightly when similar words happened previously to pass through my mind. Formless words of a thought I may have entertained more or less, but as I read Cullen's poem, the words that it held, words released and shaped by poetry, were different words, new words, more true, more alive, with more power and resonance than my poor mind and body ever could have endowed them. I hear the poet's words asking if *Africa*—itself a word and name and question—could free a mind, free a spirit to glimpse the eternal, primal source of Beauty. Not the second order of Beauty, that second order constituted by physical objects that can be rendered materially in stone, words, thread, cloth, stone, metal, flesh, wood, musical notes. Or in a bent but not broken, wind-sculpted tree on an African savanna. Despite the surpassing beauty of such material *things,* whether natural or made by hands, they are not beauty's source. Contemplating and interrogating never reach beauty's source either. But get closer. Closer to the first order of Beauty. They achieve intimations unique to contemplation and interrogation. Irreversible. Irreplaceable. Unbound. Above and beyond the mortal object triggering a response. Apart from that thing you behold or touch or hear or see that's still a captive of time, of time's inevitable dissolution. No matter how fiercely the work of art seems to stare back. Threatens to consume you. It's not Beauty. Not it. Beauty the embracing, entangling, lifting, coming home to roost as you contemplate, interrogate.

Beauty the opposite of crime. Crime binds. Robs. Destroys. Beauty frees. Our colored bodies and minds once upon a time enslaved. Cowed by our captors' crimes, weapons, language, images, ambitions, their plans for us. Captives for centuries aiding and abetting the captors' crimes, weapons, language, images, ambitions, plans. Witting and unwitting accomplices for centuries until this fraught modern moment, this confusion of purposes and intentions, name-calling, lost names, prescribed names, inevitable names, fictitious names, borrowed names and borrowed manners of pronouncing them, invented names, stolen names, this roiling, tiresome conspiracy, this collective, convinced suffering of punishment and dire prediction and undoing of ourselves in which captives and captors indistinguishable, equally imprisoned by histories, languages we share. Claims, complaints, bragging, injuries, pain couched in seemingly identical words by captives and captors. Wombs and graves of crime.

Early, early one morning, water was coming in my door
Early, early one morning, water was coming in my door . . .

Memories form and sort themselves and reform to tell the same old stories over and over of slaves and masters. And yes, yes. Not only am I a witness, I am guilty. I am the story, a bearer and teller of it. I harbor also, as each individual one of us harbors, a distinctly separate, private identity apart from membership in one group or the other. An identity resisted, refused, or unacknowledged because we fear it would be treated by others as an admission of weakness. Each of us bears this secret fear of being outed. Being alone. Hunted. Despised.

And worse, each one of us afraid of being pronounced guilty of being alone. An outcast, beyond redemption. Deeply vulnerable in terms so compromising, so permanent and unforgiving, we strive to keep them hidden from others and ourselves. Like the terms *black* or *white*. Terms burdened by the dimmed, perhaps, yet undiminished reciprocal enmity of captive and captor. The remnants of mutual despising and hatred sealed in hearts and minds. A living vocabulary of insults and deprecations so ugly, so virulent and criminal they shame both speakers and the ones spoken of. A nonnegotiable legacy too terrible to behold without shattering again hearts and minds of all victims and perpetrators of the primal bargain. Those terrors stirred up, once upon a time, each one towards the other, bound together by murderous circumstances that originally united enslaved with enslavers.

I was hollering for mercy, and it weren't no boats around
hollering for mercy, and it weren't no boats around
Looks like people, I've got to stay right here and drown

Crimes committed. Uncommitted. Denied. Imagined. Savored. Unforgotten. Undared. Unforgiven. Celebrated. Presumption and arrogance of captors. Submission and bitterness of captives. Who can say it didn't happen. Doesn't happen. Who can forget. Forgive. Destruction, death, ruination of a people. People erecting, enriching empire upon ruins. Victims and perpetrators who continue dancing the victim-perpetrator/perpetrator-victim danse macabre—the two-step, waltz, jitterbug, cotillion, rag, camel walk, hip-hop, blues, booty wobble, salsa, Charleston, boogie-woogie, ballroom, jig, hillbilly stomp, twist, minuet, jump, shuffle along, quadrille, tango, polka, bunny hop, square dance. What it is. Nameable and not. What else could my life, our lives be as they grow, proliferate, swell, suppurate, encrust, layer on top of layer growing, dying by leaps and bounds, crawling, dancing over and above the original wound, the festering sore incarcerating captor and captive.

My house started shakin, went on floatin on down the stream
Dark as midnight, people began to holler and scream
Dark as midnight . . .

Ishmael. Pliny. Mary. Talk to me. Africa talk to me. Europe, Asia talk to me. Peoples of islands, Peoples of great removals and migrations talk to me. Art talk to me, please. Beauty, please talk . . .

He shivers leaning on the *Lusitania*'s railing. Stares at the sea. Blackness where the Atlantic should be. Churning sea if he could see a sea which night and fog obscure. Impenetrable blackness must be sea because a ship rolls, sways, heaves under his feet. He recalls laughing with his mother at Charlie Chaplin, from seats in the deep rear or upper balcony of a theater, not cheap seats, segregated seats for which they'd paid full fare, the kind of unpleasant detail he chooses to forget usually when he recalls outings with his mother, but it had to be true, didn't it, colored sections, worst locations, but no cut-rate price, just separate seating, since, after all, the theater not in Paris, Berlin, London, or Harlem even, but Washington, DC, nation's capital, home sweet home.

Charlie Chaplin hilarious anyway up on the screen. Bright, bright screen in theater's lights-out darkness, dark enough to cloak his mother's merriment, if she had permitted herself, which she didn't that evening and seldom ever did, to laugh out loud in public. Rare music to his ears. Laughter probably rarer to her own ears, since he doubts she would ever allow herself to hear herself let go. No, no. No unbridled laughter, anonymous dark of theater or not. Rather, the merest titter and tut-tut, muted shivery animation thrilling through her flesh, her laughter next to him, sensible to him, yet nearly as silent as the busy, busy silliness projected on the screen, as he, she watched Charlie Chaplin, watched their unbending world bent by a funny little man. And who isn't grateful to have at their fingertips a funny little man from a faraway funny place to laugh at, teach lessons to, chase away or catch, cook, eat. Small man at their fingertips, a small man transformed, translated into jiggly pixels of light and dark.

Charlie Chaplin crossing the Atlantic, black dab of immigrant mustache above his lip, hurdy-gurdy man's clothes, consigned to take meals in steerage. Minstrel in whiteface, gliding, slip-sliding side to side, bouncing from wooden wall to wooden wall, floor of the room tipping way up then way down, tilting precariously, him teeter-totter, seesaw, careens up and down, across, back and forth, funny and funnier. Charlie bowling ball in his black bowler hat. Amuck. Ping-Pong ball. Tennis ball no net. He's mummy stiff to stay upright. To maintain dignity. Then berserk skater flying over the ice. Flip-flopping, bumping, scrambling, colliding, shaken, shivering, palsied, delirium tremens, boomeranged, paddled, batted to and fro, his dinner plate spilling, splashing other immigrants who scavenge for supper. He delights my mother. Entertains her while she sits regal, aloof as Victoria on her throne. Delights other patrons frisky in their seats, patrons hollering, pointing fingers, slapping knees, guffawing. Charlie Chaplin's unsteady fans, jerky-jerked free at last, free at last as wiggly ghost figures on the screen ha ha ha in early cinema days of herky-jerky pictures.

Even a first-class meal, first-class wine wouldn't settle properly when feet not planted securely to hold a body steady. Food, drink cavort instead of subsiding peacefully. Instead of sliding, draining away seamlessly, calmly turning to shit. Chaotic traffic jam bloats his belly. Horns honk. Sputtering, popping bubbles, flubbers, warm leaks, burps, fart crackles. Waves rolling, sloshing. Nothing sits still. Stuff churning up supposed to be stay put. His mother bobs. Tossed overboard. Frightened, soaked as she is she also frantically pats and presses down her wet hair so it won't get home before she does. Pats, smoothes, slaps, tamps down the white parachute of dress spreading, billowing, slowing her descent, dress she's desperate to keep every single inch of covering every inch of herself as she sinks. Dear Mama in the paddling gaggle of slaves tossed overboard to lighten the load of a steamer to Bremerhaven, light as a cork now, afloat, invisible now in the cold North Sea's tossing and turning.

In 1954 he will die in a hospital bed, turn to ashes. Ashes not urned. Rather shaken into a plastic bag, bag stashed in cardboard box. Box and bag passed from the executor of his will to a woman who had been a friend and writing helpmate, then passed from person to person for years waiting for somebody to claim them. His ashes bagged, boxed as, rumor has it, he had bagged and boxed, for god knows what reason, semen samples of his lovers in bags in a box found among his things by same woman entrusted with possession of his ashes by the executor. Samples of sampled males she destroyed swiftly to prevent rumors, though she kept his ashes till she knew she was dying and passed them to a niece who passed them to Howard University where other colored men who had attended Oxford honored the ashes finally with a ceremony and interment.

Odd way to remember Mama, I must admit. Tossed overboard. Not a malicious act, the ship's captain declared under oath to a Board of Inquiry. Or Inquest, it may have been called. Not a scurvy scheme to collect insurance for a mishandled cargo too rotted, too decimated to coffle ashore and sell to earn a profit. T'waz a matter of them or all of us. To save lives, t'waz necessary to lighten the load, milords. A raging storm. Leaky tub. A judicious choice. Not the slave ship captain's choice. My choice judicious—choice to beseech her company and recall my mama when and how I did, on a ship crossing the Atlantic to Europe, a voyage, a passage I had insisted, begged she share and she had complied a number of times. Even when she shouldn't have. Voyages with her invariably pleasant, even when we could not afford first class. Mama loved them. Me, too. Too late if I had postponed our maiden voyage together till after 1922, the year she passed, or till after 1954, my year to pass. Year the Court said *no*. Said *yes*. Year before, that poor boy in Mississippi lynched.

In *Etiquette: The Blue Book of Social Usage,* Emily Post, ultimate arbiter of good manners, wrote, "The person who has passed away is sometimes left lying in bed in night clothes, or on a sofa in a wrapper, with flowers, but no set pieces, about the room, so that an invalid or other sensitive bereft one may say farewell without ever seeing the all too definite finality of a coffin . . ."

D'you hear the latest about that crazy Locke and his stiff-assed mama. Well, she sure nuff stiff now. Dead for days and the simple man won't put her in the ground. Invited some her friends, some his, to a tea party Sunday past, and there his mama sits big as life on the sofa, in a gray silk dress, saucer on her lap, gloved dead fingers stuck in a teacup handle.

In a letter (cited by Jeffrey Stewart in his monumental, indispensable biography of Locke) a friend of Alain Locke quotes to Locke from a note she received from a mourner at his mother's wake, "she spoke of the very sweet, natural picture that your mother made lying there on the couch in her pretty gray dress with just a few blossoms here and there."

Oh, dear Mama. Mama Dear. I miss you so much. I do. I miss you so very much. Tears now prevent me, but tomorrow, Mama, I will write the note to the young man who hurried away. Who could not attend your wake. I must ask him why.

He stirs blackness with his outstretched left hand, readying himself, after scooting his hips close to the bed's edge, to shift his weight to his backside and fling back covers with his right hand, before kicking out his freed legs over the edge to sit up, bare feet slapping the wooden floor, bare knee touching the corner of a small, bed-height table where each night he positions before sleep, on top of a gooseneck lamp's steady, copious base, a glass tumbler only one-third full, so when he gropes for it in the dark, he won't splash the nice wood tabletop nor tablet nor note cards and couple pencils it's his habit to set out every night as he sets out water before sleep, water not to drink, but to take a mouthful whenever the need to pee awakens him before morning, mouthful he rinses round, retaining it, not swallowing it, water might trigger more undesired trips, but water relieves unpleasant dryness of lips, tongue, gums, keeping them moist until he spits the mouthful into the toilet a few paces beyond his bedroom door, in the bathroom where the urge to pee impels him far too often at night, and getting worse as he ages, disturbing his rest, delaying the deep, rare peace that occasionally awaits him when he's lucky, peace he hopes will drown him after he gropes for the squat, wide-bottomed tumbler with fluted sides which provides a firm grip, his glass appropriate for performing duties he depends upon it to perform in the dark while he's still half-asleep, still on his back in the bed, no glass raised yet to his lips, nor replaced on the lamp's pedestal, a lamp seldom switched on at night except for emergencies, Locke choosing instead to perform in darkness, choreographing in his mind a very familiar but not inevitable scenario—water, exit bed, emptying mouth, emptying bladder, then in bed again, under sheets, blanket again—seeing and not seeing, performing, not performing the act, preferring darkness, not turning on the lamp a judicious choice, as judicious as when, aboard the steamer, he decides to recall his mother, and he does and witnesses and does not witness poor Mama floating, sinking invisible in blackness of night, of sea.

[1954]

Once retired from Howard University, moving from Washington, DC, and settled into his New York City apartment at 12 Grove Street, *Smalls Paradise* the name of the Harlem bistro (or club or nightclub or bar or nightspot) he frequents. The name, *Smalls Paradise,* an absolute scream and he sometimes wishes he could holler it aloud, wishes for someone special he could trust to holler and scream with him. Somebody to laugh, scream with him because it is damned funny. Almost laughed out loud the day he heard a stranger say Smalls Paradise and suddenly, for the first time, the joke hit him. An absolute scream, whether the joke at his expense or not. *Smalls Paradise.* To share the dumb joke, somebody wouldn't even have to be acquainted with the Greek language origins of the word *paradise.* That once upon a time *paradise* signified undressed, without clothes, naked. No. Just knowing paradise a kind of happy place, happy, dappy like heaven supposed to be. And everybody knows *small* means small. Means, you know, *little* compared to big. Just possessing the general knowledge most people possess enough to get the joke. And knowing little him. Small Locke. But finding a trustable somebody with whom to laugh and scream, that's the hard, the rare, impossible part. Leaves him to laugh alone, to scream alone at his own damned self. Ha ha ha. Look. Look at that little nigger. Small, ain't he. And he loves this joint. Look at the nigger smiling and talking a mile a minute, grinning at some, ignoring other niggers sitting, coming and going out the padded little boof. Ha ha ha happy like he done died and gone to heben. And ha ha ha ain't that funnier than shit ha ha ha cause he stone small, stone little small midget, little nigger and the joint's name *Smalls Paradise.*

C'mon, Locke. I don't believe Zora Neale be sassing her white lady patron like that. Puttin her ofay Fairy Godmother in the dozens. She didn't really say *art, books, white people can kiss her black ass,* did she. And Langston bust in wearing *what.* University of Berlin, you say. Paris, you say. Richard Wright you talking bout. The Native Son Wright, right. Well, I be. And every kind of artist, you say, actually hanging out over there cross the pond. Giacometti, the cat I dig because he sculpts figures cut down to the bone, almost nothing left when he finishes and youall called him Snowman you say because he leaked trails of white plaster dust on the street between his studio and the cafe where everybody hung out. A witness. Say you and your mama got jammed up in Berlin, heard the Kaiser over there on the radio declaring the First World War. Damn.

You been everywhere, Locke. Cities most us dream bout seeing. Never will. Certainly not see like you, my man. Naming names. Taking names. Bearing witness. Fessing up.

Huh-uh. You not just talking bout folks. Talked to them. Said you teaching at University of Wisconsin, a black visiting prof at a major white school way back then, and just that fact itself would be a big deal to hear about, but on top that news you passing along, you say Paul Robeson showed up on campus with his white girlfriend Uta Hagen, Desdemona to his Othello in the big hit play they touring, both of them there, you said, cause her parents lived in Madison you said and all youall at a big dinner in Robeson's honor at the University President's home and you wanted to ask Robeson why he choose to sing spirituals so they sound as if they had been born and raised and continue to flourish and should be performed in the same classical manner, same tradition that produced Schubert lieder. Ask why a brown Paul Robeson and other brown concert artists not acknowledging in any way, shape, or form that spirituals are transplants from Africa, from bush arbors hidden in the woods on Southern plantations, and singing them had often meant risking lives, including the singer's life, but all Robeson did, you say, when he wasn't talking politics and union organizing and class struggle, was flirt and drink the whole evening.

Damn, Locke. You a lucky man. But you say at Oxford the African brothers and West Indians and East Indians teased you about Garvey. Said ha ha you American Kneegrows preaching *Back to Africa* ain't never *been to* Africa, so how you going *back*. And W. E. B. DuBois, Booker T, Bessie Smith, Horace Pippin, Mrs. Roosevelt and a couple U.S. presidents, and Duke, Ella, Satchmo, Simone de Beauvoir, Jean Toomer, Claude McKay, Josephine Baker, Ma Rainey—actual conversations with all those stars, and damn . . . hey . . . me, ignorant-ass me and the rest of us sitting round here sipping these fine Smalls cocktails, we could listen to you forever . . . thank you, my man . . . cheers, bro . . .

Home again, home again, Mama. Alone again. Miss you, Mama, more and more. It's very late and I'm very tired. Hope to fall asleep right away. Deep, peaceful sleep, Mama. Pray for me, Mama. A good sleep, and then tomorrow, bright and early, I'm going to write that note and ask why he left so soon.

ANOTHER STORY

THE WORK OF IMAGINING MYSELF to be the person I imagine is much more impossible than fiction writing. Conceiving who I am demands all of fiction writing's trickiness, dissatisfactions, concentration, and pointlessness, but no stops or starts, no stepping outside, no revision. Everything and nothing forever on the page. Work in progress without progress. Expressed in words of a language no one else on the planet speaks. Person I try to imagine being made up as life passes, as life consumed, never feels quite me, but someone or something like a weather report that drones on and on about what I already see out my window, but no forecast. Or like a beach book plot predictably unrolling page after inevitable page whether anybody's reading it or not or like a person halfway overhearing stories other people are telling in which that person is probably butt of a joke or dead or both or feels like someone I am when I lie to myself.

It's easy to mix up days and times, mix up where you are going with where you have been, what you intend to do next with what is done already. Mix up things you possess with things you desire. Age, of course, complicates the mixing up. And aging, itself, is easy to mix up with being young again, innocent again, no more responsible for getting everything mixed up than a robin or roach trying to write a story about humans.

Be that as it may, hopelessly confused and not, I lead a life that I can't quite identify as mine, but one thing I'm sure of—I know I have a daughter and love her and must hurry to her because I am her father and she is hurt and crying and afraid of losing her daughter.

My daughter's mother, the woman who was my wife when my daughter born and thank goodness not my wife now, loves our daughter at least as much as I do and probably she is already at our daughter's bedside. Though not my wife now, she doesn't stop being my daughter's mother and the woman who named her. Woman who insisted as our children grew up and learned to speak, they should call us by our first names. Not *mama, papa, mommy, daddy.* Parents just plain folks, older, bigger, yes, except people our kids would learn loved them dearly because of how we treated them, and our kids would learn to love us, and we would become a family understanding, depending upon each other, sharing bonds of mutual love as we all aged together I guess was my ex's idea. Or ideal, I should say, to be fair. In her mind family should be the result of actions, a natural process rather than a template imposed from above by big people upon helpless little ones. My ex-wife's intention clear enough and reasonable in a way, so despite my reservations, I didn't oppose her. When our firstborn, my baby daughter, started speaking, kind of cute to have that tiny bit of a thing address me by my given name, *Cyrus,* though also embarrassing occasionally when folks not family overheard or my mother or sister rolled their eyes at one another as if to ask why in hell is this child being taught a language different from the one everybody else in the family speaks.

My sister always called our father *Daddy.* Still does after all those years of him not around and long dead now. For our mother he was always *Cyrus.* Never anything shorter. *Cyrus.* Not *Cy.* Nor *Russ.* Always

Cyrus. No play with the sound of the name to turn a bit of it or some echo or rhyme buried in the sound of it into another name. *Renee* to *Ray-Ray. Cheryl* to *Rell. Tunsia* to *T.* Generations of aunts, nieces with a couple few names apiece. Alternatives not to express dissatisfaction with a proper given name, but in our family a way to give space, choices, no cut-and-dry slot for a name or a person. Room to grow, change, outgrow. To let us get used to one another on each one's own terms. True or invented. But my father always *Daddy* for my sister, *Cyrus* for my mother, as if each had learned, nay, been instructed unforgettably once and for all in some darkly frightening subterranean chamber, what was proper for a wife, a daughter to call him, and when speaking love or hate or anything in between they could put into their voices, neither my mother nor sister dared try out another name for my father.

Comes back to me now that it was much more common in our family to play with female names than male names. And I seem to recall also it was the women who conferred most of the names that stuck. A male could earn or get caught by a street name and it might be repeated at home, but didn't fit there. Lost power and edge. Street world and family world different. Men supposed to rule both and believed they did until reminded they had no home, no family if stories put home and family business in the street. Or if they looked around and found their women and children out there in the street where a man's women and children were not supposed to be, they, the men, ruled no separate world with separate rules separating places they could call home or street, and thus if they really thought about it, perhaps ruled nothing.

When I became a father, my father was no longer around, so the fact I bore the same name as my father not confusing for my baby daughter. Only one Cyrus for her to keep track of. Which she did quite well until

I, too, like my father, stopped being around. *Cyrus* gone. For my daughter *Cyrus* probably became a ghost word in ghost stories. Like *Daddy* was a ghost word in ghost stories for my sister after her father and mine left home. What does my daughter call me now in stories she tells herself.

I see my daughter on the other side of a glass wall, and she isn't there, I know. Confusion. Me getting mixed up again. She is not waiting for me in an airport lounge. Impossible as her standing next to me smiling as we stare together down at the red creature (all we can see of its flesh, a tiny, angry red fist of bandaged head poking out from swaddling, tubes, wires) that had nearly killed its mother. Not her, not my daughter in the premie ward looking down at herself, it's my first wife beside me, both of us exhausted, not quite sure whether to believe or not that one of the infants behind a glass wall, in a row of incubators hooked up to machines, had spent seven months inside her belly. Both of us terrorized still, two days after a bruising, precarious birth with no survivors almost. Impossible almost for a daughter to be alive and breathing. Impossible as it would be today for my daughter to be standing on the other side of a transparent wall separating incoming passengers from people waiting for planes to land. Impossible because she is in a hospital bed and doesn't know her father on his way so why would she be at the airport trying to find me among a crowd of arrivals.

No, it will be me, alone on my side of the glass imagining her, as once in a waiting room her mother and I had tried to imagine her, neither of us speaking, lights on all night, afraid to look at hands of a big white clock, afraid to fall asleep, as if by pure force of our wills we could keep her alive after the doctor said sorry, but I must tell you this . . . very, very unlikely she'll make it through the night and I'm sorry, so sorry to have to say it, but you folks need to know . . . not impossible . . . she may pull through . . . don't lose hope . . . she's some little fighter and we're doing our best . . . everything in our power . . . and truth is we never know for certain one hour to the next . . . but X-rays show infection spreading, spotting her lungs and you should prepare yourselves for the worst . . . not hopeless, she may survive, he says . . . she's tough he says and we won't give up on her he says and busy, busy he leaves, leaves each of us, her mother, me, as alone as we have ever been. But daughter's lungs miraculously clear next morning. *Miracle,* doctor's word after the longest night, night of not waiting for morning. No such thing as morning could exist until . . . if. No word for morning, no word for night, only utter emptiness stretching until . . . if . . . Not waiting for morning, simply alone with nothing to wait for or to say, nothing beyond emptiness. And I imagine my daughter again, here, today, at the airport to greet me because unspeakable again if she's not.

I stop at a glass wall and there's her mother, off to one side, a good distance away from me, from congestion where airport doors connect secure areas to public space. She's closer to magazines, drinks, snacks in a row of kiosks than to an automatic sliding entrance I step through, and if she sees me, she maintains her distance you could say, a discreet, ambiguous distance, not anxious to greet nor avoid me either. Clearly not really there for me, even if she is.

Easy to mix things up. Not her after all in the airport mall. Another smallish, trim woman gray hair bobbed short who from a distance might be mistaken for my ex, but a mistake probably I would not have committed before I got old. That familiar stomach cringe of uneasiness, of hopelessness each time I realize I'm confused and how easy now to stay confused.

One daughter. One son. Simple enough to remember. Though since son's daughter born same month as her father and same day, the twenty-sixth, plus or minus one, often I can't keep straight whose birthday—

son or granddaughter—comes first. A confusion I admit and joke about almost proudly, basking like a patriarch in an abundance of generations when just yesterday it seems I was a boy myself.

Son another *Cyrus*. Nobody knows the name I gave him unless they ask. He goes by his middle name. I am sure my son to this very day doesn't claim *Cyrus* without some pressing reason to fess up. Odd, old-fashioned, foreign. You know. Funny sounding. Kind of name other kids tease. No disrespect, Pops, to you or Grandpop, wherever he might be. Even proud maybe. Just I don't go round announcing it. Especially after all those years I was sposed to call you *Cyrus,* and didn't like it cause it sounded like, you know, weird, old-timey, something to get teased about when what I really wanted was just to call you Pop or Daddy or Father or whatever, you know. When you were little, were you sposed to call your father *Cyrus.* Did you obey, Pops.

Doesn't matter if I'm making up that conversation or we actually had it or one very close to it occurred, it had to have happened. Not an old man's confusion. Nor an imitation of an imitation of a talk I wish we had. Believe me. I wish things had been different.

Anyway, bag in hand, briefcase slung over shoulder, on my way to see my daughter, not my son, I follow taxi signs in the airport, join a long queue. Big airport in a big city I have been to before. *Been-to* a kind of person, I remember suddenly, not because I chose to, not because it was a word popping up instantly when I needed it. Word memory like all memories now, a hit-or-miss shambles, junkyard, graveyard, detour, sinkhole. Memory possesses a will of its own. *Been-to.* Did that word originate in Africa. Can a person be a *been-to* if not born in Africa. Better be careful. If a stray word or too many words distract me, I might find myself forgetting why I'm waiting in line. Mouth open with nothing to say when one of the guys in yellow cap, yellow vest, dangle of chits in hand, asks where you going, saahh.

Same yellow-color vests flooded Paris this spring. Not singing "April in Paris." Vests rousting people. Accosting you on the street with nobody's-business questions. Yellow vest barricades blocking traffic. Demanding answers from you as if they have a perfect right and your sole perfect right to answer. Correct answer only. And if you are not sure what the question is, they are quick and happy to tell you the answer. Yellow vests. Yellow malignancy spreading in the great metropolis. All of France under siege. Yellow fever. Yellow fever once upon a time contracted by travel to tropical places. But a trip to the tropics doesn't make you a *been-to*. Wrong direction. Do I remember reading *been-to* a word invented in Ghana. Efik slang referring to Ghanaians who had been to Great Britain and back. Word also signifying uppity, arrogant. Know-it-alls after a year, a day abroad. Believe themselves suddenly more sophisticated politically, culturally than their downtrodden, stay at home, going nowhere brethren. Act like they think maybe their color different, different color like their different accents they affect when they return home.

My guess lots of children of been-tos among yellow vests hassling Parisians. Perfect recruits. People with shitty jobs, no jobs. People angry at the shitty rich getting richer because shitty government keeps wages low, keeps taxes on rich falling, on poor rising. Second generation of colored misfits alienated from parents themselves alienated. Where do these immigrant kids of been-tos belong. Why did their families work so hard to send them away. Away to places they do not fit. Not welcome. Been-tos' children (mine?) heirs of doubled dissatisfaction.

Where's home if you have been-to and when you go back to where you came from, it's not there. Not happy there, and no happy ending elsewhere. Not comfortable. Not welcome. Permanently been-to. Belonging nowhere. Confused. Permanently estranged. Neither one thing nor tother. Like colored immigrants in my country with their air of superiority, their condescending manner when they deal with us native darkies. Big-city immigrants with an attitude, driving taxis, passing out taxi chits at the end of a waiting line last time I passed through this airport, which is not this time so don't get mixed up. Quietly wait your turn. Enjoy colors, accents swirling round you. A been-to, myself, and daughter dear, dear son been-tos, too. Daughter who waits. Peering through glass bowl, iron bars of cage for signs of life.

But no. No. Neither she nor I are fish in somebody's bowl. Not aliens. Not somebody's slave. Figured that out a long time ago. *Slave* a nasty idea that divides human beings into kinds. Absolute, eternal kinds. Old, old idea that some people have no rights other people are bound to respect. Idea that certain individuals or groups belong in a high category and others in lower categories, lower orders of humanity that qualify them as eligible for enslavement. Or eligible for worse. Or nothing. Simple as that. An idea that grants enslavers license to grant themselves license to prey upon particular groups they deem lower.

The idea of *slave* comes first—alive, festering in the minds of potential enslavers. *Slave* a nasty idea. Wishful thinking. *Slave* an imaginary creature enslavers attempt to make real once they gain power to prey upon particular individuals and groups, power to impose their will upon them. Power to separate, subordinate, discipline, and punish. Catch and cage. Swim you round and round in a fishbowl.

Where is my girl. Does she see me through the glass. Will I see her. Break through silence of glass. Silence of been-to. Silence of what comes next.

If I send what I have written so far to my editor, she would likely respond—*can't figure out where this piece going—no plot . . . no story yet . . .*

Your email received—agree completely—no story . . . no plot . . . all I can
add is maybe no character either—on the other hand, old friend, what's a
guy to do—maybe I have another (last) story in me, and my only choice to
follow it to its grave or it follows me to mine . . .

Naturally, given my color and colors of my family, I think a lot
about enslavement. Not because some of my ancestors may have been
slaves. They were not slaves any more than I am a one. But our color, of
course, since it's a quality enslavers designate as an absolute and eternal
sign of inferiority, our color, no matter what else color might prove or
not, naming us by a color means the idea of *slave* still exists. Most of
my family members yesterday and today in jeopardy. And no, I'm not
confused about color or slavery. Not mixed up about slavery by old age
as I warned you I tend frequently to get befuddled by some things. Old
fool not necessarily every kind of fool, and maybe an old fool harder to
fool than a young fool.

One way I think deeply about enslavement is lying belly down
naked on a massage table. Self-indulgent I admit. Bodywork with Chinese ladies whose skilled hands perform it during hourlong and occasionally longer sessions, me belly down, sometimes belly up, not cheap.
Such regular pampering of myself may be pure overkill and indulgence,
but thinking is not. Thinking a necessity. Especially thinking about enslavement. And no place I've discovered more perfect for thinking about
enslavement and freedom or anything else for that matter, once I pull
my clothes off and stretch out flat on my stomach, than a dimly lit,
closet-size room with a massage table. Barely enough space in the cubicle for the small Chinese woman who became my favorite, to maneuver.
The Chinese woman who waited on the other side of a door she closed
always for propriety's sake while I arranged myself on the table. Chinese
woman impatient before she starts her work, impatient to leave imme-

diately after she finishes her work, impatient because her hands with no profitable work to do as she stands waiting on the other side of the door while I undress or until I get dressed and open the door again for her to reenter and collect fee we settled upon, and a variable tip.

Impatient not a fair word. *Impatient* suggests unpleasant behavior. My special Chinese woman scrupulous. Quite aware she's on the clock, paying rent to a proprietor she calls *Boss* for every minute we spend in the room and me paying her by the hour, so she keeps a very strict accounting, but I never felt impatience or hurry in her fingertips when they were working my body. No unpleasantness. In the stuffy, cramped stall I daydreamed. Experienced enjoyable minute after minute of our time together, and nothing prevented me from imagining each minute felt as precious to her as it felt to me. Her mannerisms indicating impatience not directed at me, I chose to believe. Thus they caused me no discomfort. It's the clock ticking, the pressure to earn a living that got to her. Just as before and after our sessions, certain details sometimes bothered me. Our situation complicated by the fact I spoke only seven words of Chinese, three words or less on one of my bad days, and her English not much better than my Mandarin. Many years of rendezvous and still the languages we each spoke mutually incomprehensible.

Again, I am not being fair. Apart from our embarrassing, nearly total ignorance of the other's language, the Chinese woman and I understood each other and communicated much more than adequately well. Perfectly well, I almost wrote, to describe our exchanges, but I don't want to drop the word *perfect* into this work in progress too often. Overusing it as I overused *shay-shin-nee* (thank you), and she repeatedly injected *yoo well-cum,* into our conversations. Cute maybe, but clumsy attempts to compensate for our inability to express complex thoughts, feelings, good intentions that lack of a shared language made it impossible to address. Except with a couple fumbling, mispronounced phrases. But the Chinese lady's hands beyond articulate kneading my flesh. Quiet, graceful, understated dance of her movements transformed a tight space to intimacy, abundance. Strength in her powerful arms that twisted and stretched my limbs, also lifted the low ceiling, pushed back partitions incarcerating us. I floated in immensity. Undaunted, free. Chattering with an ancient, invisible friend. Or wondrous silent contemplation ignited—no words necessary. Able to contemplate enslavement's terror, the perils and contradictions of my naked, colored life (or hers) calmly, with clarity.

Perfect. A word like *beautiful.* A superlative you better save, warned Hemingway, for the once, maybe twice in a writer's life it may be called for, and thus perhaps earned, sayeth Ernest. Cheap shot otherwise. Bad art. Show not tell, he commands. Called us nigger to show and tell his opinion of us.

Naked, completely at ease, when exposed to her eyes first time and every massage after. Nodding no thank you to blanket, then towel the Chinese woman offered. My body in all its beginning to show age, naked ungloryness not news to her. I lay down, and no frills, she began. My penis had never before been so unambiguously, frankly, intelligently addressed. Nudged aside by back of her hand when it blocked access to muscles of upper thigh, adjusted from vertical to horizontal or vice versa by a gentle, two-finger grip when it pointed in wrong direction and complicated her view of whatever part of my anatomy she wished to treat.

When I turned over on my stomach, sometimes she sat on me, flesh of our legs touching if summer and she's wearing shorts. On a few occasions, after standing on my tensed buttocks to gain her balance, she'd strolled slowly up and down my back, bare toes gripping, flexing like fingers along both sides of my spine. I was body like I'd never been body before. All those years of life had passed and never before been as separate from myself as she taught me to be, or rather taught me the parts of myself she separated from me and returned as gifts. Parts free, truly belonging to me for the first time. Parts partly exhausted, partly yearning immediately afterwards for it all to happen again. Her hands, her work breaking aeons of silence that my body parts no longer content to suffer. Lost and found. Oh—wondrous contemplation—no words . . .

Not perfect. Nor perfectly innocent. Erection now and then. A surprise first time, and she looks a bit puzzled as she peers down, raises her eyebrows slightly before she pats me, strokes once, slowly, eyes fixed on mine bidding me to follow her gaze upward to her other hand that makes a fist in the air, then slides up and down rapidly, as if fingers curled around an invisible shaft, a carrot, stick, candy bar whatever. I see my mother's Oh, you naughty boy begrudging smile in the Chinese woman's black eyes questioning mine until I shut mine, then hardly a blink or sigh's worth of closed before I open them again and nod a no no . . . no thank you, ma'am, no. Huh-uh. Price of the ticket clearly includes anything you wish, anything you politely desire, saahh, just say so, saahh, she silently lets me know. Or says whatever words Mr. Hemingway would write into mouths of coolies and darkies, words of willing accomplices, not victims, or just plain dumb words mimed by Mr. Conrad, Mr. Hemingway to make their stories good and true.

Still having problems following plot, story . . . perhaps too many stories and plots . . . not clear where you want to go with this draft . . . why so much Chinese woman . . . does she belong here . . . or in another story maybe . . .

Married twice my story goes, or went. Color line crossing still slightly scandalous when I got hitched first time. For a hot minute after I wed my first wife, tabloids couldn't get enough. Match made in heaven. Or hell. Race bee in their bonnets got them all buzzing. Where are they now when my poor, deserted books bleating for attention. Second marriage aroused hardly a blip in press. Article in my hometown paper quoted a longtime intimate who "confided to this reporter." A changed man, he confided. So what. Any man always many men. As a woman is always many women. Simple story. Why twist it into melodrama. Me, a man with wife and children, took a second wife after love between me and first wife died. And truth be told, not certain to this day who deserted whom first.

Second wife French. Our love story created by two people from quite different places. A love also inseparable from a single place now: Brittany. Particular Brittany days, not exactly perfect, but close enough to remind me that being alive a couple minutes not a bad deal, even if price is being confused often, then dead forever after.

Still with first wife when I went to Chinese women. And went to my favorite Chinese woman, too. The one who became the sole one I visited. But she was many women like I am many men. My first session with her, once upon a time, before she found the cheap storefront with its street-level warren of massage cubicles and flophouse rooms beneath, I had stood with her at a desk at the top of stairs that rose steeply, abruptly from a sidewalk door. There on the second landing, an outgoing client, gray-haired, but younger than me, whispered loud enough for all clients sitting on two benches to hear, a half greeting, half assertion of his prior acquaintance with the Chinese woman, reminding her of a previous condition of servitude: Yu-Yu . . . little Yu-Yu. Wow . . . been a long time, little Yu-Yu. Good times weren't they, Yu. Hey . . . you still look great, Yu-Yu.

During one session, just before tearing from a yard-wide roll of paper exactly enough to serve as a sheet for the massage table, she had pointed to a small, round hole more or less centered in the scantily padded plywood slab that served as table's mattress. Inserting a finger into the hole, she wiggled it. A reproving nod for the hole, for mouths of shameless girls, once upon a time, I assumed, stationed below it on their hands and knees. Then, with a swiftness any good writer of fiction would envy, she shifted her story's point of view. As if to inspect the darkness beneath, she poked her head under the table, then quickly popped out and up, rolling her eyes, smiling, her lips imitating some character's nasty deed she would never dare.

Once upon another time, when no room in our usual inn, a friend of hers who worked there, led us, for a modest tip, through numerous sorry-assed Chinatown streets to a tall, crooked, narrow building with a low-ceilinged third floor crammed with plastic-curtained stalls. While I lay on my tummy and the Chinese woman tugged, squeezed, beat staccato with heels of both hands on my knotted calf to unkink it, people sucked and fucked, thrashing loudly inches away. Was this god-awful place new to her, I wondered, but of course I couldn't ask, and we may have come closest to making love that afternoon as we ever did. No front door for cops or *Boss* she feared to bust through. Not on that woebegone street, building. And despite respectability and cool distance she consistently projected, she definitely wasn't shy or innocent, was she. Not ashamed. So why not. Why not get it on then and there. No wife I loved then. Thus loyalty, betrayal irrelevant. Mostly we didn't, I guess, because I was confused by the fact I didn't know the Chinese words for asking. And didn't know whether I should ask or not. Or why.

Sad for both of us, I think, looking back. No choice. No freedom. Too much history behind us. Whether we did it or didn't, I had no way to tell her that I believed whatever we did do could be something more than, something other than business. More than pleasant, therapeutic business for me. Something other than compulsory business for her. Position, money, and power I possessed, though not impressive to me, made demands on her. How would she know that I did not assume that she was obliged to perform whatever services I desired from her. How was she supposed to figure out that I didn't believe the natural-born order of the universe was for me to expect, to demand, and her duty, her fate, no questions asked, to comply. If she couldn't know what I couldn't tell her, how would she understand I was not treating her as a slave. And worse, if she behaved like a slave because she believed she must act like one in order to get paid, wouldn't that make her a slave. Me an enslaver.

No Chinese words to explain myself to a Chinese woman, let alone no English words with which I could explain myself to myself. Did my nakedness begging for her deft hands enslave me. No English to explain myself to myself then, nor later to explain my past choices to a woman, a wife I love.

Freedom. Precious freedom. In this land that is supposed to be free, I must work hard to stay free. I write not only because I'm selfish and vain, but to stay free. And to get paid. To remember. To imagine myself, my children, a wife, a Chinese woman free. Hard and easy. Easy and hard. I try not to get mixed up. Confused. Hard and easy. Easy and hard. Imagining free.

Different languages not a problem with my second wife. Not only does she speak English better than I do, she hears the words I do not say. Once, when I wanted to tell her about the Chinese woman and enslavement, I worried she might get the wrong idea, so warmed up by saying something to my wife about how much I loved, respected, cherished her, would risk doing anything in my power to avoid losing or hurting her. Her eyes thanked me. She patted my shoulder, and then said, I'm touched. I love you, too. Now, tell me what you want, sir. Or what you want me to forgive . . .

I smiled back. Swallowed my story. Perhaps I should have said: Until aging's infirmities and practical-headedness suggested that separate rooms, separate beds more convenient, before we conceded to that reality, before we allowed age to interfere, during all those years with you beautiful beside me every night, those years before we let time and tides bully us, I never missed the charms of other women's bodies, nor envied the erotic luck of any other man on earth, nor missed the legendary sexual prowess and irresistibility once upon a time I attributed to myself.

I did confess to her that I believed cutting myself off from my children an unforgivable error. Irreparable, of course. I tell her that I cannot imagine why I did what I did. Deserting my children. I can't imagine who I was when I decided to leave and never return. You cannot imagine how much I miss them. Daughter. Son. And now grandkids. Do any of them ever speak my name. I can't imagine the blindness of the person I thought I was when I left. Can't imagine returning and finding no one there.

Let's do a travel book next, my dear editor and friend—I will embark on a make-believe or actual journey, then the book, TV series, movie—a winning combo. Lots of bucks, an agent assures me. On the back of some exotic beast, I will galump-galump solo through bizarre, dangerous terrain *inconnu,* reach China's Great Wall, and when I arrive, peer through its ancient stones, contemplate the billions of souls behind them. Shout over the wall's towering top, *Yu-Yu . . . Ahoy, Yu-Yu.* And what a wondrous tale if someone answers. A good story, right—my first bestseller, blockbuster—even if no voice responds.

———

Very difficult, I imagine, my son, to wish to become a writer and have a father who is a writer, especially the kind of writer who thinks himself scrupulously dedicated to the craft and art of writing and who would not praise a son's work, would not wish nor consent to read a son's story, son understands, unless work of the highest order. How you sposed to show your stuff to a guy professing such bullshit, guy on the record for professing it. His reputation propped up by such professions more than any immortal words of fiction he ever captured on the page. How, why would you risk your writing in his hands. And to top it all off, he brands you, his son, perpetually, with *Cyrus,* his phony-sounding name.

Critics would exploit a son's work—exploit his (our) name. Reduce a son's novels or poems to biography, melodrama (same treatment mine get). Our story public, easy to exploit, good copy—son a follower of father or not, better writer or not, pissed off or not by decades of estrangement, envious or cowed or keen to emulate Poppa's shining example or defeated by it. Unforgiving, angry, bloodthirsty, and determined to chop the daddy, replace him. Easy for critics to find easy things to say, easy to say nothing.

Luckily no bloody fights with my first wife in the middle of the kitchen floor need to be edited from the record, from this draft, from a story a son might write. When love changed to indifference then dislike and then terminal intolerance, I went away, cut absolutely ties with a wife and two young kids. To save the children, to spare them, I disappeared. Disappeared totally from my kids' lives, a check a month for years my sole connection and I'm not certain to this day if their mother let them know I contributed regularly, substantially (when I was able) to their financial well-being.

My absence also motivated of course by purely selfish reasons, by factors undefinable at the time I left. Emotions I haven't figured out yet. Though if truth be told, I stopped a good while ago those endless, unproductive, inconclusive ruminations and interrogations which lead nowhere other than pain.

What else is there to say. Best I'm able to do, I guess, is to finish this story. A story I'm delivering to you with words, words, too many words. Blah-blah generalities to support my side of things. Few details. Few recollected. Or perhaps details repressed, suppressed. Unavailable to me is the point. So what does my story prove. Alter. Take back. Mixed up or not. Then or now.

Language. Each possesses one of his or her own. Incorrigibly nontrans-latable.

For instance, when I hear or read the word *dog,* I see a brown and white spotted, four-footed, tired, furry rag Teddy asleep on a pile of rags in a corner behind the stove, or slunking around stinky in my grand-mother's kitchen, or scooting away from blows of a rolled-up newspaper Grandma turned into a weapon in her fist in the house where we stayed, my mother and two, three of us kids for two years while my mother and father *not getting along* we were told, and I remember my grandmother putting old, old Teddy out the kitchen door to eat from his bowl on the back porch or do his business in the alley, and later when she opened the door again to let Teddy in, she growled, *Get in here, fool,* and when he didn't come back, Grandma armed with a rolled section of the *Pitts-burgh Post-Gazette* went outside in her housecoat, remaining a very long time for a bitter cold day seemed to me, and when she finally pushed back into the kitchen, and pulled shut behind her the door and torn aluminum screen door attached permanently to it all seasons, too raggedy to repair, a new one too expensive, she stood there, shoulders shivering, cold I thought, and said, *Ted gone.*

While my children were growing up, easier to follow my daughter's life than my son's. She hooped and was great at it so there were school teams, box scores, seasons, and eventually plenty of national media coverage of what was for the most part her astounding success. My son played ball, too, through high school, and I heard much later, he was pretty good. Somehow I also learned of his intention to write. Maybe he was my source of this knowledge, but if I heard him voice either his ambition to write or a belief he possesses the grit and tools to make himself heard, it had to be in fairly recent phone conversations or emails, because only very recently, barely, have my kids and I commenced communicating again. Neither kid, adult daughter, adult son, has met my second wife. Anyway, son wants to be a writer. *Why.* Why choose obscurity. Who cares about wannabe writers, and how many aspiring writers ever become more than wannabes. Greater failure rate than among little colored youngsters who dream of stardom in the NBA.

Ambition to write, for just about anybody—colored or not, father a published author or not—a dead end. No exit. Something like being a been-to who's never been-to. Invisible. You don a yellow vest so people see you, and then they see color not you. Tough hustle, and I respect my son's choice. Proud, you might even say. Especially if he knows what the fuck he's choosing. But loving, supportive father or not, I can't help entertaining serious doubts about his vocation, or livelihood, or calling, or mission, or crusade, or effort to purify or demolish the language, or immolation, or nothing, or hype, or lie. Whatever the fuck writing is. See. I can't even say, though this very instant I believe I'm engaged in writing, and for over half a century have been engaged. Soon to leave behind reams and reams of published and unpublished words in my wake, and still can't say.

When I addressed the Chinese woman or spoke to an answering machine to confirm our habitual appointment or when I mentioned her to others as a wonder-working therapist with magic hands who managed to keep my hopeless back at least semifunctional, I called her *Yu-Yu,* same name fondled by an asshole once at the top of steep stairs. Name she'd offered at our initial session, greeting each other with handshake, smiles. A ritual she must have been instructed to perform once by a *boss* and had memorized. She didn't ask for my name, but I said *Cyrus* anyway. I didn't take very seriously the name she proffered. Too cutesy, easy, a handle, street name, stage name, brand name conveniently simple for clients to pronounce. A way to maintain her distance, her privacy, my suspicion is what I thought when I heard *Yu-Yu* the first time.

If she ever said *Cyrus* I can't recall when. She heard my name once when we met, and then many more times in dumb *me Tarzan, you Jane* monologues I performed, hoping to get us better acquainted. My index finger stabbing my chest. Stabbing, hoping my multiple *Cyrus*es might earn one *Cyrus* from her. One gleaming nod of recognition in Yu-Yu's eyes as she savored my name passing through her lips, *you Cyrus.* Yes. Yes.

Yes, Ms. editor . . . though I agree that she might not fit . . . yes . . . I find myself writing more, not less about Chinese woman . . .

———

Cyrus. I'm sure Yu-Yu heard it and knew it. I'm sure she forgets nothing. Stopped expecting her to say my name. Truth might be—I have never said hers. Only repeated a fiction. And so what. Are things ever otherwise when it comes to names. To stories. To colors. To language. Approximation the rule. False proxies. One word, one name, one story as good (almost typed *god* for *good*) as another. Words, names, stories, colors stand for what. Why. Who says. Not me, certainly. Ancient, befuddled me. Not a speaker anymore. More a listening post. But nobody much listening to me, it seems. Traffic of messages in bottles or emails or silence from readers who don't read, gossipy literary tidbits on the grapevine. Phantoms speaking each to each like human voices till they reach us . . . and we drown. Isn't that how it goes.

Cyrus difficult perhaps, perhaps impossible for Yu-Yu to pronounce. A Chinese thing, maybe. Like the Japanese thing during WWII. Story goes, since all chinks look alike, our troops in the Pacific theater of war instructed to challenge all slanty-eyed people found in the wrong place at wrong time because they might be enemy spies or infiltrators or sympathizers. Detain them and demand they repeat the word *lollapalooza.* Jap chinks unable to pass the test. No matter how much they twisted up their twisted tongues, gagged, slobbered, cursed, stuttered, wept, bled, jap chinks fail. Thus we know they are japs and they get their yellow, buzz-cut heads righteously chopped off.

The ones with their heads lopped off, the dead ones, are the only good ones, a famous Indian fighting general is said to have said. And now a president trumpets the same sentiments about people he believes are totally unlike him. If our present chief executive lives until the next election, he will be elected again by supporters who may differ here and there with his attitudes and policies, but in the main, largely practice and believe as he believes and he practices. His supporters, my fellow countrymen who depend upon the fact, and proud of it, too, that they continue to constitute a majority of those who are both eligible to vote and bother to vote.

Perhaps I should omit the two paragraphs above. They read a bit like a paid political announcement. And who will pay for it. Don't ask, son. Just do it. Speak out. Free of charge. Remember that all responsible members of fiction-writing community have a duty to let well-meaning political messages slip into their texts occasionally.

be generous and patient with me, editor and old buddy . . . maybe all the fitful starts and stops fit together if you think of them all as one story, dearheart . . . a single story whose subject is names . . .

Yes. One hopes that writing able to perform useful, civic services, my Son. But sometimes writing walks you into a darkness. I switch on the light, and there on the room's ceiling, just above my right shoulder, a huge, fat, black spider, each spindly, segmented leg longer than mine, it seems, and since killing spiders bad luck in family (ours) that raised me, I'm confused, hesitate an instant. Aware spider's aware. As astonished by me as I am by it. I don't want to scare it by raising my head nor eyes towards the ceiling. I don't need eyes, anyway. Less a matter of seeing the spider when I snapped on the light, more like vibrations filling the room's air, telling me I was an intruder in a space where something hiding or sleeping or hunting, a palpable sense of its alarm, its readiness to flee or fight. Both of us stunned, surprised, and the spider, very much swifter than I am, profits from my mixed mind. Drops to the floor. A heavy thump, unnaturally louder than a spider should make, I'm thinking, as it darts away into shadows along the floorboards.

It is with that sudden, almost appalled, ambivalent awareness I greet her, or she greets me, when she appears one night. No light snapped on. Room stays dark except her flesh glows, luminous beneath hospital gown, burka, tent, nun's robe transformed sheer by light of her body to reveal every detail beneath the darkness draping her, undraping her. She lies on her back, pillow supporting her shoulders, bare legs bent at knee, thighs cocked wide open as if she's giving birth or captive on a gynecologist's bright table, mocking me giving birth to her in the dark, me driven, urgent to see, to look, to gaze, to contemplate as if she's a painting or intricate riffs of music, I tell myself, while tiny angels in attendance upon her fly towards me, cavort, pinch me all over, my body thrilling with each small attendant's ministrations, fingers that excite my skin, intricate counterpoint danced on my flesh, angels stretching to life-size, lean El Greco figures hovering, wavering, streaming, many colors.

Ends quickly as it begins. This dream. This supernatural interlude. What else could it be, if not a dream. Angels recede. Shadowy naked figure recedes. A wave of sadness and regret. Dismal silence until I drop asleep again, scuttle away, a spider into a hole.

Perhaps I should have rammed my naked hips into a passage open suddenly between two worlds. Let everything inside me rush out. Pour into a glowing womanshape. As if I could. But no. Stop. No. Not that kind of dream. No stains, no stiff sheets in the morning. And I am afraid. She could be anyone. In the deep silence I listen for names. Hers. Theirs. *Cyrus.* Name of my beautiful wife asleep in bed beside me. She's there, isn't she. If I reach over to touch her. Of course she is there. Must be. Or have I lost her. Or has she gone away and come back weary, so I best not disturb her. With another story. Another dream of dreaming. Another confusion.

———

Confusion not the worst thing. Not always the enemy. Being mixed up can confer unpredictable benefits. Imagining myself way more evil predator than I am helps me when I need to imagine myself not quite as evil as I could be. More than once I have taken advantage—pleasant for me, pleasant also for her, hopefully—of a woman's confusion at the height of her passion, and wiggled my thumb into a previously reluctant place.

One more piece of this tale to tell. Perhaps to keep my daughter safe until I reach her bedside and everything begins to be okay again. A final, odd story about basketball. Odd enough that you may find it difficult to believe. I played b-ball for many, many years, long enough to be involved in lots of hoop stories, including numerous odd ones, but nothing nearly as strange as what I'm about to relate.

A fairly close-to-great player, whose name I won't disclose here, a name you might recognize if you are more than a casual fan of the game, a guy who was an all-American in college and graduated to the pros where he distinguished himself as sixth man on various title-contending NBA squads. A guy who hung around the game after injuries forced retirement, working as TV announcer, assistant coach, rep for sneaker and sports apparel conglomerates, b-ball summer camp recruiter, that slow downhill slide from glory most ex-stars experience, till he got lucky and landed an executive assistant's job in the league office where he met a young lady, herself a former college all-American and pro player till a broken ankle ended her pro career two years after it started. A woman smart enough to go on to law school and earn a degree before she was wooed back into b-ball and accepted a job the league created especially for a woman with her accomplishments and credentials. No doubt you may be thinking you know already where this story is headed, given what I've said so far about two extremely talented hoopsters who discover one another working in same suite of offices. They will fall deeply in love and ride off together towards a golden sunset. A youngish couple of stars the stars have shined upon, and where else would they wind up, if not happily ever after, wealthy, glamorous, endorsements galore, beautiful kids. Role models, wished well, envied, gossiped about, merchandised, idolized, made fun of by us ordinary mortals till they are displaced by another star couple whose turn it is to reign, to remind the rest of us of our ordinariness, of what we are and are not yet but who we might very well be in the next dispensation, next lottery, next alignment of lucky and unlucky stars. Our fate then different, somehow, someplace, though we will also certainly remain here, where we abide, and the change will never happen here. Here we will not ever star anywhere except daydreaming in our own minds. Or when we gaze at stars and they gaze back benignly, shine their light on us an instant.

But all that's not even close to my ballplayers' story. No, no, no.

Heirs of grinding, violent competition, the two former pro hoopsters argued way too much. Increasingly vicious, name-calling quarrels, and because the man's hands and temper quick, an aggressive, backboard-dominating power forward in his playing days, he hits her and because she's a point guard, a fighter, her mind and hands at least as quick as his, she hits back, and their combats are sudden, fierce, intense. Often brutal. Tit-for-tat in a way, but since he is much bigger than she, taller, heavier, meaner, way stronger than she, one day she lies on the floor of their penthouse in a pool of blood. Panicked, full of illegal, toxic substances an autopsy later discloses, power forward snatches their three-year-old from her crib and flees with her in his silver Maserati, driving away faster than you would believe, faster than he believes, for reasons he most likely doesn't know or believe either, after perpetrating an act he does not believe, an act he has no words to describe. Fleeing for a destination he surely doesn't know or believe, just fast, just get away away fast and faster.

And nobody else, whatever they think or believe, will ever know what the man knew or believed because he crashes his car and kills himself plus driver and passenger of another car he smashes into head-on. Only the little girl strapped in her car seat in a deep well behind the Maserati's driver's seat survives. And she barely survives. On life support, hooked to machines for a week in a hospital just as her mother once had been when her mother, thirty years before, had arrived eight weeks early, a premie fighting to stay alive, just as her daughter, believe it or not, was also born prematurely, weighing less than two pounds, and hovered for a week between life and death, just as she hovers a second time, three and a half years old, after surviving the horrific wreck of her father's Maserati, just as her mother, my daughter, hovers again in the same hospital as her daughter, barely surviving the wreck of her husband.

Not such a strange story, I think I may hear you saying. Sad as it may be, sir, and maybe a bit confusing, too, your story about star-crossed lovers, even though both members of the loving couple in your tale happen to be colored and ex-basketball stars, their story not all that odd or unbelievable. No, Sir. Very much in love, beautiful, doomed couples a commonplace of poetry, novels, even life, Sir.

I'm old. Why pretend I can guess how younger generations of readers will react to my writing. Why care. Hemingway claimed that details are what render fiction convincing. I respect the details of a story. I resist abstractions, generalizations, melodrama, soap opera, O. Henry surprises, Joycean epiphanies. If I remember facts, I narrate them as accurately as

I am able. I didn't say the knocked-down ex-player was *swimming* in a pool of her own blood, did I. Swimming would require copious, copious gallons of spilled blood. Plus require a container to pool the blood. Nope. Not that. Just a tiny red halo beginning to seep from the point guard's temple slashed open by a metal table leg's sharp edge as her skull slammed the marble-tiled floor. A nasty gash, to be more concise, precise. Not life threatening. Only a wound. But yes, a concussion when bone slams into hard floor, and a coma, an operation, followed by slow convalescence, yes . . . but like my daughter, she breathes. Her life goes on. Though it's absolutely true that a large, powerful, confused, temporarily crazed individual damaged her. Almost fatally. In spite of himself. But only almost.

You may recall, perhaps, my desperate hope, my determination, expressed at the beginning of this story to see her, my own lady star alive. And, *thank the lord,* as my mother used to say, I do reach her. My daughter still confined to a bed, attached to machines, still deeply medicated when nurse and doctor bring her daughter to her room, daughter a little girl freshly off her own life support system that saved then sustained her while similar machines kept her mom alive only three hospital floors above, three floors up, then down the hall three doors, in Room M306.

The little girl, thank goodness, responsive again to human touch, human voices, her dark eyes animated again. She hollers loudly and at length if she wants something or just needs to holler. Vast improvement rapidly because she's young, very young. Young enough to bounce back and heal with youth's incredibly speedy recuperative powers. But you can't expect her mom to do as well this soon, Olympic athlete or not. Will take a while before she rises from the abyss, makes noise, cowers, smiles. Despite her precarious condition, the story goes, a glint of a glint in the mother's eyes when nurse at bedside leans down and extends the slightly doped-up little one cradled in her arms towards the oxygen tent a doctor unzips and holds open a moment in Room M306.

Details, facts pile up. From many stories. Congregate in a single story and propagate other stories. That may be oddest thing about any story. But this one in particular. A mother and daughter both with blood type A. Shared genes. Doubled, precarious premiehoods they share. Dead they share. Both loved by a man the two of them loved and shared who nearly kills both. And will the three-and-a half-year-old grow up to be a star player . . .

Patience, reader. Contemplate the tales above. Contemplate how much the characters in them suffer to entertain us. Entertain one another. How they bury and forget one another, but continue to share. Share confusions, mix-ups of color, history, names, family. Odd. Almost un-believable. Like stories. Like me.

ABOUT THE AUTHOR

JOHN EDGAR WIDEMAN's books include *You Made Me Love You, American Histories, Writing to Save a Life, Philadelphia Fire, Brothers and Keepers, Fatheralong, Hoop Roots,* and *Sent for You Yesterday.* He is a MacArthur Fellow, has won the PEN/Faulkner Award twice, won the 2019 PEN/Malamud Award for Excellence in Short Story, has been a finalist for the National Book Award, and has twice been a finalist for the National Book Critics Circle Award. He divides his time between New York and France.